THE BIRTH OF ANARCHY

j.d. brewer

J.D. Brewer Books

www.jdbrewerbooks.com

Twitter: @jdbrewerbooks
facebook.com/jdbrewerbooks
goodreads.com/jdbrewerbooks

ISBN-13:

978-0692596920 (J.D. Brewer Books)

ISBN-10:
0692596925
First Edition

The Dedication

When my imaginary friends refuse to talk to me
you do.
When I want to give up on a story
you talk me out of it.
When I need a good laugh or a fresh glass of wine,
you bring the joy.
And that day, two years ago, when I wrote a book and didn't
know what to do next
you did.

So I dedicate this novel to my literary work wife,
the only one who understands the honor of being named
Bacon in my phone,
the woman who took a chance on a happenstance friendship,
the wanderlust vagabond who travels without borders,
the only one I trust with my book covers,
the "gal" who encourages and uplifts those willing to fight for
their own dreams…
I'd be lost without your positivity and wisdom.

Sarah Martin
you inspire.

TABLE OF CONTENTS

EXTRAS

THE BIRTH OF ANARCHY

j.d. brewer

CHAPTER ONE

The most visceral stories are the ones that have not yet been born. They haunt me in ways the known stories do not, and, trust me, I know stories that could torment the strongest of souls. I was born on them, with them, and around them, and they pump through my veins in half-lucid rivers of truth, pushing me towards the places I fear the most.

For this reason, when I was younger, I reveled in the adrenaline rush of the unwritten future. Rather than look back, I directed my attention towards forward movement because I believed the future did not have the weight of inflexibility in the same way the past did. However, it didn't take long to see a flaw in this philosophy because even the known histories had their debatable inconsistencies. In studying our nation's past, I eventually recognized that I had more stories than memories concerning my own. I started analyzing every conclusion I'd drawn from the tales I'd been fed about my beginnings. The facts ended up getting all muddled up with perspectives that weren't mine, and the truth of who I was became completely lost on me.

After all, depending on who tells the tale, truths shift, and these shifting truths make the past more malleable than historians give it credit for. This could only mean one thing. The past is just as unwritten as the future, for both places in time hold unborn stories, and the only moment you can truly trust exists between the here and now.

And right now, I could trust in the sound of the drums, the way my feet walked in step with nine other pairs. Right here, I could trust the thrum, thrum, thump, steady as a moving train. My fingers, shrouded in black gloves, wrapped around a silver handle, carrying a weight I had never known could exist before.

Yet it wasn't this object, this *thing*, that was too heavy to bear. It was the unborn stories that led up to this *thing* that wearied my heart.

The first time I held the weight of an unborn story, I was small and my father was large. When you're a toddler, you think you understand the purpose of crying. It belongs casually in every day because the manipulation of tears is the only way you know how to communicate. Yet somewhere in the depths of passing time, you learn to move past the wails and shape the noises into words, and it is with age that you learn true tears have nothing to do with manipulation and everything to do with acute pain.

Still, when I was six, I was too young to understand the tears I'd stumbled upon, but I remembered the way they formed in the corners of Father's eyes, subtle yet vivid. I couldn't have known that there were thousands of histories, memories of moments, trapped in the small beads. I couldn't have known how I'd learn to want to read these stories, rescue them from their prisons, divine their meanings to make sense of my own. Nor could I have known how his tears would bring about my own for many years to come before Grandfather taught me how not to cry.

These were the tears of something broken inside, and it was my first lesson in what it meant to love:

"Ani, my boy." Father scooped me up onto his lap and didn't attempt to hide the moisture shining in his too-bright eyes. He brushed a long, rust-red bang behind my ear, which only made the water in his eyes expand. "We won't cut it just yet," he said, as he

often did about my ever-growing hair. Mother was constantly mentioning how it made me look unpresentable for the photographers. Next to her and Zosimos' blonde, straight, perfectly lined locks, my hair always had a little edge of wild to it. It made me stand out in all the portraits, but Father never gave into Mother's logic. He said I was bound to stick out no matter what I did simply because of who I was.

"What's wrong?" I asked and tugged at his earlobe. He always did that to me when I felt bad, so it was a gesture that made sense. "Are you hungry?" I gave the followup question because I usually cried when I was hungry.

Father let out a gargled laugh. "No, I'm not hungry." And that was when he told me about my genetic history. About love leaving. About betrayal. About death.

That was how I learned Mother was not my genetic-mother and that my brother was only half-way-so.

That was the day I learned my genetic-mother's name, and, from that story on, it was a name that whispered its way along the cracks in my soul.

Once you realize that you do not have something, you begin to see people who do have it in a new light. It started when I noticed how my mother, Zosime, embraced my brother just slightly more fully than me. She'd scoop up Mos with a little more care, and when she'd say, "My sweet, sweet Zosimos," there was a special light to the words. I used to think it was because he was the youngest, but eventually I realized it was because, as much as she tried, I was not completely hers. She loved me, I didn't doubt it, but there was something missing in our connection.

Years drifted by, and I watched, and watched, and watched. I began to see mothers everywhere. I began to watch how they coddled and soothed, how they scolded and taught, and how they loved with a secret smile that only mothers have. Eventually, with just a glance, I could pinpoint the Celebrity children being raised by mothers that did not share the same genetic lineage. These were the children that were fathered or mothered genetically by someone who did not raise them and were left in the care of only one parent linked to them by blood. The genetic-Celebrity-parent simply did their stoic duty and left their genetic gifts before riding the rails towards their own futures.

These mothers I observed loved all of their children, whether genetically linked or not, but there was a subtle loss of connection. To be honest, I wasn't sure this faulty connection was the mothers' fault. I hypothesized that it rested in the children, like they knew a piece of them was missing when they looked into the faces of their parents and couldn't find a link to their own. It brings up questions, that even in innocence, shakes a child from the inside, and no matter how honestly love is attempted, there are gaps in the honesty, places where truths burrow just a little bit deeper than facts.

Perhaps I was just more aware of it because of my own situation. After all, I was the most well known of the Celebrity children, though technically my conception brought scandal to my family. It turned out that my genetic-mother was not a traveling Celebrity, birthing children and leaving them in the care of another mother. My genetic-mother died giving birth, her name lost in the cracks of time. Her name swept under the rug of indecency and shame.

When I was eight, I learned that there were more layers to my Celebrity status. Father and my genetic-mother were a part of *Project Prometheus*. The Genetic Engineering Guild had altered their genes involving intelligence. I was one of the ten offspring coming from those concentrated alterations, and they called us New Wave Perfection. The G.E.G. had originally been cautious with Father's partnering because of his unconventional beginnings, but Grandfather had lobbied for Father's genetic gifts to be properly utilized. Father went on to carry out one of the most profitable Celebrity Tours in his generation. It went so well that the G.E.G. gave all *Project Prometheus* children a Celebrity Tour. They called the unconcentrated offspring between *Project Prometheus* members and regular Citizens, Halfsies. Of course, the Republic didn't know the significance of these children until it was too late to protest.

Still, I was different, even from the other New Waves. I always had been. My conception made me different to a whole new extreme. I was born out on the Tracks, and the wild stained me like a birthmark I had to constantly prove I was better than.

My actual, legal mother? The woman I called Mother? Well, she was more regal than the word regal itself. In proper fashion, she could say all the right things and love me in all the right ways, but it was never enough. It was so subtle a difference in love that normal people with normal brains rarely noticed it, but I was observant to a fault. I could see the hiccup in the familial framework that structured the Republic, though I was smart enough to never speak of it to anyone.

These observations built up a volcanic mountain of questions, and it took me five years to figure out who to ask of them. To ask Mother was to ask a brick wall, and there was no way I was brave enough yet to attempt the conversation with Grandfather. As for Father? Just the mention of my genetic-mother brought his eyes to a place of pain, but, eventually, my own pain could not be contained.

That was how, when I was ten, one of the most important unborn stories came from my father's best friend, Uncle Ty:

"You knew her?" I asked.

The Victory Garden on the west end of the Colony was our favorite haunt, and, like always, I was having trouble keeping up. It was as if I couldn't grow into my own feet, and my knees told tales of how tall I would eventually be but wasn't quite yet. Uncle Ty never slowed down for my growing bones, and I often found myself tripping over my shoes in an attempt to keep his stride.

Uncle Ty got that crinkly look on his face—the one he always got when he looked at me. I could never tell if he was content or distressed to see me. Yet, even though he wore both expressions openly on his face, I knew he loved me.

"I knew her well," he said, pausing next to a large, bronze statue of a young man situated in the midst of tomato plants. Their

red, orbed bulbs looked like shiny ornaments against the neon bright green of their leaves. The sun ran rivers along the carved bronze of the statue. Without having to read it, I knew the plaque underneath the statue's feet read Leo Solano and that the inscription would continue to list his contributions to Humanity. I studied Leo Solano's expression, a carving set in one final story. How did they fix a countenance like that? Who got to choose the emotion he'd wear in a stone-cold immortality?

Leo Solano used to be a ghost in the peripherals of history. Everyone knew he was important enough to have statues built in his image, but no one really understood why until this year. Recently, the Council of Manipulation had begun to release hidden documents about his role in the founding of the Republic and his contributions to the Genetic Engineering Guild. Now, the topic was so widely discussed that no one could escape the implications of his influence.

Yet when I looked at Leo Solano, I hated that I knew more about this man's histories, many generations gone, than my own.

"How's that possible?" I asked.

"We lived through many adventures together," Uncle Ty said.

I tried to imagine the stories behind these adventures he spoke of, but I had no real images to grasp onto. It wasn't fair that he and my father had these gifts, these memories of her, and I did not. I sat on the bench that faced the statue and tried to be patient.

Uncle Ty sat next to me. "I wonder, how after living a life full of choices in a world full of choices, Leo Solano was able to give up the most important one."

"What was the most important one?" I asked.

"One day, you will be old enough to understand. One day, we will have the harder conversations. But for now, know that your genetic-mother was kind, brilliant, and bold, and, although you do not have memories of her, know that she exists within those three gifts you've inherited from her. They will make all the difference in your world."

I swallowed. The unborn stories were there, but encrypted by whatever sense of duty Uncle Ty felt towards my father and, *perhaps, my genetic-mother. A new question escaped my lips before I understood the gravity of the answer that followed.* "Did you love her?"

"Like wind loves air," he whispered.

None of the stories I had provided comfort. Through the eyes of my father and the eyes of his best friend, I saw two sides of love—two sides I didn't quite understand. They contradicted each other in Propriety, and it made me consider all the rumors about my birth being unsanctioned.

By that time, I understood the sting of rumors when they were slung at you like sticker-burrs in the wind. My entire life, I was a primary talking point for the gossip-geneticists. Their favorite debates orbited around two scandals. First, they claimed I was unsanctioned. Secondly, they claimed I was an abomination for being one of the New Wave Perfection offspring.

I could not remember a single moment when I was allowed to just be Anicetus Petrakis, human boy. I had always been defined by how I was born and what my birth meant for Humanity.

I was trained to find humor in the rumors, but then, when I was eleven, I heard the ones about treason. It suddenly became the only question that mattered. Could it be true that my genetic-mother was not who Father said she was?

I explored vid-feed after vid-feed, tugging out half-facts and missing-truths, getting nowhere but everywhere in the search for who I was. Every time I thought I found truth, it crumbled into lies when I tested the limits of its facts.

A year later, I was unapologetically eleven, and my grandfather was unapologetically ancient. The fluidity of youth versus the constancy of experience was forever a combustible combination between the two of us, but I was learning how to speak like a man. I had to coax the unborn story out, but, with Grandfather's version of things, I tasted the hinges of hate as he swung open a different door to my genetic-mother:

"What did she look like?"

Grandfather set his fork down. The question brought a sour reaction to his smooth wrinkles. "I knew these questions would come, but must they come now?"

The food on my plate was neatly untouched, and white ceramic barely poked through the helpings of ham, potatoes, and green beans. I examined the holes as if they were holes in the story of me, but it was time to look up and ask the big questions. Not even my starched grandfather could force them into submission. "I haven't been able to find pictures," I said.

"I erased them from the databases."

"That's what Uncle Ty said," I replied.

"Paramonos and Tycho have trouble viewing the situation objectively, and it took me years to clean up after their messes," Grandfather said.

I could only nod. "Their messes," translated to my existence, and Grandfather never sugar coated that my sudden appearance was a political nightmare for my father when it came time for him to run for office. I learned not to take offense to it. Politically speaking, my presence had been an obstacle before it became an asset. Grandfather was always saying that the true worth of a Politician was in their ability to spin negatives into positives or turn setbacks into advantages.

"Be not clouded by ignorance. Objectivity will bring about pure truths." I whispered the phrase Grandfather coined for Father's first campaign. I did it in a way that looked unplanned, as if I was coming to a conclusion for the first time in front of him, but each word was planted in the air with a fresh sense of political choreography. I said the phrase again, louder and clearer, before adding, "Objectivity is what I seek. How can I remain objective when I haven't explored any side but my father's and Uncle Ty's, or, forgive me for saying, yours? I know you didn't completely erase her because genetic files are sacred, especially with the plans you have for me. To wipe all traces of her existence would only invalidate me, and you wouldn't risk that. I seek facts, not stories. All you have to do is un-classify the files for me, and I can learn the truth about my origins. The more I understand about

where I come from, the better I'll be at directing where I go." I kept my voice steady and devoid of hope. To let hope take the reins would only cause the old man to ignore the request completely. It would give away that I craved to see my genetic-mother's face rather than the information behind it. I had to play the role of the Politician he was training me to be in order to get what I wanted.

Grandfather sighed and reached for the tablet that was never out of reach. Despite being the Prime Chancellor and no longer having an official active role in the government, his hand was felt everywhere in the Republic. As far back as I could remember, he had his tablet nearby in case an emergency popped up.

As he fumbled along the screen, I wondered when I'd get access to the newer tablets. He was one of the few who got the newest tech first, though this upgrade was technically old. Most people had no clue that the three-dimensional capabilities that allowed a picture to hover above the screen actually predated The Great Disaster, but that just went to show the power the Council of Manipulation had. Grandfather once explained that access to too much knowledge made people feel smarter than they really were and made them act using dangerously false logic. The Manipulators managed access to knowledge through controlling the tools that let the populace obtain it. Grandfather had said, "There's a balance, Ani. An overly informed populace gets confused. An uninformed populace wastes away in ignorance. But one that is adequately informed? They help civilization advance while remaining manageable." The G.E.G. petitioned for the release of three-dimensional capabilities two years prior, and the Council of Manipulation finally granted it last month.

The recent technology release was still in its beta-stages and everyone, including Grandfather, struggled with how to use it. His old fingers had trouble adjusting to the commands, and they flailed on the screen. I felt a surge of impatience as he navigated a database, but it was soon forgotten as a figure projected above the tablet in three dimensional frames.

I reached up and felt my own too-long hair, and my lips quivered.

It was her.

Rust-red.

Eyes like universes exploding.

Unsteady hearts on unsteady feet.

Just a girl, a girl who never grew much past the moment being projected. But I would. I would grow beyond her time and into my own. These were now the only memories I felt completely sure of, the ones I possessed in the way my hair caught the sun or my eyes observed the unobservable. These were fluid stories, rooted in the genetics she gifted me, yet to be fully realized by my relatively sheltered experience.

Just as quickly as the picture rose into my sight, it collapsed back into the tablet. I felt the urge to protest but held it back. Grandfather had conceded as much as he would in that moment, and if I ever wanted to see the information again, I had to prove to him I deserved it.

But the way the picture disappeared made me feel a different kind of loss. He hadn't left it up long enough for me to commit her to memory, even my own highly evolved one, and I was left with fragments of the person. Had she been up one second longer, I could have preserved her to a file in my brain as a complete and whole visual. But Grandfather knew my limits, and he'd left it up for less than a second. He was one of the few people who understood how my brain worked, how any more than a whole second with a picture or text and I could have it stamped irrevocably on my memory in perfect detail. I tried not to be angry that he'd prevented me from the gift of a new memory, but a controlled rage surged through me. I knew then that I'd failed Grandfather's test. He'd seen through my carefully laid out words and taunted me with a glimpse of the information I sought. I waited for his point to come because, by the smug glimmer in his eyes, I knew he'd been waiting years to make it.

He leaned back in his chair and set the tablet aside. "Anicetus, I need you to listen to me carefully."

I stared at his stern eyes without truly seeing them. I was trying to hold onto the shape of her face, but it was like my fleeting grasp

---

on air. My chest rose and fell as I lost control of my breath. I struggled to remain patient as he explained his truths, but the only truth I wanted was the image of my genetic-mother.

"To love this woman is to love treason. Despite what we've fed the media, she was a Genetic Terrorist. It was luck that your father found her and salvaged her genetic duty to the Republic. The only noble thing she did in her short life was send you as a sanctioned gift before her fellow Terrorists killed her. Perhaps, in her heart, she was trying to atone for her unforgivable acts against the Republic by giving you up, but even that is a stretch."

"Terrorist?" I whispered.

"Ah. That's the part they didn't want you to know, my boy. You must not be fooled by your father's and Tycho's perceptions of this woman. It is in all our best interests to publicly deny the rumors being spread, but it does not prevent them from holding truth. Nikomedes Kostas is not to be mourned. She is not to be revered. And, most importantly, it will only cause you great discomfort to wallow in thoughts of things that can never be. She is gone, my child. Let the girl rest. Let the scandals rest with her."

But the scandals never rested with her. As my father pursued his political career, my unconventional inception became a bigger talking point for all sides of the political agenda. My very existence was filled with guilt because I couldn't change my past any more than I could pin down my future, and sometimes I wondered how much easier things would have been for the people I love had my genetic-mother never given me to the Republic.

Especially on a day like this one.

Nineteen years in, and the plan for my future was shifting, the design altering. Nineteen years in, and the only thing that wasn't changing was that my future still didn't belong to me.

"Unhinge, brother," Mos said. Though he was a year younger than me, he rose nearly six inches taller, and when he set his palm over my hand and squeezed, it practically swallowed mine. The gentle embrace reminded me I'd been holding the metal handle for far too long.

21

I looked up and saw my face hovering on the holo-vids popping up in three-dimensional dioramas amongst the crowd. It was almost like every Citizen in every Colony was standing with us in the moment.

On the stage above us, Grandfather didn't need to change his expression to show his disappointment. He saw me falter. He saw me slip. He was telling me to pull it together.

Behind him, nine others stood on an elevated stand. The other New Waves, with the enhanced NPTN genes—the markers linked to intelligence—were usually protected from the limelight as much as possible so they could focus on their respective trades. But today, Grandfather thought they'd give the Republic hope, an image to show what everyone was stoically sacrificing for. One New Wave, Alexandros Lampros, was meant to be a florist, and his contributions had already solved several plant-plagues in the Victory Gardens. By the time he was nine, he'd even created new water-efficiency systems for the bio-domes that fed each Colony. Another girl, Myrrine Kaya, was meant to be a Manipulator. She was trained to exist everywhere but never be seen. Despite her genetics, she lived in the political shadows learning the histories. But my eyes were drawn to Eudocia. Her core nurturing plan had involved genetics, while mine involved leadership. Her true love, like mine, rested in the solitude and quietude of the labs, and I envied her. Ever since I learned how DNA worked, I dreamed my genetic studies class could become more than just a hobby. I wanted to move along her path so badly, but she was destined to head up the G.E.G. while the world always thought that I'd lead the Republic. Eudocia and I were the only two New Waves raised in the same Colony, and she was the only one who could keep up with my speed of thought in class.

Eudocia? All of us? We were expected to rule, our brains nurtured to live within the world of politics and science.

I half expected her to send me an encouraging smile, but I knew better. One would never come. She stood there with a face as placid as a statue just as the others did.

"Ani, unhinge," Mos said again.

Unhinge. Mos and I spent our entire lives masking our words with proper form and hidden meanings, so that it was habit to, more often than not, speak formally in every situation. Grandfather always said, *"You never know just who is around the corner trying to get a soundbite of you sounding extraordinarily ordinary."* When we were younger, Mos came up with a signal—a word—that we could use to let each other know the coast was clear. Mos had always been my safe space, and I was his. He was the one person with whom I didn't have to worry about the vernacular of the powerful, and sometimes, when it was okay to unhinge, we even played around with slang we'd overheard on the vids.

But this wasn't about words, since there was no time for them. Mos wanted me to know he was there for me, that he was just behind me, that I could hand him my suffering if I needed to. But there was no longer a safe space for me to unhinge. The whole Republic had been given front seat tickets to the tragic scene of our family's agony, as if it was their pain, too—as if they had a claim equal to our own.

The holo-vid above the stage was humongous, turning me into a hovering giant above the world, and though there were seven other people with me in the plot of grass below the stage, my face was the focus. My replicas held matching expressions, and I tried to translate the look on my face. How did I get those circles under my eyes, those shadows upon shadows of worry? I lifted my chin in the proud angles I'd been trained to mimic, and just in case the microphones were on, I spoke as properly as I could. "Forgive me brother, I know not what came over me." I loosened my fingers but could not bring myself to release the cold metal to set the casket down on the ropes.

It was lighter than it should have been, but then again, it was just a prop. The bombs were very efficient when it came to blowing Father clear to the sky.

Father had always been invincible in my eyes. For all his strength of character and body, he couldn't stop the vice-tight grip of death when the end set its sights on him.

23

I never should have watched the video, but morbid curiosity got the best of me. I opened the file and saw how Father greeted the two Senators that supported him in the 30th. They sat to watch the choir sing the Song of the Republic, and my eyes were drawn to a brown haired girl with bright blue eyes. She was over-enthusiastic with her singing, belting out every word from her tiny little diaphragm. Father let out a laugh, and I knew it was because he found the kid entertaining. He had this thing about children—a joy he found in their presence. I loved the way his guard fell down around a story that made no sense to anyone past the age of six and how he could understand it despite the age difference. Growing up, he never got that confused look adults got when Mos or I would talk from the imagination.

Father was smiling when it happened.

The blast of explosion. The way smoke billowed as easily as clouds before a storm. The way shrapnel destroyed the image. The way fire consumed the colors of song. The way charred staging was the only thing left in the wake.

That vid became a scar on my memory.

It was Father's end when it should have been a new beginning. I should have seen it coming. The Patriots hadn't even attempted to tolerate the Absolution Bill he'd passed after the data-leak, and this next stage was even more frightening for the public to accept. Despite the threats, he developed this new Act, and he'd practiced the speech he was meant to give that day to an annoying exactness. He didn't know it, but I'd witnessed him pacing in his office, saying the words over and over again so that he wouldn't trip over a single one.

Words that would never be spoken.

Words that would explode before the definitions could ever be known.

I shouldn't have watched the vid, but I wanted to see if there were clues I could find where others could not. Something that could give me a hint as to who was responsible. Something that could make me forget that in many ways it was I who was responsible.

I rewound it to the beginning.

There was no body in the casket before me, but the Republic demanded the pomp and circumstance of a funeral. Our people needed to bury their Chancellor to truly believe he was gone. It was as if they couldn't have a swearing-in ceremony for the Interim Chancellor unless it happened over the dead body of the last one.

My face bounced back from the shiny black coffin. The other men and women carrying their piece of the charade waited for me. They were instructed to let me go first, to follow my example. I looked to the soldier opposite of me, his mask just as shiny, pristine, and black as the coffin. My reflections bounced back everywhere, and I had no idea where I existed within the shell of all the versions of me being sent back to the boy still holding onto the coffin. Maybe a part of me felt that if I didn't let go, I wouldn't have to move, and if I didn't have to move, then none of it was real.

I sucked in a deep breath as I let go. There was a hollow sound to the coffin as it landed on the ropes that would lower it in the tomb, but my limbs felt heavy, as if my hands were still gripping the metal handle.

As far as funerals went, we were in the last stretch, but I knew it was far from over. This would not be the average funeral. It was difficult to believe that the hard part was still to follow, as if anything would ever be easy again.

Rewound.
Pressed play.
Shook hands.
Sat down.
Kids sang.
Father grinned.
Explosion.
Smoke.
Fire.
Gone.

Rewound.

I turned the way Grandfather made us practice over and over again the night before. Mos and I had never been in the Militia, so a Military funeral was not one we were equipped to be a part of.

It wasn't as if I didn't want to follow Father's and Uncle Ty's footsteps and partake in a Tour of Duty, but my face was too recognizable for anything other than being a Public Relations puppet. Grandfather had said, since that was the case, it made more sense to learn everything I could about leadership instead, that I should learn to control puppets rather than be one myself. It was no surprise that he'd been grooming me to follow in the family footsteps of the politically correct, and I was growing used to the sculpted movements of Politicians.

I completed a manicured turn, and one boot moved to greet the other as I reached out to grab my piece of the green and blue flag. We walked it off the coffin—the empty, empty coffin. I tried to swallow, and behind the gulp rested unshed tears. How did you say goodbye to an empty coffin? How did you put someone to rest when they ended so violently? Or had my father already found peace the moment he ceased to exist?

For as smart as I was, I couldn't figure death out. For as smart as I was, I knew no one ever had nor ever would.

Clear of the coffin, I stepped toward the masked soldier opposite of me and released the flag to his trusty hands, then grabbed the bottom of the fold. Hand over hand, the flag condensed into a triangle. It was as if they could fold up a person neatly and tuck their past away in the yards of colored fabric, but I knew my father was more than the flag they placed in my hands.

Rewound.
Pressed play.
Shook hands.
Sat down.
Kids sang.
Father grinned.

Blue insignia.
Should have been red.
But it was blue.
On the collar.
Every child wore the blue insignia.
Explosion.
Smoke.
Fire.
Gone.
Rewound.
I found what the Militia had missed. Or did they miss it on purpose?

The clue was with the twelve children in the choir standing on the small set of bleachers. Their robes of red flowed all the way to the floor, swallowing them whole, and below the collars on their sternums rested a small circle. The Militia insignia. Inverted. Turned topsy-turvy. Not in its vibrant reds, but in a horizon blue.

It was the brand of the Patriots, marking themselves on the very children they'd sentenced to death.

And when I paused the vid right before the explosion, I saw that the blast began as a collective of twelve tiny bursts above twelve tiny hearts pushing out from the insignias and tearing my world apart.

I looked up to the stage above the burial plot. Corinna Tantalos stood near Mother and Grandfather. She was dressed in her new Chancellor Reds, and four Manipulator Stars rested above six Senator Stars on her chest. With each new office held, leaders wore their old Stars under their new ones as a resume of their experience, and Corinna, like Uncle Ty and Father, held every title she'd served as carefully as she would hold broken glass. Today, Uncle Ty would pin her with the Chancellor Stars, and they would gleam on her uniform the way silver stars pulsed in the night sky.

To give up her seat at Manipulation to serve as Interim Chancellor sent shock waves through the Republic, but I saw it coming the moment I discovered my father had been blown apart.

In the four Chancellor elections my father won, Corinna Tantalos was the only true competition, and last year, she'd been appointed to the empty Manipulation seat. I felt the hand of Grandfather with the appointment. What better way to distract her from seeking the Chancellor's office than to give her one of apparently equal value?

Manipulation was a job only few were given, a job perhaps even broader and farther reaching than being a Chancellor. Yet, unlike a Chancellor, Manipulators were subtle in their actions, using time as a tool in the implementation of ideas. The Council of Manipulation had five appointed officials holding office until death, given the keys to all known histories so they could best strategize and inform leadership concerning the Republic. They were the only ones able to veto the Chancellor and the Senators in a four-to-five vote, and they advised the drafting of laws by the Senate, directing the course of an entire nation behind the scenes. Most Citizens thought the Council of Manipulation was just an antiquated homage to history. They believed Manipulators were figureheads who preserved the past. But I'd known for a long time that preservation was not their purpose. Controlled advancement was. Only a handful of Citizens truly understood the power they wielded.

Even still, most Citizens felt the oddity in the event. To give up a lifetime appointment for one that was not guaranteed was unprecedented, but Corinna Tantalos often did the unexpected. It worked for her.

I studied Corinna's face and searched for traces of my own. When I was younger, there were rumors that we were genetically related. Grandfather's Public Relations Specialists always found ways to discount it, but it was hard to deny the gossip-geneticists comparing our genetic similarities in the commentary feeds. When I was younger, Grandfather used it as a lesson in seeing past rumors, and I eventually doubted that Corinna and I were related. However, given recent events, the fiction could not hold up to the genetics. Now the whole world knew Corinna Tantalos was my father's genetic-half-sister.

Part of me wondered how she felt, standing over the memory

of her genetic-brother, holding no claim to him the way he held no claim to her. Did she hate him? Did she understand him—who he was?

I followed the steps that pulled me up on stage, Mos at my heels. We were met at the top of the stairs by Mother, and I stretched out my hands to offer her the folded flag.

The red lightning streaking across the whites of her eyes was the only sign of her heartbreak. In the days of queens, I had no doubt she would have been among them, and I wondered if I'd ever be as good as she was at hiding my emotions. She cupped my cheeks before taking the flag with her slender hands, then she moved towards the podium.

She pulled her chin up and spoke in a clear voice that projected into her holo-vid replicas. "I present to you the Council of Manipulation and the new Master Manipulator, Tycho Tripoli."

It was another adjustment in the ranks. Uncle Ty had been on the Council of Manipulation for years, and he'd been voted to take Corinna's title when she left her seat to become the Interim Chancellor. Uncle Ty left his spot open for a new Manipulator to be voted into the Council, and the Republic was in the thralls of debate over who it could be.

I hadn't seen Uncle Ty all day, and I wondered how he felt about not being able to carry the casket. He should have had the honor, yet he had a larger role to play in the day. He could not be the bearer of death when he needed to be the bearer of change.

A door slid open from the back of the stage, and Uncle Ty led out four other council members. It was the newest addition—the one that filled in the gap when Corinna and Uncle Ty's new appointments called for a readjustment—that caused the crowd to gasp. There'd been rumors that they were letting in one of *their* ambassadors into Manipulation proceedings, but this woman's presence, with her wild braids stretching into a million woven strands down her back, finally confirmed it. She wore the same blue Manipulator robes and the same calm expression, but she was as wild as her hair. She was as wild as the last time I saw her.

Uncle Ty adjusted his pack, and I copied his movement. I felt awkward under the added weight. It wasn't that my pack was too heavy, but more that its bulky shape threw me off balance. I'd been practicing carrying one all month, ever since my seventeenth birthday, preparing for our sanctioned camping trip, but it wasn't until I'd hiked all day with it that I started to grasp the gravity of it all.

Uncle Ty noticed my discomfort and smiled. "The bulk was the hardest part to get used to, until all of the sudden, I no longer noticed it. Part of being a Vagab—a Terrorist—involves carrying a pack the way a snail carries a home."

I nodded, letting his slip of tongue go. Usually these slips were intentional, but something in how he caught himself made me realize that for the first time, Uncle Ty made a misstep in his speech around me.

"Eventually, the pack became a part of me. Eventually, I only noticed it when it was no longer with me."

I could tell there were things Uncle Ty wanted to tell me, but he held back. He carried secrets like he carried his pack—burdens he ported so long that he didn't realize how many ways they weighed him down. With every story he let loose around me, I could see tension float away from him, and I took on the weight of his answers, mixing them with my own secrets—my own burdens that Uncle Ty would never understand.

Being in the forest made his tongue loose, and I was already considering questions that would work towards my advantage. We hiked up the hill in relative silence, and I let him have space to think, knowing I needed to give him a moment before I pushed some more.

He was taking a big risk for me. Though our trip was sanctioned, I knew we were going off course for my own purposes, and if we got caught, it'd be a scandal of epic proportions. If we were lucky, the headlines would read, Manipulator Tripoli and the Face of New Wave Perfection Caught Canoodling with Terrorists. If we were unlucky, the headlines would tell a different story that ended with a needle in both our forearms. Yet Uncle Ty acted with a faith that we wouldn't get caught. He promised me he knew where we could find some Terrorists from his days on the Tracks, people who might be interested in helping me with my experiment.

It amazed me how gracefully he had leapt from the moving train the day before, his body still perfectly strong despite its path to aging. I'd seen a picture of him in a report when he was about my age. He'd just come out of his Tour of Duty on the Tracks, and there was this wild look about him. Hair, long and black. Skin, tanner than leather. Eyes, dark and bright. Now his hair was cropped and peppered with gray and his skin bore slight wrinkles, but his eyes were still the same orbed contradictions. All of the perfection that remained in his face was testament as to why he got issued a double-duty as a Celebrity.

Like Father, Uncle Ty's genetics were a true gift to the Republic, and the world never let him forget it. His Celebrity children littered nearly every Colony in the Republic. He, like the Project Prometheus children, broke so many precedents. He was one of the leading Celebrities starting the trend of double Celebrity children—two nearly perfect, non-altered parents creating even more nearly perfect offspring. Even before the shock of the Project Prometheus scandal, double Celebrities had become less terrifying. Something that was once so shocking became common practice, and Uncle Ty, rather than my Father, was the face of that change. Through Uncle Ty, the G.E.G. wanted to remind the Republic that even naturally directed children could reach greatness. The G.E.G. called these children Second Wave Perfection, and the gossip-geneticists followed the lives of some of these children nearly as closely as they followed New Wave Perfection and Halfsies. It's strange how the world can shift like that, how, in just one generation, we became desensitized to the taboo.

I ached to ask Uncle Ty about how it felt to not even have one child to show for it himself. It wouldn't be long before I was expected to go on my own tour, and it killed me to know I'd be leaving behind so many genetic gifts, never having any claim to them. Part of me wished the Republic still feared the implications

---

31

of *New Wave Perfection* to the point they'd be wary of allowing any of us Celebrity Tours. Part of me knew my genetic gifts would be valuable to the human genome in the long run, that it'd be selfish of me to keep them to myself, that, like my father before me, I had to do more than just believe in Humanity before self.

The biggest part of me wished I could make the same shocking decision Uncle Ty did when he gave up his rights to parenting. He allowed his last Celebrity child to remain with the mother, and he even got out of a partnering situation in exchange for his second Celebrity Tour. His Public Relations Specialists said it was because Tycho Tripoli's focus needed to remain his duty to the Republic, and the Republic alone, but I had a feeling Uncle Ty didn't want a traditional family. I had a feeling that something bigger was broken inside of him. Maybe, if he had to be a father to one of the children, he would have a daily reminder of all the others he left behind. I could see the comfort in being allowed to forget, but I wouldn't get out as lucky as he did. I'd already learned my fate, my partnering, my tour-duties, my expectations for Humanity. My situation would never allow me to take his path.

"Niko loved this place," he finally said, and my breath caught in my throat. If words could sucker-punch, these knocked me breathless. "Your mother and I came here several times. It was a very special spot for us."

It didn't escape me that he called her my mother, leaving genetics off the doorstep of the word. I knew it for the intentional deletion it was. I became afraid to speak, knowing that if I did, I might shut the story down, and I so desperately wanted to hear the things Uncle Ty was never brave enough to say. I felt like he was getting closer and closer to trusting me with the entire truth. It was something I'd been working so hard to gain.

"Did you know that your mother had been flagged by the G.E.G.? She grew up thinking there was something wrong with her, and she could never see how perfect she was. Brilliant. Beautiful in that unconventional kind of way."

With every word that wanted to still me, I forced my steps to continue. As much as the topic froze my insides, I knew that if I

---

didn't keep up, I'd miss something. Uncle Ty's pace, as always, was fast and steady, unwavering and unfaltering. He fell back into his Track-legs, making every step count in terms of distance and speed and energy expulsion.

"Your grandfather? He tried to... He ordered... He—" Uncle Ty struggled to formulate sentences. Each one held stutter-stop pain pulsing in every pregnant pause. His feet stilled and he cocked his head.

"He ordered what?" I prompted, stopping right next to him.

"Hear it?" he said instead.

"Hear what?"

Then I did. The noise was like the first clue to a puzzle. It was a plucky note of a taut string being tuned before a torrent of what might have been music meandered through the leaves. I recognized it as a ukulele and wondered how something so small could produce a note so twangy. I stepped towards the sound, but Uncle Ty set his hand firmly on my forearm to stop me.

"What is it?" I whispered.

"The Stilling Song. Follow me." He pushed himself up against a large boulder to the left of us and motioned for me to join him. When I saw what was on the other side of the rock, the view pacified my racing mind. It was a lake the size of a large swimming pool with water so black it mirrored the blue sky perfectly. On the shore stood two boys. The oldest was about my age, but much larger in frame. His broad shoulders reminded me of a slender pit-bull, and his bright blonde hair made me think of lemons. The younger boy was about twelve, with hair the color of pock-marked bricks and eyes the texture of green granite. His head hovered near the elbow of the other, and I could tell the younger would one day grow just as large and tall as the lemon-headed one. Perhaps they were brothers, but perhaps their similarities were born out of growing up in the wild together. They were the perfect specimens for the debate of nature versus nurture.

Uncle Ty shook off his pack and knelt down next to it so he was still covered by a smaller boulder and some shrubbery. I tore my eyes from the scene and followed his lead, not missing the fact that there were tears welling in his eyes. "It's about to begin," he whispered.

I nearly asked, "What's about to begin?" but then one voice sang out, as another one harmonized. The oldest boy sang the first lines, while the younger layered in the second lines so that before one ended, the other began:

    "You're just a song bird
        I can't see
  Yours is a sad song
      Woe is me
          Woe is me.
      I'm free.
  You take joy when you
      See me cry
  Yours is a glad song
      When I die
          When I die.
      I die.
  Freedom takes my
      Heart beyond
  But Death is a stilling song
      For Vagabonds
          By the Bond
      We are bound
          By the Bond."

The song stirred my blood and my palms became sweaty. When the train-track sound of a harmonica chased after the ukulele strings, I discovered where the name of the song came from. For as chaotic as it was, it ripped through my heart like a clamorous calm, and as the younger voice sang the chorus again, I was surprised to recognize notes that carried traces of my own voice, as if I could sing the same song in the same key with the same understanding. When the harmonica cut out, I think its absence was the thing that broke me. Or maybe it was the leftover chords of the ukulele or the way the two boys brought death to life in a single song. There was something unmysterious and truthful about it.

Uncle Ty pushed away a few stray tears with the back of his hand. *"It's a funeral song,"* he explained. *"Someone was executed this morning in the 88th. She was an important comrade of theirs."* There was a twinge of deep-seated pain in his words.

"You know—knew—who it was?"

"A woman named Claire." There was a stark contrast in his expression as he became torn with the rest of it. *"I knew her, and her death has been a great shock to the Vaga—Terrorists."*

The name Claire solidified in my memory. I knew of this death, but I worried as to why Uncle Ty showed so much sadness over the victory. Was he the traitor Grandfather suspected in this? I decided to prod and try to find out. *"Even small victories are one step closer to ridding the world of Terrorism. These nano-bots will help us root out the Terrorists themselves. Why cry over one loss, when we know we are about to cause so much more?"*

His chin snapped up. *"Do not throw around words you cannot fully understand."*

"What I don't understand is how you can be upset about one Terrorist's life? Especially when she threatens the well being of the entire Republic."

"Ani, those are not your words."

He was right. If only I could tell him the words that were mine rather than echo Grandfather. Perhaps, in hearing Uncle Ty's voice shiver, a part of me re-felt the guilt Grandfather had attempted to talk me out of the month before.

Uncle Ty examined my face before he continued. *"You can't possibly get it, yet... but one day you will. You see, Claire blamed me for many things, most of which were not my doing. However, this? Her death? This one was on me. Because she trusted me, she accepted a fate that never should have been hers. She walked right into it, knowing she'd never walk out again. And Claire's is not the only death that is my fault. As a leader, you will experience this. To carry the weight of the dead, any dead, is to carry an irrevocable responsibility. All life is sacred, all life is important, and every death is a sacrifice, whether willingly or unwillingly made. All* deaths should be mourned and respected. One day, you will have choices to make, and, until you become the cause of someone else's sacrifice, you will never truly understand what it means to carry the consequence of responsibility."

I closed my eyes. If only Uncle Ty knew all the things I was already responsible for, and all the things I had yet to be responsible for. Revelation was just around the corner, but I didn't want to think about how Uncle Ty would grow to hate me for what I was fated to become. Could it be possible that Uncle Ty was the traitor Grandfather said he was, or was it an unhappy coincidence the Uncle Ty claimed responsibility for and mourned this Terrorist's death? I wanted him to say something else to disprove the dots that were connecting in my mind, but the fact that he thought he was at fault in this told me of things I didn't want to believe. It was the glue to Grandfather's suspicions, but there was more to it than that. How could Uncle Ty ever know that he wasn't the one responsible for Claire's death?

I was.

There was a bigger question I needed to ask, but someone else spoke from the boulder above us before I could formulate it.

"Well, spoken," it said.

I looked up to see a man, ragged beneath a dark, black beard.

Uncle Ty stood. "Polo, you know my sincerity all too well."

The man, Polo, jumped down and cupped my face in his palms. "He has his mother's smile."

"Cut it out." Uncle Ty grabbed Polo's wrists so he would release my face.

"What's going on?" I asked, stepping back from the strange man with a severe disrespect for personal space.

"Well, by the celestial powers vested in me, I am here to test out these nano-buckets."

"Puns? Really?" Uncle Ty sighed.

"Don't be so sullen. One day, you won't take yourself so seriously." He turned and whispered behind his hand as if it was a secret, though he meant for Uncle Ty to hear everything he said next. "Sometimes fear causes us to think we are more important that we actually are. This dude has way too many fears, and way too much self-importance."

"Polo..." Uncle Ty warned.

"Calm down, Xavi. I'll get to the point. She's here," he said.

Xavi. The way the name fluttered from Polo's mouth made me cringe. It was so foreign to the ears that it made me wonder what kind of person this Xavi character had to be out here all those years ago just to fit in. And the way Uncle Ty bantered with Polo pointed to a deeper bond.

"She's here?" Uncle Ty asked, his face lighting up with shock. Polo faced me again. "Buckets, my boy. There's someone you're overdue in meeting."

CHAPTER TWO

Celeste took her place next to Uncle Ty. The closer she got to Corinna, the more elements of their faces connected them to each other. Hair. Skin. Eyes. From the moment I met Celeste in the woods, there was no denying the fact that she was related to Corinna. Then, she let me give her the nano-bots and proved that even my genetic lineage was interlinked with hers. Though I had not taken the nano-bots myself, Father had. Through DNA, these two women were related to me, but this meant more for the Republic than it did for me.

Uncle Ty held a tablet in his hand and projected the sworn oath of the Chancellor into the air. He swore Corinna in, a speech I'd heard every four years my entire life. Except, instead of my father, this woman stood in a space that did not belong to her. It was over too soon, and the world chanted with her, "Humanity before self."

While my mother wore a mask that said nothing, my uncle wore one that said everything. The contradictions ran in a thousand different directions on his face, making him a thunderstorm and the eye of a hurricane all at once.

I blinked, glad I did not have to say anything yet. It was almost time and my throat swelled just thinking about the words I'd have to push out. To distract my mind from the tears wanting to come, I looked out into the crowd and tried to live within the shock of change. Yet the faces I saw hovering in haphazard lines were a mix unlike anything I'd ever seen at a funeral. On the stage, we were mechanical marionettes. Out there was an entire world of chaos.

I needed to let the faces blur. It was a trick Grandfather taught me right before the first speech I ever gave. *"It's easier to think of them as one massive object than an extreme number of souls with lives and stories all their own. Humanity and the human are two things that feel wrong to separate, but a Politician must be able to see one without the other—to preserve Humanity over the human—in order to save both."*

I let each face blend into the next, not wanting to commit them to memory. I knew that if I scanned back and forth, never letting my eyes stay put for too long, they'd become a blur, one entity in my memory anytime I had to recall this day.

Faceless faces.

I found comfort in them.

Until something shocked me out of the all the faceless, and one came into focus. A flash of color. Green eyes—clovers swimming on a granite surface, marbling into a neon too bright to be real. I locked onto those eyes, and before I could take in the rest of her face, there was a long wail of a trumpet to mark the close of the funeral and the commencement of the swearing in. Just like that, the eyes were lost to the crowd.

Corinna had taken the podium and the world inhaled the change. "You are expecting a speech from me. You are expecting me to make promises. Yet it is not my place to be the owner of what comes next. It is not my place to speak for the sons of the dead. There is someone here, someone needing to deliver a message that connects to a greater design. It is my hope that we honor this young man for his bravery, for it will be his words that bring us through the darkness shrouding us all."

"You're thinking so hard, you're about to have an aneurysm."

I yanked the earphones away and let them dangle over my shoulder. *"Mos, you startled me."*

"Unhinge, brother. No one is listening." He grinned and continued in his easy speech. *"Seriously, though, making your brain explode will not solve any world problems."* He stretched his back, and I heard the crackling of spine. I often wondered what it felt like for him, as a giant, to grow into the mass of a body that contained him. It was probably similar to my own, indescribable growing pains within my mind.

"My brain is tougher than you give it credit for."

"You're listening to them, right?" he asked.

I nodded. *"I know you don't believe it, but they have their own language."*

He reached for the tablet and examined the data I was looking at. *"Haven't your nano-bots caused enough ruckus? I mean, it was supposed to be a thesis project, not something that'd—"*

"It's not a ruckus. It's truth. The Terrorists may not be what we think they are. They may be a—"

"Control group. I've heard the theory plenty enough, Ani." He was trying not to be worried, but the information I was uncovering scared him.

I sighed. *"Then how can we deny it? Think about it. What does every experiment need?"*

"Ani—"

"If the Colonies are cultures for studies in Genetic Advancement, it means that they are the experimental groups. But in all of my research, not one Colony is left unchecked. Where is the control group then?"

"Ani, please," Mos begged. *"Don't let these nano-bots take over your brain."*

"Har. Har. You get funnier the older you get."

"And you get funnier looking the older you get, but you don't hear me rubbing it in." He unplugged the earphones from the tablet and turned up the volume of the feed so we could both hear it. To most, it sounded like static, but to my brain, it sounded like singing.

I closed my eyes and listened as the nano-bots transmitted the data, the strands, the letters and sequencing that spiraled into DNA. I heard the unborn stories they told, and I knew it was nearly time to let the world hear them too.

This particular stream proved the owner was a seventh-generation Terrorist, born and raised in the wild. Genetic Engineering Seminars at Institute always claimed that all Terrorists were escapees from the Colonies. They always told us that people were rarely born in the wild, and if they were, they were not likely to survive their first year. Yet, this feed, and hundreds of others, suggested that a large portion of Terrorists had never been Citizens. Each stream of data connected back to a Citizen at some point, but it wasn't always a direct offspring. It only proved my belief that breeding in the wild was encouraged.

It also made me wonder where this happened? It couldn't be easy to raise babies out in the wild without a safe harbor for their more formative years. When I posed this question to Grandfather, he suggested it happened at the Vault.

As the Council of Manipulation let loose new stories of the Solanos, the Republic began to digest them in the small doses they were given. The Vault was the newest acquisition of knowledge that gave Citizens roots to their origins.

The original Vault was a legendary lab, rumored to be the place where civilization rebooted after The Great Disaster. In the wake, as is the natural order of things, humans sought out other humans, and Solano Industries had created a safe haven for the survivors in a city that has since lost its name to time. The Vault was crucial to the Republic after The Great Disaster as it reinstated laws in a lawless land. Survivors craved civilization, and civilization demanded structure. To get this, the Founding Families were willing to give up certain freedoms for the advancement of Humanity.

According to the Council of Manipulation, they have sent archeologists to search high and low for the Vault, but they still haven't discovered where it was. They had theories that it existed in Texas, but even some of those names were lost as history was

41

rewritten or hidden. Even the ancient borders were uncertain after the Deletion Cancers set fire to most of the world. The saved documents indicated only two initials for the home of Solano Industries.

A winding S.

A mountainous M.

The mystery of the Vault became the new bedtime story for children, but, within our generation, the Terrorists took the name for themselves. It was now the fabled home base of those living in the fringes of our world. Now, instead of archeologists in search for a lost city, the Militia searches for the hub of Terrorism. Some spies have even said the Terrorists claim to know where the original Vault is, but the only truth that existed in those tales was that Terrorists took a piece from the very heart of the Republic's history and forced it to belong to them.

Mos' smile faded from his face, "Seriously, though. I know you miss the old man, but do you need to take this so far?"

I thought about Instructor Aeschylus. I remembered the way he always wore a half-lidded expression whenever he'd narrow his brow in thought, the way he'd always challenged me to think beyond my own intelligence, and the way he died, so quiet and tired and done with life. The gossip-geneticists insisted he made a mistake in the lab—cut his finger on a dangerous slide and couldn't be cured. He was my thesis mentor up until the past month took him away from me, and that rumor was hard to swallow. Instructor Aeschylus was far too procedural and cautious in his lab to be done in by a simple mistake.

They didn't let me visit him before he died, but Grandfather described him for me. He said Instructor Aeschylus' eyes were bloody and his voice was cracked, refusing to move words out past his lips. Grieving his death, as painful as it was, worked towards my advantage. It made it look like I was obsessing over this project because I wanted to honor him.

In truth, he didn't matter when it came to this. I couldn't abandon the research if I tried. I was so close to seeing something so hauntingly big.

"Can I ask you something?" Mos asked.

"Does that question count as the asking?"

He ignored my deflection with a smirk. "Why create the anti-bot serum?"

"Simple answer for a simple question. In order to convince the Terrorists they should participate willingly. They needed to feel safe in doing so."

"Then why put the tracking feature in the nano-bots at all?" he asked.

"Just as simple an answer. So the signal can get picked up to transmit the data. Plus, the trackers gave the Militia incentive to help administer it to captured Terrorists without killing them, just like the anti-bot serum gave the Terrorists incentive to take the nano-bots voluntarily. Both measures ensured that the most people, Terrorist or Citizen, were given the serum in the first place, whether voluntarily or involuntarily."

The thing I didn't admit was that the tracking was an unforeseen side effect, a slight tweaking in the design that accidentally allowed tracking to be a function. Less than an ounce of the serum that held the nano-bots not only recorded genetic makeups but also allowed the Militia to monitor movement, but it took me longer to figure out where the mutation in design happened so I could create the anti-bot serum.

In the eyes of the Republic, I got to experiment with genetic data and the Militia gained access to the whereabouts and dealings of traitors. When Grandfather found out about the tracking feature, he thought it was intentional and encouraged me to continue the work. Rather than tell him it wasn't and risk him shutting everything down, I had to come up with the other side of the serum to make sure no side but my research had the advantage. I knew that getting the Terrorists to voluntarily take it would make the process happen faster, and depending only on the Militia would severely limit how quickly the serum would spread.

Of course, I neglected to reveal this anti-bot serum to the G.E.G. to go along with the playing-both-sides exercise Grandfather had been aching for me to learn. Unlike the nano-bots, the anti-bot serum did not undergo production in the G.E.G. labs, and I had to give samples of the anti-bot serum I developed on my own to the Terrorists taking the nano-bots voluntarily.

"Well, why tell the Terrorists about the trackers in the first place?"

"Because it made them think I was willing to betray the Republic. It made them more likely to trust me enough to take them."

Mos paused the feed and nodded. "You are Grandfather's protégé alright. He's always saying that sometimes you have to play your hand to both sides to get the results you want in the middle."

"Why do you think he let me spend so much time on this thesis when Genetics is not the field I'm permitted to follow? I had to make him believe there was a political lesson involved. I had to explain my plan to get two opposing sides to unknowingly work together." It was the only truth I was permitted to share. The other truths were so confidential not even I knew how to think about them accurately.

My brother stood up and frowned. His green eyes hovered under light eyebrows, standing out against his tanned skin. "I overheard Grandfather last night. He's going to pull the plug on it."

"Mos, this was always part of my hypothesis when I created the nano-bots, and I have proof now. I can't ignore it. The fact that the Terrorists were not eradicated after the nano-bots spread only supports the theory even more. The government needs them to exist, and the data shows that they are more valuable genetically than we think them to be." This was the surface truth, but Mos could never know the rest. Not yet at least. I said the right words here, placed the right inflections there. Every sentence moved pawns on the chess board. Each letter knew there was a bigger endgame.

I wondered if Mos could read through my expression. I wondered if he was meant to. It wouldn't have been the first time we'd been placed on opposite sides of a story.

I glanced at the feed on the screen, at the anomaly that

indicated an essential genetic shift. Mos had no idea he'd been listening to the goldmine of information.

Mos frowned and shut the tablet down. "Please, promise me you'll drop it."

"I can't."

Before I could move towards the podium, Mos stepped before me and wrapped me into a hug. "You can still change your mind. Right here? Right now? It's the only time you can. Once we say it, once we commit, there's no turning back. *Unhinge*, brother. Think beyond. There are other ways. We have other ways."

We. He was still including himself in the decision as if he had any power in it, but I had already started down this path. I had already turned my back on the future that had always been so clearly laid out for both of us.

I already knew what he did not. That world, that future, was gone long before we were born.

As much as I wished it was different, easy was never meant to be the path for me, not when right and wrong were so blurred along the edges. I held unborn stories in my hand and in my heart. Stories that bled out from the past and threatened the future in ways no one, not even my brother, saw coming. Stories I ached to tell him but couldn't because I'd never put him in danger with these truths. Not like I had my father. How could I pretend not to know what I now knew? How could I pretend I did not do what I had done? What had to be done to save Humanity? What eventually led to Father's death?

And how could I pretend there weren't greater genetic terrors Humanity faced than the carefully cultivated fears of the Terrorists?

"I can't turn away from the truth. It's far too valuable for me to be fickle with." I pulled back and looked at him. I needed to memorize his face in this moment. There were subtle changes going on in his expression, looks I'd never seen before, and I connected the way his eyes never changed, no matter how much his face did. The colors were just like mine, and we used to see

—

45

the world so similarly through matching pupils, but ever since I leaked my findings, he'd been torn between protecting me and bashing my brains in. For as liberal as his philosophical musings were, he believed in structure. For as stoic as my musings were, I'd destroyed the very structure I claimed to believe in.

He opened his mouth to say something, but nothing came out. Instead, when he stepped back, he created an orbit of space around him.

Mother stood near the podium, and I tried to ignore the fact that her usually placid face had let distraught emotions wage a subtle war on her wrinkles. She hid emotions well, but I knew the simple signs of struggle in her heart. She stepped forward and hugged me, and I caught the familiar smell of oranges and lavender. I catalogued it with all the other times her smell gave me comfort. Collective memories piled on top of each other, giving me a larger sense of calm, and in this moment, she gave me what I needed.

Because I needed to know I was loved, that I was forgiven. I needed to know that in hurting them, I was saving them. I was saving everyone.

She squeezed my arms and backed away. "Look at that stoic face. So much like your father. Ready to sacrifice yourself, but you are my son, Anicetus. You—"

"The boy is fine, Zosime," Grandfather interrupted. He stepped next to me and clasped my hand in his. Though it was a gesture that showed respect, his fingers held mine tightly. His stare pinned me down, making sure I understood.

I did.

"You must control the Control!"

"Ani, shut the vid off," Mother said from the kitchen.

But I couldn't pull my eyes away from the screen. The fires. The riots. The trampling. Though Citizens appreciated structure, they sure were quick to tear it down when they feared a shifting political world. So easily, they traded calm for calamity, setting sail on a wave of anger. It'd been months since the first riot, and no matter what Grandfather said, whenever I came face to face with the reality of anarchy, it unsettled me.

I heard Mother as she sighed and made her way towards the den. She sat down on the couch next to me as another face came on the screen. "Patriots must unite against Terrorism. These lies are the spawn of—"

The rest of the message was lost to Mother's command that shut the vid off. "My sweet boy, your heart is too big. You made a mistake, but it was they who made the choice to destroy. They blame it on you because they are too arrogant to take responsibility themselves. Do not let this change you."

I let her wrap me in her arms and tried to let her perfume soothe me the way it used to. It didn't work. It only rattled me more, reminding me that I didn't deserve to be loved by her right then and there. I deserved to watch the fruits of my labor, the chaos I bred.

The very chaos my father was working tirelessly to fix by getting the Absolution Bill passed.

"They will never trust you again, you know." Grandfather's voice pulled me from her hold as he walked in. These were choreographed words. He'd told me just yesterday that it was time to place this particular seed, but I hated what this seed was destined to grow into. "You'll never rise here. All that training wasted. All that time I've spent shaping you—"

"That's enough," Mother said.

"It'll never be enough. The boy has blood on his hands now. He started the anarchies with his treasonous act. He birthed it into the world and ripped the Republic apart with the click of a button. I should have known it was in his veins. He's his mother's son."

"I am the boy's mother."

The way she claimed me should have comforted me. The words were right, the intention correct, but something troubled me about how much she wished she believed it herself.

"If only that were true, Zosime." There was no pity in his face, but the cold calculation sent silent shivers down my spine. He walked towards the bar and poured an inch of whiskey. He twirled it in the glass and examined it through the crystal. "The boy must face atonement if he hopes to survive this. He may get rebellion from his mother, but he gets how to be a Politician from me. The boy knows I speak truth in this."

I nodded like the puppet I needed to be. The Politician side of my lineage knew all too well. The years he spent cultivating my intelligence, the months spent analyzing strategies in leadership, the childhood lost to being the face of New Wave Perfection. Grandfather didn't need to say anymore, and Mother finally knew what I was expected to do in the name of the Republic. She'd heard the plans for the Act that was yet to come, and I watched her expression as she finally put it all together. Her face hardened as she searched for the words that would extract her from the corner Grandfather had backed her into.

Before she could, Grandfather asked, "May I have a word with my grandson?" It wasn't a question but a command. He rarely asked for permission for anything he did.

I watched Mother fold under the weight of it. She squeezed my bicep, kissed me on the forehead, and left me to Grandfather's words. I was jealous she could escape. I knew she'd go straight to her home laboratory to work. Father had it installed before Mos had been born so she didn't have to spend all her waking hours at the G.E.G. She always buried herself in work. I loved the way she donned her white lab coat the moment she entered her lab, the way she began each session with a ritual intensity and a belief in pure science. She felt in control there, and I was just a reminder that she couldn't control everything.

Grandfather moved towards me. He thrummed his wrinkled fingers on his glass, and I held onto the last moments before I had to admit I understood the part of his plan he'd neglected to speak of when I agreed to participate. I wished I could pretend ignorance, but I was too brilliant to play stupid. It was just that, for the first time, I felt the urge to pause, even though I couldn't put the brakes on now. "If I do this, do I have to give up everything?" It was an inquiry that could not feel the weight of the question mark attached to it. The answer I already knew pulled me into regret.

Grandfather took a sip of his whiskey. "Even Zosimos. Would you really want to tarnish his chances? He'll have to step up where you cannot, and he won't be able to if your shadow darkens his light."

I shook my head.

"You'll get it all back, if we play our cards right."

"It's not that," I whispered. I knew where he was going, and not for the first time in my life, I wasn't sure if I completely agreed with it.

"You get the first part, but do you understand the second?"

"Yes, sir."

"You will root them out. We must find the head of the snake so that the traitors can be eradicated. You can't go back now, or the Republic will crumble. Do you understand me?"

"Yes, sir," I replied. I thought of all the snakes rearing their heads in a crumbling world and thought of another question. "Grandfather? Why do you let the Patriots continue? I know it's in your power to snuff them out."

"Why do the Patriots bother you so?"

"Just because they are not the enemy we fear the most does not mean they should be allowed to continue as is. There are too many movable parts in this game, too many variables not within our control. We should let the Citizens know the greater threat. It may unite them."

Grandfather smiled. "Why do we let this confusion continue then?"

I sighed as the answer presented itself. "Because you don't want the real enemy to inspire people to believe in them. It is why you call them the Unnamed. To give them a name is to give them the power of existence, and once they exist, they will pose a greater threat. It is better to deal with them in secret. The Patriots are a distraction from the real threat, so we let them make noise."

"Well done."

I nodded. "But, Grandfather, you know something new. It's been a long day. Can we skip the banter and get to it, please?"

I couldn't tell if it was pity or compassion that crossed his face because neither was something he ever felt towards me. Even still, he let the disrespect slide. "We know who the leader is, now. They call her Lynk, and if we do this right, you can stop her from destroying everything we've built."

"When will I be sent out?" I asked.

"We'll need six more months to cultivate the situation. I'll let you know when it's time."

I swallowed the dryness in my throat and felt a shudder rip through me, but I stilled it as I let my family go. I didn't need to see in order to know the three-dimensional versions of myself walked stages across the entire Republic, and I needed to look the part. I needed to appear strong and determined though weakness threatened to cripple me.

As I stepped up to the podium, Uncle Ty and the other Manipulators slid through the door at the back of the stage. I knew I shouldn't take offense. Their role in the swearing in was complete, and the Council needed to appear disinterested. I knew Uncle Ty had to keep his distance in this, but part of me hoped he'd find a way to stay.

I clicked the button on the podium that would project my voice more clearly to the holo-vid versions of myself. Everyone would hear me as if we were having a simple conversation in a cafe.

I felt the moisture in my eyes choke the back of my throat. It had nowhere else to go since the tears weren't permitted to fall, and I needed to bite them back.

I blinked and in between the movement of my lids, I saw the faces of chaos and the birth of anarchy.

I blinked and saw my hands as they typed in the commands to hack into the G.E.G. database to cross-reference my nano-bot findings.

I blinked and saw the world burn.

Grandfather had never explained that part of the plan. How could I have known the realities of idealism? That it had the potential to be more destructive than conspiracies? How could I take back a deed misspent? How could I not see the birth of anarchy speeding towards me, black clouds of the inevitable storm? I had to have known, right? In all of my training, hadn't I been brought up to bear the burden of chaos so that Humanity could find peace in my stead? I must have had an inkling, a suspicion, a premonition... I had to have known what I would cause, but, for once in my life, I let myself hover in denial for a little while. I told myself there was no way I could have predicted what had happened.

I blinked and the time for denial was over.

"Your grandfather will say that sometimes, it is necessary to lie in order to protect the truth," Uncle Ty said. "You'll be told to deny intention. The smart move, politically speaking, is to do so. You'll see your grandfather's logic and do as he asks. Just promise me you won't let the lie become the truth for yourself, that you'll always remember the reality within all the fiction you'll be asked to tell. You meant no harm, yet harm was done. These deaths are on you, my boy, but you can still honor them by doing what's right in moving forward. "

He refused to hate me, even for this. I wanted him to. I wanted to tell him all about Claire and about the plan so he could get all the hating out of his system in one fell swoop. It was out of ignorance that Uncle Ty still loved me, and it was out of ignorance that he was going to be blindsided when the truth finally revealed itself. I knew it'd be the blindsiding that would make me lose him forever.

For now, the only wrongdoing I could claim was this data transmission spreading throughout the Colonies.

"Did I ever tell you about my father?" Uncle Ty asked when I tried to speak and found I couldn't. "No? I guess not. He's a hard topic to talk about, but he is important to my story. Most people think I began my Tour of Duty on the Tracks a year early because the G.E.G. wanted my Celebrity Tour to start sooner rather than later. My Public Relations Specialist spun the story that the faster I completed one duty, the faster I could move on to another. But really? It was to prove I still belonged, that I wasn't a traitor. You

see, my father had been tried and convicted of treason that year. It was a quiet trial and execution, so the rest of the world never learned of the depths of his betrayal, but that didn't mean that the people who counted didn't know."

He paused and let the information sink in.

"For the cherry on top?" he continued. "Just before this happened, I was responsible for getting a girl Rehabilitated. I held her hand. We got caught."

"You—"

"I broke a law while my father broke another. In the wake of those two disgraces, I thought I had to prove my loyalty to the Republic on a greater scale. I set out to show my genetic line was still deserving of prestige in the face of all my family's indiscretions. I wanted to secure my status as a Celebrity and the Caste I'd grown accustomed to, and I needed to do something bold. So I worked hard and exceeded beyond the tests so that I could be released into the wild early."

I swallowed. This story revealed that we were tethered to each other in similar guilts. He knew what it meant to have a traitorous parent and how it made you feel the need to prove you belonged to the Republic despite your origins. After all, I'd been trying to prove to Grandfather my entire life that I was worthy of being a Petrakis, and I did everything in my power to show that he had scoured all remnants of the negative Kostas blood from my mannerisms through his carefully guided nurturing.

"I have followed my father's footsteps by becoming a Manipulator, but I had to work ten times harder to prove myself worthy of the job" Uncle Ty said. "I don't talk about him often, but he told me things he shouldn't have. He explained how the Republic was born—the things it must do to maintain power, and he claimed that the fall was near."

"What fall?" I asked, shivering at the word. I knew he was trying to give me this information gently, and that he had practice in being the speaker of secrets. He always held them like precious stones, waiting for the right moment to send one skipping across placid water to leave its marked ripples wherever it landed.

"To generalize the concept, you must first remember that we live in a world of cycles. Power is just one of these cycles. It shifts into a set of hands which then wields it over another group of people in an act of oppression. This continues for a time before the oppressed get tired of being oppressed. They eventually fight for power. They always gain it. Then they, in turn, oppress the oppressors in the name of fairness. After all, you can't have power unless you take it from someone else. As generations pass, the once-upon-a-time oppressors forget they had ever been in charge in the first place. All they see is their lowered status, and the only direction they can look is up. From this angle, they see people complacent in their power, living in a comfort that is just out of their reach. They crave it. They fight for it. They always get it back. This cycle is an absolute and unavoidable fact of human nature, so that authority is never permanent. You see, every anarchy is just like the one before, and every cycle is rotated by the same two genres of people: those who work to maintain power and those who work to take it away."

The cycle of power was a topic we'd touched on in our *Advanced Manipulation Seminar* at Institute, but I never let the idea of it scare me. I knew that the Council of Manipulation protected the Republic from such simplistic shifts through our Caste system. As unfair as it seemed to some, our Caste system gave structure. It gave people something to strive for. It gave Citizens the hope of fluidity in situation, that if they worked hard enough, they could earn a position through generational patience rather than steal it. But I knew some of the poorer Colonies had trouble accepting it, and I knew that, had I grown up in those Colonies, I might not be so happy with my lot. Even still, Citizens wanted for little and were given everything they needed to cultivate their genetic gifts so that there was no need for revolutions.

Uncle Ty knew I understood the basics, but he wanted me to review them in my head. It was a common tactic whenever he or Father or Grandfather were trying to teach me. They had to make me work for it. My brain always needed to earn answers to make them feel real.

"After analyzing histories," he continued, "my father came up with a formula. He called it the Triggers of Descent, and these triggers were always the things that set fire to the cycle. As a Manipulator, you learn that the only way for those with control to keep it was to concede in some ways so that those they ruled over felt they had a voice. The moment people feel completely powerless is the moment they have nothing to lose. The manipulation of balance so that power shifts happen gradually is an attempt to save the most lives when facing the inevitable. In school, you are told this is done through a well maintained Caste system, but have you ever heard of the Small Anarchies?"

I nodded. "After the Deletion Cancers, there were large uprisings against the Republic. People questioned whether the Genetic Engineering Guild could truly be trusted in handling Humanity's advancement."

"Think Anicetus. Come to the conclusion that rests there."

I swallowed.

"What happens when there are too many deformities in the genome?" Uncle Ty asked.

I blinked. There it was. A new, unborn truth hiding just under the surface of history. "The Deletion Cancers weren't an accident, but a culling."

Uncle Ty sent me a sad smile. "The Small Anarchies were larger than history gives them credit. You see, human nature calls us to the fight. Every day, we fight to survive, we fight to hold onto our Humanity, we fight to pull ourselves into greatness. But for one group of people to be right, we need one group of people to be wrong. After the Deletion Cancers, Citizens believed the G.E.G. to be in the wrong, and they started to fight against them. That was, until they focused their anarchist energy elsewhere."

I laughed. "Brilliant. Absolutely brilliant."

"Time is always on the G.E.G.'s side, Ani. Now that this is out, we have to be clever in righting a wrong so foundational to our system."

I wanted to be shocked, but it made sense. If this was true, then it meant my findings revealed more than just a control group.

It suggested that my hypothesis had another layer and that the war against Terrorism was a farce designed to give Citizens something to rally against. It was human nature to need an enemy to stoke the fires of patriotism, and the Vagabonds were the most obvious target. After the Deletion Cancers, when the Small Anarchies bubbled up from the seams of the Republic, threatening to tear it down from the inside, the Manipulators, in trying to solve the unrest, must have decided to use the genetic control group for a different kind of control—the control of chaos. The Manipulators encouraged Citizens to place their anxieties outward rather than inward because they understood that people feared what they did not understand. Rather than fear those with control, those in control directed fears to those without it.

"The first rule of Manipulation is that when you let pressure release rather than force it to build up, control can be maintained. Small anarchies are encouraged, as they are more manageable than full blown rebellions," Uncle Ty continued. "This was why my father was arrested. He predicted a large-scale rebellion. He said the Republic's tight hold on the path we were on would only lead to the death of our nation. He claimed that if we started the gradual change sooner than later, the Republic could maintain the ultimate power, and he started leaking the rumors that we were close to genetic perfection and that the G.E.G. was hiding it out of a greed to maintain power. He wanted to make the G.E.G. the scapegoat— the sacrifice to a small anarchy.

"Soon, the other four Manipulators turned on him for his plan— accused him of being disloyal to Humanity for such treasonous actions. And since the Manipulation chair is held until death, the execution was expedited and quiet. Most of the world thinks he died of a heart attack because no one could find out he was trying to jumpstart a power cycle."

Uncle Ty sighed. "I can read your mind, boy. Execution is not in the cards for you. I've already talked to Manipulator Tantalos, and, believe it or not, the Council of Manipulation has seen this coming. Granted, it's not in the fluid way they'd have liked everything to go, but all five branches of the government,

---

55

Manipulators, Senators, Militia, G.E.G., and your father have accepted that the cycle is in motion. We all want to do things in a way that saves the most lives, starting with yours."

I already knew this. The quiet trial would not be my fate, but I would be sacrificed in another way. As the face of New Wave Perfection, my role would be a lot more public. One thing I had on my side? Despite the look of things, I was no traitor.

"Friends and Citizens of the Republic." The first words wobbled when they came out, but my voice soon steadied. "I must apologize for the fear and confusion that has occurred over the past year. My discoveries, though pure in intention, became the birth of anarchy. They have caused chaos, destruction, and death, including my own father's. My irresponsible procedures in my experiments led to the transmission of data that was, at the time, unconfirmed and unverified. Although I had no role in the unsanctioned sharing of this data to the Republic, I—"

I swallowed. I hated this falsity, but I moved past my moment of stutter.

"—I can't apologize enough. Though the data should have gone through a verification process before being divulged to the public in a manageable way, how the information was shared does not negate its validity. The fact that it was released prior to this process was a gross malfunction within the databases."

It was a stupid lie. How could anyone possibly believe that a simple malfunction would send out this information in a massive tsunami too powerful to call back? I hated the story and the way history would be forced to tell it. Yet it was the only way for the next part to work.

I looked down to the stage below me. I needed to stop blurring the faces. I needed something, anything to ground me to the truth because I felt like someone else was speaking the words for me. I swallowed, my mouth becoming achingly dry. Then Mos stepped up next to me and put his hand on my shoulder. I didn't want to say the next part, and he didn't want to hear it. His hand told me to turn back. His squeeze reminded me it was my last chance to do so.

I didn't want things to change forever.

I couldn't stop change from happening.

I lifted my head up, let my chin direct my words outward.

There they were. Those floating clover eyes, standing out from all the blurred faces. I zeroed in on the face. Her skin was a tanned cream and her hair was a wild bronze. It finally sunk in that *they* were here amongst the Citizens. Not just in our government and on our stages, but in our crowds. They were the proof of change, not nearly as subtle as I expected them to be. There were Terrorists—no, Vagabonds—watching my forced confession for themselves. The woman was older and wore a slack-jawed smile that may have meant pride or may have meant hope. The definition remained unknown as I found my words again, but I couldn't tear my eyes away from hers.

"The truth? It deserves to be honored. Although this was not how I intended my research to be shared, the data can not be denied now that it has been verified beyond a doubt. It does not escape me that these truths were hard pills to swallow. Since the Deletion Cancers, the Citizens of the Republic were led to believe that those living on the fringes of our society were a threat to our genetic purity, and it is hard to remove a fear so many generations in the making.

"These beliefs pit family against family in an uncivil war that goes beyond the small anarchies we've experienced this past year. This war has waged for generations, but the data does not lie. The people living on the fringes are not Terrorists, but a control group in one larger genetic plan. They are not our enemies, as we once thought, but a valuable piece of Humanity's genetic puzzle. They are Vagabonds, drifters by design in our large-scale genetic experiment, meant to serve as a control group to our Colonies. But this is *not* news. You've heard this so many times this past year, and you've had plenty of time to come to terms with these new realities. Vagabonds play an equal role to the genome experiment, and therefore deserve equal rights."

I closed my eyes and saw the explosion behind my lids. The

way my father blew apart into an infinite number of pieces, taking the start of his Donation Act campaign with him. How could I finish what he'd started? I opened my eyes and saw a different explosion. How could she be so far, yet her eyes stand out so much? Green on green on green, like looking at the sun hitting meadow grass right after a summer rain. I tore my eyes away and tried to make the faces blur again.

"Experiment," I whispered, though the microphone made it heard by all. "We should not be offended to be associated with such a word, for experiments are the very foundations from which our race was saved from extinction. What our ancestors did, they did out of a stoic love for Humanity after The Great Disaster. They designed the Colonies to cultivate genetic diversity, while they encouraged Vagabonds to live their haphazard existence. There have even been times when the depletion of their population has altered the course of our own. Their genetic realities have impacted the decisions the G.E.G. has made in partnering practices and diversity encouragement. All along, the Vagabonds have been a reflection of our scientific advancement. Where they succeed in diversity has a direct correlation to how the G.E.G. manipulates genetic paths. No matter how scared we are in the face of change, we need to remember that the moment Vagabonds can breed without large scale genetic deficits is the moment we've cured the greater degradations of Humanity.

"It is time we put the word human back in Humanity! The war against Terrorism is not the war you think it is." I shook my head and pounded my fist on the podium for emphasis. "This. Must. Stop. Each execution that has happened this year, and every year before, was one genetic possibility lost to us. I get it, I do. There are a million reasons to continue this uncivil war, but all of them pale in the light of truth and the reality of Humanity. Rather than condemn Vagabonds as Terrorists, we should celebrate them for their genetic value to the greater good."

I paused and let it sink in. It was the biggest truth, the most important one. We should have been more direct with it from the beginning, and maybe my father would still be around. Maybe the anarchies would have dissipated sooner had we attempted to replace fear with understanding right away. But my father's Public Relations Specialists begged us to play it close to the chest, while Grandfather argued that allowing the small anarchies now would prevent a much larger scale one later and that to hold off would give me time to work the grassroots side of the Bills and Acts that needed to pass next. Grandfather convinced Father to tiptoe around things, and the entire time, I watched the circles growing black under his eyes, the color of stress on his perfect face. And when it was time, Father finally made a stand—one that made it so he never stood again.

But I was learning that taking a stand was a powerful thing. It gave you balance. It gave you form. It gave you confidence in the path you were set on.

And this was my stand.

"This past year, through the Absolution Bill, the Republic has granted the Vagabonds lands in the form of Territories. This has caused a chaos within our borders that appalls me. As Citizens, we pride ourselves on being enlightened, stoic beings, atypical of our species by denying instinctual reactions to destroy that which we do not understand. Yet, when faced with a real truth, the Republic has done the typical. We have reacted from impulsivity and relied on base fears. We disproved our ability to put science before the self when we set out to tear each other apart. We are a people built on a respect for facts, yet when given irrefutable, scientific proof, we wish to bury our heads in the comfort of the uncomfortable past. We want to point fingers rather than recognize our own wrongdoings, and, in trying to hide our own shortcomings, we have caused the birth of anarchy.

"In regards to the Vagabonds, our nation has acted atrociously generations deep, and it pains us to recognize it. But denying it won't make the facts go away. Saying that we honor truth, then not backing it up with action, does nothing to foster the changes our nation needs to heal. The anarchies must stop. We need dialogue. We need a new version of peace. And we need nonviolent action in the pursuit of truth."

There was a buzzing in my ears that grew louder until I realized it was silence.

A seeded silence.

It had taken root and was growing beyond anything I'd ever experienced before.

It was as if the entire world had gone quiet at my voice, and it made me feel powerful, like I was rising up behind the legacy of my father.

But those eyes. I landed on them again as the faceless came back into focus. They were louder than the silence, floating above dirty cheeks, ghosts coming alive in the shadows. And she cried, tears that grew bulbous in the corners of all that green.

"My father believed in truth, and it cost him his life," I told her. She seemed like someone who understood what it felt like to lose someone. She seemed like someone who, even if she grew up worlds apart from me, could just get how much it hurt to lose a father.

Ghosts. They were everywhere in my peripherals. Father's death was never part of the plan. It had been a risk to ask him to bear the brunt of change, but both he and Grandfather had said it came with the duties of being a Chancellor. I couldn't help but feel his death was on my hands, stained in the cracks of my palms forever. He haunted me. My perfect memory allowed me to rewind the image over and over and over again, every detail cutting at my heart until it became numb.

"Last week, he was meant to announce the passing of a new Act, and I am here today in the shadow of his memory so that I may share his mission with you today. It is an honor that was never meant to be mine, but it is an honor I take on in remembrance of my father, the late Chancellor Paramonos Petrakis. Through my words, I hope you can hear his as I present to you the Donation Act."

Father spread his hands wide against the desk as he spoke into the cameras. I leaned against the wall, knowing it was a tactic to make him seem bigger in the camera lenses. This was his signature move after getting past the pleasantries and gentle openings of every speech.

This signaled the important part and forced everyone to move to the edges of their chairs, to lean in just a little closer to make sure they didn't miss a word.

"The Absolution Bill will grant Vagabonds rights to four Territories in the unused, southwest section of the Republic, giving those who wish to stop running a home and a central location for their own government. Each Territory will be allowed two Senators within the Republic proceedings so that we may build relationships between Vagabonds and Citizens. There will be a framework of sharing, allowing Vagabonds access to Scientists, doctors, and health specialists to maintain their genetic safety while still protecting their genetic gifts from scientific manipulation. This will ensure that genetic responsibilities are being fulfilled on both sides, and, just as we will continue to plan paths to genetic greatness here in the Colonies, their genetic lines will wander their own unhindered paths in the Territories.

"Vagabonds will be given ration cards for use within the Colonies. These will be considered Reparations for the plight we have caused their people for generations. Some may earn more credit in exchange for services, such as, but not limited to, maintenance of the rails, work in the Victory Gardens, or serving as Diplomats and Ambassadors."

The door opened to my side, drawing my attention away from my father's speech. Onesimos Leventis stepped in, dressed in his perfectly pressed suit, and leaned up against the same wall I did.

"You and your grandfather think you're so clever," he said.

"Far from it," I replied.

I never understood why my father trusted Onesimos so much, but he led the Advisory and was in Father's ear about most issues. I could see the strain of the subtle, yet not-so-silent war Onesimos waged against Absolution. Maybe that was why my father kept him around, to play the role of the devil's advocate, but there was a fine line between being an advocate and being the devil himself.

I felt the heat of his breath as he leaned in closer. "I know it *wasn't an accident." His words were steady, though his breath shook with anger. Onesimos' placid rage used to terrify me, but somewhere over the past month, I had forgotten how to be afraid. "If it were up to me," he added, "you'd have a needle in those perfect veins of yours."*

He set his palm on my shoulder as if he were comforting me, but the squeeze let his cleanly cut nails dig into my flesh. I didn't give him the satisfaction of a wince as Father's voice carried between us.

Onesimos accompanied the squeeze with another whisper. "There are true Patriots, everywhere. You think you have rid us of Terrorism because you changed their names to Vagabonds? You think you can make a wild bear as tame as a kitten? Terrorism isn't dead. Thanks to you it just got a stronger foothold in your fragile world."

I spread my hands to both sides of the podium to make myself appear larger. I wanted my father's features gifted to me by genetics to be prominent. I wanted to enhance the mannerisms I'd inherited from him so that the world would take me just as seriously.

As I placed pressure on my palms, I thought about that day Father announced the Absolution Bill. It made me wish I was announcing Onesimos Leventis' execution instead. I hated that he invaded my thoughts in this moment—that in talking about my father, my mind raced towards explosions and the way Onesimos disappeared the exact same day.

This?

This was just the first step in stopping people like him.

"The Donation Act will work in conjunction with the Absolution Bill, and in honor of my father, it has become my mission to make sure it passes successfully." I smiled. Here came the word choreography. Here came the movement of my voice that would weave the spell of change in every ear.

"Under the passage of the Donation Act, Citizens are given the choice to donate their genetic lines to the control group." I paused.

The pregnant pauses were important. I needed Citizens to take the information in and digest it while they still chewed on it. Too short and the news would feel unbelievable. Too long and they'd choke on the information.

"This is not a decision that may be taken lightly. Ask any veteran who has completed a Tour of Duty. Should you decide to shift loyalties, the life of a Vagabond is harsh. Very few survive such extreme discomfort, and the novelty will wear off fast. Once it does, you will not be able to get back what you have given up. Do not mistake the romance of being a Vagabond for their realities. Their freedom is not devoid of chains and rules, just as their culture is not devoid of expectations and boundaries.

"According to the Donation Act, all donations of citizenship must be documented by the Department of Human Relations. Upon Exodus, your genetic gifts will be harvested and preserved for the use of Humanity's genetic advancement. No person will be allowed to leave without extensive counseling and a month-long preparation course for the wild. This will be the grace period where you can return to your Caste and station without consequence, but once you make the Final Exodus, you will lose your status as a Citizen completely. Anyone leaving without going through this process will be considered a true Terrorist for stealing their genetic potential from the genome.

"I urge you to remember that your contribution to Humanity is more valuable within the Colonies and that too much Exodus into the control group may dilute certain progresses, destroying the very function it was created for. For this reason, the Genetic Engineering Guild may deny certain applications for Donation until certain genetic duties have been met that may go beyond the harvesting of genetic gifts."

I paused again. Mother tapped my elbow, but I didn't look at her. I couldn't risk seeing those eyes trap me to indecision because the decision had already been made. Instead, I held onto the clover eyes in the sea of the faceless. I needed to be accountable to somebody. I needed to remember that what I said next was not just for my family, but for every faceless human who couldn't see the larger terrors yet to come.

"My late father has left me with many gifts, but the one I value most is the belief that a leader must put action to words."

Mos shuddered next to me.

"For this reason, I will be donating my genetic lineage to the control group and forgoing the assignment gifted to me by the Department of Human Relations. I have discussed this with my proposed partner, and she sees value in this sacrifice. I knowingly understand the consequences of this decision that I give up my rank and Caste within the Republic as I strive to foster relationships between their Territories and our Colonies. I do this as a sign of good faith, and it is my hope that my example will put pause to the anarchies fueled by fear so that we, as a people, can direct our energies towards the promotion of Humanity... in all forms. I do not propose you follow me into the wild, but I do propose you follow me into understanding. Vagabonds are not our enemies, but our brothers and sisters in advancement.

"Atonement is in our hands. Let us not fade into ignorance, for it will destroy us all."

Any speech I've ever attended always received a reaction. Grumbles of complaint or agreement. Shifting bodies under their own uncomfortable weight. Gasps of shocks or nods of the resigned.

But as my last words left my mouth, there was nothing. The world remained still in its own tumultuous chaos. I couldn't move, trapped by a different stillness that fell across me. It was her eyes. Eyes that pulled me through the hardest speech of my life. I nodded at her, as if to thank her, and my movement broke the spell that shell shock had over me.

I turned and left the podium. I wanted to avoid witnessing the moment reality sunk in for the rest of the world. One foot in front of the other, Mos and Mother followed me through the doors at the back of the stage, behind the barricade of Militia that kept the people, who'd begun to swarm like red ants, at bay.

CHAPTER THREE

Eudocia Vallis looked down into the kennel.

I guess I always knew it would be her. When your mother heads the G.E.G. you tend to overhear things like the G.E.G. wanting to concentrate the New Wave lines. It was as inevitable as the Celebrity Tours awaiting us before our Commitment Ceremonies. Being partnered with Eudocia was as political as it was scientific. We were both the most famous out of all the New Waves, and when Intention Day rolled around, I felt Grandfather's influence all over the match. Of all the other New Waves, Eudocia was also the only one who had a brain working at my speed. Our nurturing had been more holistic than the others, and, unlike our peers, we'd been encouraged to explore as many academic paths as possible. We both saw this partnering for what it was. Our chemistry levels were incompatible, but the G.E.G. paired us anyways. Our public personas meant more than our hearts, and the condensing of the New Wave lines was too important for Humanity. We both knew we couldn't contest the partnering without doing severe damage to our future careers.

I studied her face from across the pet shop. In school all week, she'd been bragging that if she placed well, her parents promised her a puppy. She waved the word "if" around like the decision wasn't already set in stone, and she mainly only bragged when she thought I was listening. I wondered if she was playing a game with me, and if so, what was her intention?

I'd known her my entire life, and we orbited each other in perfect Propriety, polite and indifferent until the time came for us to be more. It was as if we had a silent agreement that since we were expected to spend our adult lives attached at the hip, then we could spend our childhoods giving each other emotional space when we could. Sure, I knew little details from a lifetime of being satellites around the same world, and we'd interacted plenty during Gruel Ball matches and dialogues in class, but we never let the other in where it counted.

Forever wary. Never trustful.

I didn't know if that was the product of our nurturing plans or the result of our fears for the future with each other.

Knowing the partnering was inevitable didn't stop my heart from sinking when I opened my letter that day. At school, we blushed more than talked, but even our blushing was calculated. It was the proper thing to be politely embarrassed, though we'd both had time to come to terms with our realities long ago.

Her friends were a skittery mass of giggles, and my brother was a solid wall of support. He'd been so sad for me all day, worrying about how I would react, but I also knew that the letters reminded him he'd have to go through the same thing that next year.

It was stupid to show up at the pet shop, but I figured you could tell a lot about a person by what kind of animal they choose to spend their life with. I wasn't even sure I liked dogs, and I definitely didn't like the idea of having a pet running haywire in my future.

But was that the whole reason she was getting a puppy in the first place? Was she trying to give me a clue inside of her carefully sculpted persona? Was it a political play? Was she making first move to show she'd make decisions as final as my own when it came to our Commitment?

I looked through the aisle of dog food and tried to peer at her through the bags. I saw the wisps of silver-gold hair braided perfectly along the side of her head so that the final rope of hair fell across her right shoulder. Emerald earrings, the color of her eyes, caught the fluorescent lights on her cream colored lobes, and her smile spread evenly across her face.

As I watched her, I wondered if I'd ever love her the way I was supposed to. I waited for the chemicals to start beating through my veins, the attraction to come. I heard it happened sometimes, despite Propriety Meds, that just by looking at someone you knew you were fated to be with, the excitement would come and the anticipation would make the time until you could be together last an eternity. But I knew that even off Propriety Meds, I'd never feel that reaction towards her. I hated to admit that I was frustrated I only blushed out of polite necessity and not excitement when I saw her.

The shopkeeper bent down into the kennel she hovered over and picked up a little white ball. It had a brown spot on it, as if someone had given it a bruised eye. "If you're looking for a small breed, these Jack Russells are the smartest. Very trainable, if you do it right. Loyal, but slightly bossy."

"I know," she said.

I grinned. Of course she'd done her research before stepping one foot into the store. She was a New Wave, like me. Research was practically a genetic side effect. I had to admit, it'd be nice to spend my time with someone who thought as I did—someone who just "got it" and understood what it was like to have a brain operating at a different speed.

The man still tried to push the sale. "I like to think of these guys as the come-back-kids. They were nearly overbred to the point of extinction—"

"Due to genetic inbreeding in order to meet popular demand. Health problems soon became associated with the breed and their popularity fell, but not before they were nearly extinct. What is not so well known is that the same thing happened to them long before The Great Disaster. This is the second time Jack Russells have

had to sidestep extinction. *This breed is proof that with proper genetic manipulation, anything can bounce back.*"

"*Ah. A future geneticist, are you?*"

"*Yes, sir.*"

The man grinned. "*Wait! I know who you are!*"

Eudocia had the grace to blush. It was just as purposive as any other time she blushed. Humility was a useful tool. It made people feel comfortable when we pretended we were humble. At least we had that in common.

But I knew another secret about her that she never meant for me to figure out: she hated the limelight as much as I did. Like me, she never had a choice in it. The G.E.G.'s Public Relations Specialists made her the female face of New Wave Perfection in the same way they made me the male face. Our paths had been entwined from the moment the news leak happened, and every elevation in my status exacerbated hers.

If she'd been partnered with anyone other than me, she'd be able to hide behind her lab coat and step away from most aspects of fame. Instead, rather than being the one looking through the microscope, she was destined to a life under one, even more so than most New Waves. Being the partner of a future Chancellor guaranteed a miasma of cameras waiting to catch her being "extraordinarily ordinary."

She could have escaped the abyss of public scrutiny with a different pairing, but, as it was, I was a curse on my future partner. What was I doing spying on her? Couldn't I let her have these last moments of peace? Couldn't I leave her to this one thing and let her choose a pet for herself? Didn't she deserve a source of joy that was completely up to her?

Didn't I?

I backed away from the dog food and snuck back down the aisle towards the back doors.

I left her to the one choice she had any control over.

"Should have known you'd be up here," Mos said.

I tugged out the earphones, and the soft static became a

discreet buzz on my shoulders. My legs dangled over the ledge, the ground a few stories below us. Once, Mother caught us up on the roof, and the consequence was four months of daily labor in the Victory Gardens. *"Do not put your genetic gifts in danger. Your intelligence is far too valuable to the Republic for it to be splattered on a sidewalk,"* she'd scolded. However, I was more than decent at hacking biometric locks, and she couldn't keep us from our spot no matter how hard she tried.

I couldn't explain it, but I felt safe up here. It had something to do with the wind, the lack of a safety net, the adrenaline of doing something slightly dangerous. There was something alive in it, which comforted me in ways nothing else could.

"I would ask if you were listening to the Flaming Flamingos' new song, but I know better," he said.

I ignored the jab. He knew I hadn't listened to music in a long time. Every spare minute had been wrapped around listening to a different tune, the song of experimentation and the chords of discord.

"Pretty sunrise." He sat down next to me and dipped his long legs into the air.

"They are overrated," I said, even though I had to admit that I was jealous of the way the sky was being set on fire. I wanted my heart to burn in the same way, but sometimes, especially lately, my life felt like a series of muted moments, dulled by the murky waters of time that I had barely begun to navigate. Not for the first time did I feel like a pawn in Grandfather's political game, unable to move for myself. That's what it's like to live in the in-between, to wait for a decision, once made, to come to fruition. That's what it felt like to be caught between old dreams and new realities, the past and the future, the here and the now. I knew the dullness I felt wouldn't last long because every day, the sun rose higher, drowning in its own flames until it fell from the sky, and every day, we were just as trapped as it, glued to a solitary path, to rise and fall, constant and dependable yet ever changing. Here and then gone.

Everything was a cycle—stories set in motion with the same

barely altered plots just waiting to be played out by the next generation. Below us, the world woke up. People walked towards work, grumbling into the dawn of day, trusting in the pure clockwork that made the Republic tick. The world always moved on, with or without you, and while they began their todays, I was stuck with the consequences of my yesterdays.

"I brought them," Mos said. "You sure you want to do this?"

There Mos went with his second guessing again. "It's the only way to keep it clean out there."

"I've seen many a Terrorist with long hair." He presented the scissors, dragging them from a small bag he'd brought with him. Then he brought out the clippers and turned them on. The buzz radiated from the battery. The blades were subtle yet sharp. I'd never cut my hair before. Father never let me, and I never wanted to. Now, all it did was remind me of what I had lost for the preservation of the Republic.

I sighed. "Vagabonds, brother. We must speak in new languages." I tied my hair back with a rubber band. He'd have to cut the ponytail first, but I knew he wouldn't be sentimental about it. It would land somewhere near the Victory Gardens, and perhaps a bird would build a nest with it in an apple tree.

Mos got up and rested the scissors above the rubber band. I felt the hesitation and closed my eyes. "Do it," I said.

"You sure?"

"Mos," I warned.

The slice that came was quick and sharp, and metal squeezed against metal. Weight fell from my scalp and wind caught what was left—chin short, feather soft, whipping across my forehead and eyes. The cutting from then on had no purpose other than to get my head ready for the clippers. The weightlessness made me dizzy, and I gripped the ledge of the roof with my fingers as the strands blew away from us. When the scrape of the clippers vibrated against my skull, I knew it was nearly done, and when it was over and the noise died down, Mos sat down next to me. His legs landed against the brick, and the easy smile he normally wore was gone. I resisted the urge to feel my scalp with my hands, though I could feel, without touching, the stubbled remnants of hair that used to be. I felt the tickle of change. I gripped the ledge of the roof and swung my boots against the brick, not wanting to speak about what was to come.

We sat there a little while, just like this. The fire in the sky faded to an early morning blue. Birds sang happy songs in the trees. Streets became pregnant with Citizens, ready for an ordinary day once again.

But my last days as a Citizen approached. There'd be a farewell party for me that night, though the party had nothing to do with me and everything to do with appearances. After that, there'd be a couple days for me to say my private goodbyes before I had to leave home forever.

"You're really going through with this, and there's nothing I can say or do?"

I couldn't answer. Answering would be too real.

Mos held out a banana he retrieved from the bag. "You missed breakfast."

I laughed and reached for it. The soft yellow peel gave way at a slight tug. "You always look after my stomach."

"It's what brothers do."

"Ah!" I pulled the earphones away, and the Flaming Flamingos became a static-filled buzz over my shoulder.

"Unhinge, brother. You need to eat." Mos held out an apple. "Must have been bad for you to miss dinner."

Leave it to Mos to dig right in. I didn't pretend to not know what he wanted to talk about. "I saw her today. She was choosing a puppy."

He looked down, over the ledge, and let out a whistle. "You're basically getting partnered with a—?"

"Puppy!" I groaned. "She's getting a dog."

"Which means you're getting a dog."

We kicked our feet against the wall and let the implications of those small facts sink in.

"Do you ever wonder what it'd be like if the Choice Act ever got

passed?" Mos finally asked.

I sucked in a breath. "It won't."

"It could work if we alter the parameters a bit. Consider it like this. People could choose no matter what, and when it came time to procreate, they just go to the Department of Human Relations for their eggs and—"

"You can't just go shopping for offspring like you'd pick up shoes at the store," I said.

"Why not?"

"Our partnering system is the fundamental foundation to the Republic. You take structure away, and the system will crash. Chaos. Disorder. Anarchy."

Mos sighed. "Those are Grandfather's words. You speak like him."

"And he speaks logic."

"Did you ever consider that Grandfather thinks as he does because he is afraid of change—that for all his knowledge, he is blinded by the comfort allowed him by the status quo?"

"I may sound like Grandfather, but you have Uncle Ty in your ear now." I kicked my boot against the rust-red brick. It felt good to beat at it, knowing that it was unmovable and strong underneath me.

"Just being objective." He reached out and put his arm around my shoulder. For a little brother, at the age of fourteen, he dwarfed me in size, and the muscles of his arms protected me from the anger forming inside.

I didn't want to be partnered with Eudocia Vallis, and my Intention Day left me feeling everything but at peace. I wanted to rewind time, go back to being fourteen, take away my fifteenth birthday and the cursed gifts that came with it.

"I wonder what it's like," Mos said.

"What what's like?"

"I read about it. The way someone would meet a stranger and chemical reactions tugged them into a million explosive directions."

"That's what Propriety Meds are for," I replied. I was more thankful than Mos could ever know for the daily pill that curbed *certain hormone filled urges.*

"I remember, Cosmos, Pamphilos, and you last year. That little experiment?" Mos laughed, reading the memory on my face. "You thought I didn't know, but I overheard you talking about it one afternoon. The way you described being off Propriety Meds made it seem so painful that I never forgot my meds from that day on."

"Well, I'm glad something good came out of those four weeks."

I bit into the apple, feeling the skin tear under my teeth. It was the bitter kind of green. Mos knew I hated red apples, the way they were too sweet and always dulled my taste buds. The crisp brightness of the green ones, on the other hand, always woke me up.

"I saw the disappointment on your face when you saw her name. You hid it well for the cameras, but I knew that expression, the resignation of following through with what was expected of you," Mos said. "A one year long Celebrity Tour when you turn 20, then a partnering with Eudocia Vallis, who will, when she turns seventeen, also go on a three year Celebrity Tour while she finishes her studies, and—"

"Did you memorize my Intention Letter or something?" I asked, but the way his face fell made me regret my sharp words.

"She's not so bad," Mos said. The edges of his eyes softened, and the colors collided. There he was, my little brother, one year away from being considered a man.

I needed a subject change fast. My reaction to my partnering was not setting a good example. "It doesn't matter. Our fates are not ours, brother. It's the price of protecting the Republic."

"I'd like to think that somewhere, somehow, people experience the freedoms we do not. Just think, if the Choice Act ever passes, you and I may not be at liberty ourselves, but future generations will be. Imagine choosing who you procreate with!"

"It won't happen," I said. Couldn't he see that it would never pass? It was a hidden Act for a reason. It was a fail-safe sewn into the original Constitution should the world have the means to be genetically responsible without the G.E.G. It was revisited every five years by the Council of Manipulation to see if it could be

applied to the upcoming generation, but every time it was up for consideration, it got shut down at the source and never made it to Senate. By this point, revisiting the Act was more of a polite tradition to respect our ancestors' hopes, to slightly consider them before setting them aside. No one would ever dare discount the G.E.G.'s necessity.

Mos sighed. "History tells us there are other ways to govern."

I thought about replying with the fact that History also tells us how any major shift in government usually began with an uprising and unnecessary death, but I didn't engage in his argument. We both knew the Choice Act would be voted down that next month. The alternative would only knock us irreparably off course, and the Manipulators would never let that happen.

I hated that Grandfather told us about the Choice Act last week. He always called us secret carriers in training, and he constantly added intel to our vault of information as tests. He wanted us to learn to bear the weight of responsibility one bit of information at a time. He loved to see what we'd do with it. How would we use our knowledge without sharing it? How would we keep the intel sacred, even if sharing it would make our lives easier? Or if we chose to share, how would we manipulate it to our advantage? Sometimes he gave Mos and me the same secrets and sometimes he gave us separate ones before he'd pit us together in debates. He loved seeing how we'd maneuver the situation based on what we both knew and did not know.

The Choice Act was a secret Grandfather shared with both of us, and I wondered what his end game was. What conclusion or discussion was supposed to come of it, especially right before my Intention Day? Was it a sick form of torture? Was it a way to let me know that I'd never have the freedom to choose during the very week my fate was sealed?

No. There was something more useful to learn.

"Promise me something," Mos said.

"What?"

"That when the time comes, you won't let it harden you."

"Harden me?"

"The way it did Father."

I laughed. "Father's not—"

"I know that love is defined by the relations deemed appropriate by the G.E.G., but I have a theory there are other aspects to love. More instinctual aspects. Father loved your mother, you know. Your real, genetic-mother. Not like he loves mine. Father braces himself before they kiss goodbye. He thinks he doesn't, but anyone can see his love for my mother is out of duty. And just like Father, you are in love with duty more than yourself. You'll try to dutifully love Eudocia out of it, but you won't be able to. We both know they paired you despite the chemistries being off, and an instinctual love will tear at you with every act of proper love you attempt with her." Sadness fell across his face, and I knew he could see his own future as he looked into mine. *"You carry your past, hidden in your core. You were a child born out of an instinctual love, and to live your life without it will destroy you."*

I felt the pulling sense of discomfort and adjusted my feet as if that would help.

After Mos cut my hair, I spent the morning in the labs, giving my last samples before I underwent the Exodus Counseling. I'd been feeling off kilter ever since the Propriety Meds left my system. In the normal course of my life, after my Commitment Ceremony, I'd have been properly weaned off the medication, but the nature of my situation didn't allow for that. The G.E.G. needed me to leave genetic gifts, and I wasn't able to do that while my urges were muted. Thinking of it made me flush with shame. Four weeks ago, I spent a morning learning how extraction worked, and every other morning since, I'd been required to give samples. I had to wait after each time, stewing in the sterile room, acting as if the humiliation of watching the extraction vids didn't bother me.

I knew debates would happen soon enough. After all, if the G.E.G. could use samples to ensure diversity, were Celebrity Tours still necessary? The answer would remain yes, for a while at least. The Republic couldn't take much more change to the framework, and the Celebrity tradition had been hard won. Genetic lines had struggled for generations just to spawn a Celebrity, and after all that work and sacrifice, it would be nearly impossible to make people frown upon the honor.

It didn't matter anymore. At least I wouldn't have to do my Celebrity Tour with this new twist of events. I preferred it this way.

I looked around the room and realized I didn't care about anyone in it.

I felt tired.

Exhausted in ways I'd never felt before.

Embarrassed that I still felt the tugging urges more often than ever despite the morning spent in the labs.

The last place I wanted to be was at a party.

I missed the calming pills that curbed the tension within my body, and some of the dresses the girls wore distracted me. My eyes kept landing on how the fabric hugged curves or—

"Your hair," Mother whispered. Her voice redirected my attention far away from where it had been landing. This whisper was the only break in her demeanor I'd get. Immediately, her face stilled into a sedated smile for the cameras.

"Ah, Mother. After all these years of complaining, you don't like it?" I tried to joke, but it didn't work.

Mos slung his arm around my shoulders and laughed. "I should hang up my political dreams and become a Public Relations Specialist. This new look is stunning. He's even wearing a bow tie, Mother. A *bow tie!*"

"Mos was quite persuasive about it, too," I said. Ever since I turned ten, I refused to wear bow ties. It was my one act of rebellion until Grandfather turned it into a trend. With the help of Public Relations Specialists, he specially made shirts for me that would look fashionable at tux-specific mixers, and looking around the room, I could see the trend still ran strong. But today, I wore one of Father's bow ties. It was like I needed him with me, noosed around my neck, tying me together.

Mos straightened my bow tie and winked at Mother. There it was, the laugh that needed to come. Mos was so much better at making her smile.

"Looks like change is happening all over the place," a soft voice said from behind us. "Headlines will read: New Wave Finally Gives in to the Penguin Look."

I turned to find Eudocia, dressed in her go-to emerald greens. The ballgown fell in waves to the floor, giving her an ephemeral look as she walked.

"May I speak to Zosimos?" she asked.

Mos grinned, squeezed my shoulder, and moved to her side. They walked towards the stage where the Flaming Flamingos were setting up. I knew it was Mother's way of giving me a gift before I left, of giving me one thing in my party that belonged to me.

The sight of Mos with Eudocia made me happy. After Intention Day, she spent a lot of time at our home studying under Mother. Eudocia and Mos became friends, and it didn't take long to recognize how he looked at her. As they walked away, polite conversation hovered between them, but there was something soft in her eyes when she looked at Mos. She'd never once looked at me like that, but to be fair, I never looked at her that way either.

"They will make an excellent partnership," Celeste said as she approached. She was dressed in a ballgown that rivaled Mother's, but even at an event like this, Celeste was untamed. "I hear you have something to do with the arrangement?"

"I had genetic proof to back it up," I said, grabbing a glass of champagne as a tray passed. The only time Mos' expression relaxed when I told him my plan was when I mentioned he'd get Eudocia in the deal. It was meant to soften the blow, and as I watched them laugh, I knew that it had.

Mother moved closer to me, like she was protecting me from something. It was strange she felt the need to do so. Something about Celeste made her uncomfortable. It wasn't that Celeste was a Vagabond in Manipulator's clothing. It wasn't even that Celeste represented all the changes she feared. It was something deeper, perhaps even personal.

"So, Buckets—" Celeste said, causing me to choke on the sip of champagne I'd just taken.

"Anicetus," I corrected her. I hated the nickname she used, but I had a feeling she knew that.

"You'll learn to shed that mouthful soon enough. The Tracks are calling to your soul, boy. It'll change you. Let it."

She was just trying to get a reaction, Not from me, but from Mother. It worked, though you'd have to know Mother to recognize it.

"I think you'll find my son more durable than what awaits him on the Tracks," Mother said. Her voice was so calm that only I could see the rage coursing through her veins. She always used her disinterested voice when she was at her angriest.

"One can only hope, Zosime. Even still, I need a word with your son. May we chat?"

"Chat away," I said.

"Privately?" She nodded towards the door that led out of the ballroom.

I scanned the room again. I wanted to talk to Uncle Ty, but I hadn't seen him since the funeral. I knew he had to appear objective, but I didn't expect him to stay away, especially when other members of the Council of Manipulation were at the party. I had hoped to say goodbye, and I worried it wouldn't happened as the days ticked away. Didn't he owe me a goodbye?

I set my glass down and kissed Mother on the cheek. "I'll be right back," I said.

"Take your time. General Tripoli just arrived anyways. There are a few matters we need to discuss," Mother said, nodding towards Uncle Ty's uncle. General Tripoli was a salty old man, straight spined and formal, yet kind. He helped raise Uncle Ty when his father died, and he'd been at our house for dinner many times. I always felt half-scared and half-awed by him.

Celeste smiled as Mother walked away. "She's scheming."

"She's not the only one," I replied.

"Forgive me. Vagabonds are wary of geneticists, for good reasons, as you know. Your mother being the head of the G.E.G. does little to calm old fears. No worries. I'll try to be better about it. Follow me?" she asked, but she'd already started walking towards the doors.

The way she moved so fluidly hid any purpose or intention she had in direction. I wondered if it was a skill she picked up on the Tracks—how not to leave a trail, especially in the midst of a crowd. No one noticed us leave. The hallway was quiet compared to the music that had begun to pour out of the ballroom. I caught the first chords of an old song, *Somewhere Over the Disaster.* Part of me wanted to go listen to it with Mos and Eudocia. The rest of me knew I needed to walk away from the familiar song.

Celeste didn't stop at the boardrooms, which surprised me. I didn't bring it up as we walked away from them, though. I figured she'd let me know when we got to where she wanted to chat. It seemed appropriate that I was following her blind, since, thanks to my speech, she would have a hand in the course my future took. She turned down the service corridor, and we entered the spiral stairwell that led to the kitchens. Celeste paused and lifted back a tapestry that ran along the wall, then she tapped on it until she a hollow sound radiated back. She placed her hand on a chunk of wallpaper. A hidden biometric scanner washed over her hand, and there was a clicking noise before the slide.

"Seriously? Hidden tunnels? Aren't those only used in spy vids?" I joked.

"How do you think your family would escape a *Terrorist* attack on the Capital?" She wobbled the word "Terrorist" so that it became a counterfeit version of chilling. It was off-putting to be around an adult who mocked. Grandfather always said that mocking sarcasm was a sign of a dull wit, but I knew Celeste's wit was razor sharp underneath the words she used.

"If it's to protect us from *Terrorists,*" I parried, "why do you have access?" I followed her into the opening and waited for her to meet the question.

"How do you think I got in for my rendezvous to plan all this?" She didn't leave time for my reply as she disappeared into the hall that was lined with soft flood lights. As I followed her, she asked, "What do you know about Lucas Solano?"

"That's a strange topic to bring up." I wanted her to go back to the comment before, about her planning. Which moving part to all of this was she connected to?

"Not so much. Indulge me, Niko Junior."

My nostrils flared at the name, though it was so slight most people never noticed when it happened. Grandfather said it was my one giveaway as he taught me to control my expressions.

"There it is. Her fire. It's in you, you know."

A fire did rage inside, though it was sobered by the thought that I shared personality traits with a genetic-mother I'd never met.

She shifted the direction of her words into another question. "What do you know about Lucas Solano?" She tried again. It was a tactic. She fluttered from topic to topic, not letting me pick apart the previous topic as I adjusted to the next.

Each word banged on my teeth on their way out. "She and Leo Solano were the first official partnering done by the Genetic Engineering Guild after The Great Disaster. Together, they created the First Five—five unaffected offspring in a genetic line for a new genetic future."

"Text vid answers? That's what I get for all the effort put into shaping that big brain of yours?"

I tried not to let it get to me. What did this woman know about how my mind was nurtured? "Given the circumstances, you will have to forgive my muted desire to analyze historical events more holistically." Though I removed the anger from my face it raced through my body. I would outsmart whatever test she was putting me through. I just had to let my patience win over my frustration.

"Indulge me? After all, this topic is the birth of our world, my boy. Everything that has happened since The Great Disaster has hinged on this girl's decisions, but there are big things most people don't know about her. Understandably so. People have the habit of reducing an entire being into what history demands, just as, I imagine, your own story is already being sewn together for the books. What will they say about Anicetus Petrakis? Boy genius or just a boy?"

My own story was being sewn, all right. I was the New Wave who toppled the world order. What was it like to be a normal

Citizen? To know that your stories would never be trapped by the words of historians? To know that you weren't notable enough to be noted in the the footnotes of history? But I grew up knowing that a figment of my image would survive beyond me in an inadequate immortality. What would the historians dictate about what I set out to do next? If I succeeded, I could redeem my place in history. If I failed, I'd forever be the villain. If I was lucky, they'd write me out of history completely, but I was never that lucky.

"Did you know that Lucas used to be considered a boy's name?" Celeste asked. There she went again, flittering between topics. It was as if she knew my brain liked puzzles, like she was testing how quickly I could piece seemingly random bits of information together.

"I think you may be mistaken," I said. Every Lucas in the known history had been a girl, but then it hit me. Every Lucas in the "known" history. What about the unknown?

"Lucas' mother hated gendered expectations," Celeste continued. "She wanted her daughters to not be defined by a stereotype. At the time, women had been fighting for equality, and I'm sure you, more than anyone, have already considered the power behind names, Buckets."

"I already have a Track name?"

Uncle Ty grinned. "Given to you before you could walk."

"By her?"

Uncle Ty glanced at my father before checking the room for Mother. They both took a knowing sip of their whiskey, wanting to avoid the discussion that would follow if she overheard them telling me about my genetic-past. She kept insisting that I wasn't mature enough to understand it, but I knew it had nothing to do with maturity or age. She wanted my genetic-mother buried in the tombs of the unspoken past.

Uncle Ty tapped the Militia Stars and Senator Stars under the Manipulator Star. Next to them rested a Celebrity Pin, and I knew that one day, I might wear matching titles. These duties cut into him, pulling out rivulets of light and dark that came with carrying the knowledge of responsibility.

But these secrets about my mother belonged to me. I would not let either of them keep the stories from me any longer.

"I think the boy is old enough for his first nip of whiskey," my father said. "After all, his Intention Day has already come and gone." He reached back and filled a half an inch into the crystalline glass from the decanter. Not even the brown amber of the gesture could distract me from this new piece of information.

I already knew my genetic-mother gave me the name Anicetus. I understood its meaning well. Unconquerable.

Names, like all words, held meanings, and those meanings became definitions of character. My name tethered me to my creation, my flaws, and my strengths. It connected me to who I was, how others saw me, and how I saw myself.

In the Colonies, we held onto our names and let them hold us to an ultimate truth of self in relation to Humanity. Even a nickname as innocent as Ani sometimes tore at me because it cut off five letters—C-E-T-U-S—that anchored me to a complete definition of myself, to a complete duty and an unconquerable stoicism in the pursuit of Humanity before self.

Whoever held a monopoly on the stories behind Buckets held pieces of me, and I wanted them back. To discover I had a hidden name that could balloon me away from Anicetus left me feeling like a drifting orbiter around my personal truths, especially when I had no understanding of the unborn stories behind them.

I always felt bad for the Terrorists who wandered the outskirts of our nation. They had no such anchor within the many names they carried. They tethered and detached as they approached different situations, and they carried as many names as they wished. These nicknames allowed them to move in and out of responsibilities, hiding who they were from some and revealing who they were to others. In a way, controlling their own names and definitions was just an example of how they could alter meaning and apply it to any truth as they saw fit. One moment, they could be one person, the next, someone new entirely, shirking the responsibilities of the persona they'd previously occupied. It felt dishonest to be able to unhook from one identity to strap on the next.

I had this theory that Terrorists wandered still because they lacked an understanding of who they were. They changed so much they never understood what they believed in. They lived so entirely for themselves that enlightenment never had the chance to cut through, and they moved so constantly that hindsight became useless. They couldn't pause long enough to contemplate truth or Humanity. After all, how could someone worry about the survival of Humanity when they were barely able survive themselves? Because of this, they knew not the harm they caused. If they ever opened themselves up to the possibility that they were hurting Humanity, they'd become so irrevocably affixed to the truth that they'd have no choice but to turn themselves in to the Republic.

However, the Terrorists, like my genetic-mother long ago, never turned themselves in. They shied away from understanding their responsibilities to Humanity and fought hard to live on their own terms so they'd never have to face the consequences of their actions. They relied on their movement to let them move on freely from the truth.

I took my first sip of whisky, and I sputtered at the fire that surged through my throat.

"It wasn't your mother who called you Buckets, but a friend of hers who gifted you the name," Father finally said.

"A friend?" I asked.

Uncle Ty laughed. "He was an insufferable boy back then, but one you couldn't help but like despite his quirks."

Father shot Uncle Ty a look, and I tasted the unborn stories beyond the singular sentences. They both had the talent of walking the fine line between telling the story and withholding it. What kind of friends did my mother have out on the Tracks? And how did Father and Uncle Ty fit in with them?

"This friend of your mother's was the one who brought you to me after—" Uncle Ty sucked in a breath, leaving the clue to dangle in the air before he took another sip and continued. "He tried to warn me that you'd be buckets of fun. It only took me an hour to *learn that babies excrete far more than they intake. I was beside myself, unable to figure out how to keep you clean the entire day. I had to travel with you, and I wasn't properly equipped to deal with an infant. Military training didn't exactly cover the basics."*

At this, my father let out a laugh. "I don't think any of us were prepared for what came next," he said, refilling his glass, but I recognized the expression they shared.

They both wore it in an uncomfortable understanding.

The joy of having me.

The pain of not having her.

It was strange, but not impossible, to imagine boy Lucases running around in the world. It was possible that one person could take expectations of a name and flip them simply by being important enough for people to want to imitate her. But that was not why Celeste brought up the gendered names. There was a clue there. She wanted me to hear the plural and all that it implied.

"Lucas' mother hated gendered expectations. She wanted her daughters to not be defined by a stereotype..."

Daughters.

As in more than one daughter.

As in a sisterhood.

Yet the history feeds never mentioned that Lucas Solano had a sister. Celeste wanted me to bring this up, and I wondered if I should play into what she wanted.

Celeste came to a stop and drew my attention to a wall.

There was a painting there. A spindly, spiky plant with tiny green leaves sprouting from ten different arms that shot up from the base. Red buds hung from the haphazard tips, and, although the paint was faded, it was surprisingly well preserved. Across the plant, in not so neat letters, was painted: *Be a fucking ocotillo, ladies!*

Celeste then pointed to all the paintings that followed the first. They lined the walls on both sides in ancient splashes of color. A pinwheel was next, caught in a blast of air like a windmill, and, like the first painting a sloppy script was scribbled across it. *Goonies never say die!* Bronze feathers drifted from black eyes down a brown cheek like teardrops. *They cannot tell us who to love, Papalotita!*

I reached up and tugged at my bow tie as if I was straightening it rather than trying to give myself room to breathe. I hated wearing them. I hated the way they constricted around my neck. I read the painting in front of me again. They were secret messages, the meanings lost to time. Some of the words felt oddly traitorous, and it was scandalous to think of them painted within the Capital walls.

"Xavi told me that some folks on the Council of Manipulation believe these should be painted over, but the notion never passes during meetings. It always comes down to the fact that erasing these would be to erase one of the few, true reflections of Lucas Solano. Not as the world knows her, but as she knew herself."

"What in the stars is an ocotillo or a Goonie? And why would she deface her own paintings?" I asked, stepping up towards the pinwheel.

"I think the ocotillo is that odd plant, though I can't figure out what a Goonie is. I can, however, answer the other question, but I think it'd be better if you figured it out on your own. Take your time, by all means."

So that was how she was playing it. She was testing how long it'd take my observation skills to kick in. I saw it quickly, but I spoke slowly. "The handwriting from all the journals of Lucas Solano is different from the handwriting painted across these paintings. Someone else defaced her work."

"Just as the Republic has its history, so do we Vagabonds. In fact, we hold some of the missing pages to your own books." Celeste spoke of unborn stories, the kind of histories that intrigued me. To know I'd walked past this hidden corridor with unspoken histories countless times before, unaware of the clues just within and just beyond my reach until now was frustrating.

"You are right. She did not write across her own paintings," Celeste said. "It was her sister."

There it was again. The misplaced idea that Lucas Solano had a sister. "She didn't have a sist—" I cut myself off. I knew better than anyone not to rely on the stories of the past. A sister could have easily been written out as anyone else non-essential to the story.

"Her name was Tommy."

Relief flooded over me. Celeste had simply been confused. Who knew how accurate the stories she had access to on the Tracks were? Tommy wasn't Lucas' sister. "That was her first daughter's name," I offered.

"Who do you think Tommy Solano was named after?" Celeste countered.

"Sisters?" I mused, trying to imagine them. I thought about Mos and how we always laughed at the oddest things. How we had our inside jokes and sacred secrets. How we were inseparable. How, if I ever had a son I was allowed to keep, I'd want to name him after Mos to honor him because Mos was someone worthy of trying to emulate.

But now, that would never happen for me.

"There is this other side to your own history, a hidden balance unknown to Citizens that propels current events into motion." Celeste stepped closer to me. "Balance is a fundamental hope. It is an elusive desire that all humans seek, but the search for balance involves navigating contradiction and the tensions that contradiction births. Think on it this way. You can't have attraction without repulsion. You can't have a brain without the heart. And you can't have a love of Humanity without betraying a love of yourself, or a love of yourself without betraying your love of Humanity.

"A coin always has two sides, and Tommy was the other side of Lucas' coin. She was the first *Terrorist*, and she led the first rebellions against the Genetic Engineering Guild. Tommy didn't do this for the altruistic reasons one might think. She simply wanted to convince her sister there was another way to save Humanity, but Lucas had already begun to believe in the necessity of genetic cultivation."

I wandered along to a painting that looked like a canyon cut through a desert. Across it was scrawled, *Life always finds a way to survive!*

"Why would Tommy turn on her own sister?" I asked.

"Betrayal is not so black and white. Consider that, perhaps, Lucas turned on Tommy? But I guess that's how history works, right? Betrayal is in the eye of the writer and the written is in the control of the powerful."

"We have less than a mile left," Father said, though there was no real reason for the update. There was a twinge of sadness to how he said it, as if he realized that the closer we got to the destination, the closer we'd be to having to turn around to go back.

I followed the crunch of his boots with my own and felt pity bloom in my gut. He rarely had time for hikes these days. We used to do it all the time when I was younger. He claimed that being outside helped clear his head, and I had the suspicion he snuck off on his own sometimes when he really needed a moment alone. In a noisy Republic, the silence grounded him. He taught Mos and me how to sit still under the trees, and I found myself doing it often, outside or on the rooftops, as a tiny habit woven into my day.

We had an understanding with our security details. We'd disappear into his Quarters Car, then slip out through the hidden door just past his bed.

With the reelection happening and the campaign trail layered on top of his already intense responsibilities, I saw the strain resting under the dark circles of his eyes. I convinced the Public Relations Specialists and the Conductor to stop for the morning, knowing our next speaking event wasn't until late in the evening. This little break was perfectly placed after the last four weeks of non-stop movement.

It felt good to walk after the three-hour ride on the motorbikes. They were the newest addition to the trains that allowed the Militia to cover more ground during Terrorist searches in some areas, but Father and I borrowed a set and used them to traverse along once-upon-a-time roads to reach this particular trail. There had been hints of broken asphalt where sand shifted over in places, but the desert had a strange way of preserving things that should be long gone. If I imagined, I could pretend I existed before my time, back into the past with the ghosts of before riding along a summer road.

"How is it that you knew I needed this?" Father asked, lifting up his leg onto the next rock.

"Maybe it was because I needed it," I replied. Taking on his burdens where I could was the right thing to do.

"I know this isn't easy," he said.

"It's not hard."

At this, Father laughed. "I suppose we don't know any other way."

"I suppose we don't. I've been accepting it, though."

"Accepting what?"

"That this will always be my life. I know I should be used to it by now. It's not like anyone lied to me about what to expect, but sometimes, on the campaign trail, I get jealous. I see normal people, who are stoic in less holistic ways but stoic enough. They do not have to sacrifice everything about themselves, if that makes sense. They care about Humanity, but they do not carry it as heavily on their shoulders." I took a deep breath. I'd never brought this up with him before, but watching him was like seeing into my future. He was me in perfect suits, shaking hands, giving pretty speeches, denying personal wants on every level. "I'm not complaining. I know I have it better than most, but—"

"Someone once told me that everything has its chains, even freedom. No matter what you do, son, you will always be asked to give up one pair of shackles for another, and to escape one situation only lands you in another. What's important is that you learn how to be at peace within the prisons you have chosen for yourself."

"You act as if there is a choice here to make," I said. I didn't mean to sound sour, but the words came out before I could moderate the tone. It was like I'd been upset over this, but didn't realize precisely how much until I started talking about it. It was strange to be saying all this to his back, but maybe that was what was making me brave. I couldn't see his facial expressions or tell if

he was approving of or disappointed by the topic.

"You are young—thirteen—so you think everything is predetermined. You'd be surprised over how much power you have in your own free will." His words floated over his shoulders, bouncing with every step he took.

"Choice? Because of who I am—who we are—I've never had much of one. Do you ever wonder what would have happened to me if my genetic-mother hadn't died when I was born? Would she have kept me? Would I have been a Terrorist rather than a Politician? Would I have grown up with fewer expectations?"

"Those thoughts have plagued me more than you'll ever know. She had these friends out there, friends who would have done everything in their power to raise you up in their beliefs of freedom. But, Ani, don't be fooled. Your life wouldn't have been much different. Sure, you would have learned to live in the wild and ride the trains, but, because of who you are, you'd never have been allowed to live in the shadows. You have always been fated to lead, but that doesn't mean you don't have choices. No matter who you are, life is full of them."

Father let this sink in for a few minutes. We walked in silence and let the sun add more layers of tan to our already dark faces. Both our eyes always turned brighter shades against the darkening hues of our skin, his a grayer-green, mine a steeper emerald.

I squinted as the sun rays bounced back up from the desert ground. I imagined the alternate reality. I could see my dark skin and red hair, bright eyes, and a stoic heart, leading an army of Terrorists to tear down the Republic. Yet one decision landed me here instead.

Rather than me, the image turned into someone else completely. Though faceless and nameless, I knew enough to know they existed. A boy or a girl, with an equal yet separate conviction, was being groomed to lead their people, just like me.

"Every kid out there is someone." I didn't know why I said it, nor did I care how redundant the statement sounded on the surface. It was like a moment of common sense that had never made sense to me until I put the thought to words. I suddenly had

a deep appreciation for whoever that boy or girl was, the one who was like me, the one who could not claim their life as their own but had choices to make that were bigger than they were.

I wondered if they felt the same about being trained to lead a cause that belonged to people generations gone. After all, I wasn't even sure if the ancient causes belonged to me in the first place because being born into a belief tended to make me feel more like I belonged to it instead.

Did people feel ownership over a cause because it was right or because it was habit? Did this boy or girl question their wars in the same way I did, or did they believe without the fear of being wrong?

Father was perceptive. He knew exactly what I meant by the statement. He knew about the people I thought of. "I call it the other side of greatness," he said.

"The other side of greatness?"

"Yes." Father paused and turned to face me. "On the other side of greatness, there will always exist people just like you or me. Politics and beliefs are nothing without thoughts and the actions of people to bring them to life. To believe in something so fully, there must be a contrast to compare it to. Ideals need a tug of war with people on both sides of the dichotomy believing with equal intensity that they are right because, without opposition, there is nothing to direct us towards our own sense of balance. True leaders respect this other side. They recognize the people behind the ideal despite the ideal itself. It is a form of forgiveness, even in the midst of war."

"But how can you fight an ideal when you see the people behind it? Why fight if you've already forgiven them?"

"That's the true burden of leadership. To know that, despite your attempt to understand them, you are right to wage war against them with all your heart. You know this fight to be true because, only in empathizing with the other side, can you fully understand and believe in your own. In the end, it will grant you the peace to trust your beliefs and protect them at all costs."

CHAPTER FOUR

"Perfection isn't what you think it is," Father said. We sat on a flat rock and stared at the chasm opening before us. "I mean, this canyon looks perfect, right?"

It was more than just a canyon, and it was more than just perfect. It was colors layered on top of each other. It was a haze of optical illusions. It was too big to fit into description, to capture with one glance, to understand the sublime weight of size. There were just some things that were too hard to believe, even in the midst of seeing.

"But look at all the broken stones, shifting sand, and cracked rocks that go into the view. Then listen to the independent adjectives: broken, shifting, cracked. They are imperfections, right?" He picked up a misshapen rock that rested at his feet. "People don't come to places like this to see one perfect rock. They come here to experience the whole sight and often forget about the flawed elements that go into its creation. It's the textures of diversity that make things perfect. It's how each different rock fits into the bigger picture that counts. That's where perfection exists, especially within Humanity; not in the individual, but in how the individual connects to the whole. Sometimes, we forget that *even the most genetically flawed individual is important to Humanity's cultivation."*

He handed me the rock, and I felt the curves under my thumb. I looked past it to the yellow wild flowers blooming against a backdrop of red and purple and orange hues.

"This is what Humanity is, my son. A conglomeration of flawed individuals—the imperfections that make perfection possible."

Celeste reached out to touch the painting. For a brief second, I could almost see her in the very desert she looked at on the wall. I wondered if she and my father knew each other before he died—if he'd attempted to see his other side in her. So much of how she spoke made me ache for him in that sharp-stabbing kind of way.

"The funny thing about it all is you have no idea how the true story mirrors your own so fully," she said.

"Excuse me?"

"There was a boy named Adan who grew up with Lucas and Tommy. They thought he was dying in from genetic impurities after The Great Disaster, only he didn't die. When the three of them met Leo at the Vault, he promised Lucas a chance at a better future. Adan pushed her towards the other boy, believing he was dying anyways. He refused to let her care for him as he deteriorated because pride does funny things to boys, Buckets. Remember that. It'll come in handy one day." She winked at me, but there was a bite to the advice. "Adan was cured, but, by then, Lucas had already left with Leo for here, the seat of the new Capital. By the time Lucas discovered Adan hadn't died, she'd had her first child, and she was already the face of the Republic. She was tied to a new duty, to do what she thought best for her child.

"Her sister never stopped fighting for her. Tommy snuck Adan into the Capital through these tunnels to convince Lucas that she didn't have to be what others needed her to be. When Tommy saw these secret paintings that Lucas had done, like a hidden journal to her own pain, Tommy had hope that they could talk Lucas into taking her child and leaving with them. Tommy knew her sister better than anyone. She knew that Lucas would need time to mull over anything Adan told her. So she sent Adan in and waited in the tunnels for him to return. While she waited, she scrawled these messages as reminders in case Lucas refused to listen, so that every time Lucas came into the tunnels, she'd be faced with the memories she'd turned her back on. I assume they were tidbits from their life before The Great Disaster, an attempt to remind Lucas of who she was, but not even her sister could change Lucas from who she had become."

Celeste was an amazing storyteller, and I felt like I was in the tunnel with Tommy and Adan as I examined the paintings. Whether true or not, the messages were a vivid picture of desperation, yet I still failed to see what my own story could possibly have in common with this one.

"I can only imagine how Lucas felt when she saw Adan again, to discover that he had not died after all. But Lucas wouldn't leave her son, nor would she take him—or the daughter she carried inside of her—to be raised in the wild. She loved Adan in ways she'd never understood until she thought he was gone, but she couldn't risk her children's safety. She couldn't have cared less for the Republic, but she knew staying was the best chance for her kids to survive."

"You mean to tell me that the most influential couple in the Colonies—"

"Had Adan showed up before she gave birth to her first child, he may have had a chance to convince her of another way. However, mothers become selfless in the face of their children. They give up their own desires for their children's futures, and, becoming a mother did big things to Lucas. It made her realize there would be grandchildren and great-grandchildren. She was scientifically brilliant for her time. She began to think in the long term. She believed that if she turned her back on the Republic for her immediate desires, she would condemn her children to a slow and sure generational death."

"Adan," I whispered the name, and the other connection came to life as clear and vivid as the paintings in front of me.

"Yes. When Adan found her, could not convince her otherwise.

93

He saw the baby boy in her hands, and knew the right thing to do was walk away."

Uncle Ty stopped in front of a painting of a girl holding a bouquet of flowers, except, instead of flower heads, the stems folded out into DNA sequences. On the walls around us, paintings hung in perfectly squared frames at the History of Genetics Museum. I'd been looking forward to seeing G.W. Kontos' work because he focused his colors on the multi-hued nature of DNA. On every canvas, spirals twirled like galaxies, floating through veins or dancing in the eyes. The colors reminded me of how my nano-bot-prototypes sounded.

"Who is this girl supposed to be?" Uncle Ty asked.

I looked at the face, freckled, blue-eyed, red-haired, dark brown skin. These were the trademarks of Lucas and Leo Solano's children. All five of them had the same features in varying degrees with the exception of the first born—the one and only boy. He had black hair, blacker than night, like an absolute black that could consume the focus of an entire picture frame.

"That's Tommy Solano," I whispered in the direction of the girl. "The second child of the First Five." I knew her face well. The childhoods of the First Five had unfolded in front of the new media that grew out of the ashes of The Great Disaster. I felt a kindred spirit with the girl in the painting for this reason. I understood the pressure of having all eyes on you from the moment you took your first breath. In this picture, Tommy Solano was a just a child. In her future and my past, she would become the first Chancellor of the Republic. Her three sisters and one brother would also hold roles in the new government, shaping it into the world as we knew it.

"Do you think our systems are what she envisioned when she helped create the Republic?" Uncle Ty asked.

"What do you mean?"

He stepped up to the painting. "All this time, we've measured Humanity by the DNA within each person. We have made this practice the foundation of our society."

"What's the alternative? Go extinct? Self-preservation will not

allow it."

"And where has self-preservation gotten you?" He lifted his hand as if tracing the flowers with his pointer finger. "This self-preservation you speak of has nothing to do with preserving you, Anicetus, the boy. It's about preserving you, Anicetus, the Citizen. Self implies singular, yet your definition takes the self out of self-preservation. It implies that the self belongs to everyone else."

I sighed. "Collective self-preservation is just a broader way of saving the self. You know this better than anyone. I'm not sure I understand the direction you're hoping this conversation will go."

He shook his head. "What if I told you this questioning has nothing to do with the questions I'm asking?"

"Then I'd prompt you to figure out what it is you truly want to ask me. I may be a genius, but even I have my limits. I can not give thoughtful answers when questions do not warrant them."

There was a smirk on Uncle Ty's face that reminded me of the expression Adonis Solano wore in the painting behind us. "I asked Mos the same things. Did you know you both had canned responses?" he asked.

"As Father would say, we are cut from the same cloth."

"And what cloth is that?"

I opened my mouth to answer, but couldn't find one. It was just a saying I thought I understood. It meant we were my father's children through and through, but as I stared at the blue-blues in the DNA sequence flowers on the canvas, I shuddered. I turned around and saw the painting of Adonis Solano, right across from Tommy. I stared at the black hair, the dark narrow eyes, the glasses resting on the rim of his nose. Suddenly, my mouth fell open in shock.

"You see it, don't you?" Uncle Ty asked.

Freckles pattered across the boy's cheeks, and he was slender and toned, in that slightly muscular way. Dressed in a brown sweater with an orange, metallic leaf necklace resting on his sternum, he held a DNA spiral in cupped hands. The color theme reminded me of the canyon my father and I hiked to a year back. The reds, the purples, and the oranges were muted in vibrancy.

"We often forget that a million different fibers go into making one piece of cloth," Uncle Ty whispered.

"How can this be?" I asked. What Uncle Ty suggested couldn't be true, but what if it was? Adonis held none of Leo Solano's traits in his features. Not one.

"Are you and Mos truly cut from the same, exact cloths? Are you equal in every way?"

"That depends on your definition."

"I prodded Mos in the same, exact way. I brought him to this same, exact place. You know what he saw when he looked at these two paintings. Mos didn't come close to seeing the things you figure out so quickly."

I glared.

"You know you are superior, though you pretend you are not. You know you are more perceptive, though you downplay it so he feels like your equal. But you are not cut from the same cloth because, when it boils down to it, you can see beyond the fabric when he cannot. You can see the fiction in the facts, Ani, and, pretty soon, that's going to be the most valuable skill you have at your disposal."

It couldn't be true, though the images of Adonis Solano tore him far from the grasps of his father's genetics. If Adonis Solano was not really a Solano, then how had he been created? Who was his father? And worse, what would happen if this became common knowledge? Surely, someone had suspected? Surely, there were genetic tests on file that showed the discrepancy?

I asked all these things of Uncle Ty, but he bit his bottom lip as if it would protect the answers he knew. When he finally spoke, he said, "There was a time when the word family went beyond genetics. People formed patchwork quilt families all the time, and the world still functioned, though chaotically," he finally said.

"And in that chaos, genetic mutations put us on the path to extinction," I reminded him.

"But, Ani, my boy. We still do this! Why do you call me Uncle Ty?"

My teeth snapped as I clamped my mouth shut. He was right.

Tycho Tripoli was not biologically related to me, but he and my father grew up together like brothers. In fact, when I was younger, I thought they were brothers. It was why I started calling him Uncle in the first place. They never corrected me, and by the time I knew better, it was habit.

"And Zosime? Is she any less your mother than Niko?"

I stared at Adonis, his telltale genetics tearing him away from his four sisters.

Uncle Ty threw a few more questions my way. "Why would Leo Solano protect and claim this boy as his own? And, is it disrespectful to the Republic's foundation that he did? After all, Adonis was technically an unsanctioned child within one of the founding families. Was parading the boy around as one of Leo's own a traitorous act? A kind one? One done out of love for the boy or his mother? Perhaps Leo didn't know or refused to believe?" *Uncle Ty shook his head.* "With all the science breaking down the formula for human creation, we forget that Humanity is far too complex to be solely considered on the basis of mathematical sequencing. The science of hearts explains how the arteries work, how the atrium and ventricles pump, and how the blood moves through the veins, yet none of the science can accurately predict what the heart will truly want in the end."

I had no reply to this. Only questions. Who was Adonis' genetic-father? And what did it mean that the founding family was built on a lie?

Adan.

Adonis.

One story strengthened the other.

I almost asked why it was not better known. After all, Lucas choosing Leo over Adan for the sake of her children was the perfect example of a true sacrifice for Humanity. Perhaps it could have been used as a source of inspiration during the Republic's beginnings. Then again, to propagate the story would have only drawn attention to the oldest Solano boy. It would deny Adonis' genetic line its due place in the cultivation of genetic purity.

If what Celeste said was true, with the stroke of a pen, our known history wrote out a betrayal of the heart and a sister.

It was possible Celeste was lying, but it was also possible she wasn't.

"Your own story can be felt in this," Celeste said again. "Niko? She loved Xavi with all her heart."

My nostrils did that slight flaring thing again, and I steadied my breath to keep it from being too obvious. I had my suspicions about Uncle Ty having love for my genetic-mother, but according to Celeste's claim, there was something deeper than a one-sided affection on Uncle Ty's behalf.

Celeste didn't back down. "Xavi loved her, too, but he was torn by his sense of duty. He pushed her away, and had he not been an idiot, you would not exist."

I shook my head. "You're wrong about that. My parents were genetically predisposed to... my father set out to create me. I was not an accident."

"According to your omnipotent grandfather, of course."

"They planned to create me." I held onto the truth of that statement because if that one statement were untrue, it would unravel too many stitches that held together the core of who I was.

"I can't deny the oddity of that. Of all the strings connecting every personal fate, Niko met Flea, the only person genetically engineered for her, but the only reason she met him was because I interfered. I was trying to protect her from Xavi because I knew he was a spy. I played on his loyalty to the Republic and manipulated him a little too perfectly. He broke Niko's heart, but there's the cold-fisted irony. In trying to save her from the Republic, I sent her right into its arms. Within the day Xavi and she parted ways, Niko encountered Flea, and by the time I found her again, I was too late. You happened, Anicetus. You. Happened."

How dare she imply such a thing? Though, if I was honest, it was a guilt that teetered on the tip of my tongue every time I thought about my genetic-mother no matter how rationally I'd learned to look at the situation.

I straightened my spine and found strength in standing taller.

"You act as if I intentionally killed her, but according to what you've just told me, you are more guilty than I." I bit back the growl that wanted to attach itself to the words.

Celeste took my hand in hers, the way Mother did when the only thing I could feel was small. It made me uncomfortable, but I fought through it.

Despite my biting tone, she read the guilt in my face. "You. Happened. We all focused on you, pulled you through the woods and made sure your life was safe. I don't regret a single moment of that because I believed, with all my heart, it was the only way. And Xavi believed it was the only way he had left to prove he loved Niko better than Flea did."

"Flea, as in my father? As in Paramonos Petrakis?" I was tired of her nickname. I ached to hear her call him Paramonos just once. Flea was such a horrible name, and my father's memory deserved better.

Celeste laughed. "Your mother talked very fondly of him when she stopped being angry at what he'd done."

"Did she love him, too? The way she loved Uncle Ty?"

Her eyes softened. "Lucas and Adan and Leo? They are impressions of your own story in so many ways. The girl loved both boys. Back then, second loves never negated first loves. Loves stayed with someone indefinitely, shifting according to the necessity of time. I guess that is something that has never changed for it is a fundamental truth of human nature. But we have an opportunity here. We can change the results of the same story that loops in our peripherals. We can learn from them. Be better than them. I'd like to think that future generations will be able choose the self without the shroud of guilt that comes with it. That the sins of our ancestors can finally be washed away by the right kind of progress so we can move forward with sure steps into true freedom."

"I'm sorry for Claire," Uncle Ty said.

"Xavi, she knew what she was getting herself into. Save your apologies for when you see her on the other side. You would have

saved her if you could, but her cause was bigger than herself. Not even you could have stopped her once she saw her path." The woman stepped towards me, closing the subject Uncle Ty had tried to open. I shivered at my uncle's Track name. I knew it was a name that connected him firmly to his hidden past, and I wondered what these Terrorists saw when they acknowledged him with it—as if he was one of them and not a high ranking official in the Republic.

How could they move so easily around him? Not a single one of them wore tense expressions. Or was that just a product of training in the same way I had been trained to hide my own fears?

"I'm Celeste," she said as she pulled me into a hug. She smelled a little familiar, like earth, like... home. It made me feel safe and lost all at the same time. It made me livid that she had the gall to wrap her arms around me like a son. "The last time I saw you in person, little Buckets, you fit in my hands! Now look at you!" When she released me, I saw a familiar expression on her face. I'd seen it on my own face in pictures and vids. I'd seen it on Father's face when he smiled and Mos' face when he frowned. We shared the same cheekbones and the same smile.

"Are we genetically—?"

"Ah! You're as sharp as everyone says! You've already guessed it before those little nano-bots of yours."

"We are genetically related?" I finally pushed out the question.

"See. No need for those nanos now! Turns out, I'm technically your genetic-aunt." She tilted her head and examined my face. "Okay. I can tell from that expression that you still require proof. Hand that serum over."

I looked over at Uncle Ty. He shifted uncomfortably from his left foot to his right. I'd never seen him so agitated before. I'd put him in an awful position by asking him to help me pretest the nano-bots with the Terrorists. Every moment spent with these people was one treasonous moment too many for him. Especially if Grandfather was right about the Claire situation. So many questions vibrated along my spine. Maybe Uncle Ty truly was a traitor. Maybe he was still on Grandfather's radar and knew it, which would make this extra dangerous for him if he was truly disloyal to the Republic. *But if that were the case, why was Uncle Ty risking everything to help me in this? It wouldn't be prudent, and the strategist in him would never allow it. But if he wasn't a traitor, why was he so sad about this Claire woman dying?*

I wondered if it was possible to hate and love simultaneously because Uncle Ty sure was giving it his best effort. Then again, he never wore his thoughts on his sleeves. Maybe his sorrow was all part of his role out here. Maybe he was simply pretending to be empathetic to a Terrorist's death to preserve a relationship he could manipulate later.

"You have it, I assume?" she asked.

I pulled the serum from my pack. It was clear, but I knew the life that lived within the liquid, the mechanics so microscopic that no one would notice their presence. "Just a teardrop is all that's needed."

"Celeste, let me go first," Polo said.

"No. I trust Xavi." *She held me with an unwavering stare.* "And I believe in you."

I didn't drop my gaze as I handed her the vial. Uncle Ty gave her that nod I knew all too well, and they spoke in the unspoken language that came from years of working along side someone. It made me shiver.

She hovered the dropper above her tongue and one landed on a tastebud. "My bared teeth are broken chains, no?"

Immediately, my tablet buzzed with life. I now had my first Terrorist reading, and it was fascinating.

I became so distracted by the information streaming from the nano-bots that an hour or so passed as I examined the data. I didn't notice Uncle Ty step away, and when I finally looked up, I saw that his pack was no longer leaning on the tree where he'd set it. Surprise startled me, and I began searching for him, scared he'd left me in the hands of traitors.

Polo noticed the fear from where he sat against a tree and said, "Relax, boy. It's an old Track habit. Never leave your pack if you can help it. Things shift so fast out here that you never know when people who mean you harm will show up." Memories crossed like shadows in his eyes. I recognized that haunted look, the way it always existed just under the surface, waiting to break through the light and tug you back into the pain of the past. His eyes drifted towards a cluster of boulders as if he could see a memory play out against their ancient curves.

I let Polo have his moment, and looked towards Celeste. "Here's the anti-bot serum," I whispered, following through with my end. She would not allow me to track the Vagabonds, and she wanted to be the first to see the tracking beacons die on my tablet before she'd permit anyone else to take them. She may have trusted her life to Uncle Ty, and by extension, me, but that didn't mean others would without proof of their safety. I saw it for the test that it was, and I wondered if she knew I was passing it on purpose.

Celeste sat up a little straighter against the rock she leaned on, and reached out a slender hand for the vial. She held the dropper over her tongue, and slid it back into the vial. She stowed the serum in her pack with the rest of the vials I handed her. The other part of the deal was that I brought her a large supply of the anti-bot serum and divulged the secrets of its replication process, though where she would make it was beyond me. There weren't exactly labs out in the wilderness, unless she was taking it to the Vault.

The idea made my heart race. The bigger end game kept peeking its head out from underneath the surface, but it was like catching dust in the wind. Every time I tried to wrap my fingers around it, I only opened my hands to find them still empty. I wanted to ask. I wanted her to just tell me where the Vault was so that all of this could end before it even started.

As the trackers inside Celeste died, I sighed over the fact that the data would be incomplete, but it was better than no data at all. The anti-bot serum flushed the nano-bots out of the blood, making sure they climbed out through the pores like sweat. I turned off the screen when the purple lights disappeared from the data feed. Just as the screen turned black, I heard the chords of the ukulele pick up on the tails of a strange, floaty laughter. I hadn't heard it often in my lifetime, but it was Uncle Ty being completely amused by something.

Being out here was loosening his bones, letting him breathe. To think of Uncle Ty in his befores—the befores that were built up by a different life with different experiences—was startling. I knew he'd been out on the Tracks for years upon years, but I never understood all the nuances of it. What was it like to have to survive in the wild? To live a double life? To build trust with these people only to destroy it in the last moment for the good of the Republic? To slide the needle in the arm of someone who trusted you even if it was for the good of Humanity?

Sympathy, or maybe it was pity, tore through me. I knew this feeling well. Back home, Uncle Ty had so many responsibilities tying him to duty, but out here, no one was watching him. He could laugh without boundaries, and I wondered what part of it was real and what part of it was carefully crafted so he could fit into the situation. Then again, it didn't matter. I so desperately wanted to be around that version of Uncle Ty, like it could give me words to the stories that did not belong to me.

I began to prop myself up so I could walk towards the edge of the lake, but, before I could stand, Polo leaned forward from the tree he sat against, stretched out his arm, and put his hand on my wrist. I shook it loose, tired of all the strangers thinking they had the right to touch me.

"Give him a moment," Polo said.

I stood up. Who was this man to tell me how to approach Uncle Ty? He couldn't possibly know what my relationship was to him.

Celeste stood up and blocked my path. "Don't take offense, but the moment you walk down to that lake, you re-hook him back to duty. Xavi has so few moments of absolute freedom with the path he has chosen, and, though we have landed on opposite sides of the war, a Vagabond respects freedom in the rare moments someone—anyone—finds it."

"Are you ready for your training?" Celeste asked, changing the subject and dropping my hands.

For most people, this training was the grace period, and the Vagabonds put in charge of it had been instructed to be as harsh as possible to encourage those considering leaving the Colonies to remain Citizens. I understood, yet didn't know for sure, what that meant for me.

"I'm ready," I lied. The weeks end would begin the shift from my before to my after. Today, I rested in the hovering place between two realities. Part of me wanted to get this part over with.

Waiting was torturous.

"You and I both know there is no turning back for you," Celeste said. "This is not the same trial others will receive because others will have the option of reintegration. Yet you will receive the same training others will get because it's still important if you are to be a true Diplomat. You need to understand the people you represent, and you won't be able to do that unless you understand the same realities they do."

I appreciated Celeste trying to give me a heads up about the trials I was about to encounter, but I suddenly realized she was taking me away from my last moments with my family. She'd have plenty of time later to reiterate her points and go over her plan for my introduction into the wild. The thought of receding time gave me a panicked urgency to get back. I looked for a pause in the conversation to remind her of this, but she began walking further down the hallway before I could.

"Your guide through this may come off as a pain in the ass, excuse the expression. I've known this girl her entire life, and she has the wit of her father and the sarcasm of her mother, and the tact of a—" The pause was not going to happen anytime soon as Celeste spewed out more information.

"Wouldn't this conversation be better left for—" I tried to cut her off.

"You know her father, Polo. You've met him the day you met me. When his partner died, I was one of the many who helped him raise his new born. Needless to say, she is like a daughter to me, even if I want to strangle her half the time. I would tell you more, but it is not my tale to tell."

I was tempted to quip with, but you just did tell me. Instead, I saw the information for what it was. Celeste was planting clues in subtle trails for me to follow. She wasn't telling me this girl's mother died so I would have an automatic empathetic link with her. Celeste wanted me to know I'd be teamed up with a girl instead of a boy. She was warning me that I'd be doubly uncomfortable. I had to praise for the tactic. What better way to test my commitment to Propriety than by putting me in a very improper traveling situation?

"I fear there will be times that you will think it unfair of me to pair you with such an explosive personality. But it is what it is, and I had my reasons."

We reached the end of the hallway, and she placed her palm on the wall. Another biometric scanner read the lines of her hand and a door slid open. Light fell on a cluster of vines that created another wall over the entrance. Celeste pushed through them and assumed I would follow. Why was she taking me outside? Before I could figure it out, her head popped back through the miasma of leaves so that she appeared to have a floating head. "Come on, boy. I don't have all night."

I parted the curtain of ivy in front of me and pushed my way through. On one side of the vines rested a hallway that led back to my family, and on the other side were black eyes, miniature abysses floating in the dimly lit dark.

"My biggest giveaway was my accent. I trained for months and months to scour it from my voice so I could hop on and off it as easily a train," Father said. "But it never fooled anyone. By the time I got out there, everything I'd learned had shifted, taking the ground from under my feet."

Mos took a note on his tablet. Since he'd turned fifteen, his fingers were always in the way of intention, and the tapping was awkward. He was interviewing Father to gather ideas for his debate that next week, but we both had an ulterior motive. Mos could have picked any veteran, but Father rarely talked about his

Tour of Duty. I suggested that it was the perfect opportunity to hear a little.

I felt bad for Mos. He ached to be a spy, just as I had, but his face, like mine, was far too recognizable. Grandfather made sure of it. "I refuse to make the same mistake twice. Unlike your father, you boys lived your life in the light from the start. I made sure the whole world knew your faces," *Grandfather had said.*

Out of the corner of my eye, I witnessed Father shooting me a quick look. I tried hard to act like I wasn't paying attention as I poured over my own mechanics research. I pretended well enough because Father continued answering Mos' questions.

"But how do you hold onto language if it's constantly changing?" Mos asked.

"The first thing you learn on the Tracks is that you can never hold onto anything too tightly. It's the fastest way to make whatever you're clinging to... die."

My head snapped up in a stuttered shock. My genetic-mother existed in that pause. Did that statement mean he felt responsible for her death? I knew he still loved her in spite of himself, but did that pause suggest he had truly considered becoming a traitor for her?

"Where did this word come from?" Mos asked. I wanted to shake my brother, tell him to go back to the last answer and dig in. With the perfectly placed question, Father could continue down that nostalgic vein! How could Mos skip over it so easily? How could he be blinded by a fascination with one, stupid word?

Father looked at the tablet where Mos pointed. "It's a newer variation."

"I figured that much, but from where did it originate?"

"Linguistics trace it back to a country that existed nearly one-thousand years ago. Scotsway or Scotsland, I think. Once in the old Americas, it mixed with Latin roots, possibly an old language called Spanish."

Mos grinned. There was a new speaking point for his debate, and he quickly typed a thought down. "Amazing! Think on it. These three letters have their own broken history, allowed to live long past the word's origin only to morph to a new situation. Older than the Republic itself, it's kept alive by the Terrorists of all people!" He opened his mouth and failed the pronunciation again.

"Try it again," Father prompted. "You almost have it."

"Eye."

Father laughed. Mos had a way of bringing out his joy the way I brought out his sorrow. I felt the frustration scratch behind my eyelids. There Mos was, botching his chance—my chance—to get a little bit of insight into Father's past, and I sat there trapped, listening to him try and fail a word on repeat.

"Aye," I finally spoke, nailing the inflection perfectly.

"Way to go!" Mos was genuinely pleased I got it, oblivious to the snarky way I'd done it. He stood up from the table and set the tablet down. "Anyone else want some water?"

I shook my head no, and tried not to groan when he disappeared through the door. I heard him saying 'Aye' in every type of inflection he could. Normally, I found his fascination with language endearing, but today, I wanted him to choke on every word he said. I rubbed my temples and looked at the clock. I was half-frustrated I'd been cruel to my brother, half-frustrated he'd probably try to perfect that word over the next hour rather than get back to the bigger questions.

"It's not easy being a genius. In fact, it makes it difficult to be around people," Father said.

"Difficult?" I asked, unsure of what he meant or what prompted him to make the statement.

"You'll forever be smarter than everyone around you, but being smarter does not mean what you think it does. What you assume brilliance to mean will give you an excessive confidence that'll cause you to do stupid, stupid things. You think that, because you are smarter than Mos, you know better. However, my son, thinking like that will become your greatest weakness. You must remember that being smart means little without imagination and thoughtfulness."

"I wasn't trying to be—"

"What? Inconsiderate? A brat? A know-it-all? Yes, you were.

You were reminding Mos that he isn't a New Wave—that he is so close to perfection, but even in that closeness, he is far from it— only half the brain in comparison to you. You call him a Halfsie without saying the words, and it's cowardly. You do not know yet that there is a difference between being smart and wise, and it will take you time and experience and failure and heartbreak to learn how to live on both sides of intelligence. Just because you are smart, it does not mean Zosimos is not. The advantage he has over you is that he is not told he is a genius. This makes him quest for genius despite the world telling him it's out of his grasp, and this quest has turned him into a questioner. Even when he thinks he understands, he asks. He works for it. For you to be annoyed by him plaguing me with questions or doggedly trying to master a word is a tragic waste of your talents."

I felt the shame seep into my joints. As he got up from his desk, the chair scraped against the hardwood floor, and I felt the weight of his body shift the leather couch when he sat next to me. He took my hand in his, and the pressure of his grip, which was meant to be comforting, only reminded me how unfair I was being to Mos.

"Think about the inspiration his questions might birth inside of that thick skull of yours. While you may have the skill of digging through the information presented, he has the talent of drawing the information out that you need to dig through. You just learned something, didn't you? Not just a word, but something about your genetic-mother?"

I didn't try to push the tears back. I didn't want to hide how hurt I felt. I was tired of wearing that stupid mask Grandfather always placed on my countenance. I wanted to feel the desire for more racing through me, and I wanted to be allowed to want. I wanted to embrace the hunger in my gut to know all the missing facts, but everyone who had the answers wanted to keep me leashed to a world without them.

Father frowned. "You have questions you don't know how to ask yet. Some I can never answer. Others I will when you are mature enough to ask the right things. For now, I'll give you a truth *in good faith. If things had turned out differently when you were born, I would have selfishly tried to give up my world for a her, and I am not entirely sure I would have been wrong to do it. But the remarkable thing about your genetic-mother is not in what I would have given up for her. It is in what she gave up for Humanity. In sending you to the Republic, she made her loyalties known. In the midst of tragic lost, she held onto her stoic beliefs. Sending you to me was an ultimate test of love, not just for you, but for your genetic future."*

"New Wave!" The girl reached out her hand. "Put 'er there."

I wasn't sure how to respond, so she grasped my hand and shook with the vigor of an earthquake. Behind her, the labyrinth wall spread out after a line of lemon trees. I knew the labyrinth stretched a mile out. Mos and I used to get lost in it when we were boys, but now we knew that garden almost as well as we knew ourselves.

"Nice speech, by the way. *Very* moving." She glanced at Celeste and winked. "Data leak was a malfunction." She laughed, and it was like spoons being spilled out of a drawer, clattering on tile. "Like anyone would believe a New Wave could accidentally do something so monumentally stup—"

"Cut it out, Hucksley," Celeste scolded without bite.

The new name dug into my lobes. It had such a harsh sounding K right in the middle of a curvy U and a slithering S. Mos would have been fascinated by the winding name.

"Malarkey. He'll have to get used to me real quick like. No time for him to be a mopey sad-sack on the Tracks, unless he wants to get pushed off within the day."

She let go of my hand, and by the limited light, I could see traces of Polo, the genetic links she shared with the man with the beard. There was even something in her stance that matched his, only it was more feminine and fluid. She was seventeen, possibly barely eighteen. I wondered what kind of line her other traits came from and immediately wished I had my tablet to see if she was even in the database.

A wide grin spread across Celeste's face and she shook her head. "I suppose you have a point."

"So, shove off. I got it from here," Hucksley added.

There was a pause in my breath. "You cannot possibly mean—?"

"Aye, the boy is quick. Can't slide anything past him. I'll have to be careful with this one," Hucksley mocked.

I shook my head. "Now? I haven't even had time to say goodbye."

Hucksley's face was devoid of pity. "Time for goodbyes? There's never enough time for goodbyes because neither time nor goodbyes exist out here."

"I can't leave Mos without—" I couldn't tell what was stopping my words. I'd never felt panic to this degree before, and I wasn't prepared to leave. Not yet.

"You can, and you will," Hucksley said.

I looked at her, finally *seeing* her, and realized I was in a standoff with a tornado. Those eyes, her eyes, ripped through me, and, even though I wasn't moving, I felt movement in my veins.

I blinked for respite, as if each dark flutter could add up to an entire moment of dark peace. I needed to collect my thoughts, but this movement inside was different, as if it wanted me to wake up.

I looked beyond her towards the shadow filled leaves of the labyrinth.

Now.

I couldn't leave now.

Not yet.

"Got you a present, New Wave." She pulled out the nickname again. I tried to find my voice to tell her to stop talking for just a second, but nothing came forward. It was as if she'd stolen my words completely, leaving me lobotomized in thought. The only thing I could process was the, *not yet*, on loop. She approached a lemon tree, but the area was too shadowed to see what she was getting. "Meet your first survival challenge," she said over her shoulder.

Why did she keep talking? Couldn't she see I needed a

second? Of course not. No one ever thought to give me time to process. It was well known that I could take in most information nearly as fast as a computer, but what most didn't know was that sometimes my emotions struggled to keep up with the data.

I felt Celeste shift next to me, but I couldn't take my eyes off of Hucksley as she came back into the light. In her arms was a small ball of wiry fur. "Meet Bixby. I saw in the vids that you and your future partner had a thing for Jack Russells. Thought I'd give you something to keep you from feeling homesick! She wasn't easy to nab, so you better take care of the little crapper."

A feeling of distrust danced in my gut. "You stole her?" I hated that my voice found itself right then and there. I hated that this girl thought she knew who I was and what I liked off of the vids that featured my life. I also hated that, at the same time, she probably knew a lot more about me than she was letting on.

"Sorry. What's that saying about old habits? By the Bond, I have good reasons. If Celeste would kindly shove off, I could get started with them." She set the dog at my feet. It began to sniff the leather of my dress shoes and explore the shoelaces. The pup had a corded rope tied around it, and Hucksley held the other end loosely.

"Stars help you, boy. I'll leave you both to it." Celeste put her palm on my shoulder and squeezed.

"But—"

"No turning back now," she whispered. "Move on. Move forward."

"Wait!" I said, but she'd already slid through the vines. I heard the click of the door and tried to breathe. How could Celeste leave me like that? No warning? No preparation? Dressed in a stupid tuxedo and a stupid bow tie?

These questions took up the entire forefront of my mind, and it made me miss the fact that the little pup was about to squat over the tip of my shoes to mark her territory. I gently kicked her away before she could do any damage, and as the pup yelped, Hucksley yelped in a different way. Laughter made her face soften into the smooth lines of a brilliant smile. It startled me, how shifting her face was, moving in and out of expressions the way a translator moved in and out of dead languages. She twisted the corded rope and the puppy moved its stubby legs to obey the unspoken command. She picked up the pup and said, "Aye, dog. You must learn that shoes are a man's home out here. Peeing on them is just not nice." Then her face hardened as she looked directly at me. "You'll be trainable or you'll be dead."

Mos knew he had his opponent by the throat. "Take the Terrorists, for example. The language of Terrorism is ever moving as a way to trap spies. Being unable to actively communicate, in any social circle, causes you to be unsuccessful in that sphere. Based on this fact, spies stick out like bruises on a day-old banana. Vice-versa, Citizens can recognize spies when they enter the Colonies to steal if they listen carefully enough.

"On the militaristic level, spies must quickly adapt to the mutations of language or be known for what they are. However, the greatest problem with the current Linguistic Training Model for the Militia is that it operates on antiquated data. They train spies in accents that might be a generation too old and neglect to take recent connotation shifts into consideration.

"The Terrorists encourage the tearing apart of definitions and the manipulation of meaning at a more rapid rate than in the Colonies, where language is more controlled. Through classical education, Citizens are trained in a more preserved language where the mutations are slowed by a reverence for Propriety.

"I postulate that, much like genetics, language evolves over time. We must think of language like our genetic gifts. It, too, is passed down from parents to children, generation after generation, and, generationally speaking, unintentional and intentional mutations can change, alter, delete, or add words and phrases just as effectively as mutations in the genome. Knowing this, the Terrorists' manipulate and degrade the language Citizens know into a baser form, yet an equally powerful form."

Darius scoffed. He wore that inane look of confidence. The poor sucker thought he could wiggle through my brother's argument to win the debate points, and I couldn't wait for Mos to knock him out of the competition. Darius looked down at his podium, then sent the crowd his practiced grin. "You can't possibly mean to compare language to a live organism! Language is just a means of communication. It is no more alive than this inanimate podium. Words can only move if a person wills them to."

"Strange how language works, isn't it?" Mos knocked his hand on the podium in front of him. I was proud at how un-calculated he made it look. I sat up straight in my chair, knowing he was about to end the debate with a carefully placed retort, and when it came, I had to hold back a laugh. "But I disagree with you here. In fact, I might just have to argue that words move people more than people move them."

I looked at my shoes, at my slacks, at my jacket. I reached up and felt the tight noose of Father's bow tie. Hucksley stepped close to me and pulled on the bow, unraveling it so that it hung from my starched collar. "You ready?" she asked. I tried to ignore the fear her closeness scorched into my skin.

"I'm hardly attired appropriately for this," I said.

"Glad to know the vids didn't downplay your intelligence at all." She nodded towards the cluster of lemon trees that guarded the labyrinth garden. "Part of me wants you to suffer through the blisters those stupid shoes will give you, but then I'd have to hear you be a bitch-baby about it. That pack sitting next to mine is yours. The clothes and boots? Yours too. You'll still get blisters, but if you complain, I'll push you from a train myself." She stepped even closer and tugged at the deflated bow tie so that it slithered from the collar. She twisted it in her hands as if she was contemplating something, then she bent down to tie the black silk around Bixby's neck in a clunky bow.

I knew I should have felt a little better at having the right clothing, but it still didn't negate the fact that I'd just been tossed out of my home. I turned to face the wall of ivy, looking for access to the door. I may not have deserved much, but I knew I deserved a proper goodbye. Or at least, Mos did.

Hucksley reached out and ran her hand along the back of my arm, sending a tingling through my nerves. I couldn't explain why my sternum began to vibrate, and I didn't know if I wanted to. It hit me that it was the first time I'd ever been left completely alone with a girl, and I didn't know how to process how close her body was to mine as she stepped closer behind me. Her fingers closed around my elbow and rested there as she spoke, her words landing on the back of my neck.

"I will not feel sorry for you, New Wave. I won't pity you, and I certainly won't give you time to grieve. There is no room for it out here. It is time for you to leave. It is kinder for you to do it without all the fanfare. I get it. Politicians have a flare for the dramatic and everything is a big show, but, out here, reality is different. Think like us. Consider questions like us. What will your words do for your brother? For Vagabonds, life is about action, not useless words. Most importantly, survival is about fluidity—movement, and it's time for you to move." She tugged at my elbow so I had to turn away from the wall and look at her. The depth of her eyes swallowed me, sweeping me up in her logic. She pointed to the lemon trees, and in their shadows rested my new home.

A bulky pack.

Understanding anchors us all to moments long after the fact. You don't often recognize the importance of new seconds until they've faded well into the past, but I had a strange feeling about each step I took behind the girl with tornado eyes, that I was being swept away into a future that had no resemblance to any I could have imagined. The wind shifted slightly, and I felt serrated shivers down my spine—the pull of anticipation as I approached my new world.

Hucksley stopped by my pack and threw a shirt in my face. "Lesson one? There's very little privacy out on the Tracks. When you have to change, you have to do it without expecting anyone else around you to give a crap."

CHAPTER FIVE

I thought about punching a wall.

I thought about chickens in the Victory Farms getting their necks snapped.

I thought about how crumbs always got stuck in Instructor Aeschylus' beard.

That was the one that got my focus back on the genetic debate.

Cosmos and Phoibe stood before us, presenting their arguments, and there was something about how Phoibe moved her body behind the podium that distracted me.

I felt a deep thrumming of annoyance for Cosmos and Pamphilos with their self-destructive dares and how they always found a way to pull me into them. It all started when Pamphilos found out that part of Militia training was to be taken off Propriety Meds. "It's so they can learn to deal with urges out in the wild. My cousin tried it for two weeks, and I bet I could beat that record." *Cosmos, of course, countered with an,* "I bet you can't," *and the next thing I knew, all three of us were fighting to see who could last the longest.*

Pamphilos went a week before he got back on the meds, but

Cosmos and I were still in the running to win. Our competitive natures kept outdoing our desires to get our testosterone-filled mood swings under control. The last three weeks, I'd been distracted enough in class that lessons actually felt like a challenge. I half expected Instructor Aeschylus to pull us aside and punish some sense into us. He had to have known what we were doing by how oddly we were behaving, but weeks went by and the talk never came.

How did people manage before Propriety Meds? They'd only been around for eleven years, and some Citizens even argued it was too much of a crutch. But in watching Phoibe, I found myself wishing I could get back on the meds while simultaneously wishing they had never been invented in the first place. Maybe then I would have learned the old fashioned way how to curb urges. After all, Humanity had had these feelings since before the dawn of civilization. There had to be a more efficient way to stop my body from controlling me.

It amazed me how calm Cosmos was when he had been paired with Phoibe for this assignment. How did he work so closely with her without going completely and utterly insane?

Phoibe ran her fingers slowly along the podium. She sent a sly smile towards Cosmos, and part of me wondered if she knew what she was doing. Did she know he was off his Propriety Meds? Was she using it to her advantage? No. It would be too improper. No one would dare impropriety just to get an edge in a debate.

Her voice wove through the desks straight into my toes. "Transgenics is a scary word, one we have been trained since birth to fear. Dissenters worry about the implications of redefining Humanity. By allowing Transgenic exploration, they say we risk creating humans that are no longer human. Yet definition is a product of perspective. Let us consider New Wave Perfection, with their slight tweaking of genes. By following this logic, does this not make New Wave Perfection inhuman?"

My eyes focused on hers. They were a strange sort of yellow-brown, like honey drizzled from the pupils. I hated this line of conversation. I'd spent my entire life hearing people debate my

Humanity, and I knew better than to take offense. After all, how could the public truly understand how much I'd given up and how much I'd still give up for Humanity? That in so many ways, the things I constantly had to do to prove my Humanity made me more human than any of them? Though sometimes, it made me feel less so.

"In our Institute alone, we have witnessed the nurturing plans of two New Waves and a handful of Halfsies. Many find their intelligence intimidating because they make even the smartest of us feel sub-human."

I glanced to my left and saw a few tablets raised. Here was another vid that'd make its way into the viral world—yet another debate that touched on my abnormalities. To my right, Eudocia sat and bore it. I wondered how she felt about it all. I wondered if she could look through cold, scientific lenses to examine her own Humanity. Did she question it as much as I did? Then I wondered why I never felt that tugging sensation in my groin whenever I was around her. Why wasn't fire singing through my bones when I saw the way light caught her eyes or the softness of her hair? She was my future partner, and I felt nothing in the way of a tethering, a pull, a feeling.

"Does this mean our natural inadequacies invalidate their advancement? Should our fears negate the possibility that exists within them? It is a genetic truth that people will have strengths and weaknesses, but should the fear of our own inabilities force us to condemn those who are stronger than we are? Those who are genetically more perfect than us? I think it's morally reprehensible that we completely discount the potential of Transgenic Therapy."

Cosmos stood with a calm confidence, but there was something wild in his eyes. "What we witness in the New Wave Perfection is a tweaking of a human gene, not a replacement. Every part of every New Wave is human, but to move genetic attributes from animals to humans is—"

There was a hitch in his voice, and Pamphilos whispered in a laugh-cough behind me, "He's going to cave soon."

"—not only irresponsible but also treasonous to Humanity. To

give a human the sight of an eagle or the hearing of a—" He stuttered for a breath as Phoibe leaned against the podium to rest her chin on the back of her hand. It caused her backside to be highlighted by the fluorescent bulbs above, and Cosmos' eyes landed right where she'd intended them to. I recognized the smirk she wore, and had to admit she was clever for doing it. There was no mistaking it. She somehow found out we were off our meds, and she manipulated her opponent's weakness. A calculated act like that would have made Grandfather proud despite the gross impropriety of it.

I cocked my head and studied her more acutely than just how her body made mine react. The G.E.G. did not create Propriety Meds for girls because they were believed to have more control over how they reacted, but watching Phoibe made me wonder if that were true. Were girls just as aware of how the chemicals raged through them? Did they have a harder time because they were not granted suppression medication like the male Citizens?

And what gave Phoibe the audacity to use that against Cosmos? How did she know what to do with her body to distract him so? It almost felt like she was taking revenge on him for taking the gift of Propriety Meds for granted. It was as if under this Transgenic debate, she reminded him of a very real debate happening in the media the past month.

Should women be granted Propriety Meds?

"Ex—exc—excuse me," Cosmos whispered and bolted towards the door.

Phoibe sent a subtle wink my way, and my blood ran cold. I finally knew what side of the debate I stood on.

Pamphilos lost it in laughter. "That's going to be all over the vids now!"

But all I could do was watch Phoibe's backside as she stood straight up and think about snails. Gooey, slimy, slow snails.

Hucksley didn't watch me change, but she didn't leave me alone either. She busied herself with Bixby, throwing leaves at the pup to chase. Bixby stood on her hind legs, bicycling her legs in the air in an attempt to catch a leaf in her mouth. The clunky bow on her neck looked ridiculous.

I looked at the clothing left for me. The boots were most definitely mine, and I was glad she'd be wrong about the blisters. I'd hiked more than she could have expected in them. Not many knew about my trips with Father, and no one knew about the time Uncle Ty took me to meet Celeste, but the shoes were the only familiar thing I'd been allowed. The clothing was soft but uncomfortable—thick pants and a thin shirt. The wool socks made a noise against my eardrums that scratched my nerves. I tugged them over my toes and focused on the boots, on how the laces crisscrossed until finally being knotted above the ankle.

My suit was now a crumpled heap on the ground, and I picked up the fabric, felt the starched structure in my fingertips one last time before draping the pants on the full branches of the lemon tree. It felt wrong to leave such nice clothes on the ground. The black contrasted with the dimly lit brightness of the yellow citrus, and I looked up to the dome above us. I knew it let in the sky while keeping the labyrinth and all the fruit inside of it climate controlled for maximum yield. The labyrinth was the most decorative Victory Garden in the Capital, and I wondered how Hucksley intended to get us out without going straight into the city.

Hucksley picked up the dog. Its fat-footed paws clawed at the air trying to find purchase where none existed. "Your dog, your responsibility." She commandeered my pack and secured Bixby in it. The puppy protested, but quickly curled up on the jacket that was balled up on top of whatever else was in there. The pup had her head poked out of the flap that covered the zipper, and I worried it would have an accident all over the belongings inside. Then I wanted to kick myself. Taking care of a dog was the last thing I needed on top of everything else I had to deal with.

"That's not my dog," I said.

"If you can't take care of a pup, then how do you expect to take care of my people?" Hucksley shouldered her pack as if the topic was finished and began to walk towards the labyrinth.

There was more to the dog then just proving myself, but

Hucksley wasn't about to tell me what it was. I didn't engage in the argument she expected. Instead, I pulled my pack onto my back. Bixby wasn't fazed by the movement. How did she so easily accept the uncomfortable situation? Even on my back, the dog had settled in for the ride, like she knew better than to argue. As I followed Hucksley, I felt uncomfortable everywhere. The pack was heavier than that first trip I'd taken with Uncle Ty, and I wondered who packed it in the first place. What was in it? What could I take out to make it lighter?

The dog would be my first choice.

"Hold onto my strap," Hucksley said, reaching out for my hand. She moved a belt that was pulled through a corded loop on top of her pack and wrapped my fingers around it. The touch was light, but I could feel the raised lines of fingerprints against my nerves. "We are about to leave the light, and my vision is slightly better than yours."

"There's floor lights in the labyrinth," I reminded her.

"Not tonight. Celeste had them shut off in case anyone saw us leaving."

I hesitated.

"You have to learn to trust me out here. You won't survive without it."

I wrapped my fingers around the belt like a new lifeline. It tugged me forward as she pushed through the hedge. Suddenly it felt like a leash, as if she was trying to train me like the stupid dog shoved in my pack. But then again, maybe that's all I was to this girl. Something to be trained. I had to hold back my pride and let her think it was possible to do so.

The girl moved seamlessly through the dark. She didn't make one wrong turn as if she knew exactly where to go. The only exits went into town, and I didn't understand why she stopped against a tall hedge farthest from the city lights. An orbed glow wrapped around the buildings, as if beckoning us into its safety. Hucksley moved her hands into the hedge, spreading out the branches so that the leaves moved around her body like water, then she disappeared into the sea of black-shadowed green, pack and all.

The belt pulled me along with her, and we landed on the other side of the labyrinth.

She didn't pause there, but tugged me out into the trees. Every once in a while, she'd warn me about an obstacle underfoot, but mostly she let me stew in my own thoughts. Hours passed, and I wondered how Mother and Mos reacted when they realized I was gone. Did they feel betrayed, or did they know this was coming?

I kept thinking about the family I'd lost. I couldn't fit it into my brain now that it had happened for good, and as I followed Hucksley blindly, I became blinded by loss, wondering where I belonged or if I'd ever belong again.

The Colony stretched out before the platform. Father was nervous, and I couldn't understand why. He was never nervous, except for here.

The people of this Colony were slightly strange in appearance. Everywhere someone existed, curves bloomed around them. The men had round cheeks, but the women were round in other ways. Watching them crowd the platform made me thankful I'd already won the Propriety Meds bet. I'd lasted an entire four weeks before Cosmos caved. It was just in time for the campaign trail to begin, and, if Cosmo had known I'd never put myself through a campaign season off Propriety Meds, he could have held off a little longer to win the bet. Then again, Intention Day was looming right around the corner, and, seeing as all three of us had just turned fifteen over the past few months, I had a feeling I wasn't the only one relieved the experiment was over before that happened.

It was a different kind of victory for me. It wasn't about getting the coveted tickets to see the Flaming Flamingos concert that mattered. Those tickets could have easily been obtained in other ways, especially since Father had already hired them for the Forest Gala that year, and I would get to eat dinner with the entire band for a photo-op. Winning wasn't even about the bragging rights, especially since I hated talking about and reliving those uncomfortable weeks. The biggest win for all of us was in our severe reverence for taking our Propriety Meds now. We hadn't complained about the daily nuisance or the fact that the girls didn't understand what it was like to have to take a daily pill. We just took them and were glad for them.

Father wiped a bead of sweat from his forehead and patted my shoulder. His dark cheeks found a way to look pale.

"What's wrong?" I finally asked.

"Nothing," he said, but I saw through it.

"Whatever it is, let me help."

"Do you know how many children I genetically have?"

I nodded. "An unprecedented 39."

I didn't have to add that out of the 39, he only got to keep us two. It was so rare that a Celebrity got to raise two children, but there was nothing normal about my existence. I happened before his Celebrity Tour began, and since I needed a mother, they let his Partnering happen before he went to fulfill his duty.

"Did you know that I was never meant to be a Celebrity?" Father asked.

"I've heard the rumors."

"They are true to an extent. Your genetic-mother was supposed to be the only match I was ever supposed to get partnered with, but your grandfather knew it wouldn't do well for my political chances to be a single father. He lobbied the G.E.G. He can be very persuasive," he said.

"I've had experience with his persuasive measures," I replied.

"Sometimes I wish he never intervened. Do you know how difficult it is to campaign in the Colonies I visited on my Tour? To know that out there, my sons and daughters watch me, not knowing they began from me? Or, if they do, they know they are unable to meet me? I won't pretend it won't take a toll on you when you have to go through it. It's the most difficult part of being a Celebrity or the child of one. You and Zosimos are lucky to have grown up knowing who and where you came from on both sides. I never got that luxury. I only got rumors and speculation until the truth finally came out."

I looked out to the crowd and wondered if I had a half brother or sister out there waving back at us. I examined face after face in *the search, but there were too many souls to pay attention to just one.*

"The world thinks Celebrity Tours are an honor, but there was another reason my father wanted me to partake." He shuddered, but hid it in a sculpted wave to the crowd. Onesimos Leventis was giving his standard introduction speech, the one that went on far too long and made the crowd impatient for Father's words.

"What is the reason?"

"People important to the cultivation of Humanity have no room to be distracted by their bodies, and when human bodies are young, they are hungry. Becoming a Celebrity is based on potential to make advancements for Humanity just as much as genetics. Celebrity Tours are meant to wash out desire from love. It takes the act of reproduction and turns it into a duty, like it should be. It makes sex a tool rather than a pleasure, and after experiencing the consequence of leaving child after child behind, it teaches us that there's a difference between bodily lust and proper love. By the end of the tour, most Celebrities are just plain thankful to settle down with one other person. The wanderlust of desire is toned down, and they are able to focus on their duty to Humanity instead."

It made sense. It was something I'd actually thought about during the weeks off Propriety Meds. It had been so hard to focus on my research and classes at Institute. It felt like I hadn't been much use to the tasks I'd been set to, especially when I was around some of the girls. I could see the logic behind getting those urges out of the system right away. The Celebrity Tours were just an attempt at turning a human flaw into an asset.

I looked back at Father. He controlled his breathing and his expressions, but I knew I needed to dig deeper. "That's not the only thing upsetting you. Tell me, please."

He sighed and dropped the hand he'd been waving at the crowd to lean in and whisper, "I never told you what Colony your genetic-mother was from. Thanks to that grandfather of yours, her name and this place were the only things the G.E.G. kept sacred from the media when the Project Prometheus *data leaked."*

"This one?" I asked. It was the last Colony I'd have ever thought to cultivate my genetic-mother. Then again, despite the bodily flaws in the genetic pool here, it was a Colony known for natural intellectual brilliance. It suddenly made more sense than any other Colony that produced New Waves, and I made a mental note to trace the other New Wave lines to see if they all came back here at some point in their genetic past. It wouldn't be hard to do now that Grandfather had given me access to some of the confidential G.E.G. forums and databases.

Father nodded. "I avoid it when I can, but the vote here is pretty important. Surrounding Colonies trust this populace to understand the intricacies of government and often follow their lead. To skip this part of the trail would make me lose for sure."

I concentrated on each step, refusing to give Hucksley the satisfaction of a stumble. She mumbled things under her breath, a slow and steady stream of words that only she could hear. Was she singing to herself?

What had I gotten myself into? Was she even sane enough for this? Was I insane enough for it?

She finally paused and set her pack down. It was a relief to let go of the belt. My fingers felt cramped from holding onto it so tightly.

"Xavi said you can jump the trains. Is that true?" She broke the silence.

"I'm proficient."

"Sheesh. You have to stop that crap."

"What?"

"*I'm proficient.*" She lowered her voice to mimic mine, and she was surprisingly accurate in the imitation. It was like her ears could pick apart the nuances of my voice and commandeer them.

I bore the brunt of the insult. Rather than respond, I tugged off my pack and set it at my feet. It was time to let Bixby have a go at a fern. So far, I'd prevented accidents by letting her down about every twenty minutes. Bixby was reliable in her clockwork ability to let out a stream that would make a river jealous. I squirted water from the water bladder in my pack into the cup of my palm. The pup lapped it up, and her bump-laden tongue tickled my skin. Bixby was a solid Hucksley buffer. Anytime Hucksley would show distaste for me, my pace, my words, or my existence I pulled the dog out and focused my attentions on it.

I wanted to see where I could push Hucksley. I knew how to shift into the very language she wanted. I also knew I'd only do it when the situation suited me. For now, how she reacted to my petulance would tell me about her character. For every torture she sent in my direction, I countered it with an exact Propriety. She had to know I understood the game, possibly more so than she did. I knew how manipulation worked, and I refused to let her use it on me.

"Try it this way. *I'm a'right at it.*"

I unknotted the leash from where I'd wound it on my pack and bent to tie it around Bixby's neck. It was probably time she learned to walk a little. After all, she couldn't be carried everywhere her entire life. I didn't know much about dogs, but I was pretty sure training included teaching Bixby how to walk in step with me.

"Your brother, Zosimos, right? Didn't he do an entire study on how our language works out here?" Hucksley hovered over where I knelt with Bixby, a dark shadow under dark trees in a dark night. "His winning speech was played on repeat on the debate forums that entire month."

I shouldn't have been surprised that she had access to the vids. With solar technology, tablets could be charged anywhere sun landed. After the G.E.G. re-released the tech, the self-charging tablets had been nicked left and right, and this memory made me hope my tablet made it into my bag after all. But then I wondered how the Vagabonds got past the locating capabilities of the tablets when someone accessed the vid-web. They must have had someone who could hack the system.

"He's sexy, you know. The way he put his hands on that podium? Made a lot of girls out here wish he'd put those hands on their bodies just like *that.*"

"Leave Mos out of this," I warned.

"It's surprising, really. All those looks and brains! Who knew someone that pretty could be that smart? You had to have helped him on that research, seeing as you're all New Wave and he's all Halfsie."

I stood up so that I towered over her and tightened my grip on Bixby's leash. There was something solid to the cord as if it tied me to the very ground we stood on. I couldn't see her, but I could sense her closeness. I tried to ignore the fact that she smelled the way her voice sounded.

"I'm surprised at how little faith you have in the intelligence of a Halfsie," I said.

"Look at you, all taut like a pulled wire! Loosen. Up." She reached out as if to grab the leash, but her hand landed on my forearm instead. It made my lungs forget how to work, like she sucked every intention away from my words so that I could only see the things she planned on taking. She took whatever she wanted. My space. My words. My goodbyes. And right then and there, my dignity.

There was a tugging in my gut, a chemical reaction raging just under the surface, wanting her to never take her hand off my arm ever again. My vision grew cloudy, and nothing else seemed to matter anymore. Her fingers trailed down my forearm, along the back of my hand, and I couldn't control the hitched breathing or the growl growing at the back of my throat.

She tugged the leash from my grip and backed away. "Come on, Bixby. Lets give New Wave a moment to learn how to control himself."

I couldn't even watch her recede into the shadows. She left me alone in the stark darkness of an ending night, trying to calm the blood going to places it had no business going. It had to be the Propriety Meds leaving my system. It was the nature of having been on the drugs for half my life. To quit them so abruptly— again—made it difficult to control the side effects.

I wanted to go back.

I wanted to return to my world and all the structure it offered, but there was no taking back the things that had happened. My new reality left me with an urge-filled body, and, as much as I hated not having my bearings on it, I hated the embarrassment of my reactions even more.

Hucksley had recognized it. She knew exactly what was happening to me and tried to manipulate me into feeling off-kilter. Since she couldn't win with her words, she relied on her touch.

I patted my cheeks, trying to knock it out of me. Then I remembered the last trick. The one I'd discovered right towards the end of our Propriety Med experiment.

Better than counting ceiling tiles.

Better than thinking about snails.

Better than imagining crumby beards.

I concentrated on the escape. I whispered the first poem Father made me remember when I was learning to read. The words tumbled out as the sky shifted to that horizon color that made everything look dream-riddled.

"Silos rise like castle keeps
In the emerald fields of broken mesquite.
In the frack-jawed caliche
They plant new trees
Of rust coated flowers,
Those oiled machines.
Amongst cotton bulbs and bobblehead rigs,
Semi-beasts dance ancient Texas jigs.
But wait for the crash, for it is sure to come,
With a bigger boom than the starting one."

Hucksley's laugh rang out like cosmos colliding. The soft-sharp bell of it sounded like her fingers felt, and my face burned in fire.

Would she even steal this moment from me? I swallowed and tried to repeat the poem.

"Poetry? That's how boys cope in the Colonies? That's rich. Abner's going to die when he hears."

How could she hear me? I was whispering it, wasn't I? And why was she mocking me? Was she that cruel?

And the answer to that helped the tension in my spine deflate. She was manipulating me, even still. I felt a determination so thick wash over me, and I tightened the strings of my pack. I wouldn't let this girl, or my body, distract me from what I'd been set out to do. If I acted like she didn't bother me, then she wouldn't win.

"Let's keep going," I said, walking towards her voice on the other side of the next set of trees.

When I got to her, she tugged Bixby at the leash and slowed her pace so the pup could keep up. The sounds of the forest settled around us, and I tried to pay attention to where my steps took me rather than the world I was leaving.

Finally, the dawn fell away, shedding the skin of night behind it, and, just as the sun began to hover above the colors of its rise, we stumbled upon the Tracks. I looked down the long line cutting around a bend in the trees, and it felt good to be out of the woods.

Hucksley handed me Bixby's leash before she began walking along the Tracks in front of me. The clunky bow tie was a lopsided mess on the pup's neck, but she panted out a smile as we followed Hucksley.

As we walked, Hucksley braided and unbraided her hair. It snaked around her neck until it disappeared around her left shoulder. She fidgeted as if she were afraid to ever stop moving for even one second. Her opposite shoulder glimmered with sweat.

"So, was that the Texas Eulogy?" She threw the question over her shoulder, trying to pull me out of the silence I'd wrapped myself up in. I couldn't see the expression on her face, but her neck was smooth and slender but speckled with lines of dirt. It vibrated when she spoke.

"Excuse me?"

"Humberto Galvan, right? *Silos rise like castle keeps—*"

"What do you know about Humberto Galvan?"

"Probably more than you do about why he, in particular, made it into your historical blogs," she said.

It was odd she knew the name. Humberto Galvan's poetry was ancient, slightly older than the birth of the Republic. Before The Great Disaster, there had been a wealth of great writings, but after, there wasn't an adequate way to save the known histories. There was no true rhyme or reason for the stories that spoke beyond the graves of billions. What writings remained was simply a matter of those left at the end of the world, saving what spoke to them and passing it on to their children.

Texas was a distant title—a place long ago faded into nothingness. I knew there were other names for places our Colonies now rested on, but, like the stories, only some of the names had been remembered. As borders shifted, older ones no longer mattered. Texas was remembered only because a few of the founding families were born there, including Lucas and Leo Solano, so it made sense that the Texas Eulogy would make it into the mix.

"In his time," Hucksley continued, "Humberto Galvan wasn't anyone special. He was a shop-owner. A small-town man living a small-town life who dabbled in poetry to pass the time. He was actually killed in the first rounds of The Great Disaster." Hucksley started to undo the hair she had just woven together. I realized it was more than just a fidget, like her fingers were working out something more twisted than her hair. Her mind was elsewhere and everywhere, but the braiding and unbraiding kept her in the moment with me.

I laughed. "How could you possibly know that?"

My eyes traveled away from the way her hair loosened, and I swallowed. Her pack swayed with the movement of her hips, rhythmic as breathing, and I quickly tried to concentrate on my boots landing on the planks rather than her shape moving against the backdrop of train tracks and forest.

"Vagabonds have access to our own histories, but we also have the ones leaked to us from your very own Council of Manipulation. There are shifts in public thought happening. Surely you've seen it. Why do you think all these hidden documents about the Solanos have been released these past few years? Come, now, New Wave. Haven't you taken—what's it called—Manipulation Seminars?"

"I figured there were sympathizers in the Council," I said, but didn't elaborate further. She wanted me to be upset that there were spies in the Council of Manipulation. She was trying to see how I'd react to it.

"Humberto Galvan was from a little town called Terlingua," she added.

Terlingua. The pieces fell into place. Lucas Solano's hometown. Humberto Galvan must have known her as a girl, and he must have meant something to her for her to save his poetry and bring his name into a fame as lasting as hers.

"He was Adan Galvan's father. Do you know about him yet?" Hucksley asked.

Adan. The name flapped against my skull, a fish out of water. Why did Celeste and Hucksley feel the need to expand on this story? For once, I was tired of talking about the past and all the inconsistencies that kept being dug up. As much as it normally intrigued me, I needed to get Hucksley back into the now. It was the only way to get the information I needed to find the Vault.

Then it struck me that Hucksley had played a different hand. She wanted me to know she was cultured. Well read. Smart.

She didn't need to. I was perceptive enough to figure out she shouldn't be underestimated, but there was something more. I wasn't seeing the connection yet, but it wouldn't take me long.

"I have sufficient knowledge of him," I said.

She paused in front of me and turned. Rather than mock the Propriety in my words, she said, "Hand me the pup."

I looked down at Bixby. She waltzed beside me, prancing over the rough rocks in between the planks. It was about time to put her back in my pack before her paws got too raw. It was something I could empathize with. My own feet were starting to feel weary.

Hucksley countered my puzzled look with an explanation. "I'm going to take Bixby for this jump onto the train. I want to make sure you don't kill her on her first day out just in case you're not as talented as Xavi says you are." She bent and hooked the dog under her arm. She twisted the leash from my grasp and wrapped it around her wrist to shorten it.

"Jump? There's not a trai—"

The horn trumpeted through the trees, three long blasts following each other in succession.

"How did you know?" I asked.

"Sometimes hearing isn't about listening for the obvious things. You may open your ears and listen for the train. I open my ears and listen for the birds."

Sure enough, there was a dizzy chirping above us that I hadn't noticed until she pointed it out.

"Surroundings, New Wave. They'll tell you everything you need to know." Still, she wrapped a smile around her face that said she was holding back something more. She peeked around my shoulder to check on the train. It was just a speck coming in our direction. She stepped back into the cover of the brush and motioned for me to follow.

"We don't need to hide. The Absolution Bill grants us fair and free access to any train," I reminded her.

"And what if a Patriot is on board? Do they believe in your silly Absolution Bill?"

I closed my eyes. Explosions in the brain. Red fire. Red blood. Screams never having time to escape. "I suppose not," I whispered.

"All a law is is a piece of paper, and a piece of paper means little to those living out of reach of its enforcement. Your Absolution Bill means nothing to the people doing what they've always done— living how they've always lived. Life out here cannot be summed up into what the Republic *allows*. That has never been our way, and it never will be. That piece of paper has nothing to do with we, Vagabonds, and everything to do with making your people feel better about the atrocities they've inflicted on my people for the past centuries. Your politics are laden with pretty words and stoic ideas, but that does nothing to address reality. It doesn't negate the generations of hate still running rabid out of a simplistic habit. If that train has Patriots on it, they won't think twice about killing us being against the law."

I followed her off the Tracks and into the tree line. I stepped over a fallen pine to squat with her behind it. The brown leaves of dried death clung to the hollowing branches, refusing to fall to the ground in defeat. I wanted to speak, but I forced myself to listen.

"There is no in between for you out here. You have to commit. You have to mean what you say."

I closed my eyes, and I wanted to tell her I did mean it. I wanted to mean every word, but I knew she'd see through the lie. She was right. I wasn't out here for her people. In the end, I was out here for mine.

"Look at me," she whispered.

I couldn't. I knew I was lying to myself about something else, something that involved my Grandfather. The suspicion thrummed along every vertebral bump on my spine, and if she'd just stop talking, I could figure out exactly what it was. But, with her voice moving against my eardrums, I couldn't find the clue that'd unravel the entire hiccup in Grandfather's plan. I couldn't decipher that hidden thing inside of my heart that made me distrust him in this thing, of all things. Something felt so very off about how everything had started to play out, but my duty was a set course.

"Look. At. Me." Hucksley reached up and placed her palm on my cheek. The touch was soft, and I felt her breath land on my nose. I pried my lids open and steeled myself from yanking my face away. Instead, I tried to read her tornado eyes. In the muted shade, the darkness of her irises trapped the light and became their own black holes, sucking me towards her. Over the dead brush, the train rumbled past in a cadence that blurred behind the face she forced me to see.

"You aren't being noble. You. Are. Running. You are running from everything you're afraid of, and that is why my people will never trust you."

Hucksley dropped her hand and pushed herself up, her intention for me to follow clear. We moved back towards the Tracks, and she ran along the side of the train, her unraveled black hair flailing behind her, her pack bouncing uncomfortably. Bixby trembled, tucked between the curve of Hucksley's hip and arm. My feet stilled as I watched how naturally she moved. She grabbed the short ladder near a closed door to pull herself up as if she, her pack, and the dog weighed nothing. She climbed up it, using only one hand to let go and grab each rung so Bixby didn't fall. How she moved looked like habit, like she always jumped on trains one-handed.

For the first time, it occurred to me that I didn't have to follow. What if I turned around and faded into the trees? What if I turned my back on all of it?

She looked back just as I thought it. "Don't make us miss this ride!" she yelled.

I started running. Even if I tried to stay put, Hucksley would only get off the train and follow me. I had a feeling she'd be able to track me easily in these woods. She probably had more experience out here than I could fathom. I shook the idea away and started to run. I couldn't turn my back on it all, even if I wanted to. Hucksley didn't know this, though. She had no idea what it had been like to grow up in my world. How could she even pretend to understand who I was or what was in my heart? Hucksley, who had lived a life with nothing but her own choices, couldn't possibly understand what it was like to have only one.

One choice that wasn't her own.

Humanity before self.

Always with that capital "H" and that lower cased "s" to remind every Citizen which was more paramount.

My father had been wrong about choices. They never existed for people like me. Perhaps it was that reminder that pushed my feet to catch up. I reached out my hand and grabbed onto the lazy train. The metal felt heavy on my fingers and reminded me of cold door knobs and sweaty coffin handles. Openings and closings. The things that happened after one false step and one mistimed moment. I yanked my body up and pulled myself onto the ladder under her. I had to crouch, my feet on the last rung, my hands three above that. The Tracks blurred underneath me, and for a millisecond, nothing else but the movement of the train existed.

Hucksley tried to hide her approval, but I knew I'd done everything right. My brain had this way of breaking down seconds and understanding the un-time-able offense of poor timing. Uncle Ty only had to explain it once, and, like most things, I picked it up quickly.

"Brains and agility?" she mocked as she slid the ring on her pointer finger over the lock. It was a biometric scrambler less than the size of a pea. It made me wonder what other tech she had access to.

The lock beeped. "You sure the NPTN was the only thing they screwed with?" she asked.

"How do you manage to take every attempt at perfection and turn them into flaws?" I asked, and immediately regretted it. It came off as cocky, as if I thought I was actually perfect and better than everyone else. No one except Grandfather had ever gotten under my skin like she was doing, and I reminded myself to be more impeccable with my words.

Sure enough, she took it how it sounded. "Out here, perfection doesn't exist, not even in you." She pulled the door open and disappeared into it. I sighed and followed.

Hucksley leaned against a tower of crates with her pack at her feet. There wasn't much floor space between the crates and the open door—barely enough for her to slump down against them and set Bixby in her lap. She thwarted the pup from climbing up and licking her cheek.

I set my pack down next to hers. On both sides of the open door, a space like a disjointed hallway ran the span of the car, but it would have been too claustrophobic to sit in its safety. The only option I had was to sit as she did on the opposite side of our packs. At least they created a stumpy wall between us. My feet nearly reached out the open door, and I had to bend my knees and hug them just to fit.

Bixby managed to clamber from her lap and demanded access to mine by scratching at Hucksley's pack. I reached around and obliged her. I rubbed the tiny triangle ears between my forefingers and thumbs, and the pup leaned into the petting.

"It's cruel to bring a puppy into this," I said. I wasn't sure why the thought occurred to me, but had Hucksley not stolen Bixby, the dog would have gone to someone like Eudocia. She would have gone to a safe home with plenty of food and love, but out here, Bixby was stuck with a boy who didn't even know if he liked dogs and a girl who wanted to use her as a training tool.

"Maybe we should drop her off at the doorstep of a Citizen in the next Colony we come to. You know. Give her a chance at a better life?" Hucksley offered. Her voice softened as she looked around the packs to examine the dog in my hands, and, for a second, the only word I could think of was beautiful.

Hucksley was beautiful.

I grinned. "Exactly! It's not right for us to expect Bixby to survive in such harsh—"

"—conditions! At the next Colony we should—" she stole my thought. My heart fluttered. Perhaps she could be reasonable and see beyond herself. "—give Bixby up. It'd be the stoic thing to do," she finished.

I stopped rubbing the ears to scratch Bixby's neck. "She'll have a better life for it," I whispered, surprised to find I cared enough for the pup to want her to have a more comfortable existence.

Hucksley's smile hardened. "Like always, your words are fool's gold. Just because your mother made the choice to hand you over to the Republic does not mean you were better off for it, New Wave."

"Rest it flat on your thumb. Support with the pointer," Uncle Ty said.

I wound my arm back, keeping my hand even, and let the flat rock fly. It skipped once, twice, five times on the water. I laughed. It was so simple.

I never got to do simple things these days.

"Why wouldn't Celeste let me give the nano-bots to those two boys?" I asked.

"She didn't not let you give them the serum. The boys chose not to take it."

"They chose not to take it?"

He laughed. "It's not the same out here as it is in our world. Someone in the position of power tells the Republic to do something, and Citizens comply, but someone in the position of power on the Tracks can never demand. They rule based on trust, and they never violate a trust if they can help it. Leadership is more fluid out here. It's not a series of yeses and nos for the greater good. It's a series of suggestions for the personal good, a displaying of information so that every Vagabond can make a personal choice to partake or decline. In fact, not every Vagabond is forced to enlist for their cause on such a fundamental and complete level the way Citizens are."

"So those boys knew what was being asked of them and decided it was not for them."

"Strange concept, isn't it?"

I nodded, and threw a perfect stone to skip in perfect hops along the surface. I thought about choice, and how sometimes, even if you wanted to choose differently, other forces could still make it feel impossible. After all, the stone, once thrown, could no more choose to change direction than I could.

"I taught Niko how to skip rocks," Uncle Ty said. "It was not one of her talents."

I felt my mood plop into the water like the stone I'd just thrown.

"This was our lake. Our spot. I loved her here. I loved her everywhere we went."

"Is that why you told me about Adonis not being a Solano?" I swallowed. Was it possible that Father was not my father? That he took me in unsanctioned because he loved my mother despite knowing I was really Uncle Ty's genetic-son? Did Father claim me because it was the only way the G.E.G. would let me stay in the Republic?

Uncle Ty read every question attached to the one actually asked. "Use that big brain of yours, Ani. In that, you'll know the truth. You are your father's son." He skipped a stone. Seven hops later, it landed one last time.

He was right. I shared none of Uncle Ty's characteristics and too many of Father's.

I didn't know if I was relieved to know my life wasn't a lie, or if I was disappointed. It might have been freeing to discover I wasn't Father's. It would mean I wasn't technically the genius everyone said I was. I could have just been another Republic genetic cover up like Adonis Solano, and it would have taken some of the pressure of expectation off of me.

Or would it have?

If my reality had been different, I would have had to live up to expectations I could never fully meet. Which would be worse? Being as great as I was supposed to be or falling just short of the greatness the entire world expected.

"But you wish I was yours?" I whispered.

"If I hadn't been a colossal idiot, you would have been mine. Then again, you'd be someone completely different, and the you I am speaking to would not exist. Not to mention, I'd have turned myself into a Genetic Terrorist by having an unsanctioned child." He laughed and shook his head. "It doesn't mean you don't belong to me in some ways."

"How so?" I asked. I was curious about his admission to willingly become a Terrorist for my genetic-mother, but I was more troubled by how he claimed me as his in light of this love he had for her.

"Name the one person who has been with you every step of the way," Uncle Ty said.

"You."

Uncle Ty nodded. "Polo brought you to me, right here. Right in that spot over there?" He pointed to the edge of the lake. "I found out Niko was gone. Right in that spot, Polo handed you to me and told me to protect you. And I've watched out for you, my boy. I've never left your side when it mattered. In many ways, I am as much your father as Ono is, and if I'd been smarter than your mother, I'd have never given you to the burdens inflicted on you by the Republic."

He threw another stone. And then another. He let me dwell on the thoughts, let me drown in them the way the stones did as they finally sunk below the water's surface.

The pebble skip, skip, skipped. Could he really be the traitor Grandfather thought he was after all?

"She changed her name to Wind." His words skip, skip, skipped. "She didn't want to be known as Knucs. As Niko. As

anything else besides something ungraspable. She wanted to be free for once because she'd never been free her entire life. But I wanted to catch her. I chased the Wind, and by the time I thought I had her in my reach, she was gone. Everything she was had morphed into everything she left behind."

My heart skip, skip, skipped. "Me," I whispered. "She left me behind."

"Even if I wanted to, I couldn't turn my back on you, but by the time I thought of a better way, it was too late. I couldn't get you out of the situation I'd planted you in."

I closed my eyes and sat down in the shallow water. I wanted the coolness of it to wrap around my navel and calm me down, but it felt like my skin could boil the entire lake until it evaporated into parched sand.

"These nano-bots, Ani. They are going to show you things I think you already know deep in your joints—things you're not ready to accept just yet. They are going to point out the grand flaws in the G.E.G.'s design, and you are going to have to decide what to do with it. Your mother was born a Citizen, but in the end, she was a Vagabond. Your mother's story is not the only one that went this way. Perhaps Terrorists are not what you have always thought them to be."

I couldn't be hearing this. Uncle Ty, for all his prestige and stature, was speaking completely traitorous thoughts, and I could see the fissures in his loyalty despite the fact he'd passed Grandfather's testing of it.

"Your father never told you this, but it's now time I did..."

And he spoke. He brought an unborn story to life. A story about how my maternal-genetic-grandparents were murdered by Grandfather because he was insulted by the pairing. A story about how Grandfather accused Nikomedes Kostas of Genetic Terrorism over hypothetical research. How my genetic-mother ran, and how Uncle Ty found her crying in the woods.

It didn't matter if I could believe the story to be true or not because he had possibility on his side, and sometimes, possibility was a truth all on its own. I knew Grandfather in such fundamental ways, and I knew he'd take care of monstrosities and atrocities as he saw fit, regardless of the consequences. Could all of this have been prevented if Grandfather hadn't tried to control it?

Uncle Ty left the story there. He stepped out of the water and let me have my space. He'd planted the seed long ago, but now he'd given it light and air and water to expand past myself into the greater inquiries.

Maybe my genetic-mother was not a traitor.

Maybe Grandfather was.

Or maybe they both were in their own ways?

Maybe...

"You're thinking about something," Hucksley said.

"It happens to the best of us."

She wiggled her fingers in front of Bixby and made the pup dance. The traitor had demanded back onto Hucksley's side of the pack-mountain between us. "If I were a betting soul, I'd bet your ration of peanut butter that I know what you're thinking about."

"I'm not a betting soul."

"Oh, I've the strange feeling we have similar souls if you pay close enough attention."

Bixby landed on her four paws, then nudged Hucksley's knee. The pup was hungry, and I wondered what we'd feed it. Hucksley had the same thought because she reached into her pack and pulled out a small sack of pebbled food. What would happen to the pup when we ran out? It didn't seem wise to have a dog out on the Tracks because, out here, survival of the self had to be hard enough.

Hucksley fed the dog out of her palm, and when Bixby finished, I felt my own stomach rumble. "So you're saying I have peanut butter?"

She pulled open a side pouch in my pack. "Amongst other things. Keep in mind you need to stretch what you have for at least a week." There was a jar of peanut butter, some tuna fish, beef jerky, granola, and dried fruit.

I raised an eyebrow.

"This is a feast out here. May not be your ribeyes and poached salmon, but it does the trick in a pinch," she said.

"I'm not complaining. Thanks for the food." I reached in and grabbed the bag of jerky, pulled it out, and offered her a piece.

She took it and tugged on the meat with her teeth. "You're thinking about your father."

"My brain is a little more complex than that," I admitted.

"How does it work?" she asked.

"How does what work?"

"This super human intelligence everyone keeps talking about."

I contemplated answering. It was a question everyone wondered, but the G.E.G. had always discouraged me from discussing it with anyone but them.

"Do you really know everything? Or at least think you know everything?" she prodded.

"Not at all. In fact, I'm painfully aware of how little I truly know." I moved the words around the jerky between my teeth and stared out the open door. Green trees had blurred into a large field of corn, their heads heavy laden with ears. Some of the major crops were still maintained outside of the Victory Gardens, and I loved stumbling upon them. Neatly planted rows popped up year after year, carefully straight and dependable.

"That must be humbling," Hucksley replied. "Is that why you're not as cocky as I thought you'd be?"

"You don't find me cocky? I'm pretty sure you do."

She grinned. "Not in the way Ollie and Abner get when they are trying to prove themselves." She slid in the names, like she wanted me to get used to their presence despite their absence. "Most boys out here are out of their minds confident. You seem moderately so."

"My nurturing plan was very carefully constructed so that I never grew too cocky. Apparently, my genetic-mother went through something similar, only on a greater scale."

Hucksley sucked in a breath, paused to think on what I'd said, and chewed on her jerky before moving past whatever surprising information she'd just gotten. "Is it like turning on a computer? Or does your brain constantly run?"

"Neither."

"What does it feel like to know you are smarter than anyone you encounter?"

"What does it feel like to know you're more obnoxious than anyone you encounter?"

She let out a laugh. There was something familiar about it, something known to me, and it made me sad. I'd laughed like that once, but I hadn't in years.

"Does it make you feel superior?" she asked. There wasn't aggression in the question. Just curiosity. "I mean, you have to feel it, right? Superiority? Growing up being told you're the closest thing to perfection in our generation."

"I never asked for this," I admitted, and the admission shocked me. The only person who really and truly understood my feelings on the issue was Mos, and it felt like a betrayal to open up to a complete stranger. "As you know, I have a brother. We have different mothers and different talents. Growing up, I hovered between feeling guilty about being smarter, feeling annoyed that he wasn't as smart, and feeling proud that I was so brilliant."

"And now?"

"Now, I just accept it. It's not something to be boastful about, nor is it something to be ashamed of. It simply is. I was created for this purpose, and the only way to honor the gifts I've been given is to try and do right for Humanity by them." I swallowed the jerky I'd been working on, and I was tempted to grab another piece. Instead, I thrummed my fingers on my thigh and willed my stomach to feel full.

"You still didn't answer how it works? How your brain is different? Or do you not know?"

"I know." I'd spent years trying to figure out what made my brain react differently. I devoured genetic comparison studies. I took a million intelligence tests at the G.E.G. I asked strangers to put their own thought processes into words. I finally started being able to articulate the differences inside of my own thought processes, but it was never adequate. My explanations were full of generalizations and analogies so that the reality of it was buried behind half definitions.

The best description I ever figured out was that my brain worked in simultaneous layers. When it came to reading or visuals, I could take pictures with my mind. I could leaf through them on demand, finding answers I'd already encountered instantaneously when the right questions drew upon them. But when it came to processing information, I could trace the path—every mistake, failure, and success—towards understanding. One discovery never discounted another, just as one thought could never replace another. It was as if they existed simultaneously in the catalogue of information my brain collected, and sometimes I wondered if my head would ever run out of space. Once I learned something, I knew how to connect it to everything else I had previously learned. Sometimes, this part took a while. I could feel the premonition of realization, which pushed me to work harder to encounter whatever truth lay hidden in the question. Then I'd analyze these answers. How did they relate? Differ? Compare? This moved me into being able to predict outcomes, come up with hypotheses that went beyond normal hypotheses, and connect normally unrelated experiments. And though I knew the truth of it in my heart, not even these explanations fully explained how my brain worked in words, which was why I'd never tried to explain it in full to anyone but Mos. Mos, who never judged me when I was inadequate.

"Well?" Hucksley demanded. She held Bixby out to me. The dog had the attention span of a fish, and I had a feeling it wouldn't be long before she wanted back in Hucksley's lap. I avoided touching Hucksley's fingers as I retrieved the pup.

"You won't understand it," I finally said. "Just keep comparing it to a computer."

She raised an eyebrow, and I expected her to fire back with something snarky. Instead she said, "We should get some rest while we can. You look like crap."

CHAPTER SIX

"What about the Patriots?" Mos asked.

"They are harmless fanatics, afraid of change. Don't legitimize them. They don't deserve the power your worries give them." Father buried his face back into his tablet, and it cast a blue-hued glow across his cheeks. He pressed his thumb on the screen, giving his biometric signature on a form, probably an agreement needed for the Absolution Bill that was in the works.

"Then again, fanatics have a way of getting fans," I said. I wasn't trying to be pessimistic, but how could Father not see the uprisings picking up speed? Each convert worked to convert others, so that a small group had suddenly become large. It was the tug of debate, the change of collective mindsets. This alteration in belief weighed down on me, encasing blame in the capillaries of my own heart. Why hadn't Grandfather put a stop to them yet? They were getting too bold.

Mos grinned. "I see what you did there. Fans. Fan-at-ics."

I sighed. He kept trying to cheer me up, but it wasn't working. I had to let him think it was though, so I joked back. "I know I technically got all the brains, but could you try to pretend you're a bit more quick on the draw. Father has a genetic reputation to *uphold."*

"You may have gotten the brains, but I can do a lot with all my beauty, brother." Mos tugged at my hair and sharp prickles raced along my scalp, but I gave him what he was after. A not so unwarranted chuckle.

I woke up when the explosions came into my dreams. Vivid brights burned the back of my lids, and I opened my eyes slowly to try and get my bearings.

Hucksley came into focus. She stood at the edge of the doorframe, balancing on the balls of her feet, her arms outstretched for balance. There was a lost look in her expression as the wind hit her face. I'd never seen someone look so sad, and I knew I was witnessing something she never meant me to see. There was a beauty to the pain, like she wanted the wind to tear it right from her skin and take it far away. Her arms fell down, and she placed her hands on her stomach, like she was forcing herself to stand up taller, straighter, like she was bracing herself to face whatever was barreling her way next.

There it was.

The weakness.

When Hucksley felt what she understood to be freedom, she dropped her guard, and watching the world zip past did this for her.

It felt wrong to capture such a private moment, so I closed my eyes again. I stretched out my back and let out a groan to warn her I was waking up.

There was definitely a crick in my neck, one I'd feel all day. It's strange how easy it was to pass out in that position when exhaustion tugged at my toes. The wooden boards of the crates weren't exactly the softest. What was surprisingly soft was the Bixby's wiry hair under my hand. Soft, puppy snores hovered over her nose, and, when I stretched, she nuzzled closer to my thigh in protest.

"She got attached easily enough, huh?" Hucksley asked.

"What are you doing?" I asked as she adjusted her body.

"Stand up, and I'll teach you."

"To balance? I'm positive I can manage such things without instruction."

"Gah! *I can manage such things.* Quit being a tool-bag-dingle-hopper before I *manage* to throw you right off this damn train." She pivoted her body so that her legs spread and her balance shifted. Her hands landed on her hips, and whatever moment of weakness I'd witnessed was swallowed within her carefully crafted persona. "You'll never learn to surf if you don't know how to keep your feet underneath you, crap-nugget. Oh. Wait. *Pardon me for my use of such foul language. Permit me to rephrase. You will have difficulty grasping the concept of this particular balance-based sport without proper instruction.*"

I held back a smile and stood up to secure Bixby to a crate. It wasn't very heavy to lift the top one and shove the leash between them. The last thing I needed was for the dog to go prancing near the door and fall out because I wasn't paying attention. Bixby cocked her head at me. There was a brown spot around her eye that traveled the length of her forehead and stopped between her ears. Ears that were triangular and all hearing. She opened her mouth and panted, like she was laughing at me. I never knew dogs could smile like that.

I turned away from the towering, rusted crates and prepared for what came next. I felt a kindred rope of compassion loop around me, and I wanted to take away the sadness I now knew rested underneath that shell of Hucksley's strength. "No need to be a, what was it? A tool-bag-douche-bucket?"

Her expression lightened when I gave her the words she'd tried to pull out of me all night. It was a gift, but I lost something the moment I spoke in her expectations. I hated to admit it, but the real reason I didn't use Hucksley's language was because it felt like the final betrayal to the Republic. I'd spent my entire life being proper around strangers, and my language tied me to home and duty. To give that away so easily to someone who hadn't earned it felt disloyal.

She kicked a foot out the door to feel the wind against it. She closed her eyes to the movement, and I studied the way absolute happiness took away the intense look of determination she usually wore. "The boy gets clever! *Why Bixby! I'm shocked. Are you not? How does he know such words like douche-bucket!*" There was something free inside of her sarcasm, and the way she switched in and out of dialects was a testament to her cleverness. She looked ridiculous. Her hair whipped at a face that wore a mocked surprise, and it made me miss my own hair. I imagined what it would feel like to be torn apart by the same wind ripping through hers. Instead, the bareness of my scalp still tickled. I reached up and scratched it with my nails, the noise of it disconcertingly rough.

Hucksley moved away from the ledge. "Get a spine, and, while you're at it, get your bearings. Today's *proper instruction* will involve surfing."

"Surfing?"

"There's been too much heavy in your world to last a lifetime. It's about time you lived a little." She motioned for me to step closer, but I felt wobbly on the moving train after sitting for so long. I took a deep breath to steady myself.

Hucksley noticed my discomfort. "Stand through it. Don't let it unbalance you. The hardest part is ignoring the open door. I know you've been on trains plenty before, but you've never felt the adrenaline of being next to the reality of its speed. It's the lack of security and safety that's making you feel unsettled."

"I would hardly call this unsettled," I said.

She smirked. "Feel the vibrations at your feet? They speak to you. Everything out here has a language, even if you don't know how to translate it."

"Terrorists have different translations for the languages of love," Pamphilos said.

"Yeah, but, if anything, we've just proven that their kind of love is just a chemical reaction," Cosmos replied. "When I look at Phoibe now, I'm only annoyed with her."

I took a bite of my avocado, but something was missing. I reached over for a lemon wedge and squeezed some juice on it. When I took another bite, I found it more satisfying. I scraped the spoon along the husk as if it were a proper bowl and prayed the conversation would change. I didn't want to think about how we reacted without Propriety Meds half a year ago, but the scientific method was drilled into our habits. Pamphilos wanted to analyze every moment as valuable data. Normally, I'd be all for treating life as one big experiment after another, but losing control of my body was the last thing I wanted to relive.

Pamphilos was determined to keep the debate going. "True, but they believe their bodies speak truth. In their language of love, to not pay attention to what your body tells you is to deny something pure within yourself. It's how they sniff out spies. Spies can't speak this language, both verbally and physically. Even if the Militia alters the Linguistics Training as Mos' debate last year suggested, that's only part of it. Citizens are too reserved in how they work their bodies to completely infiltrate the Terrorists."

I swallowed my last bite and nearly choked on the acerbic taste of lemon juice. "You mean to tell me you were just using us as part of your Militia thesis!"

"Why do you think I only lasted a week? I needed to observe you two."

I had to laugh at the admission. The three of us were elbow deep in our thesis projects. I was so close to being done with the nano-bot prototypes, and I ached to find out if the G.E.G. would approve their production. Pamphilos, on the other hand, was obsessed with military strategies, and he was going to do big things for the Militia one day. I wanted to deny his theory, but I knew enough of Uncle Ty's story to know that Pamphilos had a point. He had interviewed several spies fresh off their Tour of Duty, as well as veterans with years of distance. Between the two genres of spy, he spent hours analyzing the different perspectives and experiences.

"The Terrorists use this body language against spies," he continued. "Honest Citizens, no matter how prepared, get confused by these impressionable feelings, and some have trouble remaining objective to their duties. That is when they are in the most danger of losing themselves to the Terrorists' cause. We *have lost so many spies to a carefully crafted seduction."*

I got up and tossed the rind into the compost bin and the spoon into the dish receptacle. I was proud of Pamphilos for getting his thesis accepted into True Consideration. Every year, the Militia chose one thesis to put into actual practice, and Pamphilos was one of seven left in the competition.

"That's why I'm going to win," Pamphilos told Cosmos behind me. "I'm going to suggest we send partnered spies out, people who were meant to be together in the first place. This way, any accidental offspring or indulging of urges can do no harm to the genome and spies can live out there without the chains of guilt."

Cosmos laughed. "That's just brilliant!"

"I know," Pamphilos replied. "I may even be smarter than Ani!"

"No one is smarter than me," I replied, not sitting back down at the picnic table. "Lets get to the intake room. Coach will make us run ten mule-tucks if we are late again."

Cosmos groaned and got up from where he sat on top of the table. "Why are we still playing Gruel Ball again?"

"Because you're not fast enough for track," Pamphilos offered, ducking a punch Cosmos sent in his direction.

"I have a friend who claimed that once," I said. Thinking of Pamphilos and Cosmos made me feel the pang of loss. This past year, they'd been kept away from me. I constantly missed the easy way I was allowed to act around them. They never asked me to be perfect. They left that expectation for the rest of the world to demand. But when I leaked the data from the nano-bots, their Public Relations Specialists thought it best for their chances if they kept their distance. I couldn't begrudge them that. In fact, I encouraged it. Keeping their friendship for an extra year wasn't fair to them if it meant it could ruin their futures. Cosmos and Pamphilos were kind in trying to argue, but in the end, they stayed away.

"Sounds like a pretty smart friend," Hucksley said.

I grinned. "He'd love to hear you say it. He liked to think he was smarter than me."

"Was he?"

I laughed. "Sometimes."

She nodded towards my boots. "Now, feel it? Plant your feet for just a second. Get used to the rhythm. Close your eyes if you need to."

When darkness wrapped around my pupils, I fell into the cool rush of shadows behind my lids.

Respite.

I felt the vibrations of the moving beast underneath me. It was faster than when we'd first gotten on.

Velocity.

Speed.

Trajectory.

Yet despite all the physics that could be picked apart to describe the movement of the train, there was something alive about it. Something unmeasurable.

"Never jump off at this speed. It's an okay speed for surfing, though. Just avoid surfing anything faster than this. There's a cusp that makes the act equal parts dangerous and equal parts reasonable. Too slow, and you might as well not be doing it. Too fast, and you might as well be committing suicide."

I felt the hiccup in speed, and there was a slight change in vibrations at the base of my feet.

"Track rhythm. You feel it?" Hucksley began to hum along with it. There was a thump, thump, thump to the mechanics pushing the wheels along, but it was her humming that buzzed along my rib cage. Safe behind closed eyes, I did feel it. I felt the way my veins bubbled up and over, how my entire body connected and felt at peace with the world speeding beneath me.

"Movement is our home. To stay still is to die." Her words grew closer in proximity, but I wasn't afraid this time. I only wanted to be inside the darkness of closed eyes and the thrumming at my feet. "Now, spread your feet shoulder width apart, don't plant them. Stay on the balls so you can roll with the movement. Bend your knees slightly."

I balanced my body as she suggested and immediately felt

steady, as if my body moved with the momentum rather than against it. I felt my hips sway to catch the impact from my legs, and my head no longer rattled.

"You're a natural. I guess all that Gruel Ball paid off," she said.

I shouldn't have been surprised that she knew about my extra-curricular activities. Even things meant to be fun had a purpose for Grandfather, and he cultivated my image to an exactness.

Thinking of Gruel Ball and all the strength and balance exercises that were a staple at practice was surreal. It was yet another thing I had to give up after the leak. As the small anarchies took root in the Republic, I had to start letting go of the things I found joy in. I had to move away from my befores and into my nows, giving up the people and things I loved most about the world I knew in order to save it.

"Remember, the best Wielder is someone who can read their opponent and anticipate the path they may choose to take based on choices they made previously," Coach said. I groaned. He'd said it so many times before, and I knew who'd speak next. The discussion was clockwork, and part of me suspected Cosmos would ask the next part just out of a pregame tradition.

"There has to be an element of luck involved, though." Cosmos sat up straight and stretched.

I looked at Pamphilos then, who mouthed the canned response Coach gave. "There are only actions and reactions, boy. Luck is about as valuable as shit out here."

I stifled a laugh as Pamphilos crossed his eyes, but his display sent a twitter of snickers through everyone else.

We all loved the way Coach talked. He claimed his crassness was because of his years as a spy. He had had trouble ditching the accent once it had attached itself to his language habits, and, every once in awhile, it showed up when he was excited or on a rant. It mainly showed up in his name, though. No one really knew his official name. He shed it just like the Vagabonds shed their names and was reborn into an idea rather than an individual. I had a feeling his true name carried scars of things he needed to forget,

The Birth of Anarchy

things that happened when he was a spy. I could have easily looked it up in the databases, but pity made me stay away from the search. Sometimes even curiosity was inappropriate.

I held the square ball in my hand. It had rounded edges, but I still hadn't figured out why they called it a ball since it wasn't circular. It was hard to carry, but that was the point of it.

Gruel Ball was all about carrying a box-shaped ball into a box-shaped room in the center of a box-shaped arena called the Lab. They made the ball bulky on purpose so that it was difficult to grasp and provided an extra disadvantage during obstacles. It basically made your body inefficient by taking at least one limb out of mobility, and anything to do with climbing often required quick thinking.

It would be my first game as a Spike. I'd been a Wielder for years, and I usually got to manipulate the rooms that led to the center of the Lab. Each obstacle room moved on a track much like an elevator—if that elevator moved sideways on a conveyor belt. The Spikes ran the ball through each obstacle course. If they got through one, they were met with the next one placed by the other team's Wielders.

While Spikes needed to be sure of foot and good at solving problems, Wielders needed to be sure of mind and good at creating problems. They had to enter a room two plays out so that it could be locked in on time for the Spike. If the obstacles were too easy to solve, the Spike could outrun the placement of the rooms. When that happened, they got a free ride to the center of the Lab for five points.

Cosmos asked another question, getting another canned response. He and Pamphilos were the other two Spikes. Even though it'd be nice to experience what they did every game, I had never wanted to be one. I had the mindset of a Wielder, but that's why Coach insisted I'd be a better Spike. He said I'd be able to anticipate the people trying to anticipate me.

I wasn't sure how to feel about stepping into a new position. Nervous? Resentful? Determined?

Gruel Ball was supposed to be the one thing I had to myself, the one game that wasn't about the Republic or my role in it, but not even Gruel Ball belonged to me anymore. I had the feeling Grandfather had something to do with the roster change.

"Enough chatting, ladies and gentlemen. The Lab is calling!" Coach said.

"And we must answer!" the team said in unison.

I got up with everyone to get into position. Before I could get to my starting door, Phoibe approached me. "Any last minute pointers, Ani?" she whispered.

It was the first time I had considered how she felt about the change in position. It probably didn't sit well with her either. She was the best Spike on the team, and now she had to give up her spot so my grandfather could prove some unknown point.

My whole life, I'd been frustrated with Grandfather for how he manipulated my world. How could I not notice the way these things rippled out, touching innocent people? It felt like I left victims in my wake with every step I took towards Grandfather's idea of greatness, and I didn't know how to apologize to Phoibe for getting caught up in something that had nothing to do with her.

I cleared my throat. "Just be sure to balance out the difficulty. Pay attention to the obstacle's Strength Ratio, most of all. For every three rooms in play, you have to make sure you stay within the difficulty level range. Some people risk it. They say that if you give your Spike the hardest obstacle right off the bat, they won't get past it, but I never like to underestimate people. Sometimes the better strategy is to lull them into a false sense of self-confidence. Give them something moderate. Then something light. Then something that knocks them out."

Cosmos patted my helmet and held up his red ball on his way to the starting door he'd drawn.

"Any advice for me?" I asked.

She blushed. "New Waves never need advice. You'll be fine."

If only she knew how untrue that statement was.

There was a blinking red light over tunnel number six. It was the lot I'd drawn out of the ten evenly spaced doors. On the other side of the Lab, ten more doors would let our opponents in when *the lights turned blue.*

I positioned myself on the line and held my breath as the red blinking sped up. I had to be quick. I had to be smart. I had to be ready.

The blue light came on, the door slid open, and I moved through it to find a chasm ten feet wide. There was a small basket on the wall opposite of me and a rope that spanned the gap.

I examined the basket.

The only time the ball was allowed to leave a Spike's hand was if the basket was present, and the basket only appeared during the highest difficulty rooms. If I threw the ball, I'd be able to walk the tightrope better with all limbs. However, if I threw and missed, we'd lose the point right off the bat, and I'd be in the penalty box for five minutes.

I took a deep breath.

Play it safe?

Risk it all?

The clock on the door at the other side of the obstacle clicked away the seconds. I only had eight minutes to solve each room, and I'd already wasted twenty seconds trying to make a choice.

I wound my arm back, steadied my body, balanced it for the best aim, and threw.

"This doesn't account for the wind. In here, you're all nice and cozy, but up there, the wind creates its own version of speed. You can anticipate the train. It was made by man. You can't anticipate nature." Hucksley put her hands underneath my arms and spread them out.

I opened my eyes to the touch and tried not to shiver. I didn't think I'd ever get used to the easy way people touched each other out here or the way she stood so close to me without a second, bashful thought.

"This stance will help. You'll use your hands to balance you on top of the train before lifting your body up. Like this." She stepped back to show me, completely unafraid of how close she was to the ledge of the open door. She knelt down to demonstrate standing up from a crouch, then she walked me through it a few more times. I picked up the movement fast, crouching, balancing, and standing.

While I practiced, she double checked Bixby's leash and whispered, "Stay, girl. We'll be back."

Bixby cocked her head in the same way I caught myself doing. Hucksley couldn't possibly mean we were going to surf now. The train had picked up speed past the point she said was safe. Before I could point this out, she had already braced herself against the door frame, climbed up to the roof, and disappeared. Then, her head reappeared. Her hair flailed into a cone shaped by gravity—a slanted tornado whipped by the wind—while her face flushed from the blood rushing into her cheeks. "Coming?"

I shrugged at Bixby. "Stay," I said for good measure, hoping that the dog was as smart as I suspected her to be. It felt strange to leave our packs and the dog, and I wondered if it was a smart move as I approached the door. But if Hucksley had done it without a second thought, then perhaps I should trust in that.

I pulled myself up onto the roof easily enough, trying to ignore the force of wind that threatened to knock me off the train if I lost my grip.

Hucksley stood on the roof without hesitation, her stance angled so her body gave less resistance to the wind. Slick, black hair whipped her pecan hued cheeks, and I could nearly feel the adrenaline radiating off of her.

She was fearless.

I discovered I wasn't as fearless as I wanted to be.

I crouched, feet and palms planted firmly on metal. Even though the sun had imprinted heat into its surface, I kept my fingers tucked into the warmth. The jolting sensation of burn kept me alert. This was different from what I'd just practiced. Higher. Nothing to catch me if I lost my balance. Slick, sun soaked metal instead of shaded grainy boards.

Hucksley knelt down and held my eyes with hers. "Choose the things you fear, or they will choose you."

I sucked in a breath. It was a belief she carried that I could tell had been passed down like heirlooms, and I wondered who taught her to be brave when everything screamed to be the opposite. The words did not belong to Hucksley, but to someone who came before her. Perhaps the same someone who once taught my father about fear. I'd heard him say the same thing once, but there was so much sadness in the words that I never heard him say it again.

I tried to stand but got nervous. I planted my palms back on the rumbling train when the wind hooked my shoulders and promised to topple me. The rushing air sent me into a frenzy of blinking.

"That's how it'll be, aye?" Her eyes flared with the inflection in her voice before something shifted in her expression. She moved fast and landed a solid punch against my jaw. It knocked me backwards, and I lost my balance to fall against the thrumming roof. The thump, thump, tha-thrump of the train picked up speed. I tried to prop myself up on my elbows, but she was already on top of me, twisting my body so that my face hit the metal. How someone so small could do that so easily sent waves of shock through me.

I'd let my guard down.

It never occurred to me to be worried about a physical attack from her.

I tried to push myself up, but she'd already taken my hands behind my back and pinned my hips with her thighs. She used my shock to take me down, and, now that she had the advantage, she wasn't going to give it back. I stopped my brain from spinning, and I quit struggling. She was either testing me or trying to kill me. Either way, losing my head over it wasn't going to help. As my body stilled, she tightened her grip. She squeezed my wrists firmly behind my back and used an arm to hook them before pushing a free hand into my face.

"What are you doing?" I asked. I kept my voice even, and non-pulsed.

But instead of an answer, she grabbed my ear, yanked my head up, and slammed the side of my forehead into the metal.

A collective groan escaped the team as we watched the playback feed from yesterday's game.

"Wait for it! Wait for it! Here it comes!" Phoibe yelled.

"The best part for sure!" Cosmos yelped as I threw the ball and it landed perfectly in the basket.

"And… Face paaaahhhh-lant!" Pamphilos added, clapping his hands together for the sound effect as I took one step onto the tightrope and fell into the chasm. My face hit the netting first, making the entire team explode in commentary. Did we have to watch the vid five times?

I blushed and remembered the feel of mesh netting on my cheek, the way it was unruly as I clambered over it to get to the wall. The wall had been slippery and nearly impossible to climb. I had to creep up the section that had two parallel cracks running up it, using them as finger grips while I used the corner to prop my body up. Each hand and foot worked a different wall so that I looked like a flying squirrel shimmying up the metal. My fingers barely fit into the cracks, and nothing about the act looked graceful.

I fell two more times.

The entire team was enjoying it far too much. The only ounce of reprieve came from the few looks of pity Phoibe shot me.

Coach let them hoot and holler with every mishap. Despite the perfect throw, I had completely missed that there was a thin ledge running the length of the wall. It had subtle handholds, camouflaged in the gray metal, which was the path I should have taken. I was an idiot to think tightrope walking was the best way to get through the obstacle.

Finally, Coached paused the vid. The three-dimensional image of me had barely reached the top of the wall, and my face looked like I'd just eaten raw sewage for all the straining it was doing.

"What a colossal mess, right?" Coach spoke for the first time during this particular rewind of the game. "What would have been the standard operating procedure for this scenario? Cosmos?"

My friend coughed back another laugh. "Tap out of the obstacle."

I shook my head. I should have known better. To tap out would have given the other team a point and me five minutes in the Penalty Box. Had I done that, five minutes would have started immediately. By not forfeiting the obstacle, I had risked running the clock out instead. I would have lost two points, spent five minutes in the Penalty Box, and lost all the time spent trying to figure out the room. The smart move would have been to take the one lost point and waste less time. I'd been lucky in finishing the obstacle within the last five seconds, but just because it ended well for me didn't mean it ended right

"What honor can come from being reckless in the dogged pursuit of victory?" Coach asked the team.

Several people shook their heads, and I hung mine. I knew why I hadn't tapped out. Sometimes I was stubborn when it came to solving problems, and my instinct usually pushed me into the folds of impossible. Maybe it was hubris on my part, a misguided belief that I could solve anything if I put my mind to it, but this game wasn't about me. It was about our entire team, and I'd let them down with my overconfidence. I'd put myself before them.

"You have to look at the Lab as a series of calculated risks. When to pursue, when to cut your losses," Coach continued.

He was right. I should have paused and recognize the tightrope for the risk that it was. I should have cut those losses.

"The prudent thing to do in this situation is to tap out, but there are those who argue that the fastest way to get from point A to point B is not always the best way," Coach said. "Anicetus could have tapped out, done the logical thing, but I want you to look at his face here."

The team grew silent at the shift in Coach's tone and stared at my contorted, animalistic expression on the vid. Did he really have to pause it here?

"But this face? That is called determination, and determination can get you out of the stickiest of situations. Anicetus kept a clear head and used a balance of knowledge and instinct to get out. He used his rock climbing skills to pull himself up on a wall that should have been unclimbable, and deep down, Anicetus knew the

Wielder had used up a large chunk of their Strength Ratio on this first room. He knew that if he got through it, he could outrun the next two obstacles before the Wielder was permitted to place his next set of three. Sure enough, when Anicetus got to the next two, they were easier—a little too easy—and he outran the room placements. Had he tapped out, he would have never gotten that fiver."

The team grew silent, somewhat shocked at Coach's praise. He rarely gave it.

"You kids are trained to use logic over instinct, but sometimes, that stops you from being great."

There was a loaded pause.

"He still looks like he's constipated there," Cosmos said, and the praise was all but forgotten in the midst of the laughter that followed.

"What are you doing?" I repeated, stilling even more under Hucksley's weight. The flesh of my cheek felt the brunt against the hot metal as the meat of her palm pressed down. There was a throb in my forehead from where it'd hit the hardest, and her fingernails scraped my scalp along my ear. She pulled up on my ear again so that my face rose before she slammed it back down.

She was slender and strong, but the only way a girl that size could pin me down like that was to strategically place her own body over mine. One wrong shift, and I could get the advantage back, so I stilled my body. I let it lull her into thinking she could keep me where I was. I let her press my face harder into the burning metal, knowing that soon her body would shift so that her weight would become too concentrated on my face. When it happened, I bucked so that she flew off me.

Even in combat classes, I always felt guilty about the sound a body made when hitting a mat, but this was louder. The soft part of her backside and the thud of her spine as it landed next to me on metal sounded different, more painful. By the time she propped herself up, I was over her. I had to straddle her to lock her down. My shin landed on her forearm. My left arm hooked her head around the neck, while my other arm wrapped around her body to secure her other hand. The weight of my chest bore into hers, and I pinned her down, keeping my body away from her hips so she couldn't buck me off.

Instead of protesting, she let out a rumbling laugh. She didn't even struggle, as if she knew this moment was coming. I didn't let it distract me, and I didn't readjust my weight in order to maintain the advantage.

"What's wrong with you?" I kept my voice calm. I kept my expression whole. I tried to ignore the way her chest rose and fell against mine and the way our faces were too close. It was strange, the fine line between a hug and this move. I'd only ever practiced it with the boys in combat classes, and it made sense why they'd keep this training gender specific in honor of Propriety. Holding her down like this felt wrong in so many ways. Even still, I flattened my ankle to maximize the weight on her forearm. It would make the blood still there and force it to go numb. Most people would struggle at this, worry about the way their arm was losing its relevance, but Hucksley just laughed some more.

"Your face! Have you ever been angry before?" she whispered. The softness of her voice made me lean in to hear her better. "Really, truly angry? Or have you always worn that mask? Because your words hold the definitions of anger, but that tone and your face never show it. Go for it. Look angry. Be human."

If only she knew how hard it was to keep my face controlled. If only she understood how impossible it was to be angry every day of my life and never be allowed to feel it completely.

And who was she to question my ability to be human? She was just like everyone else, assuming that because they'd read about me and seen me in vids, that because they'd caught glimpses of my world through the lens of the media, they knew who I was. It was a sculpted image that people took for truths. Guarded emotions, planned and dictated, that it was no wonder they had trouble seeing me in any other dimension but one. They all made me be what they needed me to be without taking any consideration to who I actually was.

Grandfather stood at the door, his hand still on the knob. It wasn't in his nature to wait for permission to enter.

I ignored him and scribbled an annotation into the tablet next to the text.

"What are you studying?" he segued.

"Arbitrary Solano," I replied.

"She was always my favorite of the First Five." Grandfather smiled and quoted her: "We all become emotional packrats, carrying every heartbreak with us even when those heartbreaks become outdated. And, although they should no longer matter as time passes, we make them matter, feeling them like tiny deaths every time we revisit their memory."

Long ago, I'd lost my awe for most of Grandfather's talents, and I knew he could probably recite every philosophical text known to the Republic. "Are you here to inflict more emotional damage onto me? I'm not sure you've done enough for the week."

His laugh was thick and textured as he sat down on the lounge chair next to my desk. "I know I always say that sarcasm is a sure sign of a dull wit, but sometimes it's endearing when you try it." He propped his left foot on his right knee. It was a classic Grandfather pose that allowed him to take up as much space as possible so he could assert his dominance. It was beginning to amaze me how being a Politician in a world that preached selflessness required an element of selfishness in its leaders. And Grandfather was selfish, acting as if every human owed his cause, and therefore owed him whatever he demanded in the name of it. Most of the time, people gave in because he shrouded every request with the demands of Humanity. He had this casual confidence about him that bordered on insane, and I wondered if I'd ever grow into his brand of self-assurance.

"Seriously," I tried again, "you didn't swing by just to talk philosophy, and our mandatory dinner isn't until next Tuesday."

"Ah. I see our dinners are a chore now?"

"Only because you've made them out to be." I couldn't help but notice how brown his socks were against his khaki slacks. They

were nearly the color of his skin—his perfect, perfect skin that the entire Republic praised nearly as much as his politics. The socks were a startling change. He normally wore black clothing. Suits, slacks, socks, shoes, to accentuate his best feature, but this brown clothing looked muted because the fabric wasn't as perfectly smooth as the skin it tried to imitate.

Sometimes, it struck me that nothing belonged to me alone. My skin came from him. My hair and my eyes from my genetic-mother. My nose from my father. But that was just the outside. Once upon a time, I hoped I could at least own my mind, but I was starting to understand that I couldn't even take credit for my own beliefs. They were all spawned by the world I'd been allowed to interact with. I owned nothing, not even on the inside.

"Why do you think I talked Coach into making you a Spike?" Grandfather asked.

I sighed and put the tablet down. He wasn't going to let this go. He had to have known he wasn't telling me any surprises. "So I understand all the roles that create a team. Only through a full understanding of all positions can I manipulate the rules in my favor from any position should the situation arise." I leaned back in my desk and rested my left foot on my right knee, and, though I was barefoot and in pajamas, I knew the pose said I wasn't intimidated by him. If I had to be made up from parts of him, I might as well use those very parts against him.

Over the past few months, I'd been growing tired of his subtle lessons, and it was time he stopped trying to manipulate me the same way he manipulated the entire Republic.

"And?"

The the prompting triggered the sinking feeling it always gave me. I was missing a piece. With that one-worded question, he had a talent for making me feel off-kilter in my assumptions.

"How did the vid leak?" he prompted.

I frowned. Someone from the other team leaked our game footage despite the strict precautions that usually kept them private. The G.E.G. was usually very adamant about privacy in our league because all the kids in it were in the public eye everywhere else. Every team even had one New Wave on it after people claimed it would even out the advantage. Gruel Ball was supposed to be the one arena where we were safe from common scrutiny because it gave us a place to fail without caution and a place to learn from those failures in private.

"Why would someone do that?" Grandfather prompted again.

I sat for a moment and chewed on the question, then allowed the answer to come out. "Someone, meaning you."

"You're most welcome." He stood up and walked towards the door. "I'll see you Tuesday for our mandatory dinner. It's time we determine which thesis you plan on exploring next month. If you stop acting petulant, perhaps we can explore something in genetics?"

I stared at the empty hole his body left when he exited the room. He didn't even have the decency to close the door behind him. I heard him whistling as he walked down the hallway, and I wanted to scream. But wanting and doing were two different things, and the only thing I had going for me was the control I had over both.

He'd taught me well.

No one should have seen that first obstacle room, but now it was on repeat across the nation. People analyzed my every move, commenting on how even my failure looked perfect. New Wave Perfection: Perfect Even in Imperfection, read one vid title.

And that was the crux of it, why he did it. Free and easy propaganda.

Grandfather wanted me to be in the action instead of behind the scenes. Spikes always got the glory, even though Wielders did most of the heavy thinking. But it wasn't exciting to watch people enter codes into a tablet. Grandfather wanted a better backdrop for my win, and I'd given it to him when I fell from that tightrope and climbed up a nearly unclimbable wall.

He could have gotten the same results using footage from a different aspect of my life, but he chose Gruel Ball. He made it clear that nothing was sacred when it came to me.

"Prove them wrong, New Wave. Be human," Hucksley whispered.

Be human. I'd spent my entire life defending my Humanity, proving I deserved a claim to it. Yet no matter how hard I worked, no one saw me as one. Especially not this girl. It was like she knew the exact button to push, but I wouldn't let it work.

Only with her so close, I couldn't reply. I couldn't think. I could barely even breathe.

"You think you've won right here, don't you?" she asked. Each word was softer, pulling me even closer so I could hear her over the wind and train, over the clouds in the sky, over the world ripping away. Her hair splayed out, waves and waves of it, lashing out at both of us. I saw the colors vibrate in the corners of my eyes. The red of the boxcar, the red of my anger. The green of the trees, the green of her shirt. The blue weight of sky, the blue weight of sadness.

I was human, but I didn't have to prove it to her. I wouldn't play into the trap she set. Everyone, everywhere, lived by a mathematical set of calculated moves, and she was putting obstacles in front of me, controlling my environment to see how I'd react to each test. She'd planned for this to happen, and, so far, I'd catered to every manipulation.

Just as the realization of this sunk in and just as I moved to let her go, she angled her jaw and targeted my lips with hers.

My hold faltered. My shin slipped away from where it kept her arm locked down, and I let her neck loose to place my palm on the metal. I pushed up with that hand, trying to get away, as if the tension and movement held me up and held me together when shock tried to rip me a part. Before I could pull my head away, her fingers landed feather soft on my face before gripping my head behind my ears, trapping my mouth to hers. She took the chance to sit up so that she could push my body back, and all my weight rested on my hands, giving her the leverage. She used it to roll me on my back, covering my body with hers, holding me down with the pressure of the kiss and the weight of her hips.

It took the wind out of me. I wanted to pull back and gulp in the rushing air as it sped up around us, but I couldn't breathe. I opened my mouth to fill my lungs, but she wouldn't even give me that.

So I concentrated on the train underneath me, trying to ignore how my traitorous body wanted to react.

Velocity.

Speed.

Trajectory.

My mouth moved on hers, unhinging into instinct.

I was suddenly reminded of how time worked—or didn't work. With her lips on mine, she pushed herself away in a fluid motion that may have taken minutes or may have taken seconds. Her weight and lips and kiss were gone as she moved into a crouch a couple feet away. She balanced her hand on the train and used it to push herself up into the surfing position.

I stared at the sky, unable to look at her tornado eyes, trying to stop my own blood from flowing. I became torn between wanting her lips back on mine and wanting to tear her head off for doing it.

"When you weren't thinking too hard, you moved up here as if you were on solid ground," she said.

I gulped, felt my Adam's apple move along my throat.

"Choose the things you fear, New Wave, or you may not like the fears that end up choosing you."

I couldn't help thinking about how easy I'd assumed surfing would be. Inside the car, I had complete confidence in my own balance, but Hucksley had used that confidence against me. She threw me off kilter the moment I hesitated, but she was right. She'd completely made me forget one fear by throwing another on me. She hadn't been trying to bash my head in or push me off the ledge of the train. She was trying to push me off a different ledge completely, the ledge of self-control.

Even still, I'd moved as if I'd been on solid ground rather than a metal bullet zipping along the Tracks. As messed up as her tactics were, I had to admire the strategy of them. In that sense, this victory was completely hers. Me, standing on top of a moving train for the first time, was yet another thing that didn't belong to me.

Neither did my first kiss.

"Now that you know you can move without falling, stand up," she ordered.

I looked at her from the corner of my eye, not ready to get up yet. I hated how she wore victory on her face, as if she didn't know how to control the smug pride ripping a smile across her face. Then again, it was possible that even this display was purposeful, like a controlled act of losing control. How could I know what was real with her, and what was part of whatever hell she was determined to put me through?

I seethed. She had no right to do what she'd done. To steal my first kiss like she deserved to use it for her own purposes was despicable. It was something I'd never get back, something I never understood the importance of until it was gone.

I picked myself up and moved into a crouch. I kept my face muted of expression as I stood into the stance, but I wouldn't show her how angry I was. I wouldn't let her have that. I wasn't afraid of the movement under my feet any longer because rage was the only thing that terrified me more. It existed in my heart so fully that I had to concentrate on something else before she pulled expressions of it onto my face.

"There's the balance," she grinned. Her smile engulfed my entire line of sight until her face dipped low. She crouched to analyze my stance and coach me through the rest of it. "Arms out in front of you. Point your right foot slightly."

I wasn't going to play this game anymore. I took a step backwards, intending to return to the car with Bixby and our packs. I needed a break from her and the wind. I was about to adjust my body towards the ledge, but a movement caught my eye.

She had been trained well, never extending her leg fully until just the right time. Her ankle hooked behind my knee, and the momentum of her body pulled my feet out from under me. I saw clouds twisting and the bright sun tilting as I landed hard on my back.

I glanced towards my left. Just past my head was the ledge.

Had I walked one foot further before she'd done it, I'd have gone straight down. Speeding earth rotated fast on its own axis as if competing with the train. Or maybe the train was competing with it, trying to outrace time.

"That's enough," I said, just as she leapt through the air. I stilled as she landed on me again, her thighs tightening around my waist as she leaned in.

This was not a move to keep me down. She had to have known all I needed to do was buck my hips, and she's go flying. What was the test she wanted me to pass this time?

Her nose nearly touched mine.

"You already tried that trick," I whispered. I used a disinterested voice, the one Mother always used when she was at her angriest, and I let hate wash away the instinctual tug to let her kiss me again. But she bypassed my mouth and whispered in my ear, the hot breath landing with every word on my lobes. I shuddered at the feel and forgot about hate. I forgot about everything but the girl on top of me.

"Pay attention," she warned. There was a slight tremor in her voice that stilled my too-fast heart. "She's coming."

"Who?" I asked.

"When it's time, roll off the ledge. Swing yourself into the door. Think you can handle that?"

I nodded.

"Follow my lead. Grab Bixby, then your pack if you can. Above all, make sure you get Bixby."

"Bixby? Who's coming?" I tried again.

"Tuck and roll, New Wave," she said, pushing herself off me to roll towards the edge. Her hand reached out at the last moment and latched onto the ledge. The momentum swung her body into the open car below us. I found myself staring mesmerized until an explosion of sound pulled me back to the reality we were in. It was a zipping, sparking noise. A bullet ricocheting off the boxcar's roof. It landed on the opposite side, so it couldn't have been meant to hit me. Militia shooters were trained far too well to miss that drastically.

My body rolled off the lip of the roof just as another thought occurred. The shooter wanted to direct me, drive me into the boxcar. I caught the ledge, knowing I was already too late to change my intention. Hucksley couldn't have recognized the possibility in the brief seconds before wrestling me and leaving me. As my body swung from the hinge of my arm into the car, I already knew Hucksley and I wouldn't be alone.

As it is with hindsight, the moment you recognize you've been a fool to let your guard down is the moment it's too late to correct the course you've set yourself on.

CHAPTER SEVEN

The nucleotide was painted red on the three-dimensional screen, the sugar phosphate backbone vacant of its nucleobases. Those waited below it, scattered in a box to be drawn from. Blue adenine. Green thymine. Orange cytosine. Purple guanine.

Mos hadn't logged into the competition yet, so I stared at the empty nucleotide and waited. It was a memory game, for which the five-prime-three-prime strand would be displayed for a minute. We were supposed to memorize the sequence before it disappeared from the screen, then we had to build the double helix from the information in our heads to match it to the three-prime-five-prime strand.

Mos logged in, and the timer blinked in the corner, counting down from five, before a base sequence flashed above the nucleotide. The race began. Within a second, I'd devoured the information before it started to blink and disappear. I went to work and pulled up the nucleobases onto the screen in the correct order.

As I connected an adenine to a thymine, it struck me that Father's other side of greatness existed everywhere, even in our DNA. Both ladder supports in the twisted double helix were inverted versions of each other, as if they tugged each other in the opposite direction to keep the entire structure from falling apart. It was the tension in the pairings—one side running upside down in comparison to the other—that provided the framework.

I matched a cytosine to a guanine, and I slowed my fingers. I heard Mos' steady breathing from across the room. He was on a roll. He had never beaten me at this game before, but he never gave up.

I matched a guanine to a cytosine.

One nucleotide could do nothing without the other bonded to it. Though different, the base pairs needed each other to be relevant.

I hated that tension and pull were a part of the building blocks of life, like it was in our genetic natures to always be in gravitational competition in order to keep ourselves from falling apart. What would happen if things stopped tugging on each other? What would happen if even our DNA stopped pulling the taut wire to keep the genome strung along its course?

Perhaps there was no other way to exist. Perhaps this tension, this fight, kept us striving. Perhaps our other sides were our greatest allies on our path to greatness even as they pulled us in the opposite direction of our beliefs.

I knew the rest of the puzzle within seconds, but I treated the task with leisure. By the end of the minute, Mos jumped up from his chair. He pumped his fist, tablet and all, into the air in victory. The sight of it brought on a bought of joy, and I set my own tablet down as he screamed, "I beat you! I win!"

It went on for a few moments, this victory of his, both of us unaware that Grandfather was about to take it away from him. "You can't just let Mos win to feed his ego," he said, folding his fingers over his knee.

My smile faded. "The kid beat me."

"You let him," Grandfather accused.

I gave him a pleading look not to ruin this for Mos. It was his twelfth birthday, and, in a way, the confidence boost was my gift to him. He needed to know he was smart. The tabloids kept comparing his progress to mine, and he kept hearing them debate what his inferiority to me meant for Father's genetic line. They always brought up their belief that Mos was a Halfsie, the partial New Wave Perfection whose potential rested just short of greatness. The gossip-geneticists liked to say that the half could never measure up to the whole.

I caught Mos crying on the roof last week. I had to take the tablet from his hands and close down the site that showed a picture of him sitting next to me, studying with our private tutor. I looked bored. He looked puzzled. Of course, the picture had been taken out of context. Mos had been working on a project all morning while I had been sequestered to one of Grandfather's tedious political breakfasts. I hadn't even started getting into the assignment before me because my mind was still on the way cilantro had gotten stuck in Onesimos Leventis' teeth, and, rather than tell him, I watched him talk, waiting for the moment someone else would.

No one did.

Mos needed a win.

I looked at my little brother as truth began to take root in his face. Grandfather was unforgivably determined to prove his point. "Mos, does your brother do you any service when he lets you think you've won on your own merit when you have not?"

I groaned.

Mos shook his head, his hair flopping about his ears in shame.

"Mos will win plenty when he enrolls in upper Institute next year. He may not be as quick as you, but it does not undervalue his intelligence, for he is far smarter than ninety-eight percent of the population. On top of that, Anicetus, for you to be ashamed of your gift and dumb it down to make others feel better does nothing to honor the sacrifices that went into your creation. By letting Mos win this silly game, you are setting an example for him to be ashamed of his very own gifts when he'll be in a situation that lets him outshine others. I recognize you were trying to be compassionate, but you failed in this. You only showed your brother how little you believe in his ability to never give up."

I stared at my hands, having nowhere else to look. I hated that *he was right. Even more, I hated that what he said still felt wrong despite the righteousness.*

"Boys, remember this. Hiding your talents because you are afraid of hurting people's feelings will never allow you to move beyond those talents. You must foster them in all ways, and you must never lie about them, unless the lie is a planned political move to manipulate the opposition. So, Anicetus, either you were trying to give him a false sense of unearned accomplishment or you were trying to manipulate your brother. Which was it?"

Mos stood up from his seat and set the tablet on the coffee table. Rather than let me answer Grandfather, he asked, "Did you let me win?"

I nodded.

"I am stronger than you give me credit for, brother. Prove you are, too. Never do that again." Mos walked out of the living room and I turned to glare at Grandfather.

"Did you have to do that in front of him?"

"The lesson will cut deeper this way," Grandfather answered as he stood. He set his hand heavy on my shoulder before following Mos out of the room.

Grandfather had been right about my intentions on both accounts. Perhaps I'd been trying to manipulate the situation, trying to trick Mos into being intellectually confident through lies so I could feel better about the sympathy I felt towards his reaction to the gossip-geneticists rants. Yet, if anything, Mos' belief in himself proved how superior he was to me.

I had to see that Grandfather had done Mos a service. For the first time, I think Mos finally recognized his own worth without a comparison to mine.

At the end of the crate-hallway, just where the open door ended and a boxcar wall began, a man stood with a pistol aimed at Hucksley's sternum. He stepped forward as I entered. If I hadn't known better, the movement almost looked lazy, but I could see the adrenaline behind his black, black eyes. The darkness of his irises only augmented the paleness of his skin, a paleness that wrapped around his jaw and rammed against the thin lines of his lips, and the sharp way his blonde hair was cut made him look bald, like he wore a sheer veil of eyelashes on his scalp.

I continued to take in every detail. Snapshots of the scene were stored in my brain in one-second intervals. Bixby cowered under the arch between our two packs just feet from where I'd entered. The pup didn't whimper. She just cocked her head curiously, waiting for things to play out.

"Above all, make sure you get Bixby," Hucksley had said.

But why?

I examined the hall behind Black-Eyes. There was a door between the boxcars that opened up to the space between the wall and crates.

When did he and the shooter get on the train? While I was sleeping? While we were up on the roof? Had they been on the train the entire time, waiting for a Vagabond to hitch a ride? The last possibility made the least sense. This man was a tracker. I saw it in his stance. He lived for the chase, and he was after me.

"Anicetus Petrakis?" he asked.

I swallowed as he reconfirmed my suspicion. "No need to state the obvious," I said, putting my hands in the air. I hoped that this would make him misjudge me and think empty hands meant an empty threat.

Watching Black-Eyes, the intention behind Celeste sneaking me out of the Capital before it was time became clear. If the Patriots were waiting for me to leave before they made their move to take me out, her forcing me to leave a few days early was meant to give me an advantage over them. Before I announced the Donation Act, I knew that following through with it would only make it easier for the Patriots to act against me. I had a feeling they'd be after me sooner than later, wanting to make an example out of me for committing their version of treason. But something didn't make sense. I'd only been gone from the Capital for less than a day, and they easily found me despite the head start Celeste had given me. On top of that, how did they know exactly where to find me?

"I wasn't expecting two of you," he moved, never taking the pistol off of Hucksley. "I guess we'll take you both."

Hucksley stepped forward and met the pistol with her sternum. Each movement was slow, sluggish, like she traveled through water.

The sight of it sent a quivering of rage through me.

There's something odd that happens to your heart when a loaded gun is aimed at you. You can't help but admit how fragile your body is, how fleeting life is, and how insignificant your individual Humanity is. One movement, one decision, one second, and it all washes away.

And Hucksley stepped up to it, taking the darkness from the tunnel of the barrel as if she'd already came to terms with the possibility of her own end long ago.

I swallowed the dry saliva evaporating against my swelling throat. In a way, I'd always had a gun pointed at me. I felt it in the way security hovered in the peripherals, ready to intercept any danger at the expense of their own personal health. My life had never been mine from the moment I took my first breath, and over the course of nineteen years, I'd been on the losing side of self-preservation. All the people meant to protect me only served to remind me that there was something to protect me from.

It was happening here. This girl took the brunt of the gun, living her moments in a way that would save me. She took another sidestep so that the wall of the boxcar was to Black-Eyes' back, and the crates were to hers. Between them, his hand held the gun steady. Her hands were unnervingly calm, limp and lazy at her sides rather than trembling in fear.

One second.

Two seconds.

Three...

It was always seconds that ruled the world.

And I saw it all with her standing against the metal.

I piled deaths on my doorstep, collecting the bones as they crumbled into sacrificial memories. I saw the invisible guns that directed the course of the nation, and I recognized my role in maintaining their aim. I'd carried death every day of my life since I clawed my way into the world and killed my genetic-mother, and, with all these lives moving towards the ever-forgetful past, I knew there were parts of me that had never been alive at all.

There was a series of truths I'd been taught to live by:

I'd already given my life to the cause.

I'd always been the property of the Republic, meant to live or die for it and by it.

I'd always been in some political crosshair.

I was never meant to live for myself.

I was always meant to live for others.

Deep down, I'd always know that the other side of life was death, and to exist on one side was to try and come to terms with the other. It suddenly made sense why death would never make sense. Like life, it was too riddled in possibility to ever pin down because life and death were equal parts great, pulling at each other in equal and opposite directions.

In some instances, one death held the potential to tug more life into existence. It all boiled down to the distinction of which death would ultimately be better for the world? My entire existence, in the quest of Humanity before self, was held more sacred than others because of what my genetics represented to science. It was this demand by Humanity to be more than human—to be super human—that ultimately made me less human in the end.

"Prove them wrong, New Wave. Be human."

But the whole world was right. Moments like these reminded me that being human was something I had never been allowed to be, but in watching Hucksley, I began to feel the twitching of humanity, the humanity with the lower-cased "h." The one that meant me and not everyone else. I was beginning to feel that what I loved and hated mattered just as much as what the Republic loved and hated. And right then and there? I hated that Hucksley carried the weight of a gun on her chest. I was done with people trying to take bullets for me, literally or figuratively.

Black-Eyes stepped in cadence with her, like they were dancing at one of Grandfather's galas. Perhaps he thought that he'd be able to aim at both of us if our bodies became three points of a triangle rather than one line with Hucksley in the middle, but he didn't see the danger he placed himself in as he moved. Or perhaps he thought he could handle the risk.

"You won't shoot me," Hucksley said. She punctuated the comment with an eye-roll. Her tornado eyes landed on his knee when they came to a stop. She wanted me to see the movement, to see that she intended to act soon.

"Alive is all I've been told," Black-Eyes said.

Smart. She was unnervingly smart. She just reconfirmed her advantage, that as long as she had the fight in her, he'd do everything in his power to keep her alive.

I sucked in a breath and balled my hands into a fist. I wanted to do something to stop the unstoppable, but even I knew there was no stoping the things that had begun. There would be no changing of minds, no bargaining, no altering of fate.

Hucksley laughed, but there was a guttural tug in her voice, a hiccup of confidence as it shuddered through her throat. She was brave, but she still recognized that the power struggle between them had not been resolved. She had one advantage on her side. He held the other.

Power.

Everything was always about that five-letter word. Who had it? Who was afraid to lose it? Who was fighting to control it? It was such a waste of energy, pulling people to do horrible things—like blow up a choir full of children—in order to call it theirs.

For the first time, I saw her for what we both were.

Kids.

We were just kids being swept up by events that didn't even belong to us. Hucksley had always been my other side, growing up in the wild, learning to fight for a cause she'd inherited rather than constructed herself. She was me and I was her, and the empathy I felt in that drove me crazy with helplessness.

Black-Eyes pushed her up against the crates, and she let the gun pin her against them. His elbow wasn't locked, so she wouldn't try to hit him above the crook of his arm. The slight bend in his elbow would only let him move with any blow and would do little to get him to drop the gun. But that gap between their bodies was what she really needed. She stepped to the right. He countered, and the gap of an open door raged behind him.

"It'll put me in danger," I said.

Mos frowned. "Give me a break. You know how to encrypt things so they are unhackable."

"And if the Patriots get their hands on the encryption codes? What then? Everyone I'm with will be in danger."

Mos walked towards the ledge of the roof. A storm was building in the east. Bulbous, black clouds built on top of each other, and lightning crackled in the sky.

"I won't write the code down. I'll remember the numbers, right here." He tapped his temple. "I may not be as smart as you, but I'm still our father's son. If you insist on going through with Donation, you can at least do this for me. I'm still smart enough to keep you safe out there, but how can I protect you if I don't know where you are?"

I sighed. I could give him this since I was taking away everything else. This request was not unfounded, and if the roles were reversed, I'd want the same thing. I thrummed my fingers on the tablet so that the screen popped up, and the three-dimensional boxes waited for my fingers to type in the codes.

I looked at the small, silver vial Mos had brought with him. Inside, millions of nano-bots screamed. I put a dropper's worth on the small, rectangular reader and plugged it into the tablet. I tracked the nano-bots down on the database and ghosted them from the server. Mos came back just as I finished.

"What code do you want?" I asked. "The more random the better."

Mos looked up to the clouds. Lightning played behind him as he pulled numbers from the charged air.

I reread the sequence as I typed it. "Remember 0-8-9-7-3-0-0-4-3-2-1-2. Do I need to say them again?"

Mos shook his head and tapped his temple. "The access is

locked away."

I unplugged the reader, and hovered it over my tongue. I swallowed, and the trackers went to work. My location popped up on the screen. I became a blue dot, a moving target on a map should anyone figure out I'd taken them.

Mos let out a sigh, but not even letting him track me gave him the comfort he thought it would. A large raindrop landed on his forehead. Another quickly joined it as I shut the screen off. A few drops bubbled on the tablet's waterproof surface, and our reflections bounced back from the darkness of the screen. We were both entering a world neither of us understood, but at least I'd always be tied to Mos. With this secret, he'd always be able to find me.

There was a movement in Hucksley's chest as she tried to adjust the intake of air into her lungs. She wanted to seem unaffected by the gun, and the calmer she grew, the more rage I felt inside. There were so many ways I'd brought this moment upon her.

Mos asked me to take the nano-bots. He made me promise, even though he knew it put the mission in danger. Only Mos knew the encryption codes.

Only.

Mos.

Knew.

The two explanations that presented themselves were that someone hacked into the database and unencrypted my unhackable codes, or Mos told someone. The most likely was the second explanation, but I didn't want to think about what that betrayal meant.

So I focused on four feet.

I focused on how Hucksley and Black-Eyes were four, lividly long feet away from me. I focused on the wink Hucksley sent me just she leaned her body back on the crates, lifted her left leg, and landed the flat of her heel on Black-Eye's knee. I focused on his body as it began to crumple inwards as she reached for his wrist and pushed the gun's aim towards the roof.

I closed the span and filled in the gap of four feet with my body. I grabbed Black-Eyes by his collar and yanked him back.

I wanted to be someone who'd hesitate. I wanted to be the type of person who couldn't compartmentalize one moment from another. I wanted to be the person who did not know how to shut down his own Humanity in order to save it in the end.

"Prove them wrong, New Wave. Be human."

But I was never meant to be that person.

I was never meant to hesitate when it mattered.

And this mattered so very, very much—to realize our lives were worth more than this man's.

I saw it in his eyes when I let go, the fear of facing his own fate alone. He didn't have time to brace himself, and I moved to the door to watch as his head landed heavy on the rock-jetties below. I could almost hear the crack of skull, and, as the train pulled away from him, I knew he wouldn't be getting up ever again.

I shuddered. All those deaths that were made possible because of me suddenly didn't matter as much. This one was more real. It happened not because I pushed a button or gave military advice but because my hands tugged and pulled and took. I stared this death right in the face. I had made it a reality for one individual, and I didn't even know his name.

I stared out the door and tried to see the body growing colder in my past. He'd become a shadowed lump, and I felt the train groan underneath us, like it wanted to stop.

Hucksley stepped up to me and cupped my face in her hands. "We have to go."

"I killed him," I whispered.

She patted my cheeks before turning towards the packs. She shouldered hers and secured Bixby in mine. "We both are responsible, but we can't dwell. We can't waste his tragic event. We have more important things to do now."

She was right. The shooter was still out there, and who knew how many others?

There was no time for guilt, though I knew it would come. I was learning so many things about the feeling lately. How it only came when time settled, when movement ceased, when thoughts had time to form around the past. It had the habit of seeping into the cracks of an ordinary day, under bright skies, behind undeserved stolen laughter. Guilt was not something to feel in the immediate. In fact, it'd be wasted in the moment of acquisition because it becomes as insincere and fleeting as the event itself. No. Guilt was best served cold after the heat of a moment dissipated.

I slid my arms through the straps of my pack, and tried to compartmentalize the other realization. If Mos had given the codes to someone, the nano-bots had to go. "Where's your anti-bot serum?" I asked Hucksley.

Her eyes widened and she grappled in a side pocket. "You mean to tell me that Celeste didn't make you take any before she shoved you out the door?"

I nodded.

Hucksley didn't dig any deeper on the matter and focused on moving forward with new facts. She reached back into a side pocket and pulled out a vial. As she placed it in my hands, she swore under her breath. I removed the stopper, let a teardrop of the serum land on my tongue, swallowed, and shoved the vial back into Hucksley's hands.

It was done.

"The train is still too fast. The jetties'll be a death sentence," Hucksley said.

I tightened the straps on my pack across my sternum so it wouldn't bounce if we had to run. Less bouncing would be better for the strangely calm Bixby shoved inside of it.

"Then why is the train slowing?" I asked.

"There may be a necessity to it. Perhaps there's a train stopped on the Tracks up ahead. Timing is everything out here, and if there is a paused train, to keep going at this speed will only cause us to collide. Either way, it won't slow down time. We have none of it left. She's probably on her way."

On the roof Hucksley had said, *"She's coming."* Who was this she? Instead of asking, I headed to the opposite side of the car that Black-Eyes had entered through. "Let's go this way. We don't know if she is on the roof or cutting through the cars to get to us, so we need to go the opposite way. If we move, we might have more time to think than staying in the car she drove us into. Your scrambler," I said, nodding towards the door lock.

Hucksley stepped past me to hover her ring over the handle of the door, and the lock clicked open. She exited through the first door between the cars, and I followed her as she stepped out onto the small platform. She hopped over the gap to the next boxcar, slid her ring over the lock of its door, and disappeared through the entry.

Before I followed, I looked down at the tracks blurring below. Earth sped fast beneath my feet.

"It's called a coupler," Agathon said.

My eyes followed the gnarled line of the train conductor's hand. The mechanisms that linked the two cars were bulbous in design, and each train slid into the other at the joints. It was strange how two pieces of metal were enough to catch the shock and tug and pull of the locomotive.

It was the first campaign trail I'd been allowed to blaze through with Father, though Mother still insisted I was too young. "He's only six," she'd said, but Grandfather'd insisted I needed to get used to my future sooner or later.

I became insatiably curious about how the trains worked, and Agathon offered to give me a tour. He was loud, like metal screaming against metal, and I could tell he was a veteran by the way his spine walked straight.

Agathon walked along the metal bridge connecting the Quarters Car to the Dining Car. A chain rope waved in movement. My tiny fingers slid over the cold links as I followed him with timid steps. It wouldn't be too difficult to slip off the bridge and under the train's wheels.

Agathon ticked off the parts of the train like memories as we walked through each car, and I wondered about the first time he learned how a train came together. I marveled at all the moving parts, each one useless without the other.

We reached the last set of cars before the locomotive, and Agathon pointed to the black-topped roof. "They call this one the Tender because trains used to be powered by water and fire. Now, it's powered by a fire less volatile, as is most things these days. Want a better look?"

"Yes," I said, and I laughed when he picked me up and put me on his shoulders so I could see the layers upon layers of solar panels. They ate up the light, trapped it in all that black, and pushed it into the wheels of the moving beast beneath us.

"New Wave, snap out of it." Hucksley clicked her thumb and forefinger from the open door she held onto. I looked up at her. How could this girl know a bigger war was blooming right under our feet? If Mos had voluntarily given the code to anyone, it would have been Grandfather. The world was so full of movable parts, and I couldn't figure out what part would click together for Grandfather if the Patriots had succeeded in capturing me. Was he, and not the Unnamed, behind them? Was that why he didn't put a stop to them? Was I meant to be a martyr for his cause? Did he intend for the war between the Citizens and Vagabonds to morph into the war between the Patriots and the Unnamed with me at the center, a catalyst, a name to cry out on the lips of war?

I leapt over the coupler to join Hucksley in the next boxcar. We slid the door behind us. There were more crates with the same kind of disjointed, dimly-lit hallway. I followed her through them, and two cars later, she paused.

"The train isn't slowing anymore," I said, feeling it pick up speed again.

Hucksley stopped before she opened the next door, and pulled at a chain around her neck. A round locket freed from under her shirt, and when she opened it, a small map hovered above us. Within a second, it caught onto a signal, and zeroed in on where we were.

"Relax," she said. "Abner made a scrambler that bounces the signal back so the Republic can't trace us. As long as I do it in fifty-nine seconds or less, we can't be traced."

She glanced at the map for a couple seconds, nodded, and closed the locket. She yanked it over her head and put it over mine. It slithered between my shirt and chest where it rested warm on my sternum, like I could feel her body heat on me. She pawed at my body so I turned around, then she released Bixby before tugging at my arm to face her again.

The pup waved its paws in the air until she was in my arms. Hucksley rubbed Bixby's ears, and her fingers accidentally grazed places that made me shiver.

"Listen," she said. "We don't have much time. There's a bridge coming up, a river that's pretty deep according to the compass. There are a couple saved coordinates in the history function. One is called *Neverland*, and if we get separated, we need to meet there. Ollie and Abner have been waiting for us. If I'm not there by noon tomorrow, you have to convince them to move on to the Vault without me. Tell them *Prometheus' Fire* is inside of Bixby."

"We won't get separated," I said.

Hucksley smiled as she tugged out a green bandana from her back pocket and tied it around her neck. She pulled it up over her nose, and her voice became muffled. "Come on. Don't tell me you've never heard of *contingency plans*." She tried to joke by mocking my accent again, but terror was in the bones of her words. She slid her ring over the next lock, and ushered me through the door. I stood on the ledge of the small platform and ventured closer to the edge of the train. Open space ripped past me.

Hucksley stood at the door opening, and held onto the frame. "It should be coming up. You have to time it right."

"Should I take the pack off first?"

She shook her head. "There's inflatable technology in the pack. Keep it on, and it will buoy you back up faster."

Of course there was inflatable technology. Everything about how the Vagabonds carried tech was subtle. Rings. Lockets. Within the packs they shouldered. All signs pointed to them having access to things that should have been far out of their reach.

"It's coming," she whispered.

I moved towards the lip of the platform and caught the wind with my teeth. The bridge coming up had no railing, and empty sky would not stop the momentum of a perfectly timed jump. I hugged Bixby to my chest, and knew I'd have to angle my body so my feet cut through the water first. Hopefully the jump wasn't high enough to break my legs on impact. The compass didn't exactly give Hucksley that information.

There was something more racing in Hucksley's expression as the seconds ticked by. The bridge was near. The time was now. I stepped closer. My toes prepared to leap, but I looked back at Hucksley just before I let them free. Something shifted in her face as she looked back through the door.

"What's the bandana for?" I asked.

"In case I don't make it off. There's a tunnel coming up. It helps to breathe in the—she's here," Hucksley said.

I turned to face her. I shouldn't be the first to jump. Hucksley had to go first. She had to be safe before I could leave her behind. Something deeper within, instinctual, jolted me from what I was about to do. I couldn't risk her being left at the mercy of whoever was after us. It was just like letting her take the weight of the gun in my place. "You need to jump," I told her. "I'll hold her off. She's after me."

"Sometimes I forget how little you truly know," she said as her flat palms landed on my shoulders and momentum pushed me back.

Air filled my lungs as I let out a startled scream.

I only needed a second to memorize her face, and the way pity and determination and bravery fell into place like broken puzzle pieces. She turned back towards the door rather than follow me off the bridge. It swallowed her as if she'd never existed on the platform.

I flailed my feet so that my body righted just in time. My straight lined body cut through the water. I held onto the scrambling Bixby, praying that she could survive however long we'd be under. Bubbles surged around my ears, streamed out of my nose, and collided with the water from the force of my impact. The pup clawed at my chest, but I held her to me tightly.

The drop hadn't been far, but the speed of the train didn't help things. The pain from the fall would come later, but adrenaline was a beautiful thing. It made every ache invisible, including the one ripping through my heart. Later, I would feel the fall all over my body and the betrayal all over my insides, but none of that mattered.

The stream of the river was slow, and whatever technology existed in my pack for floatation kicked in, gently tugging me back up towards the surface. I kicked to help it out, determined to get Bixby's ears above the surface.

I opened my mouth to the air, gulped it into my lungs like there'd never be enough of it. Bixby coughed then yapped as she shook her head. Her wiry fur frayed along the lines of her face, and she frantically kicked, terrified of dipping back below. It would be difficult to swim and keep her calm, and we were a little over a hundred yards from land. The flotation of the pack kept me upright and above the water, so I let it help. I held Bixby, and used my free hand to push us backwards towards the shore.

I didn't know what Hucksley's fate would be. What was it with the dog that she risked her life for its? Because that's what had happened. She saw that the shooter was nearing, and she stayed behind as a distraction. She had never meant to follow me off the bridge without getting rid of the threat or she never would have given me the compass and the dog.

I thought about all the things Hucksley so poignantly reminded me I didn't know about. Not knowing was going to be the end of me.

Like not knowing Mos held disloyalty in his heart.

The ache of that went beyond any pain I thought imaginable.

Mos had grown past me in size and strength, and I knew I'd never beat him in a race again. My first loss would happen today, and I was glad for it. I had a feeling he'd been holding back for a few days now, afraid of embarrassing me in front of the photographers that were always in the peripherals.

I pumped my legs harder and felt my lungs grow full with each empty breath I took. The grass tugged at my shoes and the sun tugged at my skin, but no matter how hard I tried, I could not outrun him. It was almost as if he was jogging while I sprinted, he made it look so easy.

"That's all you got?" I prompted.

I was curious. How fast could he really go when he wasn't worried about what Grandfather'd do if he out-shined me too much in front of the press? Lately, it had become clear that Grandfather's belief in owning your genetic gifts did not apply to Mos.

But I wanted the press to see me getting extraordinarily beat. For once, I wanted the world to see me being less than perfect in the shadow of my kid brother.

And I wanted Grandfather to see it and feel the sting of it.

"Come on, Mos! You can do better!" I yelled.

Had Mos been waiting for this moment? And if so, how long had it been his plan to betray me?

I closed my eyes and felt the drenched fabric of shirt against my skin as I tugged off the pack. The space under my armpits ached from where the straps had yanked on me under the water.

Bixby sniffed at some of the rocks, and I leaned back on my hands to stare up at the sky. Pebbles dug into the meat of my palms and my chest tightened. Mos wouldn't betray me like this. By me leaving the Capital, I'd already moved aside so he could pave the way into a political position. What would capturing me or killing me do? Even still, I couldn't shake the feeling that there was a hand being played that I didn't recognize.

It didn't make sense.

I paid attention to a cluster of pine needles that cut into my view of the sky and the feel of pebbled rocks under my thighs. I shuddered. I'd never been completely alone out in the wild before. The most solitude I'd ever been given was when I had to work in the labs or when I got to sneak up to the roofs. Even then, I knew civilization was within a stone's throw. Out here, on the bank of this river, it was possible to make Humanity a distant memory.

Bixby pawed at a rock, as if she hadn't almost just been drowned. She wasn't even fazed by time passing us by or the questions we couldn't answer.

I tugged at the compass on my neck. It only made sense for me to go to the rendezvous point and hope Hucksley got there within the day. I moved my finger along the map that projected and typed in the word *Neverland* into the search engine. I was ten miles away, which meant Hucksley had intended for us to get off near here anyways. If the shooter hadn't done what she did, Hucksley would be leading me through this very forest herself.

I closed the compass and stared at Bixby.

"Project Prometheus," I read again. I guess part of me always knew my brain worked differently than most people around me. The only difference was that now everyone else did, too.

It had been a month since the proof had been leaked. Geneticists had altered the genes attached to my parents' intelligence. Then I was selectively bred from their alterations.

The vids called me one of the first super humans.

When I first found out, I'd asked Father, "Was Mos?" I'd known the answer before I asked because Mother hadn't been on the partnering list, but I wanted to know for sure. I didn't ever want Mos to feel inferior, and I couldn't bring myself to think about what this news would do to his self-esteem.

"No," Father had answered. "My genetics became useful in other ways. Mos is plenty brilliant, but can you guess his other qualities?"

"Gorilla strength?"

A month later, and the gossip-geneticists had decreed. They'd come up with a name for all the Project Prometheus offspring.

"Don't let this label bother you, my boy." He tugged at my hair. It'd grown past my chin and stretched along my shoulder blades, and as much as Mother begged me to cut it, Father still encouraged me not to. I felt the same growing pains in my scalp as in my body, as if my height was trying to outgrow ten years of hair

growth. It seemed as if the ends of every strand would always be between my shoulder blades no matter how long they grew because they couldn't keep up with me bean-sprouting into each new day.

"But it's an absurd label. New Wave Perfection? Seriously?" I glared at the title on the tablet. I wanted to throw it but practiced the control Grandfather had been trying to make me focus on instead. It wasn't right that this information got leaked. Genetic details this specific and significant were supposed to be private. It was supposed to be between me, the Department of Human Relations, and my future partner, but now, the entire world knew about my extra advantages.

Initial reactions were of indignation, but our Public Relations Specialists were brilliant at their jobs. Next thing I knew, my face was peppering the vids and news casts with reports of how many advances I'd already made at such a young age. "If he could do all that within ten years, imagine what he could do in a lifetime," one Caster had said in a political debate. A little too quickly, popular opinion shifted so that the Genetic Engineering Guild was actually encouraged to continue such drastic experimentation. People were applying left and right to get their genetic lines into the trials.

I hated that it had to be my face in front of the mindset shift, but I understood why. I'd already lived a life in the limelight, being the son and grandson of Chancellors. I should have been used to every action and reaction of my life being pried apart in front of the world and analyzed, but this was different. I'd become something new to Citizens. In carving me open, flayed before the public, my body had become a museum to examine. I was now a symbol of scientific advancement and the new hope for genetic perfection.

"But none of the other New Wave Perfection got the brunt the way I did," I said. I tried to keep my voice calm, but it wobbled. Under nearly every headline, I'd been the sacrificial face of the scientific advancement, and something about that felt terribly wrong.

"It was the right thing to do," Father said, knowing my thoughts as if I'd voiced them. I needed to get better at masking my emotions. *"I'm so proud of you for stepping up here."*

I nodded. Grandfather had said the same thing. He said it was my first true test as a Politician—to take a negative news leak and make it work in my favor. "Turn every narrative into an asset rather than a setback," *he'd said.*

A leak.

Nothing was ever accidental in this world, and suddenly I knew how and why the data got out in the first place.

"It was Grandfather, wasn't it?"

Father frowned. "I wish I could say it wasn't, but we both know my father. He's always scheming."

"Sometimes I really hate him. Why can't he just leave me alone?" I felt the powerlessness grip me. The vids made it seem like everything I had was unearned. Every win in class, every advancement in my knowledge, every right answer. They said I had an unfair advantage because I never truly had to work for any of it.

"I know what you're thinking," Father said.

"You always do," I grumbled.

"You can't listen to criticism like that. Every piece of knowledge you have? You worked for it. The real tragedy would be if you stopped striving to attain knowledge—if you settle for what comes easily to you rather than work for what lies just out of reach. Never forget that even the smartest person can be challenged by the pursuit of brilliance."

"But how can I hone my brain if no one can compete with it?"

"You'd be surprised. Sometimes it might seem like you can't find someone to challenge you, but when you do, it'll make all this worth it."

"Did my mother challenge you?" I asked. "I mean, my genetic-mother?"

Father's laughter faltered. "She was the first person I knew who could make me reconsider every truth I'd ever believed in. She pulled more questions than answers out of me, but, in the end, it wasn't because we were intellectual matches. Sure, that helped, but what really mattered was that we were so different.

We'd been through experiences so opposite that the challenge was in understanding these differences enough to find the similarities within them."

What was *Prometheus' Fire*, and why was it inside of the dog? Prometheus, according to a legend, was the ancient god who gave the Greeks fire. It sparked technological advancement, plaguing the world with curiosity. Instructor Aeschylus loved visiting the story to discuss the burdens of knowledge. He always said, *"Knowledge is a great gift, but sometimes greatness does not mean what you think it does. There is an enormity involved in greatness, a terrible, sublime abyss that can suck you right in if you do not know how to respect it, nurture it, and contain it."*

What great and terrible gift raged within the tiny, damp pup? Did it have to do with New Wave perfection? After all, New Waves were created under *Project Prometheus*, and the names were too similar to ignore.

I wouldn't find out until I found Hucksley's Ollie and Abner.

I sat up and cracked my spine along the seam. The last thing I wanted to put on my back was the damp pack, but I shouldered it and scooped up Bixby.

As I stood straight, I heard a noise. It was a bird, calling out with two long *ahhhh-ahhhhs* before it rolled into a thrumming vibration of a *wacka* noise. Bixby cocked her head and yapped.

"Shhhh," I whispered, "It's just a woodpecker."

Bixby squirmed in my arms until she was free, and like a rabbit, she hopped away towards the sound.

"Bixby!" I yelled and chased after her, but the pup was fast for having such stubby legs. She darted into the tree line that snaked the edge of the river, and every time I got near, she jolted in a new direction so that I couldn't catch her. Of course the dog would choose right then and there to decide to be a runner.

The woodpecker called again, equal in tone and length.

I saw the white fur dart between clusters of ferns, then pump its little legs up a hill. The dog was determined to meet the sound, and I was just as determined to catch her before she did.

The bird sang out again, and I paused. Hucksley had said, *"You may open your ears and listen for the train. I open my ears and listen for the birds."*

I counted the seconds before the next call. Three.

The same variation of a woodpecker happened.

Three seconds.

Ahhhh-ahhhh, wacka wacka.

Three seconds.

Ahhhh-ahhhh, wacka wacka.

"Surroundings, New Wave. They'll tell you everything you need to know," Hucksley had said. It wasn't a real bird, but someone calling out a warning. The noise kept up in the same solid intervals. It had to be Hucksley trying to tell me where she was. It was less invasive than calling out for help in case she was being followed, but the bird whistles were just enough clues for me to find her if I listened.

It got louder the more Bixby ran, and clearer the closer we got. The pup darted around another tree, and there she was.

"Hucksley!" I yelled, just as Bixby stopped short at the girl's feet.

Hucksley limped in my direction, holding the inside of her left thigh with her left hand as she walked. When she saw me, she sighed and leaned against a tree. "I was hoping I'd catch you before you started. I wasn't sure if I'd be able to get there on time with this leg." She lifted her hand, and I saw the gash. Where the skin parted reminded me of smiles, of how lips opened up, sharp at the corners and gapping in the middle. Blood flowed softly down her pants.

She moved her pack so that it hung on one shoulder and pulled out a small, green box from a side pouch before letting the pack thud to the ground. "Now that I found you, I need to stitch up this wound."

"What happened?" I asked.

"She needed to take me alive. We both knew it, so I gave her a good fight. She thought she could best me using only a knife, but I wasn't about to go down again. I won't ever go back to that place."

Hucksley moved her fingers to her belt and began to unbuckle it. There was a hitch in my breath as she unbuttoned her pants. "I didn't kill her. Just knocked her out real good before I leapt. The train jetties had just ended, so I took a calculated risk."

I couldn't move my eyes away from her hands as she tugged her pants down. The blood had glued the fabric to her skin, and she sucked in a breath as she peeled it over. With her pants at her ankles, she slid down on the tree. The bareness of everything between her undergarments and her ankles made me shiver. I couldn't hide the emotion or the way my heart burned to get out of my throat. And what was worse? I hated that she could read the expressions raging on my face as if I'd never learned to control my emotions before.

"Survival goes beyond the things that make you comfortable. Uncomfortable is better than dead," she said. Rather than look at her bare skin, I stared at her face. Sweat made the dirt glisten on her forehead. She bit her lip to hide how much pain she was in, but I knew the face of suffering. It was strange to recognize a Vagabond acting stoic. She bore the brunt of pain, not out of pride but so I would not worry.

Hucksley met my expression with determination. "I'm not sorry for the impropriety. Working around the pants will only tear them more, and I need to keep them intact as much as possible. I don't know when I'll get another pair. Do you know how to suture?"

"No," I said, setting my pack down and kneeling next to her.

She opened the box and tugged out some Neo-spray. There was a *schaaaa-schaaaa* noise as she sprayed it on her cut, but she didn't even suck in the sting of air. Then she grabbed a small clear bag and plucked out a curved needle.

"Help me thread it," she said, handing the thread and needle to me.

I picked up the needle. It was small in my hands, so small I could barely see the eye—that calm, pointed oval so tiny inside the metal.

"I didn't think you had a concentration face," Hucksley said.

I grinned. "What does it look like?" The thread refused to go into it, and I had to try again.

"It looks like most of your other faces, except happier. It's like you find peace in the challenge."

"I guess I do," I said. The thread missed, and I took a steadying breath before trying again. It went in. I knotted it and sprayed it down with the Neo-spray.

She took the needle from me, and hovered it on the edge of the gash. "Time to learn something new," she whispered. "See where I'm putting the needle? This is the bite width. You want to make sure you give the needle plenty of tug, a place to anchor the thread in the skin. You enter it like this, at an angle, then follow the circular nature of the needle so that it hooks like a loop."

She talked me through it more for herself than for me. I read between those lines. The more she talked, the less room she had for expressions of pain.

"You're pretty brave," I pointed out. "I'd like to say I'd be as quiet as you had I been the one to get cut that deeply, but I'm not sure I would be."

"You learn to live with quiet pains out on the Tracks," she said. "Sometimes it's the difference between surviving and dying. For example, if I give into the pain and cry out while I sewed, someone could find us. Who knows if she and the other man were alone? Who knows if someone else followed me when I left the train?"

She nodded towards the gash, and showed me how to loop the thread into a tie. "You try now," she whispered, leaving the needle in my fingers and leaning back against the tree. I didn't want to, but I could see exhaustion turn her face pale.

I placed my free hand on her thigh to steady the skin around the hole, and tried not to blush again. There was nothing improper about trying to heal a wound. I had to stop thinking about Hucksley being an exposed girl and start thinking about her as a patient. Classifying her in that way let me dig the needle into her thigh. I could nearly hear the sick tug of thread through skin, the prick, the push, the pull, the tension, the tie. I tugged and tugged, and the needled wove its closing spell.

"Who is after us?" I asked. Hucksley needed to keep talking, and I needed answers.

Hucksley laughed. "A puppet. A pawn."

"Just tell me who you think is after us."

"You won't believe me until she's standing right over you, holding that gun to your pretty little head."

"So you think I'm pretty?"

Her jaw tensed in a quivering of pain. She just needed to keep talking, to keep holding on. "Pretty in that obvious kind of way."

I laughed. "Okay, even if I won't believe you, tell me a good story."

I took a bite of peas. Each burst between my tongue and the roof of my mouth felt soggy and uneventful. I was tired of the conversations, weary of the way Grandfather kept the questions coming.

"You have studied the art of world building in Manipulation Seminars, but how can you maintain one?" he asked.

I swallowed and answered on autopilot. "You create chaos and manipulate the populace's fear of the chaos you've created." I thought of my nano-bots and the data they had been streaming back. "For example, all these years, Terrorists and Citizens have been pitted against each other. We were trained to fear their genetic abnormalities because we needed an enemy. If we were to ever create a peace with the Terrorists, a new enemy will most likely rise to take the place of the other before the reality of peace can even be defined. It turns out that peace does very little to maintain a world order."

Grandfather placed his tablet on the table between us and pulled up a three dimensional image. It was a nucleotide, adjusted in a strange sequence. The difference was so slight, but something was definitely off about the feed streaming from it. My fork hovered before my mouth when I saw it, and peas avalanched back down to the plate.

"Who created the Patriots?" Grandfather asked. "And for what purpose?"

I sucked in a breath but couldn't answer.

Grandfather's eyes grazed the screen again. "I call them the Unnamed. They have their hands in everything, and they are pulling the strings everywhere. They are the very people who manipulated your genes without consent under the guise of working for the G.E.G. It was not easy making it seem like Project Prometheus *was on purpose. They even created the Patriots after you leaked the data.*

"Now rumors are coming forward that the Unnamed is taking it one step too far. They have actually used Nikomedes Kostas' hypothetical research to find the missing link between animals and humans at the Vault. They have begun experimenting with Terrorist children still in the womb. They targeted fetuses already selectively bred for certain trait enhancements, then modified them in the womb using Transgenic Therapy."

I couldn't breathe. Not only was Grandfather admitting how I was unsanctioned on a very fundamental level, but my genetic-mother's name bled out of the past and still inflicted genetic harms on the world long after her death.

"Selective breeding made sense to enhance human intelligence, but imagine all the shortcuts to super human strengths that exist by transferring animal traits to our own? Imagine how inhuman it may make us. I'd hoped your nano-bots could root out the experimental children so we could track them down, but they've been protected. This was why we needed to pretend to make peace with the Terrorists. I thought that if we played it right, we would have been able to get your nano-bots in the right bodies. I thought that by lulling them into a false sense of friendship, we could root out these anomalies—the abominations—before they bred, but this has not happened."

I shuddered. The Absolution Bill was a scam. Grandfather had this in mind all along. He didn't care about righting a genetic wrong by giving the Vagabonds sanctuary within the Republic. He saw the bigger dangers beyond a petty war, and manipulated situations in order to root those dangers out.

"Their leader is still faceless. We know it's a woman, but we don't know her name or what she looks like." Grandfather adjusted

the floating screen and pulled up a different document that zoomed in on the strand. There was the hiccup. The non-human addition to a very human genetic strand.

I needed air. I needed it to move my lungs. I thought about that one anomaly I'd stumbled across a few months back, the hiccup in the genetic makeup I couldn't match with natural design. I'd eventually written it off as a fluke, but what Grandfather said turned that anomaly into something much more dangerous. He twisted its three dimensional shape so that I could see he'd been reading my research along with me. It was the same reading I found myself drawn to over and over again.

The genetic abomination.

I set my fork down. I knew where Grandfather was going with this, but I asked anyways. "Where do I fit in, here?"

"If I didn't encourage you to create the nano-bots to prove the Vagabonds' worth... but to, instead, discover these abominations so we can dispose of them? If you didn't leak your data so the Terrorists could be unstigmatized... and you leaked the data so you could gain their trust instead? What is the next step?"

"Garner that trust," I whispered.

"Anicetus, by the Stars, you are going to be the Politician I raised you to be because you are our only chance to root these genetic abominations out."

"It does sound fantastical. I mean, it happened to me, and even I have trouble believing it," Hucksley said.

"Then dig in," I prompted.

Her voice sounded riddled in pain, but she never caved into it as she spoke. "Last year, I took a girl named Bee under my wing. We all knew she was a spy, but I thought I could get to her, make her see our cause. Eventually, Bee came clean and told us she was a spy. She even started talking about a boy back home, how she wished that she'd been partnered with him instead of her actual placement. Bee said and did everything right, so that I thought she was changing. Looking back, I think she used that story about the boy to fend off any kind of Claiming. Abner had a thing for her, after all, and being heartbroken is as good excuse as any not to connect with someone new."

I studied her wound. She just needed a few more goes with the needle. I focused on the next stitch and fell into the story, imagining the friendship with Bee forming, the betrayal coming.

"Bee wasn't at all what we thought she was," Hucksley continued. "She wasn't just a spy, but an observer for the G.E.G., and her interest in me went far back into my past.

"Apparently, my father came from a Colony that cultivated enhanced hearing. Simultaneously, three generations before, my mother had ties to a Colony focused on cultivating enhanced sight. I'm sure you know how that works, being all New Wave and all. Within the G.E.G. each Colony is subtly famous for one trait or another."

I was aware of these small scientific prides. It was a layering thing, a maneuvering of resources. The G.E.G. sought perfection in all realms of the senses, all realms of the mind, and all realms of the body through cultivation. Some Colonies had higher concentrations of traits within their borders, and once the concentration was thick enough in an offspring, they'd raise the child up into Celebrity status to spread the desired trait.

"My mother trusted someone once, just like I had. I guess we are all doomed to repeat our parents' mistakes." She let out a laugh that held no humor. "My mother met a woman who called herself May. She was spy who once worked for the G.E.G. When my mother found out she was pregnant with me, she went to May, who had established herself within the Vagabonds as a midwife. No one could have known that May was still working for the G.E.G., that she was sent to experiment with Vagabond children. She found ways to trace my parents' lineage and thought me to be a good candidate.

"Growing up, I always felt odd. Like I could see things more clearly, hear things more sharply. It turns out May had Transgenically transferred traits using Nikomedes Kostas' hypothetical research, bringing the impossible into possibility. I wasn't the only one. It happened to Abner, too. And Ollie was a part of a different experiment in the Colonies before Xavi rescued him, but it may as well have been the same."

My fingers paused with the needle hooked into the skin. One small story had so many possible roads to go down. First of all, who were Abner and Ollie? She kept bringing up their names like I should know them deep in my bones. Then there was the tidbit about Uncle Ty stealing a child from the Republic, the accusation of Transgenic experimentation, and the connection to my genetic-mother. My genetic-mother's name made it feel like someone had reached into my gut and yanked out my innards.

Hucksley was right when she said I wouldn't believe her. I couldn't. The G.E.G. would not have done these things. If Hucksley had been experimented on, it had to have been by the Unnamed in the disguise of the G.E.G. just like what had happened with me.

It didn't matter how it happened, though. Hucksley was one of these genetic abnormalities Grandfather wanted me to root out.

Why would she admit to being an abomination? Was Hucksley telling me all of this because she was getting woozy, losing her wits as she lost her blood? Or was she trying to dig into my skin when my muscles and brain and heart were frayed along the edges, trying to unravel me? Did she know who I was looking for? Was she toying with me by spinning a story so opposite to Grandfather's just to get inside my head?

"I didn't know for the longest time," Hucksley continued. "My mother died giving birth to me, and Celeste and Lynk helped Dad raise me."

There was the thread that unraveled the *who* in her story. Again, she said a name so cavalier, like I should find it in some hidden memory and trace each letter in my veins as fondly as she did. *Lynk*, the very leader of the Unnamed that I sought. Couldn't Hucksley see the fault in her story? Did she know that Lynk was the leader of the Unnamed? Did she know that the Unnamed was responsible for experimenting with Transgenic Therapy?

How clever Lynk was to take in three children she'd modified. Perhaps she fed them a story about the evils of the G.E.G. to ensure their loyalty to her. That's what Grandfather would have done.

I dug the needle into Hucksley's skin again and tried to make sense of the story.

But what if Hucksley knew it was Lynk who'd altered her? What if Hucksley was proud of her genetic deformities and used this story as a pity card? If that was the case, then Hucksley was the ultimate form of traitor, especially if she was that closely linked to Lynk.

Hucksley shivered, but her voice grew strong. "It was Lynk who figured it out. Abner is her son, after all. He's two years younger than me, but we developed very similarly. We hear things most cannot. We see things from an insane distance. The experiment worked, but the G.E.G. wanted to collect us when we passed adolescence. They wanted to take us into the labs, test us and collect the data. They wanted to contain us before they unleashed the next step in their genetic plan.

"Which brings me to Bee. She talked me into setting out with her, and I did, despite Ollie's advice to stay. It's just that I thought I knew better. The first night, when I took a nap on the train we'd just boarded, she knocked me out, and when I woke up, I was in a room. White walls, bright lights, cameras. I was there for six months." The way she said six months said so much more, and she shuddered in a way that made it difficult to disbelieve her story.

I grew angry with Lynk. It became clear that Hucksley didn't know that the person she trusted most was the one responsible for her pain. How could I tell her something so monumental?

I thought of earlier, how she'd worn a look of sadness while she looked out into the world, and an unborn story unfolded from that moment, that memory. She was free, balancing against the wind, and in that freedom, she remembered how easy it was to lose it.

Another possibility struck me. What if Hucksley was telling the truth in some aspects? Maybe the G.E.G. was trying to beat the Unnamed at their own game. After all, Transgenics had been a term tossed about everywhere, like the G.E.G. debates were getting the world ready for the idea. They wove in the concept into our generation, so that in a few generations, the word would not be terrifying. I also knew that the G.E.G. would not waste their time unless they knew Transgenic Therapy was possible, and what better way to trust possibility than to know it had already been tested. It was the way idea-launches always worked in the Republic. It just hadn't been on my radar with everything else stealing my focus.

Perhaps the G.E.G. was trying to finish what the Unnamed had started and Hucksley really had spent time in a G.E.G. lab being tested. The truth of her imprisonment was layered in the intensity of how she spoke. If that were the case, what things did she undergo in the lab? Did Mother know about these experiments, or was it unsanctioned, hidden within the joints of the G.E.G.?

Then again, Hucksley could just be a brilliant liar. There were a lot of those in my world.

"I'd been in the lab for six months," she whispered. "All eyes were on you this week. Celeste used your speech to get me out."

The last stitch. I sprayed down the wound with Neo-spray, then sprayed down the bandage that she pulled from the box. There was only enough for two more, which meant we'd only get two dressing changes out of the supplies we had. Infection would be a possibility. I helped her pull her pants back up, putting my hand between the fabric and the wound so it didn't graze along the wired knots under the bandage as we moved them up.

"You didn't even blush this time, New Wave," Hucksley joked as I motioned for her to zip up and button her pants.

"Just a smidge of a scar will happen if we keep it clean," I said.

"You did good." Her voice was unbroken, as if she'd simply gotten a paper cut, and I wondered how she was able to act like getting gashed so deeply was nothing. Perhaps it was the same talent needed to push someone off a moving train and act as if it had been nothing. I closed my eyes and heard the crackle of bone, the way the momentum tore past the skull, the way death blasted through an ordinary day.

"You think we can make some ground today?" I asked.

"I may need your help," she said. "But we can get a few miles in before it gets dark."

I helped her stand, then helped her put her pack back on. I adjusted the straps along her shoulders, and noticed the goosebumps shimmy up from the muted-forest green bandana around her neck. There was a pulse under her skin, vibrant under the sheen of sweat as she swallowed. She reached out and held onto my biceps to support her leg, and I hooked the straps that kept the pack tight over her chest. I blushed, trying hard not to graze her shirt. Then I clipped the straps at her waist.

I stepped back and she propped herself up on the tree while I tied Bixby's leash to my damp pack. The pup would have to walk along side us. I pulled my arms through the straps of my pack, then turned to help Hucksley, careful not to trip over the new obstacle of leash.

"Uncomfortable is better than dead, aye?" I joked, and Hucksley laughed as she slid one arm through the space between my pack and back. I hesitated before I copied her. It was the only way for her to keep a steady pace through the forest.

We backtracked, then led off on a new trail.

I couldn't get her story out of my head.

Anything was possible. I thought back to the labyrinth, the way she claimed her sight was better than mine. I thought back to the moment she heard the train long before it whistled.

"Keep talking," I said. I needed her to make me feel real again because, suddenly, I felt like I was hovering high above myself. "Where am I going?" I finally asked.

"North. The train was supposed to take us another six miles before we got off, so we have a bit to go."

I fell into her directions, and she was kind, pulling back from such heavy topics so I could digest the ones I'd just been fed. The moment I realized she knew these woods was the moment I gave complete directional decisions to her. Each step was directed by her, each turn of her design. I was her marionette, but none of that mattered. I began to feel the strain of weight between Hucksley,

Bixby, and the packs. I was her human crutch, and her bad leg hobbled between us. I lost track of time as we moved. Had it been half an hour? One hour? Several?

A new hope came under the guise of a different possibility. If Hucksley's story was true, that meant this Bee girl was after her and didn't care about me. It would also mean Mos hadn't betrayed me. But there was regret within that particular hope. If Mos hadn't turned on me, that meant I killed the nano-bots for no reason. It would mean I left Mos worrying over my whereabouts, and the thought of him worrying made me feel ill.

Maybe it was I who'd betrayed a promise... not he.

CHAPTER EIGHT

Onesimos typed on his tablet and dragged a picture into three dimensions. "Her name is Claire."

I looked at her soft face and her unruly hair. She was a generation above mine and beautiful in that wild kind of way. There was intelligence and fire in her green eyes—eyes that looked so familiar.

"She is a known Terrorist, the sister of the head of the Terrorist Cell in fact." Onesimos' voice continued dropping facts upon facts into a bucket.

Grandfather sat back at the table. "What course of action would you take?"

I closed my eyes and pondered the question, knowing that the question was bigger than what he asked. He wanted to see how I would distribute justice. "She's close to your spy?" I asked.

Onesimos nodded. "He is known to meet up with her at least once a month and is often joined by another unidentified woman. We slipped a heart monitor in the spy because we suspect them of having relations. It's not confirmed of course, but his readings always speed up for a few hours to the rate that usually occurs during relations."

I blushed, then felt sick. This spy was putting lives in danger. He could easily reproduce with this Terrorist and put forth genetic anomalies, unless, of course my nano-bot hypothesis ended up being correct. Still, I couldn't be sure until the nano-bots were active. If my hypothesis was invalid, then his actions were wrong on a fundamental level. To top it off, he was with not one, but potentially two partners. It was indecent.

"Do we know if he is loyal to us? It is possible he is doing this to gain their trust?" I asked, thinking of Pamphilos' thesis.

Grandfather smiled. He approved of the question and the fact that I considered the information from several angles. I hated this part of my education. Onesimos and Grandfather had taken to giving me real situations rather than hypothetical ones. Sometimes, if my logic was sound, they'd follow my suggested course of action in real life. How often they listened to me was an indicator of how much I was growing as a Politician.

"Though he gives intel, he rarely tells the entire tale," Onesimos answered.

"Then we need to determine without a shadow of a doubt, where his loyalties lie," I said. "Treason is not something to accuse lightly. Give him orders to execute the girl, but don't tell him the second part."

"What's the second part?" Grandfather prompted.

I swallowed. I hated the answer, and I hated myself for knowing it was the only course to take according to our laws. "If he doesn't bring her in, then try him for Treason and execute him publicly as an example."

"Okay then, how can we be sure he'll execute her? What proof can we ask of him?" Onesimos asked.

"He has to bring her in. He has to manipulate her, never letting her believe she's in danger. Then, he will reveal himself to her. He will destroy her spirit before he drags her up on stage and sticks the needle in her arm himself." The words shocked me more than anything. Being around Grandfather too much brought out the harshest side of my knowledge. He taught me about the firm fist that held the world in check. He believed in the law so devoutly

that there was no forgiveness or mercy for treason.

I knew the other side of the punishment as well, but didn't want to verbalize it within the conversation. If this spy wasn't loyal but still brought the woman in to save his own neck, there was a different level of agony awaiting him. If the spy loved this woman, killing her would haunt him for the rest of his life.

What he chose to do would be telling, but how he chose to do it and how he reacted to it would determine the fate of his citizenship. Just executing the Terrorist would not save him. He had to do so without remorse, believing it to be the right thing to do for the Republic.

The tracker they'd placed inside of him would tell the unborn stories. The heart rate would reveal intention, pain, fear, excitement.

We would know his loyalty one way or another.

Hucksley tried to adjust her weight again to put most of it on her good leg, but her face only grew paler. The heat of her skin burned against mine where her forearm slithered between my pack and my back. Her movement bunched the shirt so that her arm rested on the skin of of my back and her fingers landed my hip. I tried to ignore the way her touch felt. Whatever feelings kept raging haphazardly though me were even more treasonous now that I'd found out she was a Transgenic abomination. Hucksley was the very thing Grandfather wanted to eradicate by finding Lynk, and here I was feeling chemically drawn to her. It made me ache against the impropriety of it all.

Every once in a while, she let out a soft gasp. Her weight grew heavier on me with each step, but I refused to complain. I was too busy trying not to touch inappropriate places as I helped her keep her balance.

The dusk of sunset had arrived, making the tree cover pull us into deeper shades of shadows. It wouldn't be long before we needed to stop and rest, but the more distance we put between the Tracks and us, the better. Hucksley hadn't heard anything unusual in the last few hours, but it didn't comfort me the way it should have.

I checked on Bixby. The pup made her way along the trail with us, and I moderated my pace again so she could keep up. Her leash tied to the other strap of my pack, opposite of Hucksley. It was a chore not to trip on the rope or the girl, but the three of us managed to push through the forest.

"How do you know where to go without checking the compass?" I finally asked when she directed me left.

"This is my forest."

"Yours?"

"Closest thing I have to a home. Ollie, Abner, and I spent most of our childhood here."

"You're trying to get me used to those names," I said. It was just like the G.E.G. sliding the word Transgenics into the national conversation. Since I met her, she wanted me to know they existed in her heart, that she wasn't alone out here on the Tracks, that there was an entire community I'd yet to encounter.

"Aye, you're a sharp one." She tried to take the weight on her bad leg again.

I rolled my eyes. "Keep the pressure on me. You're going to pass out if you don't, and then we'll be in a bigger pickle."

"Now you decide not to talk like a robot?" she muttered. "Bet you never thought you'd be rubbing skin with a Terrorist like this."

She was still scheming to manipulate me like she had on the train, but things were different now. When we were surfing, she'd been playing her cards while I'd barely been in the game. With her in pain, I had the upper hand. I was growing steady feet in my new reality, ready to approach her with more calculation. If she was that closely involved with Lynk, it wouldn't be long before I was able to manipulate the situation to my advantage.

"So, you said Uncle Ty stole Ollie from the Colonies?" I prompted.

Hucksley nodded. "Ollie was Xavi's thirteenth Celebrity child. Xavi always checked in on all fifty-two of them. He never forgot any of the women he Interviewed and always worried about how they held up under the pressures of having a Celebrity child. He felt just as responsible for their happiness as he did for his children, and he often maneuvered things to make their lives easier if he could. It was why he never allowed the G.E.G. to partner him."

The alternate reason Uncle Ty never partnered was possible yet shocking. Celebrities, though they knew very intimate things about who they left their gifts to, were forbidden to contact them again unless it suited the Republic. This rarely happened.

"Most of Xavi's children lived relatively normal lives by the Republic's standards, but Ollie's mother was a bit crazed," Hucksley continued. "She had consented Ollie to experimentation before he'd even been conceived, but unlike Abner and me, Ollie was Transgenically modified for strength. Xavi didn't notice it until Ollie was three. He saw how unnaturally large the boy was growing, but by then, the G.E.G. had already taken Ollie into the labs. Xavi didn't rescue him until he was seven. He brought Ollie to Lynk, and he was raised beside Abner and me."

I listened for more. Lies or facts didn't matter in the quest for truth, and I knew there were truths about Lynk inside the story if I listened just right.

"Lynk was good with us. Every time we felt like we were less than human, slightly more than animals, Lynk never let us forget we were more than the genetics that tried to define us. She always told me, *'You're just a girl, my sweet, sweet Huck.'* And I believed her until I spent six months in the lab with May. I was never meant to be just a girl."

She paused, like she was done talking, recognizing that she'd given away too much too fast. She knew Lynk. She grew up with her. According to the stories she'd shared that day, Lynk had a son she was close to as well?

I wanted her to dig into that story more, but she wouldn't if I tried too hard. I put out a question to draw out something else and appear disinterested. "Why'd you do it?"

"Do what?"

"Kiss me up there."

She laughed. "Why do you think?"

"It gave you the advantage," I answered.

"And it finally made you react. I shouldn't have done it though."

I nodded, but her admission surprised me. To admit she was wrong was not something I thought I'd hear.

"I regret it now. It wasn't fair," she added.

I took a deep breath and waited for the apology to follow. It never came.

"I completely disrespected myself! I deserved better than that," she said instead.

My cheeks flushed. "You're not apologizing to me?"

"Why the hell do you need one? The only person I'm sorry for in that situation up there is myself."

I watched her from the corner of my eye. She was serious! My jaw unhinged, hanging so low my chin nearly hit my sternum before I caught it. I tightened my jaw and bit my teeth to keep from retorting.

"My heart belongs to someone else, so kissing you to prove a point was stupid."

What did she mean by her heart belonging to someone else? Was it one of the boys she kept talking about? Something about that thought made my lungs stutter. Why did I care? Why did the thought of her with another boy make my blood boil and my heart sweat?

"Besides," she continued, "your lips are like... I don't know how to describe it... slimy? No. Not slimy. Rubbery? Aye! It felt like I was kissing a rubber fish!" She laughed again. "Maybe I need to teach you how to do it, you know, so if you ever get that stick out of your ass and decide to go for it, the girl you try to Claim will thank me."

"Are you *serious*?"

"I've never been more serious in my entire life. There's a technique to a good kiss. A slowness that builds into a raging, sexy fire. A—"

"I'm not talking about this with you." There was a humming growing in my ears. Was it possible to see stars floating in the corners of your eyes? Could anger do that?

"Someone needs to talk about it with you. You'll never be able to Claim a girl with moves like that." Her free hand landed on my chest, like she was trying to see just how fast she was making my heart vibrate against my sternum. "You really should apologize for being such a wuss up there that I had to subject myself to kissing the fear right out of you."

She couldn't be in earnest, but her eyes narrowed as if the kiss had been my fault.

"You're angry? At me?" I scoffed.

"Darn skippy! If you'd only gotten up rather than cowering like a toddler, I wouldn't have resorted to fighting you or kissing you. Next time, get your head out of your ass and try harder."

I struggled for composure.

Again.

How did she do it? No one ever got under my skin like this.

Grandfather always said when your enemy was getting to you, the smartest thing was to pretend you understood their perspective. I tried to see the world through her eyes, but her eyes were so foreign to me. In what world should I apologize to her for her kissing me to gain an advantage in a fight she started out of impatience because I wasn't ready to stand up on a speeding train?

In what world did that make sense?

To anyone?

She waited for me to speak. She waited for me to say sorry.

I swallowed. I burned. I wanted to punch something.

And then she started moving her fingers along the curves of my chest, making the hairs on my neck stand electrically rigid. "A good kiss needs tension," she whispered.

The game. It was the game. The different languages that existed here. The ones I didn't want to bring myself to speak. I clenched my teeth, but she kept moving her fingers.

In telling me secrets from her past she made it look like she was trying to get my trust. Now she wanted to throw this trust right back at me, unsettle me, unravel my nerves.

My brain knew better. My body did not. I needed to get away

from her, just for a moment. I dropped my hand from where I had helped hold her up, but as I tried to move it out from between her pack and back, my arm got caught on the strap. I tried to slide my fingers out, but they just stayed stuck between the bunching fabric, her skin, and the weight of all the things she carried. So I tugged on her opposite strap with my free hand and turned her to face me. I held her by the waist at arms length so she was still supported, but she was still too close.

"You have to stop, or we'll get nowhere," I said. I needed a moment to get away from the tugging in my gut, the speed of the blood raging through my veins. I needed to set her against a tree so she could hold herself up for a second.

I moved her towards it, but she looked up at me and smirked. "You'll never get anywhere, New Wave. Have you ever belonged to yourself?"

I opened my mouth to respond, but caught the words just in time. I felt my fingers tense against the skin of her waist. I felt the thick fabric just above her belt line.

"Have you?" she prodded.

I knew the answer to this question all too well. It was a question that could only be answered one way. But the question gave me another nugget of truth. Vagabonds knew how to be selfish. They even prided themselves on belonging to no one and nothing, and, in doing so, belonging to everyone and everything.

In my mind, I tried to straddle two worlds—to really understand the importance of what I was doing. Was there a way to blend the cultures of freedom and responsibility? Was there a way to live peacefully and preserve the genetic sanctity of the Vagabonds and Citizens as we tried to eradicate the Unnamed? Or would every interaction between the two worlds, between the Colonies and Territories, between Citizens and Vagabonds be like this?

I'd been with Hucksley less than a day, though it felt a lot longer with everything that had already happened. I couldn't figure out if I wanted to throw her off a train or kiss her again. I hated how she made me boil, and I wanted to turn back—tell the world I'd changed my mind because Vagabonds were hopeless and uncompromising. But there was more at risk than a staged treaty and more at stake than Absolution and Donation. Fear of that kind of failure made me angrier than any question Hucksley could throw at me. The human genome couldn't afford Transgenic abnormalities threatening its genetic purity.

A new sense of calm washed over me, and I answered her question. She had to believe she was getting through to me in order for me to gain her trust and get to Lynk. Even though she'd already used the trick of the kiss and the touching to unnerve me, I couldn't get used to it. She knew this. She thought she could trap me within my body and make act out of fear of her liberal touches.

So I answered. "I've always belonged to my beliefs. Even when nothing else is present to claim me, they shape who I am." There it was. The indestructible answer she expected.

"And what if I told you your beliefs were wrong?" she asked as her pack hit the bark of the tree I wanted her to lean on while I got my bearings. I felt the scrape of wood against my forearm as I finally freed my hand.

"What if I told you there was no such thing as right or wrong? There is only perspective," I countered, placing my free hand on the bark above her head. "What if I told you things just are... life just is... beliefs just happen? That beliefs are flawed, interchangeable to a situation? That it is time for us to work together to shape the new beliefs that will help us forge this new path?" They were the right words to say to a Vagabond, though they felt traitorous as they poured out.

I leaned in closer and let her eyes take in mine. I saw it there, the way the darkness closed in around her pupils. My closeness bothered her for once.

"Then I'd say you were a Politician," she whispered.

"And I'd say... so are you."

"Don't be upset, Anicetus. You did well today. You impressed Onesimos."

I looked away from Grandfather as he came into the room. I know I'd made him proud, but that didn't make the situation feel right. Sure, I wouldn't be the one holding the needle, but I may as well have been with the order I'd given.

"You have a big heart. That's not a bad thing." He sat down on my bed and smoothed a wrinkle in the blue comforter.

I didn't care for his compliments. I didn't care for any of it. I sent someone to her death today. Me. I wasn't old enough to be given that power yet. Why did he force me into it?

"It's better that you start learning this now," he said. I closed my eyes, angry that even in this, he could read my thoughts. "You need to get used to the idea that your orders will have consequences. That you will have to weigh the good of individuals—and sometimes hundreds of people—against the good of the Republic."

I knew that we couldn't let this spy continue operating as he was. But this woman? Claire? I couldn't stop thinking about all the stories she had inside of her. How they'd be gone with the prick of a needle, never to be heard again.

"You are so like your father in this sensitivity. He struggles with this too, you know." It was a loaded statement. My father struggled with decisions involving the protection of life. Grandfather did not. Once again, the truth of the message was in what wasn't said. Grandfather never hid his disappointment in Father. There was a tension constantly tugging the two apart, and I had the impression it was wrapped around my birth. It was confusing growing up between them. I never knew which one I was supposed to be more like.

In this case, I was glad I mirrored my father. No one should be completely at peace with sending someone to their death.

"Speak up, boy. There is something else bothering you about this situation."

I looked at Grandfather and nodded. "There seemed to be some information missing. For example, the spy? Is he older?" I asked.

"What would prompt you to ask that?" I could tell from how he smiled that I was on the right track.

"Claire is a bit older, and most spies are sixteen to twenty.

Either this Claire is having relations with someone far younger than she is or this spy you are testing is a generation older than me. If the later scenario, then this spy has been leaking information for a very long time. Who knows what secrets he has traded if he is disloyal?"

"And?"

"And with age comes elevation in rank. He may be privy to more valuable information than most, which makes any disloyalty on his part extremely dangerous."

These were the justifications. I knew Grandfather wanted me to see them and verbalize them to make myself feel less guilty. But I needed to understand what this kind of guilt felt like because it would be the feeling that'd one day keep me in check.

"Yet you made the decision even when you didn't know if the spy was younger or older than the woman. Why?"

"Because if he was younger, that's just as bad. Physiologically speaking, this woman would be taking advantage of him because it would be hard for him to redirect his loyalties back to where they belong. A teenage boy can easily be manipulated by adults with more experience. Look at how easily you manipulate me into doing as you would have done."

Grandfather laughed at this. "Observant to a fault, my boy. I guess I can put you out of your misery then. I didn't tell you the entire story about this Terrorist."

I wasn't surprised. There was always room for more information to be had, but he wanted to see how I'd react on the bare minimum of it. As a leader, I'd have to anticipate the next moves based on incomplete information all the time.

"Did you know the Terrorists have Scientists of their own now? They have laboratories dedicated to their own brand of Genetic Terrorism," he said.

"I know this," I whispered. I'd suspected it for a long time.

"Claire is one of the Terrorists who help hide this lab. They call it the Vault, and we think we can manipulate the information out of her if we bring her in."

I shuddered. Manipulate was just a pretty word for torture, and

I hated that her death would not be slow. If Grandfather was sharing this information to make me feel better, it wasn't working.

Grandfather sighed. "But worse than that, you were right. The spy in question holds and extremely high rank, and he's been in the public eye his entire adult life. If Tycho Tripoli is unfaithful to the Republic, it is time we find out once and for all." He let the last bit of information sink into my bones, and it earthquaked apart the image of someone I thought I knew well.

Could Uncle Ty really be a traitor?

Hucksley was a silent sleeper. She leaned against her pack, and, with Bixby curled up in a ball on her lap, she was the image of peace. I sat next to her, trying to keep watch as the sun went down and shadows wrapped around us. I stared through the dark, afraid to take my eyes off her.

She didn't have a fever, but she was tired from the blood loss. We'd eaten peanut butter off a shared pocketknife, but I knew she needed something with more nutrients soon to keep her afloat. I wanted to put a tent up in case it rained, but she was adamant about leaving it tied to her pack in case we needed to run again.

I let the back of my head thud against the tree. I almost kissed her to prove a point earlier. I had her trapped against the very tree she slept on, but I'd pushed myself away. I wouldn't stoop to her level. I wouldn't let urges get the best of me. I could play a more evolved game, and I owed it to myself to do so. So I'd backed away and let the blood rage subside in my gut. It was slow going, like turning off the heat on a pot of boiling water and waiting for it to cool while still on the hot burner.

When Hucksley slept, she looked softer. I wanted to strangle her less, and I took comfort in the peace of her silence. It was almost like I could pretend I was alone for just a moment. As the hours passed, it got harder to stay awake. A half-hearted blink threatened to not reopen, and I sat up straighter.

In the darkness, I began to see things clearly. The blackest eyes. The cracking of skull. The volley of atrocities I was forced to partake in. Had there been another way with Black-Eyes?

Especially when there is always a hitch before the tug, the stutter of movement that happens in the middle of pulling, so slight yet so major, telling you to pause, to think? Did I have to throw him to his death?

I blinked again, half-lidded attempts to get rest. I pretended each blink was an entire night's worth of sleep. I didn't know how much longer I could last. It would be smart to wake Hucksley up so someone kept watch. Instead, I stood up and stretched, letting loose the snap-crackle-pop of my spine.

It was safe to be near Hucksley when she was asleep. I heard her shift slightly, and Bixby yipped at the movement. I reached over and grabbed the pup, felt the wiry hair in my fingers.

I wondered how Eudocia's dog fared. The gossip-vids showed her in the park with it a few times. The dog was an imperfect white, with small spots under the fur. She named it Ion, and when I met it, it bit me. That moment was on a running loop on the vids, staying true to the habit of media to report on things that never mattered as if they did.

Bixby never tried to bite me. She happily let me pet her triangle ears. I sat back down against the tree with her, thankful I wasn't the only one who couldn't sleep.

My brain kept wanting to drift to Mos. Did he betray me on purpose? Or did he trust someone he shouldn't have? Or did someone outsmart us both and hack through my defenses? Or did what happen on the train have nothing to do with Mos and everything to do with an escaped subject? Could Hucksley's crazy story be true in some aspects? Could it be true in all aspects?

There was a spectrum of realities inside of the unknowns. On one end of possibility, my brother wanted me dead. On the opposite end, the G.E.G., and not the Unnamed, was responsible for Transgenic Therapy. All the unknowns cut at me. I didn't want to figure those things out because none of the answers would give me comfort in a world that had gone dark. Not matter what, there was a growing probability that everything I'd been taught to believe was wrong, and that was something I couldn't bare to face just yet.

Walking through the forest the night before was different from this night. Moving through the things we couldn't see was less terrifying than sitting still inside of them. Suddenly, I wanted us to be walking again. I wanted us to run far away from what had happened on the train—from what had happened all my life.

I brought Bixby up on my shoulder, held her like I'd seen mothers hold a baby. The pup licked my cheek, and the world felt better. It was strange how she brought me comfort, and I felt the rough dots of her tongue again and grinned. Somehow, she had become special to me. Somehow, within the course of twenty-four hours, I felt connected to the dog, feeling like she was precious cargo to be protected.

"Ollie and Abner will be there waiting for Bixby." Hucksley had said.

With everything going on, she'd wanted me to save the dog over her, but why? I wanted to ask what *Prometheus' Fire* was. Was it another genetic modification? A manipulation like the NPTN? Or was Bixby a link in the Transgenic Therapy research?

The whistle of an owl cut through the trees, and Bixby nuzzled into my neck. She was precious cargo alright, a package to be delivered rather than some training tool for the Tracks.

"What are you hiding, little pup?" I asked.

Surely Hucksley wasn't taking me right to the Vault within the first few days of being away from the Capital, especially if Lynk was there. Surely, she would make me work harder to prove myself before trusting me with the most wanted criminal in the Republic.

But, perhaps Hucksley told me about the dog out of desperation because she thought she'd be unable to deliver Bixby when there were too many unknowns on the train. She might have, under the right circumstance, risked sending me straight to the source by giving me the compass that housed a slew of coordinates in its memory—the very compass she didn't ask for me to return. Either way, whatever was inside the pup was worth the exposure.

That meant, if I left with the compass, I could bypass all these games. I could leave her behind and take the dog. With her wound, she'd never catch me. I could weave the story that she'd been killed, and that she told me to bring the dog at all cost to the coordinates in her compass. If I did it just right, said it just right, I could put myself right in front of the individual in charge of the Unnamed. Lynk, the woman responsible for creating the Patriots as a distraction from the horrors she was inflicting on the world, the woman who sentenced my father to death.

Another owl hoot zipped through the air, and Hucksley woke with a start. "New Wave?" she whispered.

"I'm right here." And in that statement I was. It didn't feel right to leave her wounded in the forest. What if her wound got infected? What if she died?

I wouldn't be able to take it if she died.

"Where's Bixby?" she asked.

"Right here." I handed the pup over, and she let out a soft sigh once she felt the dog in her hands again.

"Why don't you get some rest? We have a while to go still, but we won't get anywhere tomorrow if you are too tired to help me along."

"You sure?" I asked.

"Sweet dreams, New Wave."

I rested my back against the tree. I closed my eyes but couldn't sleep. The bark bit into my back. I couldn't drift towards dreams. I could only think about the pieces to a million stories, the shattered glass of an unclear image, the unborn words waiting to explode into thought—into existence.

I thought about Celeste. If Hucksley had been chosen by Celeste to train me, and Hucksley was taking the dog to Lynk, then that meant Celeste was a part of the Unnamed. Was Celeste Lynk—the Unnamed, woven into the very heart of the Republic now?

I thought about Uncle Ty. If he had left his son with Lynk then that meant he was the traitor I feared he was. It meant that Uncle Ty had played us all, even when he took atrocious steps to prove himself.

I closed my eyes and thought, and thought, and thought, but

nothing made sense as disjointed dreams littered the caverns of my mind.

Mos cried, big dew-drop tears. His arms gripped me into the cavern of his hug, and the sobs ripped through him like stars being born. "He can't be gone," he shuddered.

Mos was right. Father couldn't be gone. Grandfather must have been mistaken. Fathers didn't just get blown up. Fathers didn't just disappear forever.

I tried to hold him together, but my brother fell apart, shredding into a numb nothingness.

The air on top of the roof had turned stagnant. The clouds stood still. The sun refused to set.

"Don't ever do that again," I said. I stepped us back, even further from where I'd caught him standing.

Later, he would say he was just trying to count the people walking back and forth, forth and back, pretending to grieve without understanding what true grief was. Later, he would say I'd overreacted. Later, he would say I misjudged his intention.

And later, I would let him deny how his toes slid past the ledge and the way his arms spread out as if he could fly.

For now, I would counter all the things he would later deny with all the love I could pour into my hug so he knew he wasn't alone.

"You dead? Celeste will kill us if you're dead." I felt a toe pick against my knee, gently forceful, but the voice was not one I recognized. It was a young voice, and it immediately made me think of how desert dirt dries after the rain, how it becomes clay chips under the feet and crackles in different pitches. Male, yet not quite a man.

I pried my eyes open and felt the hot beams of sun as they cut through the leaves. I stilled my body to take in my surroundings first, but I readied my feet to act.

"Let him be," Hucksley said. Her words were lazy and unworried. She knew the two boys that became the focal point of my vision.

"If I were a betting soul, I'd say he'll be a yodeler," the bigger boy said. This voice was like a bear growling, deep and grumbly, thunderous and sonorous. "We won't get three feet without hearing about how his back hurts from sleeping on the ground. He'll cry about it louder than a rabbit being screwed by a porcupine."

The three of them laughed, and a breath caught in my throat. There's a different kind of understanding that happens between people as they layer a guffaw on top of a giggle on top of a hiccup of laughter. There were inside stories to the phrase *betting soul*, and I wondered where it originated. Now that I'd heard it more than once in the last couple days, I knew it was reusable slang. Mos would be fascinated by its use.

These two boys where Hucksley's friends, but were they mine? Did they mean me harm?

I sat up straighter. The files of memory tucked away in my brain pulled up a picture of recognition. I'd seen them before when I met Celeste two years ago. They were both a little bit larger than the last time I'd seen them singing by the lake. The rust-headed one was about fourteen now.

The young one spoke again. His cracking voice found a moment of solidarity when he raised it. I could see into the future of his words, how they'd grow strong and deep and forceful. "Hell, Ollie. I am a betting soul. Wager you your jerky that he'll be a stoic little sucker."

"Deal," the lemon-headed Ollie said. The boy took up so much space that he became his own universe. He reached over and gave the kid a rub on the head with his knuckles, pulling out strands of hair from a tightly braided mass. The kid had more hair than me, thick and full and on fire when the sun snuck through the overhang of trees to find it.

The brick-haired boy leaned in. "Don't make me lose my jerky. Ollie stole the good stuff yesterday, and he never shares it."

Something about the banter made me think of Mos, and an ache ripped through me. I stretched my back against the tree, pretending I wasn't feeling the soreness that ripped through me.

"New Wave, meet the lost boys. This is Abner and Ollie. They are major pains in the ass, but at least you won't have to carry me anymore," Hucksley said.

Ollie moved closer to her and helped her stand. "I heard what they did. Did it take?" he asked her. The joking tone disappeared from his voice. Hucksley nodded, and he grabbed her chin with his fingers like he was pinching it together. "I'm sorry, kid."

Hucksley shook the hand away. "By the Bond. Let it go." She nodded towards me pointedly, and I let a clue sink in. She wouldn't be able to play her mind and body games with me when this Ollie guy was around. When she said her heart belonged to another, it became clear that it belonged to this boy by how he looked at her.

"Well, hate to cut the joys of a reunion short, but we should get moving," Abner said. He reached out a hand to help me up. I hesitated before taking it. I was so close to Lynk, and his hand in mine only reminded me of just how close.

Abner looked at my arms and whistled. "Guess she didn't share her Smells-All with you. It's the best way to keep away the bug bites," he said.

I looked at the marks left by the horseflies. I tried to ignore every sting, but ignoring the welts didn't make them disappear. Abner unshouldered his pack and rummaged through the top. I noticed a shirt and jacket in the same color he wore, forest green, solid, and plain, and a green bandana that matched the one Hucksley wore on her neck was looped around his forehead, offsetting the brick tones in his hair.

"Not one for variety?" I tried to joke. "Aren't you Vagabonds supposed to be a colorful people?"

"Aye, but green is better for the woods. Tan for the desert."

I nodded. "Guess you have no trouble blending into the trees. You're nearly tall enough to be one."

"Never took you to be a comedian," Ollie said as Abner handed me the spray canister. I swooshed it along my skin and immediately felt the soothing calm along my pores.

"Never took a Vagabond not to be one. Don't you guys find joy everywhere or something?" I couldn't figure out what it was about the mountainous boy that made me want to poke. Was it because

Ollie was Uncle Ty's son? Because he shared a secret bond that Uncle Ty had never trusted me with?

Perhaps that was the thing that pained me and brought jealousy into the forefront of my brain. I tried to find traces of Uncle Ty in Ollie, but his hair was so bright and his skin so pale that there wasn't much to work with. I could see it in his nose, the way his cheeks walked high on his face, but everything else was off.

Suddenly I recognized the jealousy for what it was. It was as shocking as jumping into ice water, crippling in a traitorous way. It had nothing to do with Uncle Ty, and everything to do with the treason of desire.

I hated the way he'd touched Hucksley's face.

I hated the way her heart belonged to him.

Phoibe walked towards me, and I felt the hair on my arms stand tall. There was a soft smile on her face, but there was sadness there.

"They changed my placement. They've asked me to join the Militia," she said. "I've come to say goodbye."

I kept my face from showing surprise, but the shock of change raged across her eyes. "I thought genetics was your specialty."

She let out a startled laughed. "Who says it isn't? Apparently they need spies who understand the intricacies of genetics. I leave for training in the morning."

I felt a splintering inside, a strange wave of sadness that I'd never see this girl again. She was beautiful in a way that was hard not to notice, even since I got back on Propriety Meds.

"It was nice knowing you, Anicetus Petrakis. There's a goodness in you, and you're going to do great things for our nation. Don't let them twist what's inside you."

I glanced behind her and saw the faceless guard waiting for her. He watched every move we made. "Don't let who twist me?"

Phoibe moved her slender hands through the air, like she was touching the entire world. "You know who pulls your strings. Don't be their puppet." She walked past me, and her arm scraped the air that touched my skin. Close, but too far. "Good luck on your nano-

bot launch."

"Good luck to you as well," I whispered in her wake, and that night I wondered. I imagined. I dreamed.

What would a world in which I could have grabbed her hand and pulled her in have felt like?

Ollie was a mountain, much like Mos. The way he carried Hucksley through the forest like she weighed nothing was impressive. Abner and I kept asking if he needed a break, but he always refused.

"Don't take offense," Abner finally said. "We haven't seen her in six months. It's been hard on everyone. Ollie most of all."

Hucksley and Ollie fell behind Abner and me, but Abner's pace didn't falter. Soon, the other two were so far behind us that we couldn't see them through the trees. Though sometimes I could hear the murmur of their voices behind us, indecipherable in conversation.

None of them seemed to be in a hurry as we hiked, as if we were going on a little stroll through the forest and not trying to outrun the events chasing after us. Abner whistled while we walked, and it reminded me of the owl I heard last night. It struck me that he'd been warning Hucksley that he was near. Hucksley had done something similar with her woodpecker call to me. The mimic of the birds was so acute it was unnerving. Thoughts of animal traits fluttered to the forefront of my mind.

"How did you find us?" I finally asked.

"Hucksley's compass on her neck, I know how to hack it and find the location. After what she's been through, we weren't about to wait for her to come to us."

There was a protective pride in the statement, perhaps a guilt that he'd let her get taken in the first place.

I let it go.

I noticed we were moving farther and farther from the Tracks, rather than remaining parallel to them. Wherever we were headed did not involve trains, which surprised me. It had always been assumed that Vagabonds lived by and near the Tracks at all cost.

The more they remained on the move, the safer they were from being eradicated.

Yet the further we got from the Tracks, the more comfortable Abner became. It went contrary to everything I'd learned about their culture.

I ducked beneath a branch that Abner walked around without a second thought. What was it like to live in a world that fit you so perfectly? He moved fluently through it, as if he owned every inch, as if every rock or tree or leaf was made to fit his body and orbit around him.

"Where are we going?" I finally asked.

"Does there have to be a where?" His fingers grazed along the crumbling bark of a dying tree. Brown flakes fell in his wake as he moved on.

I reached out to touch the same spot, felt the same tension and give as the bark broke down under the pressure of my fingers. "I suppose not, but that doesn't stop me from wondering."

"Do you ever look at something and just let it be? Do you ever leave your questions behind? Or do you want to tear the world apart just so you can understand it?"

Something about how his voice covered the whispers of Ollie and Hucksley behind us let me know he wanted to give them privacy. It was like he could hear their conversation transpiring and wanted to cover it. I had no choice but to let him.

"Just because I ask questions doesn't mean I want to tear the answer apart. I just want to understand things, not destroy them," I answered.

"Not out here. To ask why of someone or something, to ask where on a journey, is to weigh them down with your expectations."

"Expectations?"

"Aye, expectations. You expect the world to give you answers if you ask it to, but simply asking a question doesn't quite mean you've earned an answer. Appreciation does, and appreciation comes from respectfully letting something exist. Let it be. Your precious answers will come then, and only then." Abner moved beyond a tree, then around the next, like he was braiding his own path through them. I wanted to ask him how he knew what direction we were meant to go, but after what he just said, I thought better of it.

Instead, I took the hint. I watched instead of asked. His neck moved slightly as he looked up or down or left or right. He scanned the scenery for something, so I followed the directions his head went. When I finally saw the markings, I was impressed by how subtle they were. Scratches on trees. Some were under the armpits of a branch. Some were near the roots. Some were even ingeniously carved into rocks grouped in seemingly random heaps.

It reminded me of when Uncle Ty took me to meet Celeste by the lake. He had led me on a haphazard route, as if he'd known his own path by heart, as if he'd walked it so many times he didn't need reminders. And suddenly, I knew that Abner didn't either. He only looked for the markers to see how fast I could pick up finding a trail without him having to explain it.

"I don't hear Hucksley and Ollie anymore," I said as I realized it.

"They are fine," Abner said. The kid didn't seem too concerned. "We saw you two years ago at the lake." He changed the subject. "I wanted to meet you. Xavi wouldn't let me. Ollie said we were better off for not knowing you. That you were probably as square as you looked. Said you'd never fit into a round hole if you tried."

Something about his babbling made me think he was nervous, but about what, I couldn't know just yet. However, none of the conversation was unplanned. He wanted me to know that Ollie didn't trust me.

Then another thought struck me. These three only knew what the rest of the world thought it knew about me. There was an advantage in that. None of them really understood what I was truly capable of because none of them had estimated me correctly. Ollie thinking I was a square-peg just proved that, and it gave me something to work with.

"What are you grinning at?" Abner asked.

"You mean to tell me that Ollie, a Vagabond, only believes that circles and squares exist in this world?"

"There might be other shapes, but he believes yours is pretty obvious." He nodded behind us. "I guess that's the whole point of what we're doing, though? How do we get all the circles and squares of this world to morph into something—I don't know—other?"

I nodded. The kid was either an idealist or trying to see if I was one myself.

Abner stopped to check on Bixby in his pack. He had taken to the dog immediately, and he worried about her well being with an exactness that was startling. Part of me wanted to ask for the pup back. Something about letting the dog go bothered me, but I bit back the request.

"We should let them catch up to us and see if Ollie needs a break," Abner said. "Though I doubt he'll take the offer."

Bixby poked her head out of the opening to watch me from around the neck of Abner's ukulele. The case was strapped to the edge of his pack, and I wondered who taught him the instrument. What made him brave enough to play it in a world where the wrong person hearing it would result in his death?

"Do you play?" he asked when he saw me eyeing the ukulele.

"Not at all."

"I'd be happy to teach you. It's pretty easy, and very therapeutic. Also, the ladies tend to love a man with an instrument."

I blushed.

"That night at the lake. Why didn't you sneak away and come meet us? We were at the edge playing music all night. You could have joined." The shift in the conversation from girls to me not trying to meet them at the lake startled me rather than made me feel better. Was he really offended that I didn't interrupt?

"I was told to let Uncle Ty enjoy his freedom," I finally answered.

"It's strange to hear him called that. I don't think I'll ever get used to it."

I nodded. "I don't think I could ever get used to you calling him Xavi, but I suppose we'll both have to try."

Abner grinned. "I suppose we will."

CHAPTER NINE

"Who are you?" Instructor Aeschylus asked.

"I am Anicetus," I said. "Anicetus Petrakis."

"Are you sure that is who you are?" he warned.

"Who are you then?" I retorted.

"Who do you think I am?"

"Do you always answer a question with a question?" I asked.

"Do you?" He leaned back in his chair and smoothed a wrinkle from his lab coat.

"Is there any other way to answer questions?"

Satisfied, Instructor Aeschylus laughed. "Who are you?"

"Who is anyone?"

"Do you see the big picture then? The way it works?" He tapped his temple, and reached over to the cage. Inside was C-43298. Its small pink nose wove patterns in the air. Its whiskers reminded me of an orchestra conductor at the symphony. With gloved hands, Instructor Aeschylus pulled it out. "Who is this?"

"The label given is C-43298."

"And what other labels can we give her?" he asked.

"Control Group Success Story."

"How so?"

"A positively heightened GJB2 gene, happening without direction by our hands," I said. The answer scared me. Control group success stories felt dangerous, as if they invalidated the Genetic Engineering Guild's genetic direction.

"Can we trace how C-43298 got its enhanced hearing?"

"Generational necessity," I answered. "Test group GJB2 was put in different auditory conditions over the course of twenty generations."

Instructor Aeschylus nodded. He had even been working on the concept before I ever entered his lab. The worst part? Subject C-43298 reached the desired goal before any other subject we'd tried to manipulate. In fact, some of our manipulations led to more negative mutations than positive, making C-43298's success feel more like a failure for us.

"Anicetus. Who are you?"

"I am the grandson of a Prime Chancellor. The son of a Chancellor. The face of New Wave perfection."

None of my answers pleased Instructor Aeschylus. I tried everyone in my arsenal, but with every wrong response, his face grew as pale as his beard. It was the expression that bloomed above his cheeks when he was disappointed with me, except his disappointment was the worst kind. It was too controlled to ever be verbalized, but knowing it was there made me feel failure acutely.

I was supposed to be brilliant, but it's difficult to feel intelligent when you're only fourteen.

Instructor Aeschylus was one of the few people who always made me feel less than intelligent. He was just as talented as Grandfather at it.

He put the mouse down in the labyrinth. I watched it scurry through the obstacles, avoiding the grinding noises of the painful spots. If she went left, she'd run into a loud shock field. If she went right, she'd have to figure out how to climb a small wall, but there'd be no shock. From a safe, auditory distance, she could tell where the new shock fields were placed.

She went right.

"Who. Are. You?" he asked again.

"What's that song?" I asked as Abner finished the last lines. I bit into the apple he'd offered. It was red. Sweet. Barely bearable. I already missed things like real food and soft couches to relax on.

"Don't have a name yet. I'm working on it."

"You wrote it?"

"Sure did." He stopped strumming to pluck the strings a bit.

"Is it smart to play that when we don't even know if enemies are afoot?"

Abner raised his eyebrow. "*Afoot?*"

It sent a sliver of laughter through me. This kid had a knack for bringing out smiles.

"No one is after us," he said.

"You know this how?"

"I have my ways."

I guessed he did. If his hearing was as sharp as Hucksley claimed, then perhaps he could hear a shift in the forest, or how the animals quieted or loudened at the approach of someone.

Abner's strumming made me think about the lake, to the first time I saw Ollie and him singing the Stilling Song. I studied Abner as he played and tried not to choke on the apple as I swallowed it. It was all so convoluted that not even I wanted to believe it completely.

They mourned family that day.

Claire...

Then another possibility struck me. I studied Abner and now knew exactly why he looked so familiar. I hated how my brain worked, how once it made a connection, there was no way to un-connect it. Within a split second, I saw the chiseled jaw and the dark, olive skin. I saw the soft smile that was full of contradictions play on his face. Abner was Uncle Ty's, sure as the sun rose and set. "Are you and Ollie brothers?" I asked, already knowing the answer, but wanting confirmation to believe it.

"Half. Same father, different mother. Similar to your story, I understand. Like me, you know how to be half and whole all at the same time. Do you miss your little brother?"

"Miss is an understatement. I'd never pictured life without Mos before, and now that we're apart, I feel like something bigger is missing," I answered on auto-pilot while I thought about what Abner's loaded words meant.

"I would feel the same way if someone kept me from Ollie." He started strumming again, and I closed my eyes to the wide open song he sang:

"Lead me to pieces
I shattered them whole
Crumpled them straight
So you fit
Me.
Lead me to home
Since it does not exist
And I'll tear down the walls
So they stand
straight.
Lead me to stars
I plucked every one
And I snuffed out their lights
So they shine
dark.
They led me to you
And you ate them all up
Devouring lies
So they turned
True."

An unborn story bloomed in the song. The way Abner's smile moved with the words made me think of Uncle Ty. I always knew Uncle Ty carried secrets, but this one was bigger than just stealing one son from the Republic. Grandfather had suspected Uncle Ty had a relationship with Claire of an unsanctioned nature, and the boy who sat next to me only proved Grandfather had been right.

Not only was Abner a Transgenic abomination, but he'd been created out of genetic sin within an unsanctioned relationship. I couldn't wrap my head around why Uncle Ty would engage in such an act of Genetic Terrorism.

Since Claire was this woman, and Lynk was Abner's mother, that meant Claire was Lynk. Yet, the confusing thing about that conclusion was in the name. They all talked about Lynk as if she still existed.

Perhaps Lynk wasn't just a person anymore, but an idea. Could it be possible that Claire was the leader of the Unnamed before her execution, experimenting on her own children? Was it possible she sacrificed herself so willingly in order to protect the products of her experiments? And now, the Unnamed used the title Lynk for consistency in leadership, a title like the Republic used the word Chancellor?

"Want to learn?" Abner asked.

I tried to steady my voice and pretend I didn't know the things I'd just figured out. "I doubt I'd be much good."

Abner laughed. "I doubt your doubt. You're a New Wave. I'm sure you're good at everything the moment you figure it out. You know, I wondered if you'd be humble. I wondered if you'd be cocky. I think I wanted you to be one or the other. I think I hate that you are neither."

He handed me the instrument, and immediately, I realized how small and fragile it was in my hands. My fingers shook slightly. It was so subtle. All my training in how to control my emotions went into a useless hyperdrive, and Abner noticed. "You okay?" he asked.

"Yeah. Blood sugar, I think." The lie was from an old bag of tricks. My blood sugar was fine, but my heart was not. Did this boy know I was the architect of his mother's death?

"You see, Claire blamed me for many things, most of which were not my doing. However, this? Her death? This one was on me. She went into her end knowing the fate she set her mind to," Uncle Ty had said.

"This is the C." Abner put my middle finger on a string and pressed it down. "These bars here make up the frets." I put pressure on the note, and he moved my other hand to strum the strings slightly. "This is playing a chord," he added. "Down, down, up, up, down."

It sounded wrong in my hands. Not nearly as fluid and musical as when Abner had control of the instrument. But there was something satisfying in playing. It was as if I was in control of uncontrollable sound. I could see why Abner loved the instrument. It gave him something to manipulate, something that could never be evil and always strived to be beautiful.

"Good," he said, though I was far from good. I listened to how the vibrations interacted to make different sounds, and missed my nano-bots. I missed how they used to buzz in my ear as they gathered the data, buzzing their own genetic music in their own genetic orchestra. They were my song the way the ukulele was Abner's.

"A trick is to strum down with your pointer finger and up with your thumb. The movement of the wrist makes it more fluid."

I shuddered.

What kind of person sits with the son of someone he killed, playing the ukulele?

Right and wrong blurred along the edges of disjointed song.

I was responsible, but I'd never have to take responsibility for it on a personal level. For now, they blamed the Republic. They blamed the whole rather than the specific person who gave the order. When people don't have a face to blame, they make one up. The Republic may have been multi-faceted and made up of countless faces, but, to the Vagabonds, all those people were one. One big, giant monster of oppression.

What would happen if this boy knew I killed his mother?

"Here's the G." Abner adjusted my fingers into a triangle. The hold was awkward, but the kid helped me position my hands. There was something so gentle to how he worked with me. Life out here couldn't have been easy, and I wondered what tragedies he ran from when he played.

"Do you hate me?" I wasn't sure why I asked it, nor was I sure of why I had the sudden urge to know. But here I was, a representation of everything that hunted Vagabonds his entire life, sitting next to him, playing a ukulele, and all I wanted was for him to forgive me. All I wanted was the fresh start that never existed, and it was as if this boy could give it to me with his forgiveness.

His fingers hovered over mine where he'd just placed them into a new chord. "I don't know you enough to hate you."

It wasn't the answer I wanted, but it was better than the answer he could have given.

Abner cocked his head to the side. It reminded me of how Bixby looked when she was hungry or confused. "I have to admit, though, that I'm terrified of you. The world knows you are full of potential, but I know that potential can be a double-edged sword. This *potential* for greatness inside of you may not mean it'll be great for me or my people."

"Who am I?" I growled, reaching for a handhold. The route on the rock wall was too easy, and the ease infuriated me as much as the difficult question. I wanted a path to make me fall. I wanted to feel the groan of the harness on my groin, the way it tugged uncomfortably under my weight.

"Who am I?" My fingers wrapped around the jutted-toothed-grip. I pulled my weight up on it and reached for the next.

Who was all relative. Depending on the situation, I took on too many whos. I wasn't even just one who to one person. To Mos, I existed in the labels of brother, big brother, competition, hero, failure. I was so many whos, that perhaps I was no longer capable of defining myself into one. Perhaps it was everyone else's job to figure out who I was to them.

And what did who mean anyways? How could I respond with a simplistic answer when nothing in this life was as simplistic as responding to the question, "Who are you?"

Perhaps that was the answer Instructor Aeschylus was looking for.

I grunted as my hand landed on a hold. It was an easy hold, but my grip grew slippery on it. I strained my fingers but felt them slide. The tug of the harness caught my weight and bore into my thighs, inflicting discomfort on my groin.

"Who?" I asked as Cosmos lowered me.

"What," Cosmos asked, "was that about?"

"What?" I asked and laughed. Not who, but what. What was I?

If Subject C-43298 was the control group, that meant the other groups were the variable groups.

What was I then?

On the scientific level, I was a variable.

But what was the control? Or better yet, who?

Abner didn't notice the stillness that fell over my eyes. I was a murderer, of that much I knew, but holding the responsibility of the anarchies, the mass deaths, and even the death of the man on the train, felt different than holding the death of Claire in the face of her son. Abner was just a boy, and I witnessed his pain mirror my own the day they sang they Stilling Song.

"Down, down, up, up, down," Abner sang. He knelt beside me, watching my hand placement. "There you go. You got it!"

I definitely didn't have it. There was a clacking noise to my strumming and changing chords was a disaster, but Abner was enthusiastic. Then, something changed in my ears. It always happened when I learned something new. The click of understanding, the expedited learning curve that made the world seem less challenging. The strings began to work together, and Abner's smile faltered slightly. It wasn't a displeasure, but a shock.

"You really do pick things up fast," he said.

I spoke over the chords. "Life is just a series of cycles, and each cycle parallels the next. Learning the ukulele is just like learning to add. One element plus one element and those elements plus another. Building blocks. That's all learning is. But steps and intention are two separate things. You have heart when you play. I may pick up on mechanics, but heart is something I cannot learn so quickly."

I strummed some more, wishing I had a heart to begin with. Abner cocked his head and listened carefully for the difference I spoke of. I saw it in his eyes when he noticed it.

"Are Hucksley and Ollie a—a—?" My tongue became loose, and I wanted to cut it off for trying to ask the question.

"Are they—?" Abner laughed. He was going to make me say it, and part of me hated him for it. The other part of me hated myself for wondering.

"Are they a—?"

"A what?" He sat up straighter.

"I don't know how to ask the question," I admitted.

"I'll put you out of your misery then, but I have a feeling it'll only put you in a different kind of misery if I do."

I closed my eyes. He was right. I was the last person who deserved forgiveness from any of them. I craved the way her tornado eyes stirred me even though I knew it was wrong, even though I knew she was genetically tainted. Yet thinking of her as an enemy was becoming harder and harder to do, and I couldn't figure out what it was about her that made me feel in this direction. Maybe it was because she reminded me of the bigger picture, that there was a bigger mission I worked towards that made all the sacrifices mean something. All these lives I carried on my back were being carried towards a greatness. All these lives would save so many more.

"Hucksley's heart belongs to someone else," Abner whispered, the laughter deflating from his teeth. "She tried to be Ollie's, but it killed her. He loved her enough to let her go, and because of that, he got to keep her in a different way. They are best friends, nothing more."

Was it relief I felt for the answer? Was it pity for Ollie that he wasn't lovable enough for Hucksley to be his? My thoughts about her ripped a chasm in my chest. To wonder such things was traitorous. Just because I had to learn to think like a Vagabond did not mean I needed to start behaving like one, but before I could regret asking anything at all, the next question escaped. "Who does her heart belong to?"

Sadness tugged the smile off his face. "That's not my story to tell."

Grandfather shifted his stance so he could lower me with the rope. "Again!"

I punched the rock wall when I swung towards it, then Grandfather lowered me back to the ground. I felt the harness pinch areas that sent bolts of lightning through my spine.

"From the start?" I'd been stupid enough to ask the first time it'd happened last week. It didn't make sense to have to go all the way back to the beginning of the route. I'd already worked so hard to get up to the point I was at, but each time I missed, straining right where the crag jutted out and the hold rested just out of reach, falling into the support of the ropes and harnesses, Grandfather said, "Again!" Each time, he lowered me back to the ground and made me examine the holds that climbed up the uneven structure in spotted blues and greens.

He seemed amused at my anger, which only exasperated it. I turned back towards the wall and climbed up the first part with so much ease it only made me boil. The first, second, and fifth time I'd tried it, this part of the route had an edge of challenge to it. Now it was just an annoying reality, a waste of time to get to the part that mattered.

That crag.

That hold that was just out of reach.

Every day since that first day, Grandfather took two hours out of his schedule to meet me at the wall. How he had time to do it was beyond me. He'd always insisted on spending quality time with me. I missed the days when that meant he drilled me on history, philosophy, and politics. To barge into my exercise hours was an invasion that bordered on unforgivable. The time of day I looked forward to the most was being stripped away by his incessant persistence that I repeatedly climb the same exact wall until I got it right.

"Again!" he said.

I screamed. I couldn't help it. I wanted to tear the wall down with my bare hands, and I put that rage into my next attempt.

I fell.

"Again!"

And I fell.

"Again!"

And I fell.

"Tomorrow," he finally said, unhooking himself from the rig of ropes. I placed my hands on my knees and tried to catch my breath.

Ollie didn't want a break, and pointed out we were almost there, wherever there was. They fell behind us again, and Abner let me stew. He knew something was on my mind, and he gave me the space to explore it. For the first time since being pushed out of my home, someone allowed me room to think, and I didn't know how to feel about the kindness. He sang softly under his breath, and I recognized the mumbling. Hucksley had done the same thing that first night. She *had* been singing as she led me through the dark.

Abner sang like there was something about song that set him free, and I grew jealous of the peace he found in his words. There was a strength about him, stretched across his skin. It was the color of bright leather, and, when he smiled, the pity in it didn't feel insulting. Within the course of a day, I was discovering that it was hard not to love Abner. The way dirt on him seemed to lay just right in the crevices of his neck that moved when he sang. The way his cracking voice could falsetto to punctuate a note so that he could sound like a squealing pig or nails on glass. The way hope rested in his fingertips as he plucked each taut string on the ukulele. Everything about him was haunted, like secrets being held just below the surface of murky water, yet everything about him was optimistic, as if he hoped in a myriad of colors even when he knew he shouldn't.

I felt it then. Compassion for the boy. Compassion for Hucksley and Ollie as well. Compassion for how they had to grow up too fast, for how they had to lose too quickly. Hucksley, Ollie, and Abner? They were the kids raised in the wild, belonging to a cause that began generations before they were born. Like me, they had no say in the choices made on their behalf. If they were Transgenically modified, they couldn't help it anymore than me having a concentrated NPTN modification. Like me, they grew up wondering if they were human, wondering how to cling onto a definition of Humanity when they felt so different from everyone they grew up next to. Were they anymore an abomination than I was? Which definition of abomination would become the truth when events were written into history?

They were my other side of greatness, the ones I was supposed to love and understand so that I could believe in my own cause more fully. But Father's logic was faulty. In recognizing them as me, I couldn't see them as anything else. Our two causes bled together, and the entire war felt wrong.

Which way was right in the search for perfection? Was it the slight alterations in what already existed or was it enhancement through giving us what we'd never had before? Or was it finally time to just leave it all well enough alone and let the human genome do as it would?

Being around them made the answer beautifully unclear.

We moved beyond another crest, and followed the downward slope through the trees. Then he paused before a stack of boulders. "Home sweet, home, New Wave! Though you've been to *Neverland* before," he said as he moved around them. My mouth opened slightly, and I barely caught the breath of shock that rammed into my teeth.

It was *the* lake, the same lake Uncle Ty had taken me to, only we hit it from a different angle. Black water captured the clouds on its surface, and I watched a swatch of blue dragonflies play along the top. Abner had already rushed towards the edge. He let Bixby out, and immediately, she began to explore as he pulled his water bladder out of his pack.

"First rule is every time you find water, fill up right away. You never know when you'll have to leave in a hurry, and you never know when you'll find water again." He dipped the top of his bladder into the lake. "There's a filter in the spout. As it goes in, it cleanses the liquid so it's drinkable. It's good to clean the filter every once in a while with boiling water if you can risk a fire."

I tugged out my water bladder from the pouch that housed it. It was still half-full, but Abner had good logic. When we finished,

Abner sat down on the beach to stuff the water bladder back in his pack. He settled in next to the pack and patted the sand next to him. "We should chat before the others get here."

"Again!" Grandfather said, lowering me back to the ground.

I felt the soft parts of the foam flooring wrap around the soles of my climbing shoes. The padding bent under my weight when it was given completely back to me by the slacking of the ropes before he pulled and they grew taut again. I hovered slightly over the floor so that the only way to be comfortable again was to keep climbing.

"Aren't you a little old to be hanging out at the rock gym?" I asked. I moved my hand against the backdrop of people climbing. Everyone was under the age of 30, except for crazy, old man Nicodemus, but he didn't count. Nicodemus was just as likely to be talking to the hummingbirds in the Victory Gardens as painting in the town square as climbing rock walls with no ropes. He was eccentric, but everyone knew he was a genius. Next to Grandfather, all the youth emphasized the contrast. Not even being beautiful could keep a person from looking old.

"Old is as old does," Grandfather replied. "Quit stalling."

"People are going to start talking."

"And what would they say, Anicetus?"

"The tabloids would read: Prime Chancellor Petrakis Tries to Live Vicariously Through Grandson, Fails Miserably."

At this, he threw back his head in laughter, and I laughed with him before turning back to the wall.

This time, there was no frustration, just the peace of knowing. I'd figured out his game after he'd left yesterday. After a few quick interrogations of one of the trainers, I discovered Grandfather had personally planned the route. The boy admitted that the wall was unclimbable, then everything fell into place. This was a lesson with two desired outcomes. Part one was to test to see how long it'd take for me to learn control over my anger when faced with the impossible. Part two involved recognizing when someone was manipulating me. Grandfather had always meant for me to interrogate the employees and discover he was behind it all. I should have known better from the first day he showed up at the rock gym because nothing Grandfather did was just for fun. He always had hidden purposes and agendas when it came to me.

I pushed off the rock wall and lunged, missing the hold again. Knowing it was an impossible expectation finally took the weight of frustration from my shoulders. Reaching the top was not the point. Getting under Grandfather's skin was the real test.

I dangled from the rope and felt the pinch of the harness. "Again!" I said, beating Grandfather to the command. When I landed back on the floor, he made no shift in emotion and his face held the same polite smile it always did.

Game on.

"Do you have any pointers?" I'd never asked it before, assuming I knew everything there was to know about climbing. After all, it was my favorite exercise, with the right blend of problem solving and bodily exertion. Why would I ask this old man, who'd never shown any interest in it?

"Try thinking outside the lines," he offered.

"Helpful," I laughed. There was the noncommittal answer he was so famous for. I turned back to the wall. Climbed. Fell. "Again!" I said the moment my fingers grabbed only air.

Two tries later, his words sunk in.

Think outside the lines.

I looked up at the wall looming ahead of me. I'd been so focused on the holds that I didn't pay attention to everything surrounding it. There was a slight crack in the wall's foundations. I'd seen it a million times, every fall after I'd hit the wall with my fist, but it was against the rules for indoor climbing. Part of the challenge in climbing was about following foot to hand on the set route.

But Grandfather had set the route, and he intended me to think outside the lines—outside the rules.

I remember him saying once, "Politicians follow a different line of reasoning and rulings. Not out of arrogance, but out of necessity. It may seem like cheating, but you need to adjust fluidly along the firm lines created by contrasting views. Every side has its own boundaries, and to make things work, you have to be able to move between them."

There were the climbing rules and my Grandfather's rules, and this was his game. I reached the part of the wall that jutted out and placed my fingers into the crack in the surface. Both hands fit perfectly and allowed one foot to hook underneath the overhang.

It was the real world.

And as much as I wanted to live by the path, I had to recognize that the normal path was unfollowable. I had to create my own straight line between the gaps.

I pushed with my foot and strained my left hand, felt the blue shape of the hold under my fingers and pulled my body up. The rest of the wall was easy after that, but, when I reached the top, the victory tasted salty. It burned on my tongue, and I wanted to tell Grandfather he could keep his rules.

But when I reached the ground under Grandfather's careful guidance of the ropes, none of these emotions showed. I wore his polite smile, an inheritance that was either a gift or a curse.

"Now, old man, your turn. Think you can beat it?" I asked.

He unhooked the rope from his carabineer and shrugged. "Child. Not only did I plan the route, I put it up myself... without a harness."

"Chat away," I said as I lowered myself next to Abner. It felt good to sit down just out of reach of the shade. The sun was fresh and warm as it cut through the light spattering of clouds.

"The problem is, if I just flat out tell you everything, you won't believe a single word. Lynk said you needed to figure things out, like a puzzle, before you can draw a conclusion. She said you needed to think through possibility before you are open to believing something."

I held back a growl. What did Lynk know about how my brain worked? Or better yet, how did she know that it was hard for me to trust answers that did not stem from questioning?

Abner reached into his pack and pulled out a tablet. He set it in the sun to charge. He propped his pack up behind him then leaned back on it as if it were a chair.

"I assume Hucksley told you about where she's been, but I also assume you still think she's lying."

I debated denying it, but I thought it'd be counterproductive.

"So, let's pretend for a moment we are being honest with you. While we chat, I hope you keep in mind the possibility that we are telling the truth."

"I can try," I said.

"Were the Genetic Terrorists, in the end, right to release The Great Disaster?"

It was a strange question, but one I'd actually considered long ago. "If I ignore the moral implications of genocide, the act *did* save Humanity in the long run. If humans had been allowed to continue breeding and growing in population as they had been, then mutations would have caught up to Humanity. That, or they would have destroyed all the natural resources first because the planet couldn't have possibly supported such exponential growth in population."

"Tell me more about The Great Disaster."

I swallowed. "It was a culling. A plague invented by Genetic Terrorists that wiped out seven-eighths of the world's population."

"And?" Abner prompted.

"It made the Genetic Engineering Guild a necessity. With such a reduced population, the Genetic Terrorists ended up getting what they wanted in the first place. The next few governments that grew out of the decimation focused on the preservation of Humanity, not by choice but by the fear of extinction. Though there were disagreements on the best route to save us, the Republic was eventually founded. Ever since, the Genetic Engineering Guild has steered us towards this current point in Humanity through genome maintenance, protecting and preserving our genetic gifts so that our race can survive." The answer sent a wave of calm through me. Pulling on text-vid information calmed me, like I was falling into habit. I could have been chatting with Grandfather or Instructor Aeschylus, rather than a boy in the middle of nowhere.

"Do you think the Republic can last forever?" Abner added. "Give the honest response, not the appropriate one."

I looked at the boy, studied his face. What a strange distinction, to know that my answers were always a product of situation, that my answers always had a public and a private version.

"Nothing lasts forever. Civilizations always fall, even when they appear to be at their sturdiest. It is very possible that the Republic could cease to exist under the right circumstances. Or perhaps the wrong ones?"

"Xavi said you believe in unborn stories, that you recognize history can be altered to suit a cause."

I felt a shuddering of betrayal. Uncle Ty spoke to this boy about my beliefs. He had no right to do so.

"Through this theory, you recognize that history isn't set in stone. It is easily manipulated by power," he continued. "Yet when you talk about the G.E.G. you act as if they have been honest in terms of history. But who had the most to gain with The Great Disaster? Who has maintained power since the original end of the world?"

I blinked.

The answer was so clear it was unclear how I'd never caught it before. It was entirely possible that the Genetic Engineering Guild had released The Great Disaster.

Abner saw the answer in my eyes. "Xavi has told us the mission you think you're on. We know you seek Lynk. We know you think she is the Unnamed. We know you think she is a Genetic Terrorist seeking to destroy the Republic, but considering everything you've been trained to know about politics, manipulation, and world building, who do you think the Genetic Terrorists are now? Who is this Unnamed you seek?"

There was a buzzing in my ears, that rare feeling that something was on the tip of my tongue but refused to form a thought yet.

Mother's smile was a thumbnail moon. Such a slight sliver, yet always bright enough to light up a crowd. I was proud of her then, the way she stood next to Father as he raised his hand to the crowd. I had heard it said that Paramonos Petrakis always looked his best with Zosime Petrakis at his side, but watching the stage only made the statement feel fundamentally disrespectful. Mother was more than the wife of a Chancellor, and all of her contributions to Humanity proved it. For the eight years I'd been alive, I'd watched the speeches she gave and felt inspired.

Part of me wondered why Mother had never run for Chancellor. She'd be a shoo-in if Father ever decided to step down. The other part of me knew that Grandfather would never allow it. He had this subtle belief that a Petrakis by birth was meant to govern, and for as advanced as our society was, the way the government ended up working felt archaic.

Mother stood up to the podium and readied her spine to hold up the weight of her speech. "Our ancestors had foresight in some ways," she began her speech. "Perhaps not in the genetic sense Humanity needed, but in the broader sense. These turbine forests still serve their purpose, even today. Our ancestor's reliance on fossil fuels was nearly ended all because a few brave Politicians were unafraid. Unafraid of the lobbyists who controlled the purse strings. Unafraid of change. Unafraid of doing what was right for the world at the cost to their own personal comfort. They began to right wrongs they'd inflicted on the earth in order to keep it a viable habitat for future generations. When it boils down to it, humans always end up choosing Humanity over the self, and when it really matters, Humanity always chooses to save the world in inventive and self-sacrificing ways."

Behind Mother stood a tree-turbine, painted tie-dyed with snap-pea paneled leaves twirling in the soft breeze. Before The Great Disaster, they used to have competitions for engineers to create trees that were functional yet beautiful. The forest in the Capital was breathtaking, growing tree by tree throughout the last thousand or so years with each competition. By now, the new trees weren't needed. By now, each new tree was slightly overkill. By now, it was excessive.

But it was a tradition started long ago.

After The Great Disaster, the Capital's forest began with Leo Solano as an homage to his dead mother. In fact the tree standing behind Mother had been transplanted from his hometown and restructured into the grid of the Capital. Generations later, the popularity of the competition slowed until Doctor Nicholas saw potential to inspire. He said something as little as inventing a tree-turbine was an exercise in inventing more beyond the realm of what we knew. Mother especially loved the tradition, insisting on giving the opening speech every year the way Leo Solano's mother had before she'd died.

"This year's competition," Mother continued, "should remind us that with the right mindset, anything is possible. When we forego greed for the better good, we can build a better world for each other."

Uncle Ty clapped next to me. "Zosime is on fire right now," he whispered. I nodded. The way Mother spoke could inspire the hopeless, the driftless, the lost.

"She honors the science that led us here and the science that will lead us beyond. Mother believes in the sacrifice scientific discovery requires in order to preserve Humanity before self." These were Father's words, but I tried them on like too-big shoes. They felt clunky coming out of my mouth. I looked up and noticed the wrinkles around Uncle Ty's eyes furrowing. There was water flooding the corners, threatening to fall. "Uncle Ty?" I asked.

"Niko believed in the same thing," he whispered, turning his face away so I couldn't see a twitter of pain lightning across his face. The crowd applauded as Father stepped up to the podium, and Uncle Ty's expression hardened so that even I wasn't sure if I'd seen or heard anything at all.

Abner reached for the tablet and pulled up a screen. "What might happen if the G.E.G. felt it was losing its grip on the Republic?"

I swallowed again. Suddenly, I was thirsty. I reached for my pack and sucked down a few gulps from the water bladder. The answer was so clear it ached in my toes. A small population was easier to maintain, and a culling would generate enough fear to bring people back into the fold while cutting out any debate on the relevancy of the G.E.G. The G.E.G. could try to reduce the population again to make it manageable, then blame it on genetic deformities to maintain their role.

"What's the best way to spread a new disease? To discover traits to target? To disperse a new plague that only targets those they want to silence?" Abner added.

I let the questions build, knowing that they would erupt in a slew of answers soon enough. Seconds would pass and bring everything into focus.

Horror took root in my heart as one answer became clear. I didn't want it to be possible. I didn't want it to be true. But how could I deny the possibility that my nano-bots were the perfect vessel for such a plan?

"I'm so sorry, but this day is going to get worse before it gets better," Abner said. "Yesterday, I loaded the most recent news-vids. I think you'll be surprised at how the world sees you since you left the Capital."

Abner moved his finger along the video. A Caster in a teal dress stood at a podium, and when he pressed play, her voice quivered through the screen. "It has been confirmed. Manipulator Tycho Tripoli has been working in conjunction with Anicetus Petrakis, the late-Chancellor's first-born son. The Militia has issued warrants for both arrests after the following footage was leaked."

The screen cut to Uncle Ty singing by the lake with Abner and Ollie, then to me talking to Celeste and Polo by the lake. How those images were captured was beyond me, but I felt my stomach turn. The images bled back into the Caster's face. "Interim Chancellor Tantalos has yet to comment on the unfolding events, though it has been confirmed that her genetic half-sister, a pardoned Genetic Terrorist, has officially fled the Republic with Tycho Tripoli. Though the Tantalos Administration has been tight-lipped, Zosimos Petrakis has issued a statement this morning."

The screen cut to Mos. He wore a sturdy suit and stood

between Grandfather and Mother. Mother's face, placid and serene, gave nothing away. It never did. They were the picture of solidarity, the family I'd always known, and I waited for them to shoot the rumors down. Behind Mos, Eudocia stood on the stage with her hands folded, mimicking Mother's regal pose.

What absurd allegations. Grandfather would never stand to let them tear everything we'd worked towards down.

Mos smiled a sad smile into the cameras. "Growing up, I'd heard rumors of my brother's unconventional conception. I'd heard rumors that his genetic-mother was a Terrorist. But it wasn't until after my father's death that I was able to discover the great lengths his administration went to make truth seem like rumors. Growing up, I always thought I understood my brother's heart. He always appeared stoic, faithful, loyal to the cause. This past year, however, I've watched him teeter on the edge of madness. I've watched him jump off the ledge completely, only to find out that Anicetus Petrakis is an imposter. He was an unsanctioned child, a spy planted right in the heart of the Republic."

My lips moved, opening then closing like a guppy pulled from the water, and my heart grew dizzy. How could Mos say such things? How could Mother and Grandfather stand next to him, propping him up with the lies?

"I wish it weren't so," Mos continued. "But, as my grandfather often says, we cannot deny facts. My future partner, Eudocia Vallis, a New Wave like my brother, discovered discrepancies in the data streaming from Anicetus' nano-bots and, upon digging deeper, yesterday she finally unveiled my brother's treachery. The very nano-bots that led to the small anarchies will be the Republic's undoing if we do not act quickly. As part of a long played Terrorist plot, Anicetus set them on a timer that will release a plague greater than The Great Disaster this coming Monday. The worst part is that nearly every Citizen still has nano-bots in their systems. By our estimations, six-eighths of the Citizens of the Republic will be infected. Yet we are unsure if Anicetus has given even more of his nano-bots without the Genetic Engineering Guild's knowledge. It is possible that every single Citizen has the potential for death blossoming inside of them."

The buzzing in my ears grew louder. It couldn't be. He couldn't be saying this.

"Pause, Citizens. Be still. We are not lost. As we speak, an anti-bot serum is being transported to every Colony. Eudocia has been able to alter the nano-bot directives with a new anti-bot serum that promises to rid every Citizen of the plagues resting in their bodies. For the sake of your well being, the G.E.G. encourages you to go to the nearest hospital and request the serum.

"As for my family, though members have acted atrociously, I stand here before you as a sign of atonement. I vow before you to put an end to this madness. The Terrorists remain our genetic enemies rather than our genetic allies, and I encourage you to support me in the campaign against Absolution. As Patriots, we must unite."

Abner turned the screen off before the cheers rang from the crowd. He set the tablet back down and gave me a moment to feel numb.

"Let's climb one," Mos said.

I knew we shouldn't do it, but when Mos got that smirk, he was irresistible. The turbine-forest grew thick around us. Most barely worked, some fell into disrepair because they were no longer needed in the way they used to be. Our controlled population didn't demand the energy output the world did before The Great Disaster, and with competitions making even more efficient models every year, the ancient ones were left to time.

It was rare that we got away from security, that we were able to sneak away when a crowd was amuck, and it was rare that we just got to be boys. We would get two months in the Victory Gardens for this escape, but it would be worth it. My palms itched to climb as much as Mos' did, and suddenly I realized that this might be my last chance to ever beat him at something so physical. He was already about to overtake me in height, and I think we both secretly looked forward to the day he was naturally better than me at something.

"I call the asparagus tree!" I yelled, racing to the trunk of a tree littered in a collage of spray-painted asparagus. It was a strange decoration, and whoever Madame Lucas was had an odd sense of humor.

"Then I call this orangey one," Mos said. His tree was layered with what looked like rocks in several warm colors layered on top of each other. It looked like desert formations in reds and oranges and browns creating a line into the sky. The trunk had the same Madame Lucas marker as the tree Mos had chosen, and I wondered how the same artist won the competition two years in a row. It wasn't known to happen often—that an artist and an engineer could win back to back years. I also recognized the ancient nature of the broken turbines. The paint wasn't peeling and the branches weren't rusty, but only a handful of leaves moved on both trees, creaking in the wind.

Mos reached up to grab a limb, and I noticed how he still needed to grow into his hands. If they were any indicator, my brother was about to be a giant.

He didn't wait for a count off, but neither did I. We became monkeys swinging on art. We became speed and laughter and lightness in a world that was quickly becoming, for us, slow and sad and heavy.

It was an evenly matched, no-one-yet-everyone-won kind of moment. We sat on metallic branches that faced each other, me surrounded by asparagus spears and he surrounding by painted sand. Our long legs dangled into the air as we rested our backs against the sliver of trunk, and we felt the heat of metal thrum against our backs through our thin shirts.

Not even out of breath, we laughed.

Then I looked down on the branch I sat on. There were words etched into the metal. My laughter fell from my throat and landed on the poem.

"Look what I found," I said. "There's a poem here!"

"An odd place for a poem," he replied. "Read it."

I cleared my throat, struck by the hidden stories on top of a tree no one would ever think to climb in the middle of a dying forest no one would ever think to visit.

An unborn story.

"Dry is the desert that waits for the rain.

Lonely is the heart that attempts the same.

I still watch the skies for the stars and

Satellites to collide.

And I imagine their explosions to mirror my own.

I write my secrets here,

Find them in the leaves.

Truths hidden in the lies,

As we all succumb to Greatness,

One way or another."

I looked away from the poem and stuttered on the lines in my mind. Across from me, Mos frowned as he looked down at his own branch. His eyes narrowed and his breathing grew heavy. "What's genematch.com?"

"I don't know," I said.

"Mine doesn't have a poem, but a message." Mos looked troubled, and I prompted him to read it. "It says, Confirmed: The Genetic Engineering Guild was not born out of The Great Disaster but before it. Solano Industries ran genematch.com and attempted to guide genetic purity prior to The Great Disaster before the government shut them down. They created the plague to foster genetic fear and gain control. I left the documents in the panel."

I laughed. "Mos. It's a joke, obviously," I said, but Mos had already begun to climb down the tree to the base of the trunk. He yanked open the panel that led to the grid before I could reach him. He reached in.

Part of me sucked in fear, wondering if there were actually documents proving such a ridiculous lie. Part of me felt vindicated when Mos withdrew his empty hand. It should have made it easy to quell my little brother's fears on our way back to the gathering.

"But what do we really know about a past that is so far gone?" Mos asked undeterred. "It could be possible, couldn't it?"

"And it could also be possible that it was just some sick, cruel

joke, written in the knowledge that no one would ever think to climb that high to read it. A work of fiction hidden in a strange place. That could also be possible, couldn't it?"

"Grandfather wins again," Mos kicked a blue trunk as we passed it. His shoe made the metal sing.

"What?"

"He taught us to always disagree. Even if we want to agree with each other, we always err on the side of distrusting agreement."

I grinned and rubbed his head with my knuckles. We could hear the party going in the distance. The Flaming Flamingos were playing their newest hit, Genetic Monster, and rather than answer, I started singing along.

"Don't do that," Mos interrupted.

"What?"

"Act like it's normal to always be pitted against each other. Can't we, for once, be on the same side of possibility?"

"I wish we had more time. I wish I could tell you this story slowly so that you can digest it while you eat every word. But there is no time," Abner said. I looked into his eyes, found the cracks in the marble that made me think of a field of clovers.

Did Father see this coming? When he spoke about the other side of greatness that day in the desert, I'd always assumed he meant someone like Hucksley or Abner or Ollie, growing up with a different set of values and beliefs, being taught to lead her people. I never thought the other side of my coin would be my very own brother.

Mos called for the Patriots to unite. Could he possibly be loyal to a group of people who killed our father? Or was that why Father was killed? Because he wouldn't let Grandfather turn his sons against each other?

The worst part was that I couldn't be sure. Did Mos believe what he was saying because Grandfather manipulated him into believing it, or was this always the plan? Did my own brother set out to destroy me because he thought it was the best thing for the

Republic or because he wanted power? What better way to prove stoicism than by turning on your own brother for the sake of Humanity?

In the end, I didn't know if I could blame Mos, but I knew without uncertainty that I could always blame Grandfather. He never liked what I represented. I was Father's act of rebellion while Mos was a sanctioned child. We both had individual lessons with Grandfather every week. While Grandfather whispered in my ear one thing, I knew he was whispering in Mos' ear something else entirely.

My vision blurred, and I tried to keep Abner's face in focus. I blinked, wanting to escape behind closed lids.

"Abner," Hucksley said from behind us. "You started without us?"

I stood and walked towards the water. It wasn't fair that it could be so calm, so pristine. I started looking for imperfect trees, crooked rocks, ripples in the water. I turned to look at the three of them, but their faces blurred.

Hucksley limped towards me. "It's okay, Anicetus," she whispered. It was the first time she'd said my name, and I opened my heart to it. There was understanding in her abyss deep eyes, and they swallowed me whole.

Was it possible she'd always been telling the truth?

It was.

Anything was.

Shivers rattled through my body. I vibrated from the rage and the hurt of it all.

"Step away from the volcano," Ollie warned, but Hucksley reached out and took my hands in hers, anyways. She rubbed them, slowing the vibrations in my veins. Then the dam broke on my laughter, explosions caught in my throat rocketing out.

Rewound.
Pressed play.
Shook hands.
Sat down.

251

I saw my father torn apart. The dozen children blown to smithereens. A perfectly good concert ruined, a perfectly good song stolen, a perfectly good speech destroyed.

The laughter didn't push Hucksley back. Here was the reaction she'd been poking for since she met me, and I could see it frightened her. For the first time, uncertainty flooded her eyes. Those eyes. They tornadoed between us, and I finally *saw* her. It was like I knew her as well as my own fingerprint, the intricacies of how her brain ticked, the thing that tethered her to the world around her. She was me, just as fixed on her path as I was. By nature of who she was, her choices were never about her. Vagabond or not, she had never been free.

Kids sang.
Father grinned.
Blue insignia.
Should have been red.
But it was blue.
On the collar.
Every child wore the blue insignia.

"You wanted me to react?" I asked. "You wanted me to be human?"

The tears burned hot in the back of my throat, gargling my words. I hadn't let them go since I was ten. My head felt like a balloon, light and dizzy, as the tension pulled me above myself.

"Be human," she said. "You're allowed."

I shook my head, but I felt my knees buckle. Grandfather had been playing me the entire time. He was up to something so major, so earth shattering, so insane, and I walked right into it. How long had he been planning it? Since I was born? Since before?

"They are turning me into the greatest villain Humanity has ever seen," I choked out.

Then it hit me. Perhaps Grandfather even thought I'd understand his motives. What if he even thought I'd agree with them? He'd been training me to think for the good of the whole my entire life. Maybe he'd always intended for me to recognize my new role and accept it. It wouldn't be beyond him to expect me to believe in how much my sacrifice would help Humanity's reboot and save the government—save my Republic. If he were here, that's what he'd be whispering in my ear. *"The G.E.G. needs to maintain relevancy. Humanity before self, Anicetus."*

It was the new truth within that possibility. This had always been his plan. He intended to arrest me before my departure. The only crime I'd committed against him was existing as a perfect blemish on his perfect world, but he intended for me to pay for larger crimes that did not belong to me.

I landed in the sand, my knees digging into the dirt. I wanted to be swallowed by the earth. I wanted to stop fighting.

Explosion.
Smoke.
Fire.
Gone.
Rewound.

Rewind.
Reboot.

Grandfather wanted to start the world over again. Those of my generation who survived would walk the streets of Lucas and Leo Solano's world, trying to pick up the pieces of a dying world. We would have no choice but to live every day with the cry of Humanity on our lips. Every action would be tied to preservation. Every love would be chained to a strict, controlled Propriety. Our children would become the new First-Fives. Our children's children would continue to sculpt whatever world survived.

We were doomed to relive our ancestral past, and there was nothing I could do to stop it.

Hucksley kneeled in front of me and pulled me into her. Her hug reminded me of home. Hints of pine, stains of sunlight. There was compassion there, a tethered understanding.

Normally, there's a competitive nature to empathy. It's as if we think that, in order to understand how someone feels, we have to compare their tragedies to our own. We bring them up at just the right time in an attempt to tell the person we are comforting that they are not alone. However, it always backfires, making the existence of absolute empathy a myth. In a series of dueling tragedies, each empathizer tries to one up the other with who has it the worst. It's the narcissistic side of empathy, the side no one likes to admit exists.

With Hucksley, this side did not exist. She just held me together in her arms, like she could take on my pain as her own. She used no words, offered no platitudes, gave no anecdotes, pilfered no clichés, though I knew she'd been through plenty in her short life.

And I released a flood of tears into her neck. I was a volcano alright, erupting into a new understanding of my old world. I'd never get it back, and I'd never even be allowed to set foot in it again.

Everything was lost to me, but for good this time.

CHAPTER TEN

"I won't insult your intelligence if you don't insult mine," Instructor Aeschylus said.

"Fine. I got off Propriety for just a second. Call it an experiment I'll never try again."

"You know what they say about the word never?"

I groaned. *"Can we just get back to the simulation?"*

"Only after you tell me how you reacted around your future partner."

I glared. *"Do you hound her like you do me?"* It was a sore spot. Last week, I discovered he volunteered to be her thesis mentor as well. We were both about to stumble into thesis year, and Instructor Aeschylus was the most sought after mentor. It was silly but I hated the idea of sharing him with her.

"Anicetus," he warned.

I stared at the tablet. I considered picking it up and ignoring the old man's prodding. *"I felt nothing,"* I finally admitted. *"There's something off about her. I can't pinpoint it, but I think her nurturing was miscalculated. She's cold when she should be warm. Calculating when she should be—"*

"—human?" Instructor Aeschylus asked. *"Do you know who*

you just described?"

Was he implying that I was just like Eudocia? I wasn't a robot like her. "But I did feel something. For a different girl, I felt the chemicals bubbling up inside until I was so uncomfortable I could have burst."

Instructor Aeschylus grinned. "But you did burst, my boy."

I kept my face steady. He couldn't have known.

"I know." He read my unreadable expression.

I closed my eyes. I remembered the way Phoibe's closeness felt. The way my hair on my arms reached out to touch hers.

How could he know about her secret visit?

Before she left for her tour of duty, she came to me again. She snuck right into the Capital and said we could always enact the Choice and forego children together, but I couldn't turn my back on a partnering suggestion from the G.E.G. It was the surest way to destroy my future as a Politician. I told her we both needed to be true to our stoic duty as Citizens, but I was really just protecting her. She would have been dead within the week had we even attempted it. Grandfather never would have allowed it, but even if he would have, I wasn't sure if it'd be right. No matter how my body had reacted to her, there was something off in how my heart felt in relation to her.

Maybe I wasn't as human as I hoped I was.

I'd heard she was doing well.

Instructor Aeschylus moved to where I sat at the table in the lab. Something about how he shuffled his feet looked sluggish, almost sickly. I'd been so caught up in my own worries that I hadn't really considered what his age and deterioration meant. He handed me the tablet. He was letting me off the hook. He could have turned us in, ruined her future, gotten her rehabilitated like the story Uncle Ty once told me about a girl named Aspasia. Instead, Instructor Aeschylus moved along. "What happened when the polar bear populations dwindled a couple thousand years ago?"

I tried not to smile. "They began mating with grizzly bears, creating a new species altogether."

"Are they still bears?"

"Of course, but it took geneticists years to re-cultivate the original species. Many viewed the hybrids as abominations."

Instructor Aeschylus sat back in his chair and twirled his beard in his fingers. "I'm going to ask a question. I want you to answer it without thinking."

"Okay."

"Do you think they've already started experimenting with Transgenics?"

"Yes."

"Why do you say this?"

"I doubt the G.E.G. would see the harm in experimenting with animals for now."

Instructor Aeschylus nodded. "What about on humans?"

"They could, but I don't think they'll allow it yet. It's too risky, morally. I think they will bide their time, find the right moment to get the Republic used the idea, and forge forward into a new future. They always do. Look at me..."

The sun began to set over the water, and Bixby tugged at my pinky with her teeth. Suddenly, I knew what real loyalty was. It existed in this dog, this little, fearless beast that lived by a simple yet powerful rule. Love those who love you back.

"You're all I have left," I said, grabbing a leaf from the ground. I gave it a slight toss and Bixby tried to catch it with her mouth.

Did the world know that within a week—that with every setting of the sun that approached their days—they were one step closer to the culling that awaited them? How many people would the G.E.G. decide needed to go in order to cleanse Humanity? How many people needed to stop existing to justify their existence? And how did I stop it?

I couldn't.

Mos' speech held intel below the surface. This anti-bot serum they were claiming to give was just one way to get as many Citizens to take the nano-bots as possible, not an anti-bot serum. People weren't getting the cure but a possible death sentence.

They were afraid enough to trust the G.E.G., and telling people they needed the cure gave the G.E.G. the broadest reach in deciding who stayed and who went. Every death that happened, they would tell themselves that it was because of inferior genetics. They would say they are right to do everything in their power to keep their hands on the wheel of Humanity. Rather than fade into irrelevancy, they would maintain the world they trusted in. And even if I recorded a vid, hacked into the system, and told my side, no one would listen. The Republic had already successfully made me out to be the most infamous criminal of mass destruction.

How helpless I felt, knowing that even I, with all my brilliance, never saw any of this coming.

At the edge of the trees, towards my left, I saw Hucksley limping my way with Ollie. I knew that they carried more news, that more of the worst was yet to come.

Ollie bent down as Bixby ran towards him. He scooped down to pick the pup up and laughed. Hucksley sat down next to me, and hooked her arm through mine. She leaned her forehead on my shoulder, and something about the unnatural situation felt natural. I was holding onto her presence like a lifeline. How was it possible within a couple of days, to need someone so fully?

I was drowning. She was drowning with me. There was comfort in that.

"I stole Bixby from your partner's lab," she admitted. "Little Miss Perfection has a sick obsession with testing her research on Jack Russells."

I let each news drop into an already full bucket of secrets. I felt calm about it, like nothing else could surprise me anymore.

"We need your help," she whispered.

"I'm not sure what good I can do," I said. "I'm still not sure what any of us can do."

"Before your nano-bots were spread, Eudocia intercepted your research. During production, she hacked into them and put her own twist on things. The nano-bots were redesigned before they were spread. As a side effect, the anti-bot serum turned off the tracking devices, but did not purge the nano-bots from our systems. Everyone who took them still has the plague swimming inside of them, waiting to be activated by the timer G.E.G. set.

"What's more? I have a feeling she knows about the anti-bot serum you gave us and how ineffective it was. Any future dissenter can die at her command once she figures out how to reprogram the trackers in us to work again and redistributes new ones to what's left of the population. With trackers intact, she'll be able to individually target someone even if their genetics do not warrant it. It's insanity. Eudocia created this self-contained plague, and, based on the data you've collected from your research, she created a long list of Citizens ripe for the culling. Using her broad knowledge, her incurable brilliance, and her perfect brain, she created a plague that will target the mutations *she* deemed invaluable. Essentially, one girl has been left to decide who survives and who does not.

"The plague will act in stages. There are different strands meant to stagger the death toll because the longer the plague lasts, the more fear it will incite. The more terrified the Citizens are, the more likely they will be to open their arms back up to the G.E.G. for salvation."

I closed my eyes. The nano-bots were inside of me. I had a feeling they weren't inside of Hucksley, Ollie, or Abner. I would have noticed the abnormal genetic strands in the research. Was that why Celeste hadn't let me give them the nano-bots by the lake?

I knew I was safe until Eudocia figured out how to reprogram the trackers again, but I would need to figure out how to get the nano-bots out of my system for good soon.

Hucksley nodded to the dog Ollie held. His massive mountain hands enveloped the little pup as he sat down on the other side of Hucksley.

"Inside of Bixby," Ollie said, "is a second strand of the plague. We think it is meant to specifically target those of us who underwent Transgenic Therapy—that the G.E.G. became terrified of the reality of Transgenics on the human genome and wants to destroy the experiment. We think the Republic is redistributing this

---

259

new strand of the plague along with trackers under the guise of this ultimate cure. Bixby is about to enter her final days. The truth, pure and simple, is that the Vagabonds need you, and Bixby can help."

"How?"

"First, you need to hack back into the nano-bots that already exist. Reprogram them."

"But I can't hack into the server long enough to do that without them finding out where we are and shutting me down."

"That's why you work remotely. You'll have to reprogram them on an individual level. The database framework is in the tablet. If you take a blood sample and reprogram those nano-bots, then re-inject them into someone's system to kill the other nano-bots, then you can save a life one at a time.

"You can take a sample of your own blood since you've taken the nano-bots," Hucksley said. I felt the sting of betrayal again at the reminder. Not only did Mos want me to be the scapegoat, but he wanted me dead one way or the other.

Ollie continued, "You can take as many samples as you need. If you take sample of your blood and you accidentally release the plague inside of them while they are out of you, it won't trigger it inside of you. Then, once you figure out the code, you can hack into everyone's nano-bots at the Vault."

"I don't have a—"

Hucksley grabbed my hand and placed a thumb-sized reader. All I had to do was put a drop of blood on it and connect it to the tablet.

"And then what?" My heart yanked itself into my toes. "How do I do that out here, without access to the labs."

"All you need is a tablet and that brain of yours," Hucksley said. The faith she had in me made my joints cringe. "After you figure out the plague inside of you, you can figure out the new plague inside of Bixby. Perhaps we can save Citizens as we find them."

The impossibility of it all weighed down on me. Did they really expect me to save Humanity one person at a time? It was too sublimely large to even fathom.

Hucksley didn't let me dwell on that thought too long. "You can do this. It's what you were made for."

I tugged one of the earphones out so I could hear him repeat the question. The nano-bot feed poured out of my mini-tablet in my pocket as we worked in the Victory Garden. I was too excited not to multi-task.

"How many Citizens do you have?" Mos asked.

"So far? Three-fifths of the population has agreed to take the nano-bots," I said, plucking a cluster of grapes from the vine. They were bulbous, bright green universes ready to explode on the tongue.

"And the Terrorists?" Mos popped a grape in his mouth before putting the cluster in the basket.

"Don't let Agapetos see you again," I warned, glancing over at the Garden Ward. He was bent over a bed of carrots a few patches down.

"What will he do? Stare me to death?" Mos took another grape and sliced it between his teeth so I could see all the juices burst out. "How many Terrorists?"

I frowned. "I'm not sure how many are actually in their population, but we have about six hundred who have consented and nearly two hundred who were given nano-bots unbeknownst to them. It's enough to trace their genetic lines back. By the end of the year, I think I'll have about two thousand Terrorists who have taken them."

Mos stared down at his basket. "I didn't realize there were that many out there. I always assumed it was just a couple hundred. Why do you think the Militia downplays the numbers?"

"Probably so we don't over-fear them."

"Over-fear?"

The grapes were flappy on their stems as they clumped in my basket. I stared at them for a second and thought about how much to explain further. "What would be the point of being too afraid of them? In a way, the Militia wants to keep us safe, not just in body, but in mind. By hiding how many Terrorists actually exist, they keep us calm. We know that there is a threat to be concerned about—a threat to fight, but we don't let that threat dominate our every thought."

I moved away from the vine and looked down the line of T-posts holding up the heads of grapes. I imagined standing still and counting every orb, but there were so many they blurred in my vision.

Mos stood up with me. "So they keep us just afraid enough to never forget, but not too afraid so we aren't distracted from pursuing perfection?"

"Exactly."

I pricked my finger and let the blood bubble on the reader before inserting it into the tablet. I entered the database and heard the familiar song. I could pick out the colors, the vibrations, the letters of the data, but I couldn't tell where the plague existed inside the nano-bots.

I closed my eyes and remembered my research. I saw the thousands upon thousands of streams dumping data from four-fifths of the Republic's population. Then there were the couple thousand Vagabonds in the system. All these people with a ticking bomb seething through their systems.

I examined my readings. I could pick apart the data, but no matter what codes I punched in, I couldn't regain control of the nano-bots. I couldn't reprogram them.

Hours rose and set on the hands of time.

Abner built a fire.

I tried a new code.

Ollie trapped a fowl.

I pricked my finger again.

Hucksley plucked the feathers.

I bubbled blood onto the reader.

Abner roasted the carcass over the coals.

I failed at hacking the code.

All three of them settled in to rest by the fire.

I spent the night trying to undo the harm I'd done. Unknowingly, I had unleashed this on the world. If I had never created the nano-bots, perhaps I'd be on my Celebrity Tour by now. I tried to imagine that world, where I rode the rails, giving my gifts to the Republic. The opulence of the train, the extravagance of the honor.

That life would never happen.

I needed to figure out the code. I needed to right the wrongs I'd done, though none of my wrongs were forgivable. I'd been a plague on this world, a stain on Humanity, though I'd only ever intended to do right by it.

The other three slept, Bixby curled up next to Abner in his sleeping bag. The dog, my dog, had a similar plague inside of her, too. It was strange how just looking at her made me want to push harder through the night.

Knowing Eudocia, *Prometheus' Fire* was probably more efficient than the original plague she'd created. Eudocia was brilliant at layering discovery on top of discovery, and I wondered how I'd outsmart a person capable of being too clever to outsmart.

I entered another code. Another code. Another code.

I kept track of the algorithms in my head. Counted them up in my computer-esque brain, twelve numbers, in every combination possible staring with all zeros. My fingers moved like wind across the number pad, never letting them rest. I had a system in my head, but the code might take weeks to hack. I only had days.

Every once in a while, the plague would burst in the reader. I'd clear it out with the saline solution, praying that I didn't run out of the cleanser before I figured the code out. Then I'd prick my finger again, let the blood bubble up on my finger, let it drip, drip, drip onto the reader, and try again.

Dawn turned towards morning. Morning turned towards noon. The sun rose high above my head. At times, they put food into my hand. Abner thumbed a fish in a nearby creek, and protein felt good going down my throat.

But they mostly left me alone and let my fingers type away.

"Take a break, New Wave," Hucksley said. Her shadow moved

over me, and I looked up into those eyes. Her entire world rested in my hands, and I couldn't let my fingers stop moving.

"I can't."

"You must. You'll give yourself an aneurysm."

The words brought tears to the corner of my eyes. I thought of all the times Mos said that very thing. I thought of all the times I was told not to cry, and suddenly I had to let it all out of the crevices of my soul. What did Mos do? Couldn't he see how wrong this path was? I thought I knew him. I thought he knew me. What could turn him into this mass murderer?

"Can I ask you a question?" I asked.

"Does that count as the question?" she replied.

The banter tugged at elbows, made me twitch in memory of my brother. "You told me that your heart belonged to someone. May I ask who?"

She smiled. "Isn't it obvious by now?"

"Ollie?"

"Stars, no! My heart belongs to me," she said. "And for as long as there's a new world to build, I'll never be able to give it to someone else."

The way she stood there with one hand on her stomach and the other on her hip, as if she was holding in a stark pain, startled me. Something about love hurt her, and I tried to see the world through her eyes. Her mother died giving birth to her, just like me. Hucksley was marked by death, forced to carry it before she even understood it, just like me.

"Go for a swim, okay?" she said. "Sometimes doing something that doesn't require thought lets ideas come. You know this is true."

She was right. I needed to pause and step away. I set the tablet down on the sand and tugged off my shirt, unlaced my boots, and stripped down to the shorts under my pants. I didn't have the heart to blush, or the energy to be embarrassed.

The water called out to me. I walked down to the edge and disturbed the water around me. The sun felt hot on my skin, but the water soothed the burn when I dove in. It filled my ears, muting the sounds of the forest. On my back, I let the above overwhelm my sight. The clouds had burned off, and the sky had become a bright blue, perfect circle, bordered by a ring of trees. The lake's black water was surprisingly deep, and I had no concept of how far it went.

It didn't make sense that my brother would turn his back on me completely. It was all Grandfather, twisting situations to suit his own needs. Mos was smart. He had to have seen through it.

Suddenly, the true enemy became clear. The Unnamed attracted definitions like iron shavings to a magnet. It had a name so full and real. It wasn't Lynk, whoever Lynk now was. It was something so much bigger than the Republic itself. The man who always pitted Mos and me against each other and manipulated every scenario to bring the world to this point.

I couldn't take offense to it. Grandfather was good at what he did. Every new world needed tension, a balance, a fight between beliefs only to solidify that beliefs were worth believing in. I would become the coagulant to whatever world came next, the binding force people rallied against when they divined their version of history as they reclaimed Humanity.

Ollie swam laps towards my left, the same way Mos would have been doing if he was here, and I felt a deep longing, a gaping hole of missing, open up in my heart. I closed my eyes and encountered the bright darkness and buoyancy of water. What if I just stopped floating? What if I just let it all go? Did Humanity deserve to keep going? After all of this, did we earn the right to exist?

The way the sun backlit my lids made me think of Hucksley's eyes, and suddenly I couldn't imagine a world where her eyes didn't exist, where her great-great-grandchildren didn't wear the same expressions she did.

I moved my arms through the water, felt the swish and swirl as it adjusted.

Hucksley, Ollie, and Abner were still hiding something from me. For as major as what I now knew was, they didn't want to tell me the last pieces. What were they hiding?

I heard Ollie's steady strokes through the water. Mos loved to swim the way I loved to climb. He never let his size get in his way, and it turned out his broad shoulders were surprisingly hydrodynamically suited for the water. He'd won race after race, his strength making up for his body type. The moment he hit the water, it became an extension of him.

But me? I liked floating. I liked the weightless feeling that made me forget I existed. But now, I could never forget that I existed. I could never lose myself to the calm. The others had their ties to each other. Me, I'd become drifter—an outsider in every world.

In the water, if I really tried, I could imagine I was at the beach of Lake Solano. Ollie could have just been some long-distance swimmer, pushing himself in long lines along the water. If I really, really tried, I could see Mos racing him, arms broad and wide, cupping the water with each stroke.

This memory made the water feel wrong. This was not supposed to be a normal day. I was not supposed to be swimming and relaxing when plague-ridden nano-bots I had invented threatened to kill so many innocent people. Bile rose to my throat, but there was a peal of memory that jolted my head from the water. I treaded so my face could bob and hover just above the surface.

I watched Abner and Hucksley play with Bixby in the shallow water, trying to teach her to swim. They laughed, like the end of the world was not looming, like they knew I'd figure out the impossible. And perhaps they were right.

"Can we please destroy that picture?" Mos asked.

Mother had it hanging in the family hallway, the one that lead to the bedroom chambers. No one had access to this hall but the four of us, but I could see why it embarrassed Mos. It was the gauntlet of childhood, snapshots of growing pains, a survey of every awkward moment.

"I think you look dapper," I laughed.

"Are you kidding me? Look at that suit! You'd think that for as much as they pay our tailors, they'd have sewn me something that

fit."

I examined the way the grey arms of the jacket fell beyond his fingertips. "Is it their fault that you didn't meet your projected growth that year? You were supposed to fit the suit by the time you needed it for the swearing in."

"I look like a sail boat."

"You sure do, but I'm pretty sure that's the least embarrassing picture of you up there," I taunted.

"No?"

"May I direct you to Exhibit A? Swimming lessons. Week one." I pointed to a frame a few feet down. There I was, mid-cannon ball, while Mos sat on the ledge with his feet in the water, crying. "The way Father tells it? I stayed under a little too long, and you thought I was going to drown. It was the first time you leapt into the water on your own."

"Like I'd let you die on my watch?" Mos asked. "You'd have done the same for me."

"Debatable." I punched him on the arm. "Come on. We're going to be late for dinner."

I pulled up the database and tugged up the framework. My fingers hovered, hoping I was right, not yet ready to find out if I was wrong. Mos wouldn't have wanted me to die, and he'd made sure I had the nano-bots in my system.

We were cut from the same choreographed cloth, and he had laid the clues for me to figure out from the very start. Why did Mos make me take the nano-bots? Why did he make me encrypt them with a secret code—one that he didn't really make an effort to remember? Mos was plenty good at memory, but he usually needed a few readings of a strand of numbers that long.

He made sure I had nano-bots to work with. He gave me a preplanned set of numbers. He wanted *me* to remember it more than him. He wanted me to be able to save myself when the time came.

At least I hoped he did.

I pulled up the code box and entered: 0-8-9-7-3-0-0-4-3-2-1-2.

A new stream of data wove its way onto the screen. The hidden came out of hiding.

"I did it," I whispered. "I did it!" I yelled to Abner and Hucksley by the beach.

The knowledge that Mos wanted to protect me made me hope for the first time in a long time. The entire world was going to hell, drowning in a fire of lies, but one thing had remained constant. One person had remained an ally, meaning there was a bigger game at play. What was Mos attempting? Why was Mos catering to Grandfather's plan?

Abner and Hucksley rushed towards me, and hovered over my shoulder to watch me start hacking in a new code to turn off the detonations, but I was still missing an element.

Then it dawned on me. "Do we know the exact time they plan to initiate it?"

"Celeste and Xavi were trying to find out from the Council of Manipulation," Hucksley said. "But according to that news-vid, they fled the Colonies. I don't know if they got it before they left, but we know it'll happen Monday."

I laughed. Mos gave me an exact day with his speech, at least. But I needed the exact hour.

"Do we know how to get ahold of Celeste or Uncle Ty?" I asked.

Abner nodded. "They are at the Vault."

I stood up, and rushed towards my pack. I shoved the tablet into it and hoisted it on my back. "We need to go. Now."

Hucksley frowned. "I don't understand."

"No matter what I do, unless I know the exact time, I can't pinpoint the detonation. If I can't pinpoint it exactly, I risk setting the nano-bots off instead of rendering them useless. Let's hope Uncle Ty or Celeste got the intel before they escaped."

"What if your genetic-mother hadn't given you up?" Mos asked. "Do you think we would have found a way towards each other?"

I shook my head no. Father had 39 genetic children. I'd never been able to pick out one from the crowd when we'd campaigned.

Mainly because crowds were too large, and I spent most of my time blurring their faces in my peripherals. I wondered if I really tried, if I'd be able to see a face with familiar features. I was lucky to have Mos, to have a brother I knew so well, but I had a feeling that if we hadn't grown up next to each other, I wouldn't think twice if I passed him on the street.

"I know what you're thinking. You're thinking, if we haven't been able to figure out who our other 37 brothers and sisters are by now, then how would we find each other?" Mos accused.

"I didn't say anything. Don't get upset."

Mos dug his fingers into the dirt. We got caught up on the roof again, and Mother was furious. Ten extra days in the Victory Gardens. The gossip vids were loving the punishment. I'd seen vid after vid of us, dirty faced and tired.

"Did you know that Mother had four children before me?"

I nodded. Father and Mother's partnership was strange in that Father and Mother started raising a family during their Celebrity Tours. Father was partnered with a woman who'd already begun hers. Mother was four years older, and half-way through with her tour when they had their Commitment Ceremony.

"The worst part was the three after me," Mos admitted.

It was for me, too. The G.E.G. allowed Mother to return to the Capital during her pregnancies rather than stay with the intended parents. As toddlers, we watched Mother grow large with child. Then one day, it'd be over. We never even got to see them.

"Do you think we would have had an easier life if we were one of them instead of one of us? Why was I the one she kept?"

I sat back on my heels. My fingers were raw from the weeds I'd been pulling, but I could tell they weren't as raw as Mos' heart. Grandfather had been on him all week, more so than on me for once, and I knew the feeling well. I used to dream about living a life that was not my own, but I eventually figured out that it only made it harder to accept the life I'd actually been given. Besides, alternatives wouldn't have been any easier. Everyone, everywhere was unhappy with the lot in life they'd drawn. The important thing was to find the pleasant things within each piece of the life-pie we *were given.*

So I took a handful of dirt and threw it in Mos' face.

"What was that for?"

I threw another and laughed.

The vids that day would show us being kids, tearing up a plot of garden, playing war by throwing peppers at each other until the Garden Ward stopped us for a lecture on respecting the commons.

We didn't get into the water, but we wandered alongside it. The thin river bloomed along the greens of the forest, carrying melted snow from the past winter, warming the liquid as it tumbled against the rocks. The sky grew dark faster than we wanted it to, but Hucksley kept us going. The moon came out, big-faced and hopeful through the cut in the sky the river made. Abner said a bridge went over it within a day's hike, and the four of us pushed Hucksley to her limits. Even Ollie let us take turns helping her along. When she slowed too much, we took turns carrying her. When she was stubborn and refused to be carried, we took turns being her crutch.

It was my turn, and Hucksley and I fell behind Abner and Ollie.

"It's funny, huh?" she asked.

"What's funny?"

"It's only been a couple days." Her fingers rested on my hip, and her arm rested along my back under my pack. I was thankful for the shirt, thankful there was something between our skins. "Remember the last time we did this? You nearly kissed me."

I didn't deny it, but I didn't want to talk about it.

"Where's the Vault?" I asked.

"All over," she said. "The thing the Republic never understands is that Vagabonds never stand still. Those silly Territories they tried to give us were just a way to pin us down and control us. It fooled no one, though some of us played along for the show. But not even our hearts can stay in one place for long."

"Not cryptic at all," I said.

"What goes back and forth, forth and back? What can provide shelter, but never stay still?"

I laughed. "Seriously?"

"Xavi worked for years, pulling sympathizers in. The Vault is a series of boxcars that are transported on trains. They are moved to different locomotives weekly, hidden in plain sight. Xavi has people who control the inventory manifestos. The Vault, on paper, is usually basic cargo, crates of peaches, boxes of gloves."

"Clever."

"The Vault isn't a place, but the movement of place. It's hard to pin something down if it's forever moving. Ever since your speech, though, we've been consolidating boxcars in preparation for the plague. Now, all the cars are concentrated on one caboose, picking up anyone who heeds the call. A man named Loud has been spearheading it. We know that you won't be able to pinpoint the nano-bots without individual blood samples, so we may not be able to save everyone, but we can save as many people as we can."

"I want to save them all," I said. I closed my eyes and saw all the Citizens that the G.E.G. would sacrifice. I saw all the Vagabonds who didn't get on the train in time. I saw the way their blood would slow when the heart stopped pumping, the way their blood would grow thick in the veins.

Every life lost was still on me.

"I ordered Claire's death," I whispered.

Hucksley didn't even suck in a gasp of shock. "We know. Xavi suspected it long ago."

I swallowed. "Abner knows I killed his mother?"

"Claire isn't Abner's mother. Lynk is."

I sighed. I'd jumped to the wrong conclusion, and not for the first time lately. Father was right. I had a long way to go before I was wise, before I could see the world for the shape it truly took.

But who was Lynk if it wasn't Claire?

The water rushed beside us, tumultuous against the rocks steady in its way. The same rushing buzzed in my ears, and I felt dizzy again.

"Do they hate me?" I asked. "Do you?"

"Can we really hate you for doing what you thought to be

right?"

"But it wasn't right. Nothing I've ever done has been right."

"You hacked the nano-bots," she offered.

"That I created."

"You try to right what you did wrong. A lesser person would have kept a secret like Claire to his death." She squeezed my hip. "There's forgiveness to be had everywhere. How can we move past what we've all done in the name of saving the world without it?"

There was truth there, but I wasn't sure I could forgive myself.

"I killed that man," I said. "I can still see his eyes, the way they widened when he realized it was over, that he lost. He was surprised when I pulled him, and I didn't hesitate. I didn't pause. I just pushed. The train was going so fast, but I still heard the crack of his skull, the way it splintered when he landed. I'm still not sure I needed to push him. I'm still not sure there wasn't another way. But he is gone, and I am here. And all the small anarchies? All the deaths from the riots? Claire?"

Hucksley paused her feet, and forced me to stop. "Look at me, Anicetus." The way she said my given name tied me to myself. It pulled me into a memory of who I once was, just a boy trying to divine stories from other people's pasts. "You're home now. You were always meant to return to this place. You were always meant to move. Out here, we let ourselves be imperfect. We let ourselves have the room to make mistakes—sometimes tragic mistakes— then we allow ourselves forgiveness. Within that forgiveness, we try to be better than what we were." She shuddered. "Celeste always said that forgiveness was the most important gift you could ever give someone, not your genetics."

She reached up and held my face in the palms of her hands. She wanted to hold me to her truth, wanted me to believe I'd be okay. The moonlight pulled at her hair, but the world only existed in her eyes. "There's this moment in life when everyone encounters the lie that is time. It's a new encounter with self-awareness—to realize that time is a figment of the imagination. Suddenly you realize how little control you have over anything, and it's terrifying.

We stare at the universe and wonder where we fit into it. We imagine ourselves to be important until the moment we realize we are not, at least not in the sense we always thought we were."

She quoted Lucas Solano with a cadence that soothed. I closed my eyes to her voice. I wanted to believe every word she pulled up from the past and shoved into the present. I wanted to drag every ancient word into the future with me, tucked into the corner of my heart.

Something about stepping through truth made me feel connected to a possibility. I was not supposed to mourn everything I'd lost. In its own strange way, this new future promised memories of the life I could have led had my genetic-mother not given me up, even if only in the imagination. Beyond the genetics, I always felt there was something more gripping inside of me that belonged to that life, and Hucksley stirred it up. I became painfully aware that I'd always had this movement burning through my body like molten lava so that even when I stood as still as possible, I felt like I'd never stopped moving.

"Forgive yourself, Anicetus. Learn to forgive others while you're at it. The world is still sweet, but remember, even flies are drawn to honey. Don't let their darkness become the focal point of your life." Her voice hitched. There was a hiccup there, and I opened my eyes to her tears. They caught the moonlight and the secrets she still wanted to share.

"The woman who took me, the woman who altered me? Her name was May, short for Zosime."

I had no more energy to be shocked. I had no more will for denial. Of course, if the Unnamed was my Grandfather, then these experiments belonged to Mother, the head of the Genetic Engineering Guild. I knew Mother's heart, and she never did anything without a greater purpose. Did Mother truly believe she was protecting the next generations with her research? It was highly possible that she didn't think she was in the wrong, that she believed she was saving lives. Mother always did the best she could for Humanity. Perhaps she knew that a culling was coming, that Grandfather had plans that ran so deep into our family's past that there was no steering us away from where we landed, and instead of building a dam to stop the flood, perhaps she saw Transgenic Therapy as a life raft. Perhaps she thought she was doing Humanity a service. Perhaps she thought she was saving us all by sacrificing the sanctity of children.

Then it hit me. "Mos!"

Hucksley nodded. "We think she did the same thing to your half-brother as she did to Ollie."

"Come in," Mother said.

I opened the door to her office and took in the pristine white. Windows lined an entire back wall, and the Capital stretched out behind her desk. She nodded towards the chair, and as I sank into its plush comfort, I found myself dreaming.

Maybe I could be what she was.

Maybe I could be a Geneticist.

Maybe I didn't have to be what Grandfather wanted.

"I hear you are nearly ready for the testing stage," Mother said. There was a pride there, an expectation of greatness that I wanted to live up to.

"Next week I can test it on people, but you know this already. You'll be approving it yourself."

"Anicetus, I am so proud of you. You are going to do amazing things for Humanity, and I am so honored to be your mother."

I grinned. It was such high praise, and it watered my hopes.

"I just ask one thing," she said.

"Anything," I promised.

"Promise me you won't give the nano-bots to Mos, even if he begs you to."

I cocked my head to the side. It was a strange request, and I waited for her to elaborate.

"He deserves better than to be treated like an experiment. He already feels inferior to you, and to examine his DNA for all his flaws might come off as disrespectful. He'll say it won't hurt his feelings, but it may become a source of tension between you two. I doubt either of you would want that. Nor do I think you should take

them. What if Mos gets his hands on you data, sees all the things he is not irrevocably written on paper?"

Out of love for Mos, I never gave him the nano-bots, nor did I take them until he begged.

I never read his genetic makeup.

His size bloomed into my memory, and the way it compared to Ollie made me rage inside. How could Mother do that to her own child?

I looked up and examined the skin of sky, broken by pebbled stars and bursts of clouds. The moon was growing full, fat off of all the time it gobbled up.

"I forgive her," Hucksley whispered. "I shouldn't, but I do. She took a piece of my Humanity from me. She turned me into something other. I didn't think it'd get any worse, but then she stole my freedom. She locked me in a lab. She tested me. She pushed me to my limits until my ears and eyes actually bled. And just when I thought she couldn't be crueler, she got her hands on a sample she was curious about. A week before Celeste could rescue me, your Mother tied me down. She gave me that sample, and forced it to latch on inside of me. I don't know how else she modified it. I don't know if she messed with any other genes. All I know is that I'm forced into a role not of my choosing."

"I heard what they did. Did it take?" Ollie had said the day he found us. *"I'm sorry kid."*

I shook my head. "What samples was Mother waiting for?" I asked, but I knew the answer deep in my gut. How could Mother do something so cruel? I wanted to drift away from the moment, from the thing tethering me to a fact that was becoming my new truth.

As was becoming my new habit, I couldn't hide my fear. Hucksley saw the connections happen in my face. "Forgive them with me. Let them go. Let's move forward, into this."

I pulled back, and placed my hands on her stomach. It was still flat, but how could a piece of me be alive in there, growing? I remembered how she stood on the train that first day. The way she held her stomach. The way she held her sadness.

The Victory Farm in the 34th was louder than the one in the Capital, but I was excited about this one. They had a colt scheduled to be born, and I'd always wanted to see a baby horse.

"Do you know why I reinstated the Victory Gardens and Victory Farms?" Father asked.

"Yes," I said. "Before The Great Disaster, they were everywhere. The world's population was so unmanageable that food deserts were causing people to be malnourished. In the denser areas, access to fresh vegetables and fruits caused food to be supplemented and modified. These modifications led to some of the mutations that endangered Humanity."

Father laughed. "You tugged that from a file in your brain, didn't you? You have the base answer, now lets go further."

I stopped in front of an empty stall. Hay scattered the floor, and a wheelbarrow was filled to the top with manure. "The Victory Gardens were tiny bio-domes, fit-able on top of skyscrapers and in community parks. Anyone who worked them got free food, but they also regained a connection to the earth, to all things natural." I tried to elaborate, but all I could think of was seeing the colt.

"Why were they taken away after the Deletion Cancers?" Father asked.

"We forgot how important they were. We thought we no longer needed them, and went back to the old ways, doomed to repeat history. Then the plant plagues ten years ago made it necessary for a new way, which ended up being an old way. Then again, all old ways were once upon a time new ways."

Father nodded. "As is the curse of Humanity. We constantly rediscover the old and sing platitudes of its newness."

He wrapped his arm around my shoulders, and tugged me towards the stall at the end. A boy a little older than me stood there, petting the black fur, soothing the mare that was about to give birth.

"The most terrifying day I ever lived through was the day Tycho brought you to me," Father said. "I couldn't believe my eyes.

How could I have been a part of creating you? And how could something as wonderful as you have taken a part in destroying her?"

I sucked in a breath.

"It took me a few weeks to realize how much I loved you. It took me a year to understand that it was not your fault. It took me until today to realize that you think her death is."

I swallowed, and focused on the way the light bounced off the horse. Her hoof pounded against the straw, thudded against the wooden floors underneath it.

"Do not carry this guilt. She would be proud of the boy she created. She would be proud of all the things you've yet to accomplish. I work hard to be the father she would approve of. I work hard to do right by you. I do these things, like reopen the Victory Farms, so that this world remains yours. It is the greatest gift I can pass down to you. Not my genetics."

Abner shook me awake. I wasn't sure how I'd fallen asleep, but Ollie insisted we try to get a little rest. We had an entire day before we needed to be at the Tracks, and, according to the compass, we were less than half a day's hike.

"It's our turn to keep watch," Abner said, nodding to where Hucksley was trying to nuzzle up against Ollie a hundred feet away. Bixby was curled up between their thighs, soaking in their body heat. Something about it looked safe, and I was glad Ollie was there to tether her to something she knew. I couldn't imagine what she was feeling after being violated in such a fundamental way. Mother had to have been biding her time for me to give my samples to the G.E.G., but she wasted none in getting one to Hucksley the moment I gave it. Then to be asked to take me, the person who made the sample possible, out on the Tracks and pretend that she didn't carry bigger burdens than me, caused *by* me. Everything came into a sharp, clear focus. Every word. Every snarky comment. I deserved every bit of it.

The moon had fallen away from the trees, but there was still an eerie glow it cast when my eyes adjusted. Who knew blue could be so dark?

Abner pulled out the tablet and typed in a quick command.

"What are you doing?" I asked.

"Relax," he whispered.

"If you attach it to the satellite, they'll be able to ping back to our location. Turn the vid-web off," I said.

"Just because you're a New Wave doesn't mean you're the only one who can figure out hacks. I can do a lot in fifty-nine seconds. I download the vids and watch them off-line."

Before I could protest, he connected and began to load the latest news feeds. Without looking at the clock, he cut it off right at the fifty-ninth second, as if he had a perfect clock stuck in his head.

"How are you feeling?" he asked.

"I honestly don't know," I admitted.

"No one expects you to take responsibility. Being stoic out here means something entirely different."

"I won't abandon her," I promised. I knew it deep down, that if I was to do the right thing, it had to start with this promise, this moment.

"What if she doesn't want you? What if she wants to do this on her own?"

I sighed. "I don't know how to navigate this."

Abner reached out and placed his palm on my shoulder. "Aye, brother. None of us do."

I startled at the endearment. Brother. My definition of the term used to feel so black and white, but the more I thought about it, not even Mos was easily defined. On top of that, Cosmos and Pamphilos were just as much brothers as Mos was. They defined me for a large part of my life in their own ways, tugging out different qualities in my character with their friendship and teasing. For Abner, calling me brother equated to calling me friend. There was something heavy in that—a responsibility that I hadn't earned yet. There must have been a bigger test to the word. Maybe he was feeling me out or maybe it was just a slip of the tongue. I examined his face for any sign of wariness. Was he on guard? No.

This boy trusted me, and with small words he let me know it. In this trust, I felt the forgiveness Hucksley had promised existed for me.

He smiled. "The world will slow down. On that day, you'll find peace. Today, we must rage against the threat of tragedy because the end of *our* world is at *their* fingertips. Let's just focus on taking it back for now. The rest? We can figure it out later."

There were so many contradictions raging in his face, and I felt a hitch in my breath. His earnest words made me think of Uncle Ty's light severity.

Abner turned back to the loaded vid on the tablet. "The sound didn't have time to load, but maybe we can still catch something." He pressed play, and the screen cut to a stage. A woman in a white lab coat stood in front of a sacked face—an execution. Next to the sacked face, was someone I recognized without a doubt.

"It can't be," Abner whispered.

"You know her?" I asked. How could he know Phoibe?

"That's Bee," he said.

I steadied my breathing. "I went to school with her."

She moved on stage towards the person with the sack on their head. Phoibe, the girl who'd asked me to never let them twist me, had twisted Hucksley in her wake.

"Did you happen to play Gruel Ball with her?" Abner asked.

I nodded.

"You were the guy she couldn't shut up about!" He punched me on the shoulder. "That's just rich."

"You mean?"

"No wonder she cut Hucksley so harshly! Especially if she saw her kiss you!" Abner laughed.

"You know about that?"

"Hucksley tells me everything. It's kind of the perk of being her best friend. Wait until she finds out the real reason Bee took a chunk out of her!"

I laughed, but then Phoibe's face became the focus of the vid, and I saw the way her smile hovered in an expression of pride. I tried to find the facts within the tales her face told. What unborn stories existed within her? Who had been in her ear, twisting her into the creature I saw? She was never this cracked before? What could have happened to her to pull her into the rage she didn't even try to hide?

I knew that expression. It was the same look she got every time she won a debate or a game. Whoever was in that sack was important.

"Abner. Look," I said.

I felt my sternum vibrate as Phoibe lifted the sack.

"Who's stars and who's satellites?" Father asked.

"I get satellites," Mos said. "I have a good feeling about them this time."

"Then I guess I get stars," I replied.

Father made sure we had our eyes covered. Our little hands clamped over each socket as we laid in the giant bed in his quarters. The train had to stop for some light maintenance on the Tracks, and the sky was immobile enough to search. I heard the click and slide as the roof opened wide, but the warmth of the train stayed contained by the glass ceiling just below the metal.

We felt Father's weight as he crawled in between us, and suddenly I was impatient to start.

"Thank the Stars for the Scientists of the Republic," Father whispered, cuing us to let our eyes free.

I strained my eyes for shooting stars, determined to gather them up into a higher count than Mos' satellites. I wanted to concentrate on anything but what I'd seen that day. I wanted to pretend I was seven again, eight again, anything but nine right then and there.

Something bleeped across the sky. I wondered when Mos would notice that a satellite was passing us by.

I blinked and saw the needle. The way it slid into the vein and bubbled up the skin.

A star yanked across my vision. "Star," I called. "One."

"Counted," Father said. He reached down and took my hand. He knew what I was thinking about. He hated that Grandfather had taken me to the execution. "He's too young!" Father had yelled.

"You had no right."

But Grandfather felt he had every right in the world.

"Star," I called. "Two."

"Counted," Father said.

I collected them in my pocket. They were mine to keep and let go.

"Satellite. One," Mos said, determined to catch up. I knew his heart strained as much as his eyes.

"Counted," Father said.

I saw another star shoot across, but let it go. I peeked at Mos over the crest of Father's chest. It wouldn't be long before Grandfather stole this from us, too.

"Satellite. Two!" he yelped.

"Counted," Father said.

Mos deserved to be protected from all this. He deserved to never have to see the needle slide into the skin. He deserved better.

But I knew he wouldn't get better.

Another dot streaked lines across the constellations. I let it go.

"Satellite. Three!"

Abner shuddered, the tears growling out of his throat.

I yanked the tablet from his hands. "She said something! Right before. Abner, connect again. Load the sound!"

But he was sobbing too hard to focus. I placed my hands on his shoulders and shook him. "Look at me. You have to look at me!"

He shook his head, and I recognized his pain all too acutely.

I placed his hands on the tablet. "Focus. Connect and load the sound."

His fingers fumbled over the keys, and I knew he was half-blinded by tears.

"Ollie! Hucksley! Wake up!" I yelled. We would have to move soon. We wouldn't be able to stay here in case Abner couldn't mask the signal again. My warning made them stir, and before Abner could finish reloading the vid, they were with us by the river.

Braids stretched in a million different directions, grasping for the air, wild and free. "The night grows dim at five p.m.," Celeste whispered. "My bared teeth are broken chains." The camera moved from her face to her arm, and the needle slid in, like the vein was its home.

She'd found out the detonation time. She warned us, even as she left us. And like that, she was gone.

Hucksley let out a stuttered gasp. Ollie tugged her into his arms, then yanked Abner into the hug, his chest a sturdy home for the two people he loved the most.

"We can't stay," I whispered. "We have to move." I knew it in my gut. I felt instinct kicking in, pulling me towards a new reality.

I took out the thumb-nail tester and pricked my finger before inserting it into the tablet. I entered the twelve numbers, then located the time. Monday. Five in the evening. And there was the command. I hacked into it, and turned it off. Then, I readjusted the code to a new series of numbers that someone else would have to spend weeks to hack into.

That gave me a little bit of time to recreate a true anti-bot serum. And once we got to the Vault, I could change the code every day, every hour if needed.

For now, I wouldn't die.

For now, Celeste had saved my life.

CHAPTER ELEVEN

Celeste shouldered her pack.

"Aren't you going to say goodbye to them?" I nodded towards the lake where Polo, Uncle Ty, and those two boys chatted.

She laughed. "I am not a fan of goodbyes. I'll see them again, if not on the Tracks, then on the other side."

"The other side?"

"Aye, Buckets. There's always another side to what we know." She tightened the strap across her chest, and tucked a wild braid behind her ear. It wouldn't be contained.

"But you'll just sneak off in the middle of the night like that?" I couldn't fathom it. The way she looked at all of them? I could tell the connections ran deep.

"I've taught them well. They respect me enough to know they can never tie a good woman down. I'm free to go and do as I please. So are they. In the morning, Polo will leave in the same way. The boys, too. I guarantee you will get no prolonged farewells. Well, Xavi might, but that's different."

"Yet you're here, saying goodbye to me?" I reminded her.

"Then you misinterpret the meaning of this conversation. The only goodbye I'll ever say is the Big Goodbye—when the world

---

stands still for me long enough to see the other side and walk across the border into its realm. I tell you this because I only hope to teach you a new way to see things."

I looked back at the boys. They were just teenagers, like me, living a very foreign life in a very foreign world. She was wrong in this. Everyone you loved deserved the respect hidden within a proper goodbye.

I turned around to tell her this, but she already slid into the dark trees, abandoning the conversation before it was even finished.

Abner's eyes were warm. He and Hucksley sang softly while Ollie hummed along. I recognized the Stilling Song, and I remembered the short, yet profound moments with Celeste. She'd tried to tell me all along that she'd never say goodbye. And she didn't. She died with Rebellion on her lips—a message to save those she loved. She didn't grace anyone with a farewell, but with a love that went beyond her grave.

And the Stilling Song wasn't a goodbye either.

It was an acknowledgement of a final freedom.

I couldn't tell who heard the train first. Abner, Hucksley, or Bixby. All three of them turned to glance behind us long before the train ever made itself known. As it approached, Abner put Bixby into his bag. The pup already recognized it as her place, and she yapped in anticipation rather than fear.

Hucksley tapped me on the shoulder to pull me off the Tracks. "Help me down the ditch?" She looped her arm through mine and leaned in to whisper, "Did you know you're crying?"

I swallowed and tasted the salt. "I suppose I am."

"Aye, I suppose. How does it feel to be human?" Her own tornado eyes were storming in red lightning. She wasn't ashamed of her tears.

"Rotten," I said. "Can I go back to the way I was?"

She looped her fingers into mine and squeezed. "Movement. It'll heal you. It'll heal us all. Move forward with me."

"Then why call it the Stilling Song?"

"Think on it, Brainiac. If movement is the one thing that can heal Vagabonds?"

I felt a piece lock into place. "Then being still means you have nothing left to heal."

"Aye. Maybe you've learned something yet."

I helped her down the ditch and let myself cry with them. They refused to hide how they felt, and there was something raw and powerful in letting emotions loose.

Uncle Ty once said that time worked strangely on the Tracks. *"Seconds became days and days became years while the years became seconds."* He was right. Every moment hovered at haphazard speeds, and as we moved into the trees to wait for the train, I had a strange feeling of familiarity. I felt at home for the first time in my entire life, like this safe haven within freedom had always been locked inside just waiting for me to return to it.

It didn't make sense because all logic said I barely knew these people, but sometimes you discover tethers more binding than logic. We were linked now, though I wouldn't know for a while if it would save me or destroy me.

With the lies Grandfather had let loose, I was finally free from him. I had to admire his long-game, his dedication to his beliefs, and his strategic manipulations. He juggled variables without flinching. I hadn't fooled him into thinking I was doing an exercise in politics when I schemed to get the nano-bots to Vagabonds and Citizens. He'd always intended for me to do just as I had. He made it so production of the serum happened outside of my hands. I trusted that my instructions had been followed to a T, and all the while he and Mother must have been working with Eudocia to alter the programing. Had Instructor Aeschylus been in on it as well? Did he help her create the plague only to die by it?

My my head kept circling back to Grandfather.

How careful he was to make sure the timing was appropriate…

First, he made me fear that Transgenic Therapy was happening. He blamed the Unnamed and gave me an enemy to fight against. I created the nano-bots to root them out while simultaneously giving him a weapon of mass culling. He manipulated me into searching for the Unnamed, starting with releasing my findings on the Vagabonds. Then Father was roped in to create Absolution. All the while, Grandfather stoked the small anarchies until they grew too large to contain. The chaos was cultivated into one name—Patriots, and even they were ignited by Grandfather's hand. Mos' declaration at the end of his speech only confirmed it. Then came the promise of Donation, and the plan to send me out under it.

And Father's death.

Damn the stars, and the Scientists of the Republic.

Onesimos Leventis may have set the stage, but Grandfather orchestrated the symphony of explosions.

This new world Grandfather envisioned would pit Patriots against the Unnamed. Same war, new names.

I was undone now. Though the feeling of freedom was not yet ripe, I could feel it budding. For the first time, I no longer had to do Grandfather's bidding or play by his rules.

Hucksley's breath landed heavy on my shoulder. I could barely hear over the thrumming of the train, and one passed that had a rusted door on a tan boxcar. "There it is," Hucksley said.

I followed them out of the trees, and the three of them began to sprint. Abner's bag bounced uncomfortably, and I immediately worried that Bixby would catapult right out of it. I worried she'd land right under the wheels, but the pup held tight. Hucksley was before Abner and after Ollie. There was a limp to her leg, but she pushed through the discomfort to get on the train.

I had to run with them as much as I had to run for them. I felt the weight of their sadness, and I wanted to do better for them—to do better for us all. My feet moved over the gravel, and I reached the protruding bar past the open door.

I didn't know it when all of this started long before my birth, but I'd always been working towards this moment, reaching for the place I belonged. I was going to out-play Grandfather. I was going to beat him at his own game. And I was finally going to be home.

Abner's bulky frame slid into the same door Hucksley and Ollie had. I entered the car behind him, and my eyes took a moment to adjust. But then arms slammed into me, nearly pushing me back out through the door. Hands yanked me into a hug that wouldn't let me breathe.

I knew the smell that came off his shoulders. I knew the sound of his voice when he spoke. But I couldn't believe it.

"Ani," Uncle Ty whispered. "You made it."

"He did it," Abner said. "He figured it out just like you said he could."

This only made Uncle Ty squeeze me tighter. He finally released me and turned to grab Abner and Ollie into the hug. "My boys," he laughed.

I placed my head on my pack and tried to sleep, but the sound of Uncle Ty's laughter bothered me as it mixed with boys' near the water. The youngest was still strumming incessantly on that ukulele, and I wanted to bang him over the head with it.

I wanted us to move on. It felt wrong to spend the night near these Terrorists now that I had the information I needed. What if we got caught?

Polo grinned from where he leaned against a tree. "I fear for you, Ani."

"Why?"

"I wonder if we did the right thing by sending you to live in the Colonies."

"It does little to imagine what could have been when you place it next to the reality of what is," I reminded him.

Polo laughed. "You sound so much like her, it's eerie. I wonder which part of her is more dominant in you? Her head or her heart?"

"I'm pretty sure my nurturing didn't allow for either." I said it like I was proud of the fact because I would never be a traitor like she was.

"I think you'd be surprised, Buckets. Sometimes human nature can be more powerful than the ties we bind it with."

The laugh matched a memory, and for the first time in my life, I read Uncle Ty clearly. Hope was the only expression that existed in his eyes, and the contradictions fell away completely when his face shifted into love, a love so pure that it made me ache for my father.

"I've been wanting you to meet for so long," Uncle Ty admitted as he stepped away from us. He tried to take us in, moving his eyes back and forth from each face.

Abner couldn't help but laugh despite his sadness. "Speaking of, Ollie was a betting soul. Promised me his jerky if New Wave didn't complain once. He still hasn't paid up. Care to make an honest man out of your son?"

Ollie scoffed. "Sorry kid, ate it already."

Abner punched his brother in the arm, but the laughter bled out from the cracks in his eyes.

Hucksley moved towards the open door between the cars, but Uncle Ty stepped in front of her. He took her chin between his thumb and forefinger just as Ollie had. It struck me that it was a term of endearment, smaller than a hug but just as powerful.

"I heard what she did. I'm so, so sorry we couldn't get you out before," Uncle Ty told her.

"It's okay, Xavi."

"It's not. I let you down, but I'm here for you. We will all get through this together. You're not alone, sweet girl."

"I appreciate that," she said.

I couldn't take the look on Hucksley's face. It was so broken under the subdued lighting. "Why did Mother do it?" I asked.

Uncle Ty looked at me and let a hiccup of rage show. "Did you ever know Zosime to do something she didn't believe to be right?"

I'd thought the same thing, but she had to have known how wrong Transgenic Therapy was or how wrong impregnating a young girl without her consent was. She had to have seen those two things as evil, as something you just didn't do. But then again, the only thing that could shadow wrong with right was doing it for the good of Humanity.

Mother sang her favorite song. Her voice grew full, big like her belly.

There was a monster growing inside of her. Mos and I were sure of it. We could even see it move the skin along her stomach when it raged. Once, when I sat in her lap, the monster kicked me. I flew from her lap and landed near Mos on the floor where he played.

The monsters had come before. They always left. I couldn't wait for this one to be gone, too, so Mos and I could sit in her lap again.

And the monster always made her cry. She tried to hide it, but I noticed things she didn't want me to. She must have been hungry because I usually cried when I was hungry. Sure enough, I'd catch her sneaking in extra snacks, like she could never be full no matter how full her stomach looked.

Father would hold her sometimes when she cried, like he understood something I never could.

She always sang this song the moment she grew so big she was about to burst. There were notes that went beyond my knowledge. Notes like missing. Notes like longing. Notes like loss.

The one truth that never changed for Mother was that she always did the hard thing if she believed it to be right. I was too young to recognize how hard it must have been to raise a son that was not hers while she gave up child after child. I heard a debate once about the emotional trauma female Celebrities went through. It was a deeper, more scarring experience than what the male Celebrities encountered. It was one of those truths that got swept under the rug of stoicism, but something must have cracked in Mother under the weight of all that righteousness.

For her to make Mos undergo Transgenic Therapy meant she probably did it to her other children as well, and if she was willing to do it to her own children, it meant she believed in the advancement so much she was willing to undergo the same alterations. She believed in leadership through action, never asking of others what she was unwilling to do herself.

Sending Phoibe after the children who had been Transgenically modified was maternal in a way. It was possible

Mother wanted to keep her experiments safe during the culling. Perhaps, in Mother's mind, keeping Hucksley under lock and key was her way of protecting the girl, and by impregnating Hucksley, perhaps Mother thought she was helping the preservation of Humanity after the plague ripped through the world. After all, reducing the population so drastically would require repopulation attempts after the deed was done.

I wondered how Abner and Ollie escaped the dogged pursuit sent after them. Was it all luck, in the end? Or did Mother only go after the girls first?

How many others did Mother use my samples on? The question made me sick.

Mother didn't believe herself to be evil, of that much I was sure.

It didn't mean she wasn't cracked.

"Can you three give me a moment with Ani?" Uncle Ty asked. "Go get some grub, snag some rest. Your Aunt Corinna is in the Slop Car waiting for you."

"Chancellor Tantalos is here?" I asked.

"There's nowhere else for her to go right now. Your Grandfather has already turned the Republic against her. He framed her for working with you on the nano-bots, but we can talk more about that later, okay?" Uncle Ty said.

Abner nodded towards Bixby in his pack. "Mind if I take your dog?"

I smiled. A protective edge ran along my spine that hadn't existed a day ago. It looked like Bixby was mine now as much as I was hers. I couldn't pinpoint when it happened, but I'd never throw her loyalty away. I just needed to find a way to reprogram the new plague within the nano-bots she carried, but that would have to wait until I reprogrammed every human being on the train. Hopefully, with the help of the labs that were sure to be on the train, I'd be able to figure out Bixby's plight sooner.

"Go for it," I said.

Hucksley reached over and squeezed my elbow before she turned towards the door. As the three of them left the car, I caught one last glimpse of Bixby in Abner's pack. I knew he'd take care of my dog, but I didn't like the idea of her being out of my sight.

"Lynk wants to meet you," Uncle Ty said when we were alone.

"I figured as much. Isn't that why I'm here?"

"She'll meet us three cars back. Did you learn to surf yet?"

"I'm proficient," I whispered, but my feet refused to follow him. The name Lynk made me think of the hours I spent thinking Lynk had been Claire.

"Come on, boy. The wind is calling."

"Uncle Ty. About Claire..." I said.

He stepped away from the door and put his hands on my shoulders. "It was a clever plan to test loyalty, but the moment the situation presented itself I knew who was just clever enough to come up with it."

"I'm so sorry."

"Just because you're clever and brilliant does not mean you should have known better. Your grandfather was in your ear your entire life, and I did my best to counteract everything he taught you. There were bound to be cracks in the teachings, fissures where you were uncertain of the boundaries between right and wrong. Let's do better this time. Claire forgave you the moment she learned what was being asked of her. She encouraged the rest of us to do the same." He tugged me towards the door, and I followed him up the ladder. The pace of the train was so slow that balance was easy to achieve. Uncle Ty got a running start and leapt over the gap between cars. I laughed and followed him. Like me, for better or worse, he was now free of the Republic, and we both felt the chains loosening.

Three cars later, Uncle Ty stopped and sat down. "Let's take a moment, okay."

I sat down next to him, let the sun rage against my face. He wanted me to know I was forgiven. How could Vagabonds throw the concept around so freely? Why didn't they demand atonement? Or was forgiveness atonement enough? Like they knew the more they forgave the more guilty I would feel? Their forgiveness was becoming torturous.

Uncle Ty knew my thoughts. Perhaps because he understood how much they weighed on the scales of action and consequence.

"Long ago, I knew a man named Randolf," he said. "He told Niko and me about this thing called a Deus Ex Machina—the god in the machine. I used to think it was just a way to explain away coincidences or miracles. You see, every once in a while, when all hope feels lost, something or someone comes through unexpectedly to save you. Sometimes, at least. Eventually, Niko morphed the gods in her machine to simply mean when the unexpected takes your breath away. The good and the bad. I can't help wondering which direction the machine will take us in this.

"Celeste had a run in with the bad gods on our way here. We just happened to get on a train carrying a girl aching to prove herself. She shot Celeste in her Achilles heel, and Celeste made me go on without her. She said I needed to get the information back to the Vault at all costs. I tried to carry her, but she fought me as I got near the door of the train. She pushed me right out and didn't think twice to sacrifice herself." He lifted his shirt and showed me his ribs, the way bruises traced black and purple pools of blood under the skin.

"Hucksley tried to do the same to me," I said. "In fact, she pushed me and Bixby right off a bridge."

He laughed. "Sounds about right. Saving Bixby wasn't just about getting *Prometheus' Fire* to Lynk, you realize that right?"

I thought about it, and saw it clearly.

Hucksley wanted to save something that couldn't save itself. I could understand that feeling. Right then and there, I wanted to save the entire world, but so far, I'd only been able to save myself.

The train chugged along, forward on a set path into the future. It moved almost lazily, like it had nowhere important to go other than where it was in that moment. Uncle Ty and I watched what it left behind.

"Is this what the end of the world looks like?" I asked. "Are we really just going to ride it out? Wait for it to come?"

"The world won't end, my boy. Not if we survive it. Sides have been taken. We've gathered who we could, and on this train, we carry truth. We will save who we can, but so many are taking the new serum that we will only be able pick up the pieces after the culling happens. You'll save who you can here on the Vault, but there are other things to hope for."

The truth of it felt like the burn of a skinned knee. The only thing we could do was watch the old world die and find our place in the new one.

Uncle Ty patted me on the knee. "I know that, within the Republic, the cream of the genetic crop will make it through for sure. The strands of the old plague do not affect New Wave Perfections, Second Wave Perfections, Halfsies, and those who have been Transgenically modified."

"You mean I wouldn't have died, even though I have nano-bots in my system?"

"As far as I know, no," Uncle Ty said. "Neither would Hucksley, Abner, or Ollie had they taken them."

"And a lot of your children?" I asked, thinking of the double Celebrity Second Wave Perfections.

"Yes. About half of them are safe. Time will only reveal who will make it through. And, when the new plague spreads, it may not be as we fear. Though *Prometheus' Fire* will be deadly to these groups in order to give the G.E.G. optimal control, it does not necessarily mean they seek to wipe out every modified human. No matter what, we won't give up on fighting it. We still have half a week to figure out what we can do to help. And even if your grandfather succeeds in a mass culling, we won't make the same mistakes as our ancestors. We will make sure future generations know the histories. We will make sure these truths leak out like bubbles from an ancient spring so they can learn from us."

I wanted to believe him, but even I knew how history worked. Even if the world learned the truth, it'd appall Citizens for a while, but people always grew complacent. They forgot. They repeated. Everything was a cycle. The same story slightly tweaked. Meant to be played out by the generations to come. It happened, over and over and over again.

Rewound.
Pressed play.
Shook hands.
Kids sang.
Explosions.
Rewound.

How many wars would happen for our children and their children? How would power dictate the way the world burned for the next generations? And if the culling succeeded, how could we preserve Humanity without genome maintenance practices dictated by the Genetic Engineering Guild?

Uncle Ty squeezed my hand. "I owe you truths, pure and real. For once, I won't veil words, mince meanings, or sew together puzzle pieces that will take you years to figure out. Lets start this new life by speaking plainly," Uncle Ty said. He stretched his legs, then stood up. "You're about to change the world, Ani. You're about to save it even if it doesn't feel like it."

He moved to the edge of the roof between two boxcars and lowered himself below the ledge. I followed him, trying to find redemption in his belief in me. But I hadn't saved the Vagabonds. Mos had. He had been wise when it mattered. He's seen through to the bones of Grandfather's plan and given me the codes that would let me reverse the things that had been done.

I smiled as I moved my legs down the ladder. I wanted to find my brother, make sure he was okay. The moment I reversed the plague in the nano-bots for everyone in the Vault, I would seek him out. Part of me knew he was trying to find a way to save the Citizens of the Republic. It wasn't something I could know like facts on a spreadsheet, but it was something I could know, like truth in the heart. My brother was not lost to me. My brother was not lost to Humanity.

Uncle Ty yanked open the door and slid through it. I followed, my thoughts on Mos, my heart moving to wherever he might be in that moment.

"Ani, wake up," Uncle Ty whispered.

But I didn't want to. The dream felt too real to let it go. Her voice. I could have sworn I'd heard it. Reaching out through my genetic past, landing on my ears as if I'd actually gotten to hear it before.

Sometimes, when I listened to Father speak, I could hear exactly where my voice came from. I could trace all the formations of vowels and words straight to the source.

Other times, when I listened to myself speak, there were pockets of unknown that I knew belonged to her.

"Is he happy?" she'd asked.

And I wanted to scream, "He isn't! They all lie to him! He can never be happy!"

But it was a dream where I had no voice, and her question held all the power. So Uncle Ty answered for me, "He tries to be."

I wanted to hold onto the conversation, as if it were real, as if her voice could come back to life—as if she could come back to life.

Uncle Ty shook me, and my eyes opened to the dark trees above me. "Let's take a swim to wake us up. We need to head back soon," he said.

I nodded. We'd spent the night by the lake, and I never got introduced to the two boys. They had created a line of division so acutely felt though so unbearably invisible. I didn't belong. Somehow, Uncle Ty did.

The left before I fell asleep. I shouldn't have been surprised to see Uncle Ty hug them. He'd hugged me a million times before, but why would he hug two Terrorist boys?

I sat up. Groggy from dreams. Groggy from questions. Groggy from voices that no longer existed.

Maybe it was this place—this place that my mother once wandered—that made her ghost pixilate into ephemeral memories that held no ties to reality.

"Ani," she whispered.

I *had* heard this voice before, in an unborn story that stirred in my dreams.

I wanted to ask her why she was crying, but even in the dim lighting of the car, the clue was in her hair. She held out her hands, held out her heart, held out her apology like an invisible gift, wrapped in her palm.

My head grew bright with buzzing. I knew fragments of the picture, the glimpse that Grandfather had given me years before. Her genetic gifts, her hair. *That* hair. The hair Father never let me cut as a boy. The hair that grew in the same shades of rusted brick on Abner. The hair that ached to push back through my scalp in painful reminders that Father was dead.

"No," I whispered. I backed towards the open door behind me. "I don't—" I tried to speak again, but I didn't have the words to hide behind. "Who?" came the owl question, inappropriately inadequate.

Who? Who? Who?

She couldn't even answer one simple question because she carried too many names, but then I knew it wasn't so simple.

"I'm Lynk," she said. "But once upon a time, the Republic called me Nikomedes."

My thoughts didn't stay on her. They flew to Abner, my brother. A half-way-so brother just like Mos.

I existed in the realm of halves. Half-brother with Mos. Half-brother with Abner. Half-son of Zosime, and half a son to this woman. I was half in one world and half in the other, half in the past and half in the future. I had a child who was half mine blooming in a girl who would never even give me half of her heart. I was half a boy, half a man, and after this moment, nothing would ever make me feel whole again.

Lynk stepped forward. It was easier to think of her with this name. I refused to place on her the other titles, like Nikomedes or Mother. I didn't know what those words meant in relation to her.

"My boy," she whispered.

I closed my eyes to the statement. *My boy*. Did she have that claim on me? Did she have a right to say such things?

"Be human," I heard Hucksley's voice in my heart, stirring up

all the hurt I'd always pushed down, swallowing it so it stayed trapped in my gut. "Why?" I finally asked, opening my eyes so I could capture new truths about her face.

"I thought I was dying," she said. "I knew you'd have a better chance at survival if I let you go. By the time I got well again, you were already in the arms of your father and his new bride. What kind of mother would I have been to take you from that world? How could I take you from your opportunity to mold that brilliant mind of yours?"

"You gave me up."

"Because I loved you."

Flames licked my teeth, fire lingered on my breath. "Does that mean you didn't love Abner? You kept him."

Those eyes, clovers floating above her cheeks, even more green as they widened in indignation. She took a deep breath before she tried again. "Xavi tells me you have this theory about unborn stories? That you believe the past is just as unwritten as the future? Can you try to believe in that philosophy while I tell my story?"

I didn't answer. She was going to tell her side whether I liked it or not. She motioned to a small table that hooked into a wall past the door. Sitting seemed like a good idea. The seats reminded me of the Dining Car in Father's campaign train, and my body sunk into the firm cushion. With Lynk and Uncle Ty on the other side of the table, I tried to find my inner Politician. I needed to hear this story and pretend it wasn't mine.

She wore a green shirt, and her hair became fire against the coloring. There was beauty there, and I tried to see myself in her expressions. It took her a while to speak, but I was thankful for the silence. For now, I was content enough with curiosity, and staring at her replaced missing links in my genetic history.

Lynk cleared her throat, and finally began to speak. "I have spent my adult life a traitor to the Republic. I am okay with that label because it means I've never been a traitor to Humanity."

I blinked.

Rewound.
Pressed play.
Shook hands.
Sat down.
Kids sang.
Father grinned.

"When it became clear that I would not survive my pregnancy, I thought you'd be safer living in the Colonies. I knew that your gifts would be cultivated to the best of your abilities and that opportunities would be abundant there. At the time, the Tracks had too many unknown variables for me to trust you in the care of Celeste, so I sent Polo to give you to Xavi.

"After I gave you up, Xavi watched over you. I didn't know if Flea, your father, could be trusted to be objective when it came to the Republic. Even to that last day, he struggled with his loyalty, and as he began his political career, I knew I'd been right to be wary. So, Xavi guided you as much as he could. He tried to counteract your grandfather's teaching in every way he could. Think of all the questions Xavi posed to make you examine the things you'd been taught. You don't know how it tortured me to know the man who killed my parents was helping to raise my son." Her green eyes flooded, and she choked on the tears. Uncle Ty reached over and placed his hand on hers.

"Xavi found me again. By accident perhaps, but I think it was the gods in my machine. He started sneaking me in to see you sleep. You were younger and never thought it more than a dream, but as you got older, I could only see you at public functions. I've followed your life. I've paid attention to you. I've always loved you."

"You were there, at the funeral," I said. I saw the green clovers floating in the crowd. I recognized the tears in her eyes. "Why didn't you come for me?"

"I wanted to change things, but I was locked into the decision I had made. I couldn't steal you from Flea, from your brother. Not like that. They loved you so much. You won't understand until you have a child all your own. How little you learn to care for your own happiness in the face of theirs. I was miserable without you, but I did what I thought best for you."

She reached down to her stomach and cupped her shirt against it. She was swollen, like some beast was about to claw its way out of her stretched skin. "She just kicked!" Lynk looked at Xavi and grinned.

Uncle Ty put his hand on her stomach and waited. "You're going to have a sister," he said. "We plan to name her Tommy."

Blue insignia.
Should have been red.
But it was blue.
On the collar.
Every child wore the blue insignia.
Explosion.
Smoke.
Fire.
Gone.
Rewound.

I suddenly couldn't take the sight of Uncle Ty having the one thing Father always wanted. There was love there, so big and so loud, so real and so horrible. It wasn't right. It wasn't fair.

"Did you ever love my father?" I asked, not just for her, but for him, Father's best friend.

"Ani," Uncle Ty warned.

I glared at my genetic-mother. "Did you know he loved you? Every day until he died, he loved you. He cried about you. He never let you go." I couldn't stop the words once they came. I didn't know what was more evil. The fact that she had abandoned me or the fact that she had abandoned Father.

"You don't know everything," Uncle Ty said. His face grew pointed, sparking on the sharpening stone of protection.

Lynk's hands slid away from her stomach and she rested them calmly on his elbow. "Anicetus, Flea knew I was alive."

I gulped back the slew of words I was ready to throw at Uncle

Ty for being a traitor. Wasn't he supposed to be like a brother to Father? Wasn't he supposed to be loyal to him? To me?

But it couldn't be true that Father knew Lynk was alive. He would have told me. He would have...

What would he have done? Taken me from the Capital? Turned us into criminals on the run? Or would he have worked hard to lay the foundations for Absolution?

Was this why he tried to build a bridge between Vagabonds and Citizens? Not because it was the right thing to do, but because it was the only way he could get my genetic-mother back?

"Did you ever love my father?" I asked again.

Uncle Ty swallowed. "It's okay," he whispered to her.

And when the answer came, it white-washed pain over Uncle Ty's face. The resounding yes that hovered between us all. The admission that she loved two people at once. "I've lived with a split heart since the first time Flea kissed me," she said. "In the end, I left them both behind. I had you. I nearly died. Then I got better. I was about to go after you, but that was when the gods in the machine put Xavi back in my path. I hitched a ride on a Celebrity transport—*his* Celebrity transport. He revealed to me the path with your father could never be taken. Flea had just married Zosime, and they had just announced Mos' conception. I tried to make things work with Xavi again. I traveled with him on his tour until seeing him with other women became too much to handle. I left him when he was out on an Interview, and I didn't see him again for an entire year. He found me again and offered to sneak me in to see you. I couldn't say no.

She held her stomach again. "The night he snuck me in was the night I met Zosime for the first time. She was pregnant with another Celebrity child, and there was so much compassion in her eyes that I trusted her. At the time, my best friend, Meg, was pregnant with Hucksley. Meg wasn't doing too well, and I thought to ask for Zosime's advice.

"Oh, that woman was so convincing! I even talked several Vagabonds into seeing her. We fed them the story that she was a spy turned Vagabond, and because I was the one telling the story, people believed me. When Xavi and I found out about Abner, I went to her as well. I couldn't know until Abner and Hucksley became toddlers, that things just didn't add up. All these children on the Tracks that were Transgenically modified are my fault, not just because I talked their mothers into trusting the wrong person but because Zosime's foundation for discovery was my very own hypothetical research I'd done as a teenager. Meg died for it, and my son and foster children struggled with abnormalities because of it. And then I realized how you called her Mother, how you went to her with your tears, how she tucked you in and fostered you. I wanted to get you out, regardless of who it would hurt. I flew into a rage. I stormed the Capital, took the hidden passageway Xavi showed me, and collided my fist with Zosime's face right outside your door when she tried to stop me."

She closed her eyes, her body hovering before the backdrop of a lab behind the table we sat at. Tablets and microscopes and incubators and sterile instruments lined the car in a neat and orderly fashion. It reminded me of Mother's lab in our home.

"You heard the noise," Lynk continued. "You toddled out the door and began to cry, and your father came running to your call. I'll never forget the look on his face, the way he held his chest like he couldn't breathe when he saw me. He rushed to me, pulled me into a hug, while Zosime scooped you up. That was the moment I knew Zosime used me—used Abner—to get back at me for existing in Flea's heart.

"Zosime rushed you down the hall, not necessarily because she was worried about you, but because she wanted me to see it, for me to hear you call her Mother, for me to hear her call you her sweet, sweet boy. Zosime wanted to steal away your cries and comfort you in ways I'd never been allowed."

I swallowed.

This story was too raw, too real to be falsified.

"From that day on, the years pulled me back and forth. Life took me on a strange path from there. Seeing your father only reminded me that my heart was still cleaved in half. I was a disloyal brat, hovering back and forth between the two men my heart could never figure out. One year, I'd be sure Xavi was it. The next, I'd find myself sneaking into the Capital or meeting Flea on the campaign trail. I never knew how to listen to my heart. It was like it spoke two different languages, one side never bothering to learn to translate the yearnings of the other."

Uncle Ty shivered, and pity roared through me. No matter what Lynk did, she was never meant to make either man happy.

"Your father talked me into letting him keep you. He made me see that it was the safest thing for you, and I could not fight the logic. Like Xavi, he fought a subtle fight to free the Vagabonds. He wanted to erase the social barriers that kept us apart. The few times we talked about him grabbing you and Mos to join us on the Tracks, he only became more determined to change the laws. He said that the right thing to do for our kids was to change the world so they could exist within it freely. I was so angry. I knew what he wanted would not happen in our lifetime, that generational patience did little for our family that lived in the here and now. I told him if he left again, then he left me forever. Flea didn't realize how serious I was, and he spent the year trying to pass Absolution."

Lynk looked at Uncle Ty, and I saw forgiveness flow freely between them. It was strange how honesty worked, like they loved each other enough to never hide the truths of their hearts, even when those truths burned with a savage kind of pain. How could Uncle Ty stand it? How could he accept how easily she admitted to loving neither man more? Especially after having a son with her? I guess the same questions could have been asked of my father, if he had been alive to answer them.

"Right around the time Flea left me, I ran into Xavi again. The last time I'd seen him, we'd had a similar fight. Neither he nor Flea wanted to give up on the Republic. Neither of them ever saw that they were fighting for something that was already dying. But that time, Xavi was different. He said things were in motion that could bring you, Anicetus, back to me. He said that when he no longer had to look after you, he'd join me out on the Tracks for good. And for the first time in my life, I made a choice that became so final I couldn't change it if I tried. It made me realize that love wasn't about the ache of being split in two. Love was about the peace of making a decision and letting that decision build you up. Love was about the world you created with someone. Xavi and I, we are creating our world, and even though things are going to get worse before they get better, we believe in the better that will come. We have to. For Abner. For you. For little Tommy when it's time for her to face it."

She leaned across the table and placed her hands on my folded forearms. They were large against her small fingers, and her arms were short against the length of the table, but somehow, she was bigger than everything. "I loved him," she said. "Please know that I love you all. And above all, please know that I loved Humanity enough to know this day would come. The heartbreaking truth is that the human race will be better off with the way *you* are now—because of the careful way *you* were raised—than the way you would have been if I'd raised you out on the Tracks. The way you have been nurtured to approach thought would not have happened out here. You can see the world on both sides of greatness, and it equips you to save it after your grandfather destroys it."

Her fingers squeezed, and I felt loss hover in the space between us. I felt the way tears grew salty and acceptance grew vivid in my heart. And when she got up and pulled me into a hug, it felt like I was coming home. It felt like I'd always belonged in her tiny arms that I'd outgrown long ago. It felt like the missing pieces of me began to click into place. And though I wasn't sure if I could understand or forgive the decisions she made in regards to me, I knew I'd do my best to try.

When she let me go, we laughed through gargled tears. We both wiped them away in matching gestures, then I let her show me her lab. She had it set up efficiently, and she showed me where I could begin working on the nano-bots.

There was no time to explore the Vault with time disappearing behind us. The haunting questions that still existed would need to be asked later. After the world ended, there would be time to demand her unborn stories so that my past made sense again.

What there wasn't time for was to reprogram every nano-bot in the Republic.

We had to start with one person.

That one person was Polo.

He came in with a lopsided smile, rubbed his knuckles along my bald scalp, and extended his finger so I could take a small blood sample.

Then Corinna Tantalos, free of all the stars that used to litter her chest, sat down on the bench and let me reprogram the nano-bots in her system.

A man Lynk punched in the arm and called Loud, came next, but I knew this one. "Agathon!" I yelped, and my father's conductor pulled me into a hug. All the years we spent on the campaign trail with him, and now he'd lead us on a new campaign into a new world. It was hard to look into the future with him sitting in front of me. All I could see was how he would lift me on his shoulders and explain how trains worked.

And Vagabond by Vagabond, I tried to save the world.

Nano-bot by nano-bot, I tried to be better than the expectations placed on me by Grandfather.

Second by second, I grew into a new version of myself on a train that sped towards a dying world.

And for the rest of my life, I would fight against the habits of Humanity. It was time we no longer existed on a very specific and limited cycle because I had to believe that the next generation could be better than the one before, that our mistakes could be learned from so they never happened again.

Rewound.
Pressed play.
The Great Disaster.
Rewound.
Pressed play.
The Deletion Cancers.
Rewound.
Pressed play.

The Birth of Anarchy.
Rewound.
Pressed play…

I had to believe, that this time, we could do more than rewind and start over.

LUCAS' EPILOGUE

Daddy calls questions unborn stories.

Mama calls them a waste of time.

I like to live somewhere in between, questioning everything but not letting answers tie me down. I'm more inclined to leave both behind in the shadow of possibility.

The train beneath my feet pulled at my veins, like the movement wanted all of my blood to drip down to my toes and anchor me to the metal.

It was my day to scribe, my day to write down truths into the database, my day to read through histories that lost their meanings long before I was born. But I couldn't keep my mind on the task. Not when the wind called to me. Not when the sun begged me to come out and play.

Aunt Corinna kept saying it's time for me to grow up—that I was a woman now and responsibilities awaited me. But Uncle Abner was in my other ear. *"Be a kid a little longer, sugar bear. Have what we were never given."*

On bright days like these, I was more inclined to listen to Uncle Abner.

On other days, when it suited me to be an adult, I was more

inclined to side with Aunt Corinna.

I reached up my arms and did a cartwheel, flipping my body over into the wind. The warmth of the train landed on my fingertips, carving its way into my skin. I was growing faster, the more I worked out on the roofs. Apparently, my ears would keep getting stronger, my sight would never grow weak, and my heart would pump more strength through my veins then I'd know what to do with. Daddy liked to joke that I was stronger than Uncle Ollie. Uncle Ollie made me try to prove it every time Daddy said it. I still hadn't beaten him at arm-wrestling, but I knew the day was coming.

I turned the cartwheel into a flip and felt the wind catch my body. I was getting antsy, and I wondered when Mama or Daddy would take me out for another camping trip. We did it every three or so months just so I didn't go stir crazy at the Vault, but lately, the crazy was stirring everywhere. I'd been train-locked for half a year, and, even though the scenery was constantly changing, everything felt monotonous.

I stood still as we approached the ruins of an old Colony. We wouldn't be stopping. We'd zoom past it as if the broken balustrades and peeling columns were not ghosted memories of a dead Republic. I tried to imagine the Colonies filled to the brim. I tried to imagine even before that when populations of people piled on top of each other like ants, but after The Great Disaster, the world thinned out.

After The Birth of Anarchy, only a couple hundred more than thousand of us were left.

The day Daddy sat me down and tried to explain the things I'd overheard, he ached to make me understand the travesty of cycles:

"What was The Birth of Anarchy?" I asked.
Daddy frowned and set his tablet down. "Where did you—"
"Hear it?" I pointed at my ears growing into their lobes.
"Right. Looks like we should be more careful," he sighed and tapped his nose as if thinking through how to explain it to me.

I reached out and pinched his elbow. "Or you can remember that I'm the smartest six year old on the planet with superhuman hearing and absurdly perfect hair."

I loved that my hair mirrored Daddy's and Uncle Abner's and Lynk's. I loved the way brick mixed with fire and the way it always made me feel wild.

"The Birth of Anarchy was a plague that my grandfather set free. He thought the name was so clever when the nano-bots erupted into chaos. In his defense, his hubris didn't allow him to see the moment his Scientist lost control of the plague they'd unleashed. The anarchy he'd hoped to raise then quell only caused the world to cave in on itself."

"What is hubris?" I asked, twisting a curl of hair in my finger.

"When you have too much pride in something that you can never see the wrong in it," Daddy said.

"Aye. I guess that makes sense."

"Can you stay a kid just a little while longer," he asked, kneeling down so that he held my green eyes in his.

"Aunt Corinna says there's no room for kids in this new world."

"Your Aunt Corinna is just jealous that she never got the chance to be one. Have compassion for that. Many of the adults in the Vault were robbed of the very thing I want to give you." He yanked me into his arms, and I smelled the clean pine that always followed in his wake. No one smelled like home the way Daddy did.

"You can't stop me from growing up," I reminded him.

"No. I suppose not, but I'm going to try my hardest."

I was born into chaos.

While the world was dying, I was surviving. I pushed my way into the beginnings of a new world, and my family tried to pick up the pieces. With the destruction of the Genetic Engineering Guild, the world needed a New Order to help direct genetic diversity.

But in this new world, the Vault refused to dictate the definitions of love. People were allowed to choose their partners, and when it came time to reproduce, genetic defects were corrected in the embryo before birth. The Vault traveled between the four Territories and aided in fostering these genetic corrections.

Daddy, the forever genius, discovered how to manipulate the children. He promised to never use Transgenic Therapy again, but it didn't stop the Transgenically modified from existing. The population couldn't afford to shun their gifts—our gifts. Zosime Petrakis had been thorough in her experimentations, and as my generation grew into their skins, more and more of us began to exhibit enhanced traits. Our genetics would forever be a part of the human genome. My generation, like the one before, would struggle to stretch the definition of Humanity.

Humanity didn't have a choice.

Let the mating begin.

I shuddered at the thought. I was getting closer and closer to the Age of Consent. It was a birthday most teenagers looked forward to. Most were more than ready to engage in their stoic duties, but, for me, it was a birthday that riddled me with a halting kind of fear.

I just couldn't decide. Did Humanity deserve another chance? Should Daddy and everyone else at the Vault just stop with the manipulations? After all, if we were meant to survive, wouldn't it happen naturally?

A quick whistle shot from behind me, and I turned to the noise. There was the blonde hair, torn into chaos by the wind.

"You're a crap surfer!" I reminded him.

Uncle Mos blushed. "I'm not sure I'm the correct one to explain this."

I tugged at his ears. I loved it when he got all flustered. "You don't need to. I get it. You feel like you have no voice since you were the one who tried to kill the world."

"Not funny, Lucas."

"Oh, unhinge, Uncle Mos. Funny is as funny does, and right now, your face does very funny things."

Uncle Mos adjusted the bulb of the grow lamp and turned it back on. Tomato plants grew bright under the fluorescents, and I wondered if we'd be having them at dinner again.

"Talking about how Consent works is not on my list of duties, and your statement calls for a retraction, elephant-ears. I did not try to kill the world. I got Anicetus the code to reprogram the nano-bots. I tried to save the Republic."

"But you were working with the Prime Chancellor to distribute them."

"You're incorrigible. For the last time, I had to pretend to be in Grandfather's pocket because if I didn't play along, Anicetus would have never been able to save the Vagabonds, and I never would have been able to try and save the Citizens. I intercepted the new nano-bot serum Grandfather was giving out, and I reprogrammed all the nano-bots to turn off the plague—"

"But you miscalculated him." I loved interrupting Uncle Mos. He never got exasperated by it the way everyone else did.

He tugged at a browning leaf and his face grew troubled. "The worst miscalculation in the history of the world was that I didn't realize Grandfather had expected my betrayal. He never gave out the nano-bots I'd reprogrammed. When the culling came, I sat there with him as we waited. Onesimos Leventis—"

"The man who murdered your father," I offered.

"Yes. The very one, introduced Grandfather—"

"And you had to suffer through the indignation of watching—"

Uncle Mos gave me a look that sent giggles through my teeth. When I finally calmed down, he continued. "When Grandfather stood up, I listened to the speech he gave about The Birth of Anarchy, and I expected him to be surprised by how many people survived his plan. Instead, I watched the thousands upon thousands die."

"You couldn't have known he'd outplay you," I reminded him.

"I thought I was saving us all."

I knew this story as well as my own. Uncle Mos always said his days of lying were over because he spent over a year lying to everyone, including Daddy. He played the spy to learn of Eudocia's plan and to steal her codes to hack the system. He *played the spy around his grandfather, letting the old man think he was easy enough to manipulate, letting the old man think he had gained his head and his heart. He played the spy to his own mother, learning how she's Transgenically manipulated him in the same way she'd manipulated others.*

Uncle Mos was tired of wearing personalities that fit him no better than too-small shoes.

When I needed to be reminded of what honesty looked like, I always came to Uncle Mos. He never sugar coated his role in The Birth of Anarchy. I never let him forget that he was just a kid back then—that he did the best he could with the obstacles he'd been given.

"How did Eudocia do it again?"

Mos ran his fingers along a fuzzy leaf. "She was smart." It was his way of reminding me to never be too smart to outsmart being human. "While Ani worked one side of the research, Grandfather fed Eudocia his progress. She was the only one as intelligent as your father, and she worked in conjunction with his findings. Ani had to submit the serum to be produced by the G.E.G. to get the quantities he needed. During production, Eudocia inserted the plague she'd been working on all year into the nano-bots with a timer inside to go off right after Ani was supposed to be arrested. Grandfather had this plan to do a grand, public execution just as the world began to die. He wanted the survivors to rally around the memory of the greatest Terrorist in human history. I told Celeste when I found out, and she got Ani out before Grandfather could arrest him for the false charges."

"But you didn't like Eudocia like that? Not one bit?"

Uncle Mos shook his head. "The worst moments in my life involved pretending to agree with that girl."

I reached up and took his large hand in my small one. "You can cry, you know."

"Only around you. Everyone else would make fun of me," he joked. His voice choked up around the words, but there was strength inside of his pain.

Daddy had told me once, "All life is sacred, all life is important, and every death is a sacrifice, whether willingly or unwillingly made. Until you become the cause of someone else's sacrifice, you will never truly understand what it means to carry the consequence of responsibility."

Uncle Mos carried consequences like ghosts in the black circles of his eyes. I had this feeling that the more he talked about it, the more likely he'd learn to forgive himself. He carried the weight of every death on his shoulders and forgot he tried to save everyone. He couldn't foresee that the plague would mutate or that Daddy would have to race each mutation to create new serums for years to come. I made him tell me this story often in the hopes that he'd finally find the truth within the fallible facts.

It wasn't his fault.

Uncle Mos spent most of his time in the Victory Gardens, the last three cars of the Vault. He made these cars his home, his sanctuary.

The plants never condemned him.

Neither did I.

I heard a beep of an intercom. "Someone just loaded," I said.

Uncle Mos nodded. "Don't forget to do the check-in procedures before you let them through."

"Aye. Won't make that mistake again. The last time, Mama nearly murdered me. Good thing my genetics are so valuable."

"You're not that valuable," he reminded me. He always did. Uncle Mos never wanted my ego to go to my head.

I laughed as I walked out of the car and climbed up to the roof. It was always easier to run up on the rooftops than weave around the storage cars.

When I reached the intake car, I tapped at a panel on the roof. A small piece of metal slid out and let me see the tablet that connected to the cameras. An older man sat on the cushioned couch. He looked about Lynk's age, and he spoke to a boy who had to be about eighteen.

The boy was pale. I'd never seen someone with cream-colored skin before, like he was porcelain, like if I tapped him with my fingernail, he'd break. Okay, maybe that was being hyperbolic. He did have a tan and high cheeks that turned rose along the bones.

Curious.

They never brought teenagers onto the Vault.

I was about to enter the commands to scan for weapons, but the door slid open to let Lynk walk in.

I loved my grandmother. There was something beautiful about how she approached the world, like she'd never let time be her enemy. I'd heard the stories of how she'd left Daddy as a baby, how it took them years to learn what to do with the love and the fear they had for each other. How Lynk was stubborn beyond stubborn and wore her eldest son down. The hours they spent in the lab cars, thinking at the same speeds, building the world as we knew it together, finally brought them close.

Lynk walked into the car the same way she walked into any situation. Like she owned it.

"*Loud!*" *she gasped.*

"*Wind!*" *The man reached out and pulled her into a hug.*

I groaned. My grandmother had too many names. Daddy would call these new ones an unborn story. Mama would call them the Ways of the Tracks.

"*What the hell are you doing here?*" *Green eyes narrowed in those cavernous eye-sockets of hers when she noticed the pale boy. Suddenly, I had the feeling she was about to punch Loud.*

Tommy came in behind, and when she saw the boy, I saw a flush of red float up to her cheeks. I was getting tired of her haughty attitude. She thought that, because she was technically my aunt, I had to listen to her, but she wasn't even a year older than me. She was bossier than hell, and I ached to get off the train, far, far away from her.

I laughed at her expression. This was the next best thing to leaving her in the dust. I couldn't wait to use her embarrassment against her. Fodder for days.

She had it for this rosy-cheeked boy!

"*You know very well that it's time you socialize the girl,*" *Loud said.*

Lynk slapped him upside the top of his head. "*Over my dead body. Not with him."*

Loud's wrinkled hands waved emphatically with every new word that came out. "Xavi and Buckets gave me the okay."

"And those men are just as stupid as you are."

The boy sat up straighter on the bench. He examined Tommy, looked her up and down like she was some prize. Tommy was beautiful like that. I was always glad she never got my hair, though there were other features we shared. Like eyes and cheeks and smiles. Sometimes, when I really thought about it, I knew without a doubt that she was more beautiful than I was. Most of the time, when I really thought about it, I didn't care.

The boy sent a wink in her direction, and Tommy blushed. There it was. Tommy was eighteen now, right at the Age of Consent, and rather than let her live a while in the Territories, they were bringing the Territories to her.

Leo wasn't going to give up. He pulled himself onto the roof and pretended like he wasn't afraid. All week long, he kept trying to surf. I couldn't figure out how, after eighteen years, his grandfather had never taken him on a train. Apparently Loud was the quintessential Vagabond, but he never passed on his habits of travel to his children or grandchildren. Instead, he'd let his family grow roots in Territory Three. Leo was his eldest grandson, and he'd never left the bounds of his birthplace until now.

I thought about hopping onto the next car, but there was something that stilled me. If I stayed, I could make Tommy jealous beyond measure. Leo was the best way to get that reaction from her lately.

But then I felt a shift in my breath. If I concentrated, I could hear every decibel of his boots as they scraped metal. I could see every strand of highlight where the dusty-blonde mixed with the strands of bright lemon. I wanted to hate the way the sun only made him look brighter.

I read an old poem once about an angel, a harbinger of death that wore halos of the lovers he'd stolen around his neck like a string of Cheerios—whatever those were. He looked like that poem made me feel, and I had a suspicion that if I let him walk towards me, if I let him take one more timid step in my direction, he'd be the death of something sure as the sun rose and set.

I stepped back just as he stepped forward. His feet had grown steady over the week, and I couldn't tell if I wanted him to lose his balance and fall or keep his balance so he could reach me faster.

"Want to teach me how to do a cartwheel next? I've never done one." His voice was mercury, but it was his smile that made my breath hiccup in my throat.

"I don't think you're up for the task," I said. "You'll fall flat on that pretty little face of yours."

"So you think I'm pretty?"

"Sarcasm. Look it up in the dictionary."

He smirked and stepped closer.

The building wore cracks in the foundation like wrinkles, and ivy took over the brick in a simple green. Long, white columns propped up an ornate overhang, and steps led up to an ancient stage.

"Your Daddy grew up here," Mama said to me. Her eyes were tornadoes. I wished I'd gotten her eyes instead of Lynk's. She was so good at hiding her thoughts behind them while mine were always as telling as the freckles that littered my shoulders.

Tommy and I followed her through the doors. We trudged through the dust that made the marble floors surprisingly slippery. I tried not to listen to the opulent ghosts that danced in the ballroom we stepped through. I'd seen vids of it when it was full of people in antiquated ball gowns and suits. Daddy and Uncle Mos lived that world in a lifetime long gone.

I hated that Tommy got to come with us. I was hoping this outing would just be with Mama. I never got her to myself anymore, and I wanted to have a claim to her that was bigger than Tommy's. Sometimes, it felt like Mama was more comfortable around Tommy. Then again, maybe it was just guilt that I felt, and not jealousy. Aunt Tommy was born out of love while I was born out of a violation. I knew it. Everyone knew it. Mama never tried to make me feel guilty for being created against her will, but guilt has a way of sneaking into the cracks of strong hearts. I was a constant reminder of her pain, but with the world dying all around her, Mama couldn't bear to let someone else bring me up in it. The truth always settled just under the surface of my skin, and the older I got, the more I understood just how impossible Mama's choice had been. I wouldn't have blamed her for choosing differently.

I tried to forgive her for the guarded love she shared with me, or maybe I was the one who guarded my heart, afraid to love the woman I'd hurt so profoundly from the day I'd been born. Maybe I was the one who needed to forgive myself, but things like forgiveness were never clear, especially when clouded by the vestiges of guilt.

Sometimes we both forgot to be timid in our love. We'd run barefoot on the broken glass of our pasts without feeling the multitude of cuts ripping into our skin. We'd collide somewhere in the middle and let a hug or a laugh or a kiss on the forehead erase it all. Sometimes, I remembered that Mama would love me if I would just let her. Most of the time, I felt too much pain to let myself remember.

Mama led us down a corridor and opened a door hidden in a wall. She reached back and held my hand in hers, like she could see the dark places my thoughts had traveled. Her hand always pulled me back to her. She loved holding my hand. It always made me feel young to be contained in her fingers, and, anytime I needed reminding that I was still a child, I'd reach out for her fingers. It took me years to realize she felt the same when she reached for mine.

Mama always said she hated Daddy when they first met. She liked to joke about how she'd considered, plenty of times, tossing him from the train, and neither one could agree whose fault it was that Mama earned a deep scar on her inner thigh before I was born. Mama claimed it was because Daddy kissed her to make a girl jealous, but I knew Mama better than that. They never explained what that inside joke meant, and I was inclined to let them keep the story to themselves.

She fell in love with Daddy after I'd been born. She said that hearts mutate when you see the way fathers look at their children. And that's what happened for Mama and Daddy. They grew into a love that reminded me of lightening striking thunder, and they loved to fight as much as they loved to love.

Daddy always said that Mama had never given him her heart. Mama always said that her heart would always belong to her and no one else. I knew she was lying. You can't own your own heart. It owns you, and the only hope you have for happiness in life is to follow it where it leads you.

So I let her fingers pull my heart into a dark hallway, and I tried to ignore the annoying way Tommy's feet shuffled behind us. The girl never lifted her boots up all the way.

Mama sent beams of her headlamp along the wall. Old paintings were preserved in time, and she stopped in front of one with a spindly plant on it. The thorns looked so sharp in the picture that I wondered if they'd cut me for trying to touch them. Crawling across the painting were the words: Be a fucking ocotillo.

Mama grinned. "Girls, it's time to learn who you were named after."

I remembered the words: *They cannot tell us who to love, Papalotita!*

But those words were a lie. First of all because it never told us who *they* was, but mainly because people told me who to love all the time.

If I had it my way, I wouldn't love Tommy at all, but ever since I could remember, Mama and Daddy, Lynk and Xavi, Aunt Corinna, Uncle Mos and Uncle Abner and Uncle Ollie and Uncle Polo, every damn Vagabond on the train, shoved love down my throat until I had no choice but to swallow it whole and feel it.

I loved them all, even when I hated them.

And I loved even when it hurt. I acutely felt that particular contradiction the first time I heard the Stilling Song. I felt it stir my insides with a loss that made me never want to forget to love ever again. Like the day Bixby couldn't outlive her age and we hiked up to Lynk and Xavi's favorite lake and buried the forever puppy with a nice view.

Then, seven years later, we sang the Stilling Song once more. We took turns carrying Uncle Abner's partner, Aunt Mel, on a stretcher to the same lake. We dug a bigger hole, and her brown hair laid limp around her face as the dirt landed, dust particle by dust particle, on top of her tan skin. I loved her so much as we all said goodbye. I loved Uncle Abner and the way he carried the loss of his partner in a secret box within his soul so his boys wouldn't learn what their loss meant just yet. A set of triplets, Hucks, Oliver, and Digger, who'd never get to meet their mother. Three crying babies that cut through the void of death. We took turns holding them and finding rocks to layer on the mound so that animals couldn't dig Aunt Mel up.

And the entire time, I cried.

Daddy told me to never hide my tears. He said emotions were what kept us human and that the most tragic thing a person could do was try to take the human out of Humanity. So I cried out all of my pain into every rock I set and wondered what it was like to join the mass of souls on the other side.

They taught me how to love and who to love and which ways to love them.

Like those who showed up around my fifteenth birthday, just when I thought my family couldn't possibly grow any larger. Like when Uncle Ollie met Aunt Helena and they had that twerpy Zane a year before Uncle Abner met Aunt Mel and had the triplets. Zane, who cried his way into the world like it was the only thing he'd ever do his entire life. I wanted to hate the way the kid constantly screamed, the way he always snuck into my quarters and hid things, the way he always got scared when it rained and found his way into my cot then snored so hard he drowned out the very train we were on, the way he told the triplets where he went when he got scared and it became *the thing* to do.

Four little boys, feet everywhere, snores everywhere, me swallowed up by their expectations of the safety I never promised.

And those triplets who thought I was a human playground. I

wanted to hate every snotty sniffle, multiplied by three identical faces, all that hair that rivaled mine. I wasn't fair that they were cuter than I could ever hope to be. Hucks, Oliver, and Digger, who got those long eyelashes to hang like curtains above the turquoise eyes they stole from Aunt Mel. More idiot boys when the world obviously needed more girls.

Didn't they know how valuable girls were these days? But no. Everyone kept popping out boys like the plague.

And now Leo walked out here like he owned the entire train. Did that confidence charm the girls back in the Territories? He stood just a foot away, then cut that distance in half so that I could see right into his cerulean eyes. The wind tore our hair in the same directions, and I realized that if I wanted to, if I willed it, the wind could carry me right off the roof, away from the weight I felt on my chest whenever he looked at me.

There it was, the faltering nerves. He swallowed, and his Adam's apple moved along the muscles in his throat. Was he more nervous than I was? He couldn't be. He'd been at the Age of Consent for over a year now, and there had to have been other girls he'd been interested in.

Daddy always said questions were unborn stories, and suddenly, I wondered if he wasn't as confident as he pretended to be. What might have happened in his past to make him so terrified of me? And then I realized that Mama had been right. When it came to this situation, answers were the last things I wanted.

"They have hopes for us," Leo whispered. He'd gotten so close that his voice landed warm on my face, faltering against the chill of the wind. His breath reminded me of daisies and rain, and I found myself inching closer. "But I wanted you to know, I don't."

"You don't?" I asked.

He reached up and cupped my cheeks between his two palms. They nearly swallowed my face, and his fingers were warm sand against my skin. I felt the movement in my gut, the thrill of a million wings beating against my chest.

I immediately felt guilt instead of excitement. It was true then, what Tommy had said last week:

"Marco!" Hucks yelled.

"Polo!" Zane, Oliver, and Digger whispered back.

Tommy and I sat on the top bunk just out of reach watching Hucks fumble against the pull of sound. Uncle Polo had taught them the game years ago, and it was always over quickly when they played it. Zane usually missed the sounds that the triplets, with their very enhanced hearing, could pick up, but Zane was stronger and faster than they were.

I entered another annotation in the Unborn Stories database. I'd interviewed a woman named Herbal last week and was barely getting to putting her stories into Immortal Words while we kept the boys out of their parents' hair.

"Do you remember when we used to play like that?" Tommy asked.

I looked up from the tablet and nodded. "We used to even like each other," I reminded her.

She sighed. "The game was never fair."

"I can't be sorry for my genetic gifts. I didn't ask for them, and it's hard enough to live with them without you always trying to make me feel guilty for them."

"Does it ever bother you that they did that to you?" Tommy braved the question, and I was surprised at her candid honesty. Honest was the last thing we'd been with each other for years.

After I was born, Daddy and Lynk spent a year trying to pinpoint any extra modifications that Zosime Petrakis may have inflicted on me. I was a blend of old world names. New Wave Perfection meets Transgenic Modifications meets who knew what else. As a baby, it became clear that my brain grew up too fast and that my senses were acutely sensitive. For as brilliant as Daddy and Lynk were, they still couldn't pinpoint the exact mutations hidden inside of me, but there was no denying that more had been done to me.

I was an anomaly.

Normally I wouldn't admit how much it bothered me, but something about honesty earns more honesty, like you should multiply the good with more good. So I said, "All the time. Sometimes I feel so different, I could just burst. I want to be like you, but I never will be." I felt a tear bubble up in the corners of my eyes, then wiped it back.

"It bothers me, too," she whispered. "Sometimes it feels like I have half a genius brain. I always feel smart, but just halfway as brilliant as Ani. I know Abner feels it, too, like our brains want to measure up to our brother's but we never will. We work in the labs with our mother, just like Ani does, but they speak in a shorthand that remains just out of our reach. We can tell it slows them down when they have to have to reiterate or reexplain something to us."

I laughed. "I feel that way, too. Maybe if we ever stopped fighting enough to put our heads together, we'd be smarter than both of them combined."

"You are smarter than he is," she whispered. "You just choose to pretend you aren't."

"What do you mean?"

Tommy licked her lips and swallowed. It was her nervous tic, the give-up moment before she released a secret into the world. "I overheard Ani and Hucksley talking last week."

"Just spill it, Tommy." I almost felt bad when her cheeks flushed. Whatever she had to say was painful. Whether it was painful for her or for me, I didn't yet know.

"Zosime Petrakis altered your NPTN in the special cocktail she created to make you. You'll grow into a mind that transcends every human being. You don't feel it yet, but you will. You'll be so smart that being around the rest of the world will pain you."

"You're kidding, right?" I felt a flare of anger. "This is a horrible joke to play."

She shook her head. "I debated telling you. I thought you'd see it as me being petty. But if it was me, I'd want to know what everyone is hiding about me. I'd want to know that, despite all the things they've told us about preserving our innocence, they intend to mate you off with Leo."

I started laughing. It hurt so much that I had to hold my side.

"I'm serious!" Tommy insisted.

But I couldn't stop. The entire joke was absurd. We were always trying to prank each other, but I wouldn't fall for this one.

Tommy groaned. "He is the purest genetic match for you as sure as the sun rises and sets. He's the best chance you have of having kids nearly as smart as you will become. Like Hucksley, Loud's daughter—Leo's mother—had been altered by Zosime in the womb. Before The Birth of Anarchy, she was captured by Bee, held in Zosime's labs, and given the sample of a New Wave Perfection named Alexandros Lampros." Tommy swallowed back tears of frustration. It stilled my laughter. Maybe she wasn't playing a prank. "He was a florist for the Republic." She tried to push out more of the story, but she needed a moment to breathe.

If what she said was true, Leo would be the only person, to my knowledge, that could understand how I saw the world. How I heard it. How I thought about it.

I swallowed and tossed the tablet onto the bed.

"Marco!" Zane yelled.

"Polo!" the triplets whispered.

I swung my legs over the bed and began to push myself away from Tommy. If what she said wasn't true, then Tommy was being manipulative. It would be reverse phycology at its finest. If she told me everyone else was planning for me to end up with Leo, then I'd push him far, far away so she could sweep in with her pretty lips and her pretty face and win him over.

I wanted her to be lying so terribly much.

"I'm not lying," Tommy whispered, reading the accusation in my expression.

My toes touched the ladder that led down, and I wrapped my fingers around the metal. The boy's quarters was a mess of blankets and smell, and I wanted to get onto the roof for some fresh air.

"I know my place here," Tommy said. "I wish it were different. I wish Leo was meant for me. I wish the Choice was as real as they all sell it, but there are deeper things happening in the human genome. Things I can't compete against. Things you can't compete against the moment you decide to stop acting like a

spoiled brat."

Leo was beautiful, but I wouldn't give in to what Science wanted, nor would I give in to what Humanity expected.

I had plans. I had my bag packed, hidden under my cot. I was just a girl with the world spread wide before her. I wanted to sleep under the stars. I wanted to see mountains scratch the sky, taste rain on my tongue, and swim in salty water. I wanted to stop being trapped in the Vault and all the things they wanted my brain to do for the preservation of the human genome.

I wanted to see what it was like to love myself as much as I loved everyone I had been taught to love.

Leo leaned in closer, and I couldn't breathe. His words felt like stroking feathers. "They fought hard to give us a choice, right?" he asked. "But then the population cries out for us to fix it, and the word choice just becomes a pretty word. Grandpa always told me that he never wanted me to forget to be a kid. I think it's a phrase they all say to make themselves feel better for what they ask of us the moment it's time to be an adult. But I'm not ready to be an adult yet. Neither are you." His thumbs moved to brush the skin around my ears and his fingers found their way into my hair. "You feel it though, right?"

Excitement pulled my lids closed. I nuzzled into his palms and felt weightless. Maybe the wind had picked us both up. Maybe we didn't exist at all because I definitely felt my insides being ripped apart by the speed of my heart.

"I know you plan on leaving tonight, and I hope that you let me come with you. I want to see the world for myself. It'll be a whole lot more fun with you than without you."

I opened my eyes to that piece of information. "That'll defeat the entire purpose of setting out on my own," I said.

"Being independent does not mean you have to be lonely. I promise I won't hold you to any expectations," he said.

"You sure about that?"

He grinned. "Fine. I'll say this one time because I'd be an idiot not to. When you're ready for more, I'll be there. Not because they all want us to be together. Not because it'd be the right thing to do for Humanity. But because I want to be."

He leaned in closer, his lips so near that if I just moved towards him, we'd meet. I was terrified to find that I wanted it to happen. I wanted him to kiss the fear right out of me.

It could be nice to have a friend when the forest got dark and the world got lonely.

Leo smiled. I saw it in his eyes, all the realms of possibility that existed there. I glanced away before I drowned in everything he could one day mean to me.

His words landed one by one on my ears. "I like you. I think I could love you, but for now, let's just be friends."

I opened my eyes and caught the wink he sent me as he let my face go. He stepped back, and his balance never faltered. My feet were nailed to the metal, and I couldn't catch up with my breath.

I realized he was right. I liked him. Perhaps, I could even love him. The way my gut fluttered told me that I'd never leave the Vault without him—or without Tommy. Something about leaving without Tommy felt wrong.

As we all approached the Age of Consent, it was time we consented to the desires of our own hearts rather than the desires of procreation. Tommy deserved the option of freedom as much as I did.

Our parents might be hurt by our decision to leave, but I couldn't help but feel they were falling into the ancestral trap they always preached against. They may not say the words Humanity before self anymore, but the belief was still there, somewhere, driving all the research and modifications and genetic manipulations they did. They all wanted to save the world so badly that they neglected to notice the world didn't need saving.

Leo shifted his body, and grinned. "So. Hands up? Like this?" he asked, putting his hands above his head. His fingers reminded me of a halo hung around his head like Cheerios—whatever those were.

"What are you doing?" I asked.

"Learning how to do a cartwheel. This is how you did it, right?" He pushed his body with his feet and tried to land on his hands. Instead, a loud thud shattered the wind as he face planted on the roof. The laughter that came next crippled me. I fell to my knees, clutching my side, and for the second time that day, I couldn't breathe. He rolled over onto his back, and his laughter sounded like strawberries tasted. My hair whipped in red tornados as I leaned in on myself, hovering my laughter over his smile.

Then, Leo's face became shifting sand, expressions moving in contradictions, desire moving against innocence, as he propped himself up on one elbow, grabbed my neck with a free hand, twined his fingers into my hair, and trapped me into a kiss.

I couldn't breathe, but this kind of breathlessness was beautiful. It mixed with his, and I saw the world clearly for the first time.

One day, soon, we'd have to grow up. One day, soon, we might even have to be responsible for the world. But it wasn't one day just yet. For now, we were allowed to be human in the shadow of Humanity. For now, we were safe inside the arms of the here and now.

THE BIRTH OF ANARCHY

j.d. brewer

Follow J.D. Online
www.jdbrewerbooks.com
Twitter: @jdbrewerbooks
www.facebook.com/jdbrewerbooks
www.goodreads.com/jdbrewerbooks
Instagram: @jdbrewerbooks

Don't forget to leave your review and comments on Goodreads and Amazon!
And don't miss…

ON THE OTHER SIDE OF GREATNESS
VAGABOND'S PREQUEL
AVAILABLE MARCH 2016

Keep going for…

THE BIRTH OF ANARCHY SOUNDTRACK
and EXTRAS

starting on page 329!

THE BIRTH OF ANARCHY'S SOUNDTRACK

I know I'm not the only author who feels this way, but music plays such a vital role in my writing. Music inspires. It gets my fingers tap-dancing against the keyboard and typing to the rhythms.

As a final editing exercise, I spend a few minutes with a chapter one last time, and I think of a song that captures its tone in lyrics or rhythm or sound. It is a farewell for me, a way to let go of a chapter I've been toiling over for months. Part of me rejoices when I let go. The other part of me mourns, knowing that I'll soon be letting my heart out into the world for readers to do with as they please.

Although these artists in no official capacity endorse my novel (and I say this in case something in my novel disagrees with any personal beliefs they may have), I would like to give a shout out to them. I would like to thank them for giving me the energy to write The Birth of Anarchy.

Please support these artists by legally purchasing their music to create your very own The Birth of Anarchy Playlist *as you read.*

Chapter One
My Father's Father—The Civil Wars

Chapter Two
Freedom—Pharrell

Chapter Three
The Turtle Dove and the Crow—Mandolin Orange

Chapter Four
Past Lives—Børn

Future Soundtrack Favorite
My dear friend Lindsay Coffta is in the studio working on her first EP. I've been listening to her Masters on repeat, but for now, check her out on her YouTube page.
Unless you're reading this sometime after 2016. Then you should go buy her tunes.

WITH SINCERE GRATITUDE

First of all" To You, the Reader

Thank you for giving *The Birth of Anarchy* a shot. My stories would just be words on a page without your imaginations to bring them to life. If you enjoyed *The Birth of Anarchy*, please spread the word. If you haven't read *Vagabond,* the first book in the *Vagabond Series*, feel free to give it a shot. Also, *On the Other Side of Greatness*, the prequel to *Vagabond* and *The Birth of Anarchy* will be available March 2016!

Looking for a multiversal adventure? Don't forget to check out the *Intrepid Series* as well.

And, if you have a few minutes to spare, please consider leaving an Amazon and Goodreads review!

Be sure to follow me online for updates on upcoming projects and stories. Feel free to contact me if you have suggestions on how to improve my craft. I love feedback because I want to continue creating stories you enjoy.

Online Info:
www.jdbrewerbooks.com
Twitter: @JDBrewerBooks
www.facebook.com/jdbrewerbooks
www.goodreads.com/jdbrewerbooks
Instagram: @jdbrewerbooks

If you like short stories and other musics, consider visiting my webpage to sign up for my mailing list! And if you want to see adorable dog shenanigans, check out my hashtag—#puppiesaremycoworkers

Second of all: To My Friends and Family

Yes, you—who have not seen me in months. Or perhaps you have seen me but my head was still stuck in my book, and I was trying to be social but only ended up being socially awkward.

Thank you for loving me despite my quirks.

To my Husband

That's right. When I released *Vagabond*, I was just his girlfriend, and when I released *Intrepid*, I was his fiancé. Three books later, and I went and got hitched.

Writing *The Birth of Anarchy* while planning a wedding was no easy feat, but Taylor Heard was my partner at every step. He always is. The past three years I've known him, Taylor has been crucial in making sure I pursue my dreams, even when my dreams turn out to be eccentric and time consuming.

So, Taylor, thank you for loving me just the way I am— imaginary friends and all.

To my Editors

Alexandra Kelly, your feedback helped shape *The Birth of Anarchy* into what it is today. You coached me into strengthening plots, examining character motives, and picking out continuity issues. When there's 112,070 words, little things easily get lost, so thank you for your help and many phone conversations.

Amanda Austin, you swooped in for the nitty-gritty. You caught misplaced commas, clunky sentence structures, and awkward phrasings. Thank you for tightening all the crazy.

To my Forever Puppies

Artax and **Jackie** are my coworkers, and sometimes **Bob** comes over to play. **Jackie** underwent two eye surgeries while *The Birth of Anarchy* was being developed. She is well and finally free of the cone of shame.

Dogs are the best. They make me laugh, remind me to get outside, snuggle with me when I'm stressed, and keep me company when I'm in another world.

Check them out on social media—#puppiesaremycoworkers

ABOUT THE AUTHOR:

J.D. BREWER

Some people call J.D. a leprechaun, but they just don't understand that she's simply vertically challenged. There are those who say she's fiercer than a baby pterodactyl, despite the fact that she was probably a stegosaurus in another life. Others have titles for her that are a bit more generic: friend, teacher, student, family, etc.

The truth is, she spends her time gathering moments from the people she loves, and from those moments, she creates. She glues letters into words, words into thoughts, and thoughts into questions. When she's not out having a blast in the universe she shares with you, she's creating her own through pen, paper, and keyboard.

For more updates on upcoming novels and her shenanigans as a writer, follow J.D. Brewer online!

www.jdbrewerbooks.com
Twitter: @JDBrewerBooks
www.twitter.com/jdbrewerbooks
www.facebook.com/jdbrewerbooks
www.goodreads.com/jdbrewerbooks
Instagram: @jdbrewerbooks

If you like blogs, short stories, and poetry, visit www.jdbrewerbooks.com and sign up for J.D. Brewer's mailing list!

Don't forget to leave you Amazon and Goodreads Review.
Reviews truly are the best gift you can leave for any author.

It all started with a photo shoot on a warm Texas day. **Kelli Wilson Ponce** and **Nelson Nathaniel** patiently let me figure out the camera. Then we had a blast on the Tracks and made laughter the key ingredient of the day.

Once the pictures were taken, **Sarah Martin** spent hours digging through the photos with me. She helped me choose one that captures the theme of *The Birth of Anarchy* and connects it back to *Vagabond*. Then she toiled for hours to get the rust coloring in the title just right, went back and forth with me to tweak it, and made it the treasure that it is.

All three of the people involved in the book cover are tremendously talented. Check out their bios on the next page, and be sure to follow them online to keep up with their shenanigans.

Kelli Wilson Ponce

A hair and makeup artist from Austin, beauty editor for InFluential Magazine, and future-aspiring singer. Check out her Instagram @kelliction

Nelson Nathaniel

A singer-songwriter and a kickboxing, martial arts expert. Check out his jams on SoundCloud-Ninja Star Music, Nelson Nathaniel.

Sarah Martin

She is not only a graphic design artist for websites and book covers. She writes romance novels, too! She works under the pen name Olivia Savage, and her Twitter feed is the best because she only posts positive and inspiring things. Be sure to follow her there—@4OliviaSavage.